A HANDSOME REWARD

Barely aware that they were not retracing her steps to the street, but hurrying past the corral and behind the adjacent houses, Lou tried to hang back. She felt the need to explain herself. She wasn't a violent person, yet she had just attacked a man, and done so behind his back, at that.

"He was going for it," Lou said. "He was going to shoot you down with your own gun."

Walford shoved the Starr back in the holster on his belt as he moved. "Hard thing to do with an empty pistol."

"A what?" Lou demanded, pulling free of his hand. "It was emp—"

He moved swiftly, taking her by surprise when he pinned her back to the nearest building. "Empty," Walford said quietly, his voice an intimate, teasing murmur. "But thank you all the same," he added; then he kissed her.

It was hard, fast, and the most wonderful thing she had ever experienced. And it was over far, far too quickly.

"Come on, beautiful," Walford said. "Let's get back to the hotel. I think it might be wise to leave town attired as we arrived, don't you? Too bad I hate that damn suit."

AT TWILIGHT

BETH HENDERSON

LEISURE BOOKS　　NEW YORK CITY

A LEISURE BOOK®

June 2004

Published by

Dorchester Publishing Co., Inc.
200 Madison Avenue
New York, NY 10016

ISBN 0-8439-5330-6

The name "Leisure Books" and the stylized "L" with design are
trademarks of Dorchester Publishing Co., Inc.

Printed in the United States of America.

Visit us on the web at www.dorchesterpub.com.

AT
TWILIGHT

Chapter One

Piney Woods area of East Texas, 1868

March was a damn fine time to visit Texas, J. W. Walford mused ruefully as he wrung Angelina River water out of his shirt. Or it would be if spring rains hadn't swelled the river.

Or if his horse hadn't stuck its hoof in an inconvenient rodent's burrow and broken its leg.

If the sun wasn't so blindingly bright and the breeze would bestir itself in his direction.

If he hadn't run into Uriah Roane at the saloon in Lone Tree, drawn his gun, killed Roane, been arrested then tried and sentenced all in the space of a single day. Yesterday, in fact. Yet that morning he had managed to calmly walk out of the jail cell, taking advantage of the open door when a bunch of local brothers broke the family miscreant out of the hoosegow.

1

Actually that last was the only fortunate thing that had happened to him in days. He had been scheduled to be the guest of honor at a necktie party. The town had begun work on a scaffold within hearing of both his jail cell and the courtroom while his trial was still in process. The citizens of Lone Tree really knew how to cheer their prisoners up.

J. W. draped his damp shirt over the saddle he'd lugged nearly three miles already, hoping to hasten the garment's drying process. It would be clammy and uncomfortable when he put it on, but a fellow with a passel of angry men hot on his heels had no right to complain.

Or so he'd told his Union cavalry troop during the war when Confederate raiders were spotted galloping out of the morning mist, charging their campsite. What a dandy he'd been when Claire had waved him off to join his regiment seven years ago. Lieutenant Jefferson Weyland Walford all done up in Army blue, the epitome of the smartly dressed officer. He'd been far from perfect. Had grown even farther from perfection as the war dragged on. Had it been the ever-ripening flaws in his soul or his uncanny ability to stay alive while other officers fell by the score that had earned him the undeserved captaincy? The war had ended nearly three years ago, and his unseen flaws were in full bloom now, his soul gone, bought and paid for by the devil. The outward vestiges of the gentleman officer had been reduced to the faded and mended cavalry trousers and the scuffed and gouged boots he still wore.

Both of which were soaked through.

J. W. stared hard at the landscape on the other side of the river as he emptied water from his boots, looking for the posse's telltale plume of dust. Fortunately for a man on the run, even after a spring rain, the roads of East Texas quickly reverted to dusty nuisances that broadcasted their use for all to see.

Around him, spring flowers abounded in the meadow and crept up the hillsides, a spreading, ever-rippling blanket of bluebonnets with scattered patterns of prairie verbena. The Angelina reflected the blue of the clear sky, each ripple catching the sunlight and flashing it back with diamondlike winks of blinding white. Strange to find spring so far advanced in this country. He'd grown up with late snows and a sluggish start to the growing season.

If he ever wanted to go home to the more familiar plains of Iowa or anywhere else, he'd better get moving. Although the dust cloud raised by the posse's horses' hooves was absent from the northeastern skies, it could appear at any moment. The diversionary action of trekking through the riverbed wouldn't necessarily throw the trailing men off his tracks. Even though he'd added evidence to suggest a drowning by tossing his hat in the water where it could catch dramatically on branches trailing in the river, it only took a single bushwhacker's cunning to find his trail into the water and his trail out of it a half mile downriver. Particularly since he'd slipped in the mud when scaling the western bank, landing facedown in the profusion of wildflowers. The posse would close the distance quickly and a man on foot had less chance of eluding mounted and vengeful hunters than a rattlesnake had when caught in a bison stampede. He ought to know. He was a vengeful hunter himself.

No, to raise his odds for survival, he needed to find a fresh, preferably fast, horse, then food, shelter, and supplies.

And decent guns. His own had no doubt ended up stuffed in the belt of one of the hell-bent lawmen who'd arrested him. It would be damned irritating to be shot with his own weapons. The only gun he had at the moment was a relic of the Mexican War that he'd found in the livery stable when he'd stolen back his own horse and saddle. He'd used the lone ball in it to finish off his downed gelding.

No use chewing over recent disappointments, J. W. told himself as he pulled his soggy boots back on. Getting to his feet, he scooped up the still damp shirt. Survival depended on putting distance between himself and the trailing men. But which way? He only knew he'd run south from Lone Tree because the sun had been in his eyes all day. Rather than continue on the same tack, heading west seemed a worthy option. For the moment anyway, since he was in unknown territory with no way of knowing if he was headed for a decent-sized town or into uncivilized wilderness. He needed a map sooner or later. Needed to find a telegraph office and wire Diamond about his delay. With the uproar back in Lone Tree, the excitement of which had probably spread by now to neighboring Nacogdoches, he hadn't had the leisure to contact her earlier.

Damn. He almost wished she hadn't heard word that their quarry was in Texas. It was beginning to look like killing Roane had dispelled the last of his legendary luck. The Confed had deserved to die for what he'd done, but the man the raiders had called Captain, the one who truly deserved to reside with the devil, was still at large.

Buttoning up his shirt, J. W. sized up the landscape directly west. More meadows, more rising hills, patches of dense pine and hardwood forest on the horizon and . . .

He squinted at the dark dots in the sky, then shaded his eyes from the bright sun with his hand. Circling buzzards,

J. W. decided. Maybe things were about to take a turn for the better after all.

J. W. shoved his shirttail in the waistband of his sodden trousers, resettled his belt in place, and hefted the saddle to his shoulder once more. If shelter didn't turn up on his route at least the carrion birds gave promise of a rough dinner.

Louisa Burgess levered herself upright in the bed, pushing the smothering weight of a heavily padded quilt away. The clean bedclothes Widow Rosa had thrown haphazardly over the mattress the day she had arrived were no longer pristine, but clammy and stifling. With the door and windows of the tiny log cabin still barred, only a most determined breath of breeze and gleaming slivers of sunbeams managed to find a way through the barriers.

From the angle of the beams it was long past noon. She should have been up hours ago, to feed the baby if nothing else. The widow should have wakened her. Why hadn't she? Ever since local banker and self-styled philanthropist Titus Gillette had driven the woman from Peaceful to the Burgess ranch, the widow had been underfoot, poking her nose into every cranny of the house, ferreting out and examining every one of Lou's remaining treasures. Ostensibly, the woman was there to care for her and the baby but, since Rosa and Gillette had forced her to drink the horrible tasting opiate that robbed her of both strength and reason, Rosa had been more jailer than nurse. Now there wasn't a sign of the older woman.

All was nearly silent, unnaturally so, the only sound in the cabin the quick, labored whisper of Lou's own breath.

Fear trickled through her veins, growing steadily as she strained in vain to hear something, anything. Not even the

5

sound of a frustrated fly, trapped inside the cabin, reached her ears.

Lou's breath caught in her throat. Her baby! Angelina! Surely the infant wasn't entirely silent in her sleep, unless she had been stolen away! Lou pushed the thought aside, resolutely refusing even to consider such a possibility.

But where was her baby?

The flat-bottomed cradle she'd brought to the homestead from her grandfather's ranchero was not next to the bed where she had placed it. Why had the widow moved it? Where had she hidden it? The woman droned incessantly of never having had a child herself, of longing for one. Had she decided a penniless woman with no means of support could not provide for the infant? Had she left, returning to Peaceful with Angelina?

Frightened even more of the possible answer, Lou willed strength into her tired limbs. Her wear-worn nightrail clung damply to her form as she stood. The cabin walls wavered as her mind fought against the lingering effects of the opium tincture. Obviously moving quickly was not a good idea. With her hand touching the rough wall, Lou steadied herself until the fog cleared.

A closely woven blanket hung from the low rafters, creating a privacy screen between the bed and the rest of the cabin. Lou pushed it aside and, continuing to use the rough wall as a support, inched from the alcove into the main room. At least her legs had stopped quaking. Other parts of her body complained instead. Her head throbbed and her stomach was queasy, but fear overrode the ill feelings. *Where was her baby?*

Both of the narrow cabin windows were covered by boards that served as shutters, held secure inside by a thick plank that dropped into iron brackets. A similar barricade protected the heavy door. Logic said her jailer was still in residence, for the barriers could only be put in place from inside the cabin. They were removed at sunrise. Or should have been by Rosa.

If only she weren't so weak, Lou thought. If only circumstances had not placed her in the untenable position of becoming the banker's responsibility. She was as firmly in his clutches as she would have been had Frank bet her person as well as the ranch on that final fateful hand of cards.

Frank, her late and unlamented husband. Damn him and damn his memory.

Where was Angelina?

Lou breathed a sigh of relief when she found Widow Rosa dozing in the straight-backed armchair in the corner near the cook stove, her rusty black shawl gathered tightly around her shoulders and chest, her gray-streaked dark hair straggling from the topknot at her crown. A sour and all-too-familiar aroma rose from her person, but Lou ignored the signs of alcoholic overindulgence for the moment. The cradle was on the floor at the woman's feet. Inside it, Angelina was awake, her eyes amazingly bright in the dim light as she studied her surroundings.

Feeling steadier on her feet, Lou staightened away from the wall, moving softly to the baby's side. "Thank heavens," she breathed, sinking to sit on the floor beside the tiny bed.

The wave of one tiny, grasping hand and a wide welcoming smile answered her. The stench of recently soiled linens arose to greet her nostrils.

Lou glared at the unconscious woman Titus Gillette had left in charge of her daughter. Her bare foot brushed against something on the floor, something nearly hidden in the woman's trailing skirts. A bottle. Rosa had obviously found Frank's hidden cache of whiskey, indulging in the fiery liquid until she was in a drunken stupor. Lou hoped the whiskey's burn down the nurse's throat had given her a taste of what awaited her in the afterlife. The widow deserved every diabolical torture the devil devised for leaving Angelina uncared for and unprotected after drugging her mother into insensibility.

"Forgive me, little one," Lou murmured, stroking the infant's finely boned hand. She should have been stronger, should have resisted them more—for Angelina's sake, if not her own. Though how she could have accomplished this Herculean feat when weak with fever and the lingering effects of laudanum, Lou had no idea.

The skies had wept inconsolably the day she laid Frank to rest in his pauper's grave. The clouds were the only true mourners present, for she had not grieved for him. Instead, she had been relieved when told her husband had been killed. Had she ever loved him? Lou doubted it. She had loved the idea of a husband, little knowing the sort of man she was marrying.

The only good thing that had come from their marriage was Angelina, and her arrival was nearly a miracle considering how infrequently Frank had visited his bride's bed.

But come she had, a perfect angel, the salvation Lou clung to then and now. For Angelina she could do anything. Would do anything.

Anything.

As if understanding a silent promise had been made to her, the baby cooed a single drawn-out vowel sound and waved her arms excitedly.

Lou breathed a heartfelt sigh of relief. Despite the unforgivable neglect, Angelina was well.

The baby gurgled sounds that Lou associated with a request for food, then sucked loudly on her tiny, dimpled fist.

Even before Frank's death—had it been a week ago now?—satisfying her hungry daughter had been difficult. The child was growing so quickly. Soon she would be three months old. Where would she and Angelina be when that auspicious date arrived? Still under the watchful, lecherous eyes of the town banker? He might not have been the man to pull the trigger the night Frank was shot, but he could as well have done so. In accepting the deed to the Burgess ranch in that fateful card game, Titus Gillette had taken away the only source of support for her child.

Angelina was more concerned with the eminent arrival of her dinner than with a nebulous future. And so should she be, Lou decided. Having watched Frank and his cronies succumb to Morpheus's arms after too much whiskey, Lou knew from experience that Rosa would be insensible for hours yet. Where moments earlier, the nurse's dereliction had made her furious, it now offered a gleam of hope. Being free of the woman's watchful eye meant that she and Angelina had a chance to escape. One very slim chance. Even without hearing the dutiful click of the minute hand on the small mantel clock on the sideboard, Lou knew time was slipping away.

Forcing herself upright once more, Lou crossed the cabin carefully, only too conscious of the way her head continued to swim. The pitcher she kept on the rough dresser was empty when she lifted it. Widow Rosa hadn't bothered going to the well to draw water for use inside the cabin. Lou gritted her teeth in frustration. Without water she could not freshen herself or the baby. Could not hope to shake the mists that still threatened to cloud her vision

9

and steal her will. But anger was a fair substitute, if a fleeting one. Her teeth still set, Lou took a long, cleansing breath, praying for the strength to physically eject the careless, neglectful nursemaid from her home. As it was not forthcoming, she satisfied herself with casting the drunken woman a disdainful glance.

"This is all your fault, Frank," she said, staring hard at the framed photograph on the wall. It hung crookedly from its wire, as if recently taken down and then replaced with little care. More proof of Widow Rosa's curiosity, no doubt. Should she take it with her when she left or burn it in an effort to appease her soul? Lou wondered.

It was their wedding portrait. Frank's image stared sternly at the camera, his loose-limbed body done up in an ill-fitting, store-bought plaid suit, his boots nearly as disreputable looking as those he had worn around the ranch. He was seated on a stool with her standing just behind him, glowing and elated in her bride clothes. Her left hand rested on his shoulder, her newly achieved, brightly polished, simple wedding ring proudly on display for the camera and posterity.

She had been so happy that day. Happy because she was at long last leaving Rancho de la Vaca. Happy because it was her first trip to San Antonio, a place of true wonders to her mind. Happy because she was marrying tall, stalwart, decisive Frank Burgess. What a fool she had been.

She would be one no longer.

Rather than leave Angelina's cradle next to the widow's unconscious form, Lou managed to drag it back beside the bed. Not taking time to don a robe, she pulled on an old pair of Frank's boots to safeguard her bare feet on the packed earth of the yard. It was a strain to lift the heavy plank from before the door. The effort made her light-headed again but Lou forced herself to go on. It was the stuffiness in the cabin that had her feeling faint, she decided. "I won't be long, darling," she murmured to briefly soothe the baby, then lifted an empty water bucket and pulled the door open.

The brightness of the sun nearly made her stumble; the glare and warmth causing her to pause briefly. She put her arm up to shield her eyes, squinting against the light. A playful breeze swirled around the hem of her nightgown, lifting the skirt to her knees before moving on. The scent of blooming wildflowers floated in its wake, making Lou wish she had time to spare to savor the sweet, heady aroma. Spring was her favorite of the seasons, its only failing being that the frequent rains had kept Frank and his rowdy friends in the cabin rather than away.

That was all in the past. She needed to look forward to the future. If only she could picture it, dream about it, she could envision a life worth rushing to meet. At the moment there was nothing to move toward, only a situation to leave behind.

The waist-high stone wall built around the well felt nearly warm enough to bake tortillas on but the interior stone work was pleasantly cool to the touch. The refreshing scent of water and damp earth rose from the well proper. Briefly closing her eyes, Lou breathed it in.

The fixed bucket of the well was deep in the shaft, out of sight in the dark abyss, trailed into the depths by the sturdy rope connecting it to the cranking mechanism. Lou set the bucket from the cabin down and put her hands to the smoothly turned wooden crank handle. But the longer she worked to draw water, the more her strength ebbed, the more the clouds in her mind threatened to return. Dear Lord, she was so weak! Had her illness or the drug-ridden potion Rosa had continued to force-feed her drained her this much? How long had it been since she had eaten? Two days? Lou couldn't remember. Merely the effort of trying seemed to rob her of further strength.

Although it was only March, the sun seemed unbearably hot as it beat down. The handle beneath her hands blurred, then twinned itself, giving her two images upon which to focus. Would the bucket ever rise to the surface? She had performed the simple task often yet could not remember it as so exhausting before. It no longer mattered if she could see the crank mechanism. Everything around her seemed shrouded as in a mist. And yet the sun glowed ever brighter, blinding her, making her feel so . . .

Lou's hands slipped from the crank. Only partially conscious of the whirling sound the simple mechanism made as it swung out of control and the clatter of the bucket as it dove back into the depths of the well, she sank in a swoon to the ground.

Lou dreamed that a shadow fell across her reclining form, temporarily blocking the glare of the sun. Beneath her cheek the earth felt warm, but not welcomingly so. She moaned faintly and tried to move. Tried to open her eyes so that she could identify the shadow. A man she thought, an unknown man.

Or perhaps Frank come to haunt her.

Either way she felt no fear although she had learned to be wary of strangers while still a child on her grandfather's ranchero. When the shadow crouched down to place a damp cloth across her forehead, she felt comforted and protected. The twin sensations proved she was dreaming.

"Don't try to move yet," he recommended, his deep voice so unlike that of Frank or his friends. The shadowed stranger seemed a gentle man, for his tone reflected a deep, comforting concern, something she had no experience of receiving from any man until now. It made her feel safe with him.

Feeling so, Lou wondered what sort of man he would turn out to be when she could see him more clearly, could open her eyes fully. This was a dream though. Opening her eyes meant waking and losing this pleasant, if brief, respite from the reality of her life.

Though knowledge of the type of travelers most often met in the area cautioned her, the curiosity was too great to ignore. When she sensed he had moved away, Lou fluttered her lashes, letting her pupils adjust to the sunlight, then opened her eyes slowly.

He had stood upright again and was busy at the well. With the sun at his back all she could see of her rescuer was his tall male form towering over her. At ground level, where she lay like a wilted flower, his cavalry boots and trousers were visible. They were similar to those worn by men in the Army—the Union Army. The boots were scuffed and worn rather than kept at a high gloss. His trousers were stuffed into the top of his boots in the manner favored by most western men, particularly those who spent long hours in a saddle. He was probably a bushwhacker from Missouri, but one who had stolen the trousers and boots off a dead Yankee soldier. Since she had not chosen sides in the late war, nor acquired political leanings from Frank, one former soldier was much the same as another to Lou. Ex-soldiers had a way of taking out their grievances on whatever or whomever was handy. Surely, with so tranquil a voice, he could not be of such an ilk.

"Thank—" Lou croaked and was surprised to find her voice rusty and dry sounding to the ear.

"Hush," he urged, not turning from his task. "Just lie there a while longer."

But she couldn't, Lou remembered. She had responsibilities. Angelina needed her. Or was it that she needed to hold Angelina?

"I have a—" she began, then stopped when he held up a hand and cocked his head as if listening.

Lou thought he smiled, not grimly as Frank had, but with genuine pleasure.

"A baby," he said. "You have a baby in the cabin. One in need of immediate gratification from the sound of that cry."

"She's crying?" Lou tried to get to her feet and found her limbs sluggish in responding. Her head swimming only slightly, she wondered how she had missed hearing Angelina's angry, gulping cry. It had the same lingering vibrancy as a coyote's midnight howl.

"Easy now." The stranger set the newly risen bucket aside, then bent down to Lou again. "I'll do all the work myself," he said.

She was lifted in his strong arms, held close to his broad, muscled chest, and carried into the cabin. Holding the water-cooled handkerchief he had laid over her brow as a shield from the sun, Lou studied him surreptitiously from the shelter of her lashes.

His face and neck were sun-bronzed and bristled with dark whiskers, indicating he spent a good deal of time out-of-doors and hadn't seen a razor in three or four days. Around his neck was a loosely knotted, faded red neckerchief. He wore no hat, which made it easy to note that his hair was as black as her own, but softened by subtle glints of lighter brown. Or so she judged by the nearly jet-colored side-whiskers that framed his weathered face. She could not identify the color of his eyes, for he squinted in the glare of the sun as he turned toward the cabin door. Quite obviously she was still dreaming though, Lou decided thankfully, for her rescuer smelled more of bluebonnets and verbena than he did of horse, leather, or sweat as Frank had.

She nestled against a slightly damp flannel, pearl-gray shirt, and could feel the steady beat of the stranger's heart beneath her cheek. His left hand gripped her legs behind the knees and his right was under her shoulders, his fingertips beneath her arm lightly brushing the fullness of her breasts. Or perhaps she was more aware of the warmth of his hands because her nightgown was so thin. It left her feeling insufficiently covered and mortified since the bodice of the garment was stained and gaped slightly at the neckline.

The nightgown had once been the lone treasure from her wedding trip, packed away for posterity until necessity brought it from her trunk. But now, matched as it was with the tall, bulky weight of the old boots she'd pulled on, Lou knew she looked pathetic.

Yet in the world between waking and sleeping, things were rarely logical or true to life. She would soon wake and find herself on the bed next to Angelina, having drifted into this fantasy after caring for the baby.

Entertaining impossible fantasies had been the only hope for the future that she'd had for so long. She'd been creating pleasant, happy, and sometimes erotic visions since learning that the man she'd wed had lied to her. It hadn't taken long to recognize her mistake. Once the vows were pledged, the Frank who'd courted her had metamorphosed into a stranger.

But not like this stranger. Idly, Lou wondered why he

15

had dark hair and features. For the past year she had conjured up the image of a fair-haired conquistador, not a wandering border ruffian.

Angelina's cries grew in volume. The stranger took the ear-piercing noise in stride. Deftly, he maneuvered through the cabin doorway and paused, letting his eyes adjust to the dim interior. "Shh. Take it easy, angel. Momma's on her way to your side," he promised softly. "Perhaps, if you're patient, she'll sing you a lullaby."

As if distracted by the sound of an unknown voice, Angelina paused, whimpering slightly before raising her voice insistently again.

The drifter placed Lou gently on the bed, then carefully gathered the wailing baby from her crib, placing her softly in Lou's waiting arms before he stepped back. But he didn't leave the cabin immediately as she had expected. He stood there silently, observing her, making her overly conscious of each movement. And that she was lying on a mattress, hardly dressed for visitors. Lou was suddenly thankful that the cabin was barely lit.

She forced herself up slightly, supporting her weight on her elbow, calming the infant with a murmur and brief touch. Out of the sunlight, he was an even darker figure, the deep shadings of his clothing and coloring making him nearly fade into the cabin's gloom.

"Sir . . ." she began.

He smiled briefly at her, the flash of his even, white teeth visible even in the shadows. "You have a beautiful, healthy child there. Why don't you tend to her and then rest comfortably," he advised. Although his voice was hushed, Lou felt she could hear the crack of an order in his delivery. Had he been an officer?

"I'm sure you'll feel more yourself presently," he added.

"In the meantime, I'll open the shutters and fill your pitchers with water before night falls."

Before night falls. Was it so late already? There were so many things to do yet. Things she should—could!—do herself. But she didn't protest, merely waited until he was gone before gathering Angelina protectively close.

"Did you have a dream, too, darling?" she asked the child. "I thought I was having one, but this isn't a dream after all. He isn't part of a waking fantasy."

If he wasn't, though, who was he? How had he found the ranch? It was tucked into a niche carved into the woods, the cabin built with logs felled at the site long before Frank had purchased it with her dowry. Little of the surrounding land had been cleared. A narrow stretch of natural meadow fell away toward the Angelina River to the east, but neither road nor path led directly to her door. Yet that was where the stranger had fetched up.

At exactly the right moment.

Outside the open door, she heard the jangle of his spurs as he headed back to the cabin. Then his shadow darkened the entrance. The aroma of wildflowers that had seemed to cling to him before was now overlaid with that of leather, damp leather.

"Hope you don't mind me bringing my saddle inside," he said. "My horse broke his leg a few miles back and I've been lugging it ever since, hoping to find a homestead willing to sell me a fresh horse."

When she didn't answer immediately, he set the saddle and bucket of water down. "Ma'am? Are you okay?" he asked.

Since he looked ready to take the necessary steps to the bed, Lou sat up, drawing the quilt up modestly to cover her torso and shelter the now quieted baby. "Yes, yes. I'm

17

fine," she assured hastily. "I'm afraid I wasn't myself when you arrived, Mister . . ." Lou left the sentence unfinished, waiting for him to supply her with a name.

He didn't. Instead he smiled again. With the door open, it was much easier to see him, to see what a change his mouth underwent when he was pleased or amused. Though his face looked set in lines that indicated a hard life, a simple grin transposed him into a quite well-featured man.

"The turkey buzzards circling over this place didn't think so either," he said before the smile slid back into hiding. "You must have been out for a while to attract their interest."

Buzzards! Lou shuddered at the thought, picturing what would have happened to Angelina if he hadn't come along, if she hadn't come out of her swoon. With the forest at her doorstep, natural predators were a very real threat.

"Thank you for rescuing us," she said.

"You're welcome," he responded lightly. "Tell me where you want this second bucket, then I'll unbar the windows for you. It will make the place feel cheerier with late afternoon sunlight pouring through the panes. Then, if you've got a spare horse I can buy, I'll be on my way."

Lou wished she didn't have to give him the unhappy news. "We've only two horses and they pull our wagon," she said, careful to imply that she didn't live alone at the ranch, which, even when Frank had been alive, had pretty much been the way of things. Would he think that she and the soused Widow Rosa were fair game though, women alone without a man to keep them safe? "I'm sorry, but my husband wouldn't willingly part with either." It wasn't a complete lie. If he'd still been alive, Frank would have raised holy hell if she'd sold off one of his precious mares.

"Perhaps your husband will know of someone with a horse to sell," the nameless stranger said as he lifted the security bar from the front window.

With Angelina changed and temporarily content once more, Lou reached for her robe and struggled to cover herself quickly while his back was turned. "Frank may not be back until dusk," she declared, hoping that she sounded apologetic rather than inventive. Hoping he would be in a hurry to leave. She'd point the way to Peaceful, the nearest town. It wasn't much of a place, but it did have a livery stable where he could find another mount.

"Then it looks like I need to ask you one more question, ma'am," he said, staring intently at something on the prairie to the east before turning to face her. "Do you have a place where a man could hide?"

Chapter Two

The posse had made impossibly good time. Or he'd made impossibly bad time, J. W. thought ruefully. His rope had not only run out, it would probably be used to string him up. The once admired beauty of the woodland would soon be sullied by a noose swung over a convenient tree limb.

The lovely woman he'd rescued and returned to her baby joined him at the window. Even without the clomp of her oversized boots—a man's, he thought—he would have noticed her presence at his side, for the delightful scent of woman surrounded her, filling his mind with thoughts he had no right thinking. Even if she was in her nightclothes.

Get out of this mess, J. W. counseled himself, *and you can hit the nearest saloon and find a willing partner for the night.*

But it wouldn't be the same. He didn't want just a woman. He wanted what he'd once had and lost. A good woman and loving wife. Things he no longer deserved.

"What is it?" the vision next to him asked.

She had pulled on a robe, a heavy wool plaid of faded red with neatly rolled lapels, and belted it tightly around a waist that seemed amazingly slim for a woman with such a young child. What had Claire written to him soon after their son arrived? *You would not recognize me, darling husband. Your child has left his mark upon me. Nevermore an eighteen-inch waist. Will you still love me without it?* He still loved her though she'd been in her grave nearly five years.

This little mother had none of Claire's fond teasing in her tone though. She was rightly leery of him. Yet she had not grabbed up the rifle that rested against the wall next to the bed, hadn't ordered him from the premises with a load of buckshot to speed him on his way.

"The cloud of dust?" she asked quietly.

"Do you know what it is?" J. W. murmured, matching her tone.

"A posse," she answered, surprising him. "Or a cavalry troop on patrol. Which is it?"

"Right the first time, ma'am." He paused, turning only his face toward her. "You going to turn me over?"

She gestured toward the rough dinner table near the stove. A serviceable dark braided rag rug covered the rough planked floor beneath it. "You helped me," she said. "Presenting them with you seems a sad thank-you for that service. Could you move this table for me? There's a trapdoor beneath the rug."

Since finding her by the well, he had admired the long,

raven fall of her hair as it streamed over her shoulders nearly to her waist. Now he found the graceful sway of her body as she walked away from him equally entrancing.

And he was a fool to take notice of these things. The posse would be at the door in moments and he was casually cataloging her assets.

"Thank you, ma'am. I appreciate this," J. W. said, hastening over to shift the table to the side.

She stooped and, with a quick twist of her wrist, tossed a corner of the rug aside, laying bare the outline of the promised trapdoor. "I hope this will be wide enough to get your saddle through as well. It's of too good a quality to be found normally on this ranch. I wouldn't want a small detail like that to give you away."

J. W. found a fingerhold and pried the door up. There was a ladder leading down into a seemingly bottomless black pit. The musty smell of damp earth rose from the depths. Hospitable, it wasn't.

He gathered up his saddle and wedged it through the opening, dropping it.

"It isn't very deep," his hostess warned as she extracted something from her larder. "You might have to bend over a bit." Using the skirt of her robe like a cradle, she filled it with potatoes. The same slight, musty smell of damp earth clung to them. She was using it to camouflage the scent from the root cellar should the cabin be searched, he realized.

Damn, she was a smart woman!

"Now go," she urged. "The horses are nearer. I can hear them."

So could he. J. W. dropped down into the hole, staying in a low crouch as the trapdoor closed over his head. How oddly comforting the sounds of a rug being flipped back in place and a table being dragged over it could be, he thought. And how trusting of strangers both he and the beauty above were. Would they both soon regret the unreasoning impulse to play Good Samaritan?

Lou quickly put a plate and sharp-edged knife on the table by the potatoes to give her hastily conceived tableau the look of an interrupted household task. *You're a fool, Louisa Burgess*, she berated herself. The man in her cellar could be well-deserving of a hanging. He had the look of a killer although he wore no gun holster. He had been armed with nothing more than a rusty old pistol shoved in his belt, a weapon that looked too ill cared for to belong to a man who lived by the gun. And yet his eyes had been hard as they watched the telltale cloud of dust to the east. She had no doubt he was a dangerous sort of fellow, but to her he had been gentle and helpful. He could just as easily have ignored her unconscious form, stolen a horse, and been on his way. Yet he hadn't.

The bone-jarring thunder of galloping horses was nearer, more distinct. Lou checked the magazine of her husband's second-best shotgun, ensuring that it was loaded, then stepped into the open doorway of the cabin. The rifle was cocked and braced against her shoulder when the posse pulled to a halt in the yard.

The aroma of leather, horses, sweat, and dust overwhelmed the sweet scent of wildflowers in the air. The men looked little different from the desperados Frank had called friends—or the fellow in her cellar, for that matter—their attire differing only in the fabric shades they wore. This was the first time such a large posse had ridden up to the cabin. As Frank's wife, she had had a number of experiences with such groups and had begun to recognize the members of previous posses. However, that was not the case with this group of riders. They were all strangers with stern, sun-bronzed, bearded, or mustached faces. There were two things that distinguished her current guest from them, though. They were all armed, a few wearing holsters on their belts but most with well-cared-for pistols shoved inside the waistband of their trousers. Some had rifles as well, although the long-barreled weapons remained holstered on their saddles.

More importantly, they all wore tin badges that branded them as lawmen, even if hastily sworn-in lawmen. Fifteen in all she counted, a number that did little to assure her that they had the letter of the law in mind on this chase after a lone man.

The horses slowed to a sedate walk, the music of their jingling bridles and creaking saddles joining the natural rustling serenade of the trees that crowded the house. With each step the mounts took, Lou's apprehension grew. Facing down a posse had become so commonplace, she should be immune to the situation. Yet she had never grown as callous to the danger as Frank had. Frank could afford to be nonchalant for he had never been the one holding lawmen at bay.

She was only doing it again now because she was indebted to the man hidden beneath her floorboards. He could be guilty of a crime. He could be innocent. Judging him was not in her hands. The rifle was.

If the posse's leader was disconcerted at being greeted with a weapon aimed steadily at his midsection, he gave no evidence of it. A couple of the men behind him actually laughed, apparently finding a woman in robe and nightgown far from dangerous. Others turned their faces away, either from gentlemanly embarrassment or fear that she was a madwoman. Considering the state of her appearance, the skirt of her gown streaked with dust and her hair limp and straggling around her face, Lou found both reactions perfectly logical.

"I ain't in the mood fer visitors, gents," she shouted, her voice a rough growl that backed up the warning. Miss Nottingham, her former governess at the hacienda, would no doubt cringe to hear her once prized pupil speaking so, but experience had taught Lou that men rarely believed a well-spoken lady was much of a threat. A gun in the hands of an uneducated, unwelcoming frontier she-cat was another thing entirely. "Best tip yer hats and be on yer way."

"Take it easy, little lady," the head rider soothed quickly, daring to walk his horse a few strides closer. "I'm Sheriff Detmer from Lone Tree and these fellers are my deputies. We're trailing an escaped prisoner," he continued. "You seen any strangers around here lately?"

It was a difficult question to answer and yet keep to the truth. "Desperados know better'n ta come sniffin' around here," Lou snapped. Which was true. Frank's old friends had avoided the ranch after receiving a demonstration of her shooting skills the day after his death. Especially when her parting shot had blown the heel off one man's boot.

"Best ride out before I get riled," she said sharply.

The deputies stayed where they were, arrayed in a half-moon formation behind the sheriff. A few slumped in their saddles with forearms resting casually on their saddle horns. Others fingered the guns tucked or holstered at their belts. Most of the horses stood close together, like herd animals in a field, but a loner had pulled his mount to the side, upwind of his companions. Of all the men, she felt he was the one to fear.

Yet it was another one who swung from his saddle and

hunkered over the tramped down dirt around the well wall.

Lou's gaze flashed to him briefly before returning to the sheriff. She hoped he wouldn't notice the newborn flicker of fear in her eyes. Tracks. She had forgotten there would be tracks at the well.

"Walford's dangerous, ma'am," the sheriff said. "Tall feller with hair that's purdy near black and a hard-angled face with a mean expression. He's got eyes gray as the sky durin' a blue norther and is dangerous as hell, if you'll pardon the expression."

The description didn't do her outlaw justice as far as Lou was concerned. It was interesting to learn the color of his eyes, though. Perhaps he was dangerous in their eyes. After the service he had rendered her, she could never fear him. No, the only danger that threatened her was the possibility of their not believing her, of insisting on searching the cabin. Of finding the trapdoor and the man trapped beneath it.

The men ranged behind the sheriff mumbled to one another, their words cloaked by the low tones. Lou had no trouble following the direction of a few pointing fingers though, all aimed at the ground where their tracker still sat on his heels.

"Detmer," he called out.

" 'Scuse me, ma'am," the sheriff muttered apologetically. He gave his horse a command with a touch of his heel along its flank, turning it slightly so he could better see what the deputy had found.

Lou nearly wilted. Instead of waiting for the troop in her doorway, she should have taken a stand near the well. The overlong length of her robe could then have dragged over the prints made by her rescuer's boots, obliterating them or making them unclear.

Sheriff Detmer nodded over the evidence and directed his mount to face her once more. "Sure you haven't seen anybody here today?" he asked again, the edge to his voice alerting her to measure every word she uttered.

"Ain't I already told ya nobody been foolish enough ta knock on my door, mister?" She nearly growled the marginally true statement. The hidden man—what had the sheriff called him? Walford?—hadn't knocked on the door. It had been standing wide open to man or beast. "Yer irritatin' me, sheriff. And that makes ma trigger finger get mighty twitchy. It don't make no difference ta me whether ya be outlaw or lawman. Yer trespassin' and ya been warned." Lou hoped she hadn't overdone her performance. She wouldn't be able to maintain it much longer. Her arms and shoulders ached from holding the rifle ready and true. Not that long ago she had swooned on the ground where the posse's horses now stood waiting. If they forced her hand, could she keep them from searching the cabin?

Behind her Lou could hear Angelina begin testing her voice again. It wouldn't be long before the soft sounds turned into a full-throated cry. Her baby needed her. But she owed the stranger in the root cellar a debt as well.

"We ain't leavin' 'til ya answer ma questions, lady," the sheriff snapped and swung down from his saddle.

Lou braced herself against the door frame to help steady the rifle, pointing it directly at the sheriff's tin badge. "I'm warnin' ya," she repeated.

"And I'm warnin' ya," Detmer growled. "There're fresh boot prints in yer yard and they're a leadin' ta the house. That suggests ta me that ya might be lyin' ta me."

"Instead of accusin' me of lyin', maybe ya better be a

26

lookin'," Lou responded as if her temper was about to explode. "I'm a wearin' boots, sheriff."

The information didn't deter him. Detmer rubbed his chin in thought. "I take it yer husband ain't around right now."

In more ways than one, Lou reflected silently. "Ya think if he was here he'd let me take on a bunch of bushwhackers on ma own?" They didn't need to know that would be exactly what Frank would have done.

"When ya expect him back?" the sheriff asked.

"When he feels like comin' back." The words were barely spoken when Angelina increased her volume. Lou cocked her head toward the interior of the cabin. "He cain't stand all the noise the kid makes. Now I tol' ya what ya wanted ta know, so git. I got things ta do."

Sheriff Detmer pondered a moment or two longer, then asked one more question. "Mind if a couple of my men take a look in the barn? Our man lost his horse a ways back. He'll be lookin' fer a new mount."

It was a sensible request, one she couldn't really refuse. Particularly if it would keep them out of the cabin. "Suit yerself," Lou said. "I'd give those two range nags back there breathin' room though. They don't take kindly to no man but ma husband."

"Rightly noted, ma'am," said one of the men Detmer waved toward the out building, touching the brim of his hat politely.

"Yer welcome," Lou murmured with a quick nod of her head. "Leastways some of yer men got manners, sheriff."

"Yes, ma'am," he said rather contritely. "Mind if the rest of us fill our canteens while they're reconnoiterin'?"

"Long as ya don't mind havin' a carbine pointin' at ya

while yer doin' it," Lou answered sharply. She didn't relax her guard until they all rode out of the yard.

Beneath the cabin flooring, J. W. listened to the conversation, only hearing one side of it clearly—the woman's. What he heard had him admiring her more. She not only had beauty, she had spunk. Her metamorphosis from soft-spoken lady to frontier hellion didn't fool him. She was scared.

Would the posse swallow her story? Would they insist on searching the cabin? Thin rays of light crept into his hiding place through cracks between the floorboards beyond the rug, keeping the close-walled cellar from feeling like a grave. His eyes had adjusted, allowing him to see some of his prison, the roughly cut walls, tramped-down dirt floor and his saddle at the foot of the crude ladder. There were a few provisions stored, but no rugged chairs or bedding. It was the definable, lingering aromas that argued frequent use: the scent of whiskey and the pungent smell of tobacco juice.

J. W. listened closely, his ear pressed to the floorboards, trying to catch more of what was said. Instead he heard the soft murmuring of the baby, then her full-throated cry.

Had his son cried in such a way? Wailing for a mother who could no longer comfort him? If only he had been at the farm instead of away at war.

The clomp of footsteps entering the house above him pushed the thought aside. The hinges squeaked as the door was closed. Then the soft, soothing whisper of the woman speaking to her child followed.

J. W. breathed easier. She had bluffed the posse, had sent the bushwhackers on their way.

But for how long?

"Mr. Walford?" the woman called over the infant's cries.

Damn, they'd told her his name. It would have been safer for her never to have known it.

"I have to see to Angelina before I release you," she said. "Do you mind?"

Did he mind? Hell, no! She'd stayed the hangman's hand, if only temporarily. "Not at all, ma'am." Best to stay hidden awhile longer in case the posse circled back, a very likely scenario considering his tracks led to the cabin but not away from it.

With the baby caterwauling and the flooring muting the sound of their voices, J. W. knew carrying on a conversation was impossible. Instead of trying, he settled against his saddle and stretched his legs out. What he needed was a plan. A way to outwit, outride, and outrun the men from Lone Tree. They were already out of their jurisdiction yet showed no sign of giving up. How far would they chase him? Would they involve other lawmen along the way?

A horse and a map were no longer sufficient to elude them. What he needed now was a change of clothes, a change of identity. A change of—

The sound of the woman singing interrupted his thought. It wasn't the pleasant, uplifting ring of her voice that drew him but the song itself. A song from the late war.

"When Johnny comes marching home again, hurrah, hurrah," she crooned softly. Attentive to the tone of her mother's voice, the baby's crying quieted. "Hush, love. Your dinner will be served presently," the woman said.

When she resumed her song, J. W. sang along softly under his breath. He didn't notice that his hostess broke off several times to speak to the child, but continued on

29

to the final note. The tune brought memories of other voices singing the same lyrics, men's voices, as they tramped along roads and through fields. Men who laughed at a joke one minute, then were undertaker's fodder the next. At least she hadn't chosen to croon one of the hymns sung over the graves.

"Mr. Walford?" she called again. "I'll have the table and rug out of your way in a moment."

Just in time. Thoughts of so many of his friends in their graves weren't the best things for a man to have on his mind when buried beneath a cabin.

He heard the irritating scrape of table legs against the floor then the soft whisper and slap of the rug being tossed back. He wondered how she had the strength to shift the ponderous piece of furniture. How she had had the strength to stare down a passel of men thirsty for his blood.

After her brush with the posse, would she be more leery of him, afraid for her safety and that of the baby? She had reason to worry and a reason to shoot him, especially if a reward had been offered. Damn, he wished he had been able to hear the sheriff's side of the conversation earlier. It would be helpful to know what had been said. Particularly if he was now wanted dead or alive.

Unable to wait longer, J. W. pushed the trapdoor open.

She was waiting for him, kneeling on the floor, the palms of her hands pressed flat against the boards for support as she peered down at him. She was smiling softly.

"Were the accommodations to your satisfaction, sir?" she asked, her tone flippant rather than frightened or worried. Rather than ease his own tension, the query herded more memories into his mind. Visions of Claire glancing at him over her shoulder, grinning at him mischievously. He hadn't been teased by a woman in that manner in a long time. Not since his late wife's last letter.

"More than satisfactory," he answered, hoisting himself out of the cellar, leaving his saddle behind for the moment. "That was quite a performance you gave."

She shrugged and stood, using the tabletop to steady herself. Obviously, the charade she'd just played had taxed her physically. Just as obvious was the fact that she was trying to hide it.

"Would you care for something to drink? I wouldn't suggest whiskey—it seems to have a rather soporific effect." She gestured behind him, indicating a form he had not noticed slumped in the shadows in a sturdy wooden chair.

At first he thought the bundle one of cloth or clothing ready to be laundered, but the veined, dry, sun-bronzed hand resting against the rusty fabric helped him distinguish the short, squarish figure of a woman, her head slumped against her chest, a soft wheeze of breath lightly disturbing a lock of gray-tinged dark hair.

"May I introduce you to my other houseguest, Mr. Walford?" his hostess asked. "Widow Rosa isn't herself today thanks to her close association with the devil's spring water. I do hope you will forgive her."

From the tone of her voice, the young mother hadn't. Rather, she loathed the other woman.

Best if he didn't outstay his own welcome. "I appreciate what you did for me, ma'am. If you'll accept it, I would be honored to pay you for that service."

She looked torn for a moment, then shook her head. "No, I couldn't accept it, Mr. Walford. I was the one indebted to you. Shall we simply call it even?"

"Even it is, ma'am," J. W. said courteously. There was no need for her to know the debt he owed was not forgotten. He would leave a number of the greenbacks he had hidden in his boot on the table when he left, although they were little compensation for saving his skin.

With the posse gone, he should be on his way, yet J. W. lingered. "Is there anything at all I can do for you?" he asked. "Something you need carried or stowed before your husband returns?"

His hostess paused, a thoughtful look on her lovely face. It was pale, a result of a recent illness he guessed, but it was also delicate of feature, her eyes a gentle emerald green, her cheekbones high but gently sculpted, her nose aristocratic and her chin gently rounded, though currently jutting with determination.

"Yes," she said, facing him. "There is something you can do for me, although it will put me further in your debt."

He nearly waved the statement aside, but paused. "To cancel it, perhaps you can lend me some of your husband's clothes. A shirt and trousers if he can spare them."

"Of course," she answered. "You will need to alter your appearance if you do not wish to be captured. He can spare anything you need, Mr. Walford." She scrutinized him a moment, sizing him up. "Perhaps a hat, as well? I know there is one around here. Look under the bed for it, or perhaps in the barn."

J. W. stared at her in amazement as she opened a scarred wooden chest and began rummaging though the neatly folded clothing inside. Moments before she had looked ready to swoon again. Now she was revitalized and anxious to send him on his way disguised as her husband.

The sun was beginning to dip lower in the western sky. How far could he get in the dark in unknown territory? How soon would it be before her husband returned?

And what would the man do to her if he found she'd given his duds to a wanted felon?

"Mr. Walford!" she exclaimed in disapproval. "Time is ticking away and you haven't moved from that spot."

Her tone amused him. "How can I take payment for something I've yet to do, ma'am? You said there was a chore?"

"Oh, of course," she said. The items in her arms when she stood looked suspiciously like a checkered woolen suit and waistcoat. Not exactly the kit favored by a man on the run.

She set the clothing on the table, using the flat surface once again to support herself. "Actually, there are two things I would appreciate your doing, sir," she declared, slightly breathless. Obviously she was too proud to admit the extent of her weakness. "The second is to draw water for bathing."

"Easily done," J. W. said. "And the first?"

His hostess sighed deeply. "Widow Rosa," she answered. "Would you please drag her somewhere out of my sight?"

Claude Morgan settled back in his saddle and followed the rest of the posse north from the homestead. It had been a poor excuse of a ranch, the kind of place that yielded little more than a subsistence crop, whether it be grain or cattle. In fact, he would be willing to bet that the hellcat's husband was more rustler than rancher.

And that she was hiding something.

Whether it was Walford or not, he wasn't sure, but she had been a bit too wary of Detmer's intentions, and far from hospitable. On this prairie, folks were usually more welcoming simply because they saw so few fellow humans.

33

Unless, of course, the hellcat had experience of Union soldiers riding through and decimating the countryside.

Not that his own side had been downright friendly to Northern sympathizers, Morgan admitted. There had been the incident in Lawrence, Kansas, back in the summer of 1863. The one he'd overheard Walford mention before drilling a hole in Roane at the saloon. Having ridden with the now deceased Uriah Roane, Morgan hadn't been overly disturbed by the man's death. After all, his own plans depended on no one learning of the things he himself had done while riding with Roane as one of Dalhert's Rangers. Or the things he still had to do to insure that his past remained buried. Putting Roane six foot under had been an eventuality Walford had merely done him the favor of expediting.

However, discovering why J. W. Walford had taken a bead on Roane back in Lone Tree and killed his man was a mystery to be solved. One that had nothing to do with the handsome reward offered by Roane's lady friend for the scallywagging Northern gunman, dead or alive. If he read her right, dead was by far her preference in regards to Walford, though what a skinny lout like Roane could have offered her to have inspired such an outpouring of devotion was beyond Morgan's comprehension.

Still, the amount she'd named to bring Walford in was tempting enough to send half the men who'd witnessed the gunfight off in hot pursuit. Him among them.

The majority of them would drop out of the hunt in another day or two. They'd miss their rot-gut whiskey, their card games, and their women. Most likely in that order, too. He'd stay on the trail if for no other reason than to find out what Walford had against Roane. Well, that and the reward. A damn handsome reward.

Morgan settled his hat low on his brow to block the glare of the sun and urged his horse into a trot upwind of the rest of the posse to escape their dust. If Sheriff Detmer didn't circle back to the hellcat's cabin later to check out her story, he'd shake free of the posse and do it himself, he decided. The more he thought about it, the more it seemed clear that the bedraggled beauty had been hiding something. Whether it was Walford or not, Morgan decided she was worth visiting again. Could be she'd be a bit more sociable with a lone man than she was with a posse.

Chapter Three

The idea came to Lou when she opened the chest where Frank had kept his clothing. With Walford wishing to change his outward appearance, the dark trousers and calico shirts her husband had favored simply wouldn't do if he was to escape notice this close to her rundown ranch. They were too like the clothes her visitor now wore. The suit had struck her as the perfect solution, not only to his problem, but to one of her own as well.

He was peering at himself in the inadequate surface of her husband's shaving mirror, having shrugged on the innocuous coffee-toned plaid wool jacket in an effort to prove to her that it wouldn't fit. The ready-made garment had been too large for Frank's lanky build, but on Walford it fit as if cut to his own form, the shoulders the exact width needed, the sleeves the correct length. She knew that if he buttoned the boxy jacket the breadth would be perfect.

"You look very good in it," Lou told Walford. "Not in the least like a wanted man."

"I feel like a jackanapes," he said, shrugging the garment off. "It suits a drummer of geegaws. Of course, if that is what your husband is, I apologize."

"It isn't," she assured him. "Let's see how the weskit fits."

"No, thank you, ma'am. Wouldn't want to deprive your husband of his Sunday go-to-meetin' outfit."

"Oh, you won't be," Lou declared. "Frank hasn't worn it since our wedding day."

Walford didn't look all that happy at the news, which amused her. "He's a sentimental fellow then," he said.

"No," Lou said slowly, drawing the word out. "He loathed it, actually. Made me promise not to bury him in it if anything happened to him." She had nearly done so anyway, too furious over the fact that, while handsomely rewarded for marrying her a scant three years earlier, Frank had left her with nothing but debts. Now Lou was glad she hadn't given in to the temptation to conveniently forget to honor his wish.

"This him?" Walford asked, bending slightly to peer at the wedding picture on the wall. "Handsome man."

"I once thought so," Lou agreed. That once had been a long time ago, during Frank's courtship and the first few weeks of their marriage. After buying the rundown ranch west of the Angelina River, Frank had been quick to show her exactly what type of man he really was. And the word that described him best wasn't *handsome*.

"You sure there isn't something else of his I could use?" Walford demanded. "There aren't many men on horseback who wear this sort of getup, if you get my drift."

Lou turned her attention back to the chest and searched through the rest of the meager items to find the white shirt starched collar and string tie that belonged with the suit, and Frank's spare work clothes, a pair of slightly frayed dark trousers and two faded calico shirts. "Is your first priority to outdistance the posse? If so, that might be difficult since they are now ahead of you."

"They'll swing back," Walford murmured. He turned his attention to the rumpled, wilted, generous form of Widow Rosa. "You want just her or the chair moved out as well? Looks like she's wedged between the arms of it pretty good."

"The chair, too," Lou answered. She wouldn't be taking any of the furniture when she left. Just the things that would avail her needs on the road and would fit in the wagon. The list was small, very small. It had to be for a woman on the run.

"Okay." Walford left off engineering the removal of her former nurse and, putting his hands flat against the rough tabletop, leaned forward to look down to where Lou knelt by the trunk. "How soon before your husband is expected back? I'll need to be long on my way before then, especially if I have to find a horse elsewhere. You sure you can't spare one of yours? I can pay for it."

Lou dropped the lid of the wooden chest, picked up her latest finds, and pushed slowly to her feet. How long would she continue to feel so tired? she wondered. Since recovering from the nausea she had experienced early in her pregnancy, she had been the picture of health prior to the illness contracted in the rain at Frank's funeral, the ague that had allowed Titus Gillette to plant Rosa in her home. If she continued to be so weak, she would never make it on her own, particularly to the sanctuary she hoped to find in her mother's house in Mexico City.

Which was why she was forcing Frank's suit on Walford.

"You could drive slowly rather than ride past the posse and never be noticed," she suggested.

Walford's mouth twisted in a wry grin. "Under a wagon load of hay, I suppose. That still doesn't solve my problem when it comes to getting another horse."

"Ranchers and town folks alike would remember you asking for or stealing a horse." Lou set the items of clothing on the table before him. "You'll notice I even found Frank's cufflinks. He had them engraved with his initials."

Her guest ignored the items and stood erect once more. "Ma'am, I wish you'd just spit it out instead of leading me down the primrose path. There can't be much time left before your husband shows up and, if it's all the same to you, I'd rather he not find me here."

"Because of the posse's possible return?" she asked innocently.

"Because you're wearing your night things," he declared.

He sounded a bit aggravated about it, Lou felt. Or was that agitated? She was decently covered from head to toe, the collar of her robe pulled together at her throat, the wide skirt sheltering the rest of her nightgown from sight, and Frank's old boots hiding her bare feet. The mirror had told her she was pale, drawn, had circles under her eyes, and that her hair looked like a cyclone had created her coiffure. There certainly was nothing of the temptress about her.

"Frank won't mind," Lou said and turned away from him.

Walford grabbed her arm to stay her.

She looked back over her shoulder at him.

As if suddenly mindful of his action, Walford dropped his hand away. "He'll mind, ma'am. Believe me, he'll mind."

"No, Mr. Walford, he won't." Her eyes met his steadily. "Frank died last week. Now, if you'll excuse me, I'll change while you remove Widow Rosa. She should be safe in the barn, don't you think? Oh, and watch for the empty bottle on the floor, won't you? There's a small cask of whiskey in the cellar from which you can refill it if you feel the need."

Oh, he felt the need, all right, J. W. thought as his amazing hostess walked away from him and dropped the faded drape that screened the bedroom corner of the room.

A widow. A damn shifty widow at that. He understood why she pretended to have a husband, all alone as she was in the countryside. What he didn't understand was why she had told him the truth. Or why she was forcing the cheap suit on him.

J. W. glanced down at the infant who rested contentedly in the flat bottomed cradle once more. She was so tiny, so fragile. And so wide awake, peering at him from wide pale blue eyes while she waved her small arms, almost as if she was trying to motion him down to her level.

He had always been one to oblige a lady. J. W. stooped down and, unable to resist, gently touched her miniature hand. He was both surprised and pleased when her tiny fingers latched on to his thumb.

"So you want something from me, too, do you, angel?" he asked quietly, so her mother wouldn't overhear. "If I read her right, you're taking after your mother in that respect already."

The infant gave him what looked like the beginnings of

a grin, as if she was pleased at his comment, and kicked her legs beneath the baby-sized patchwork quilt that covered her.

"I'll do what I can, sweetheart," J. W. promised, "but I do need to be on my way."

The baby made a sound that could be taken as a sigh of disappointment, although he knew she didn't understand a word he said.

It would be easy to get attached to the tiny charmer, he mused. However, the posse would be back. If he was still on this ranch by then, Lady Luck would abandon him for sure.

Disentangling himself from the little one's grasp was more of an effort than he had thought it would be. She had a grip that belonged to someone twice her size. "Okay, okay," J. W. whispered. "I'll see to things. Hang around until it gets too dangerous."

As if relieved at the promise, the baby released him and fluttered her lashes, preparing for another nap. They weren't as long and dark as her lovely mother's yet, but he figured she'd grow into them in time, using them flirtatiously to twist a fellow's guts inside out. An unruly thatch of fine, soft brown hair rose up like a rooster's comb on top of her head and the hint of a delightful dimple appeared to the left of her bowed lips. No doubt about it. He was merely one of the first of the men who would find themselves wrapped around her impossibly dainty finger.

J. W. retucked the infant's blanket into place, then turned his attention to removing the now snoring older woman from the premises. The first priority was to rescue the empty bottle at her feet. Even if the whiskey in the cask below was little better than rotgut, it was going to be greatly needed after the events of this day.

Behind the thin blanket barricade around the bed, he heard his hostess humming softly to herself. Not, he was pleased to note, a song from the war as she had before, but a tune he didn't recognize. Her singing voice was pleasant, soothing, but it was her speaking voice that had the power to eat into his soul, to spin a web around him. It was fortunate that he was simply passing through, able to escape her captivating blend of southern charm and Latin lilt.

He wasn't surprised she had the flavor of Mexico in her voice. Her features and coloring argued in favor of Spanish ancestry. All but the soft shade of emerald in her eyes. Her movements were sensual, graceful, giving the impression that while Anglo women walked, she waltzed along life's pathway.

The farther away from her he got, the better, J. W. decided. Dragging the seated, drunken guest and the chair over to the entry, he hastily removed the board barricade his hostess had put back in place and swung the door wide.

"Mr. Walford?" his hostess called.

"Ma'am?" It was almost ridiculous that, although he knew her child's name was Angelina, her late husband's given name had been Frank and the unconscious woman's was Rosa, he had no idea what *her* name was. Better never to learn it.

Maybe it was Maria.

"Do you know how to hitch horses to a wagon?" she asked.

So he looked incompetent to her. J. W. held back a sigh of chagrin. If he hadn't had the process down by the time he was six, his family back in Iowa would have thought there was something seriously wrong with him. "Yes, ma'am."

"Then, instead of drawing more water, could I impose on you to hitch the team up and bring the wagon around to the door? I think it would be best to forego the luxury of a tub bath just now in favor of getting on the road quickly."

On the road? It didn't sound like she was speaking merely of his departure.

She proved it with her next words. "I should be pulled together and ready to load up by the time you finish."

Ready to load? "You're actually going to fill the wagon with hay?" he asked, thinking of his own, rather flippant suggestion of hiding beneath it.

She chuckled, a low, throaty sound that only added to his uneasy awareness of her. How could she find anything amusing after what she had been through that afternoon? Some of it on his account.

"No, Mr. Walford. Not hay but with supplies for the trip," she said.

Beginning to feel like a fly noticing it was stuck in a web, J. W. dreaded having to ask his next question. "What trip?"

"Oh, haven't I explained?" she asked innocently.

She damn well knew she hadn't.

"There isn't really the time right now to do so," she chirped merrily, giving him further reason to grind his teeth in aggravation. "I promise I will when you bring the wagon around. I hate to suggest it, but do you think you could hurry?"

For answer J. W. dragged the chair-bound guest over the doorsill, entirely forgetting he needed to check the horizon for signs of returning riders first. Fortunately, the vista offered nothing more than the sight of turkey buzzards riding invisible wind currents, circling, then dropping down to enjoy a feast hidden somewhere within the broad field of bluebonnets.

Although she would have preferred the pleasure of slipping into the cramped tin bathing tub, thoroughly washing herself from the basin and dressing in fresh clothing made Lou feel nearly her old self. Not the cowed woman who had bowed to Frank's every wish out of fear, but the hopeful woman she had been prior to marrying him.

It took no time at all to pull on the divided nut-brown riding skirt and collarless buff-colored blouse. Her corset had already been loosened to accommodate her rounder form. She had been so differently proportioned as a maiden. She could only hope that when she donned her traveling dress in the morning it would be only a bit snug at the waist. She hadn't worn it since her wedding trip, having no reason to dress nicely since Frank discouraged church attendance or "gadding about" shopping in town. Because of the foul weather she had not worn it for his funeral, choosing instead the same serviceable skirt, shirt, and the once treasured, now faded paisley shawl her mother had sent her. Drenched, she had more closely resembled a bedraggled peon in from the fields than a grieving widow.

But then she hadn't been grieving for Frank.

Tomorrow would be a different story. When they reached the old San Antonio road, both she and Walford would need to look like a respectable couple en route to Crockett. Even in the looser fitting clothing, it was a struggle to do up the hooks and buttons without help, particularly when she kept feeling so light-headed. Changing into a proper gown in the morning, even one sadly out of fashion now, would prove a challenge.

And why was she going to all this trouble when she would be much more comfortable in her everyday work clothes? Lou asked herself. "Because I want to look respectable," she said aloud, then added sheepishly, "and nice for Mr. Walford."

Whatever had happened to the vow she'd made on Frank's grave, the one in which she'd promised never to have anything to do with a man again? Surely she hadn't been ill more than a handful of days since the funeral. Not content with controlling her life while alive, Frank had managed things so that she had been helpless as a widow, too. Was it the fact that she had been trapped these past few days or was it Mr. Walford himself who'd caused this change in her heart?

Or was it simply the circumstances? He had rescued her and, in a way, she had rescued him. Had given him a second chance, if nothing else.

No doubt the feeling would pass with time. He would be well on his way soon enough, out of her life and looking for trouble. She didn't need that kind of man. She already had had one like him.

Lou struggled to fasten the bottom-most button on her bodice. She had less trouble with the hook and eye on her belt, but could see very little of the all-over effect the ensemble created in the oval of Frank's shaving mirror. She hadn't had the pleasure of a full-length glass since leaving her grandfather's ranchero. Vanity had not been possible in the rough cabin, even if she could have afforded it.

The small mirror reminded her that her long, blue-black hair was a mass of tangles. Rather than spend precious time on it, Lou brushed it quickly, bundling the impossible locks into an unruly chignon. She would deal with the remaining knots later. There were more pressing things she needed to attend to presently.

Since she had been planning to leave before the widow Rosa had come to be her jailer, the only things not ready to load were the quilt and pillows on the bed and Frank's remaining things for Walford's use. She could offer him only a couple shirts, a spare pair of trousers, and the suit he already despised. So little reward for all he was doing for her. For all she'd have to trust him yet to do for her.

His saddle was still in the cellar. She would remind him to bring it up. Space in the wagon bed was very limited. His saddle would take up a lot of room—nearly half the area she'd allowed for sleeping—but she could cope with that. The ground couldn't be *that* hard, could it? And she did have the rolled-up oilcloth to use as a protection against the weather. The rest of the wagon would be filled with the personal items she would take: a few cooking pots and ladles, a small valise with a change of clothing for herself and a good many changes for the baby, bedding, the cradle, and the remaining food stuffs she had dried and preserved.

That left only absconding with the mares and the ancient buckboard as a crime. Surely that was the way Titus Gillette would see it. He might consider pursuing her as a horse thief, but she doubted he cared what happened to Frank's spare pistol or old rifle. She intended to take those, too.

And she would look beautiful, self-assured, and fearless as she did so. Lou surveyed herself in the mirror once more, standing on tiptoe to see more of her attire, turning from left to right. A better description might be passable, introverted, and tired, she decided. Dog tired. Was that how her outlaw felt after eluding his posse on foot?

Tying the ribbons of her flat crowned straw hat quickly, Lou wrapped the paisley shawl around her shoulders, then moved quietly toward the cradle so that the heels of her boots wouldn't create an echoing racket in the cabin. "Mr. Walford," she mused aloud. "I wonder what his given name is. Anything other than Frank is perfectly acceptable, don't you think, Angelina?" she asked, stooping down.

The baby was asleep, though, looking so like an angel with her unruly tuft of hair and pink rounded cheeks that Lou was awed anew at the thought that *this* child was her own. "Sleep on, little one. You're not going to have a very smooth ride tonight. None of us are."

From outside in the yard came the sound of harnesses jingling and wheels groaning. There was a brief knock on the door, then Walford pushed it open.

He'd found Frank's second-best hat, a battered pinch-crowned cow-country felt sombrero, she noticed. He swept it off, wiping sweat from his brow with his arm. "Your other guest isn't what I'd call a lightweight," he said, then paused.

Lou felt his gaze sweep over her from head to toe and back up again. Would he like the improvement in her appearance? The candid appraisal he gave her certainly did nice things for her ego, warming her blood and adding a few beats to the tempo of her pulse. It had been a long time since she had felt so fragile, feminine, and attractive. Was it that or her general feeling of weakness that made her sway slightly? Lou gripped the corner of the table until the sensation faded.

But it didn't disappear entirely. She was far too conscious of his every movement to feel in complete control of herself. Particularly when Walford ambled toward her with the controlled grace of a stalking cougar. Rather than frighten her, the motion sent a thrill of renewed awareness racing up her spine.

He circled her, his spurs ringing with each step but his perusal silent until he was standing directly in front of her, separated by barely twelve inches of breathing space. Once again she was aware of his scent, that interesting combination of leather and wildflowers. The sheriff was right, she mused. His eyes were gray and dark as a storm-chased sky.

"Where the blazes do you think you're going?" he demanded, quite obviously irritated.

She'd been hoping for a compliment but was familiar enough with the male of the species to recognize this was not the time or place to receive one. At least not to his way of thinking. It was the near escape from the posse, the strain of dealing with Widow Rosa's deadweight and horses easily spooked by an unknown hand, she decided, not herself that caused the irritation.

"Away," she answered. "With you."

"With me!"

"Certainly."

Walford shook his head, tossed his newly acquired hat on the table. "Listen, lady. You've been ill. You shouldn't be up and prancing about. You should be in bed recovering."

"And let Rosa stagger around here longer? I think not," she declared, her chin rising unconsciously in defiance. "You need Angelina and me. Without us, how are you going to keep every lawman in the state from giving you a look over, Mr. Walford?"

"It can be done," he said evenly.

Lou wished he would back up a step rather than tower over her. She met his eyes unflinchingly. They were stormy, yes, but not angry. He was trying to discourage her from helping him anymore.

"You still need me," she said quietly.

"No, I don't."

He didn't sound as inflexible as before. Lou couldn't keep a grin from her lips when she replied. "You do."

Walford wheeled away, striding back to the front window. Silhouetted against the first vivid palette of sunset colors to appear in the sky, he was a tall, dark, dangerous shadow. An aura of menace seemed to radiate from his still form, yet Lou felt no fear. He was a killer of men. She had no doubt of that. But he had been gentle and concerned for her welfare. In his company, she was convinced she would never come to harm. Convincing him of that was another thing entirely.

After staring at the western horizon awhile, Walford turned to face her again. "This is childish, ma'am," he insisted. "You're fooling yourself if you think to pass as a grieving widow with me seated next to you on that wagon seat."

"Oh, but I don't plan to," Lou said.

Walford didn't ask what part she did intend to play. Or what his was to be. She could tell he had already divined her intention. "Just how far and wide was your husband known in these parts?"

He sounded suspicious but, rather than be put off by his manner, Lou found it refreshing. At least he wasn't using profane language as Frank commonly had when angry. Walford wasn't angry though, he was merely run ragged, she decided, so she would overlook the frustrated tone.

Gathering the now neatly folded pile of her husband's clothing from the table, Lou ignored Walford's determination to leave her behind. "It is simple enough, sir. I need to leave here and you need to leave here. While Frank was fairly well known in the area, few would recognize me. In any event, I propose we leave here at dusk and travel along the forest path as far as possible tonight before camping."

Walford leaned back against the wall and folded his arms across his chest. His ankles were crossed as well, she noticed. The pose was that of a man with all the time in the world. Which he wasn't. "And what strategy have you planned in the event *I* am recognized?" he asked. "Detmer may have wired every sheriff's office in Texas and Louisiana with my description."

"Oh, surely only as far as the Mississippi and the Rio Grande," Lou suggested facetiously as she smoothed wrinkles from the top-most shirt. She hadn't taken much care with Frank's things when packing them away. Would Mr. Walford mind? She would have to bundle them in a bedsheet, as she would her good dress and shoes. Space in the buckboard was already so limited.

What would they do if Walford was right though and a diligent deputy became suspicious of him? "Did you have unruly whiskers when you shot that man?" Lou asked and returned to rummaging in the trunk.

"That doesn't answer my—"

"Did you?" she demanded softly without turning from her task.

Walford sighed deeply in resignation. "Yes, ma'am."

Finding what she was searching for, Lou closed the trunk lid softly. "Then perhaps you can use these things to help change your appearance," she said and opened her hand slowly. The light was still strong enough that he need not cross the room to clearly see the razor and shaving brush that rested on her palm. "The soap is on the washstand behind the bedroom curtain," she added, standing up once more.

"Amazing," Walford mumbled half to himself. He moseyed reluctantly back to her side. "All I came here for was a horse," he said, gathering the shaving utensils from her. "Instead I'm becoming a clean-shaven traveling salesman with . . ." He paused, as if allowing her to complete the thought.

"Complete with a wife and child, sir," Lou added, grinning happily. She gave him a brief curtsy. It was the least she could do considering that he had surrendered to her plan. "I hope I'll be suitably gowned tomorrow to do you justice."

"You'll probably look far too good for the spouse of a lowly drummer, ma'am," Walford murmured ruefully.

"You're too kind," she said, pleased with her victory, minor though it was. "The sun will be nearly down within the hour, so we'd best hurry."

Walford wasn't about to hurry though. "Let me get this straight first," he said. "I'm getting gussied up in that stultifying suit so I can escape notice."

"Yes," Lou agreed.

"And you are going with me because . . . ?"

"I will go unnoticed as well," she filled in.

Walford rubbed his whiskered chin thoughtfully. "Why do you want to go unnoticed? You've done nothing criminal."

"But I fully intend to," Lou assured him.

He didn't look impressed or assured.

"Frank left me with nothing, Mr. Walford. In essence I'm stealing the horses and wagon from the ranch's new owner," she explained.

"A hanging offense."

Lou tried not to look worried. The possible repercussions of her act weren't something she cared to think about much, if at all. "I propose that we travel together as long as it takes to avoid suspicion. Everyone will be searching for a lone man or for a solitary woman traveling with an infant, not a family en route to Austin or San Antonio. It is purely guesswork on my part, but I assume your goal is to cross into Mexico. That is also my destination. Our traveling together is entirely logical."

Whether he agreed with her on that point, Lou couldn't determine from his face. It was as expressionless as a rock. "And you are sure you should be traveling already?"

No, she answered silently. Had he noticed how often she gripped the edge of the table to keep from swaying on her feet? "Neither Angelina nor I will slow you down. You have my word on that. Now, do you have any other questions, Mr. Walford?"

"Just one, ma'am," he said. "What in hell is your name?"

Chapter Four

He was a damn fool, J. W. decided as he tossed his saddle up into the bed of the buckboard. And he was going to be damned uncomfortable once he changed into that idiotic plaid suit. Oh, it would fit fine. But rather than become invisible, he'd probably stand out like a target at a turkey shoot. Not a feeling that sat right with a man who had a posse with a grudge after him.

Unfortunately, the lovely Mrs. Louisa Burgess was probably right about the lawmen overlooking a man in a suit.

They were on the lookout for a scruffy drifter. Tomorrow, with his jaw freshly shaven and the jackanapes suit set to bind every move he made, the disguise just might let him slip by them on the road. They had gotten ahead of him twice now, once while he hid in a maze of brambles after his horse was downed. This time they'd moved on because his hostess had bluffed them. But if he didn't make it out of their territory soon, they would circle right back on his track. As much as he hated to admit she was right, his hostess's suggestion that they pretend to be a family en route to Austin, traveling the well-trafficked road at a sedate pace, would allow him to slip past with barely a glance thrown in his direction.

If Mrs. Burgess ever let them get on the road, that was. While he shaved, she had rattled on about the condition of a particular path they should travel through the forest. At night, if that made sense. No one would expect them to go that way, she claimed. J. W. had to admit he agreed with her on that point. Only a desperate man would be foolish enough to ride, much less drive a skittish team, into an unknown forest at night. He knew why he was desperate, just not why she was.

And she most definitely was. She had all the signs. The frequent checks of the horizon, the rush to gather what she could, the refusal to rest when she was very near to dropping from exhaustion. He'd been trusting her with his life nearly the whole of their acquaintance, but she had yet to confide in him about her concerns. Not that there had been much time to do so or, as she no doubt thought, much reason to explain her need to be on the run. Still, it would be damn convenient to know whom she feared before he had to deal with them. J. W. knew the die had been cast in regard to that eventuality. Not only did he owe her, he'd had the misfortune to be reared a gentleman. No matter what the war and his wife's murder had stripped from his soul, his instinct remained the same. He would do whatever it took to protect Mrs. Burgess and her child from whatever haunted her. It would simply be an easier task if he knew what to be on the lookout for.

The near side horse, a slightly mottled bay, shied when his hostess came through the cabin door, the tails of the quilt from her bed cascading from her arms. *Damn mustangs*, J. W. muttered under his breath as he hastened over to calm the beast. His determined angel of mercy had neglected to tell him her late husband had had a fondness for range horses, not to mention an apparent lack of patience when it came to breaking them. He'd heard men claim that a fella could kill a fifty dollar horse trying to rope a twenty dollar mustang. Judging by the nags he had hitched to the wagon, J. W. doubted anyone would give twenty dollars for the pair of them. They might be marginally broken, but they still had a wild look in their eyes, and not just because an unknown hand had been hitching them up. In the event Mrs. Burgess needed to sell them, she'd be lucky to get stage fare to the next town out of the deal.

Judging from the meager possessions in her household, the lady wasn't exactly flush in the pocket. She was going to have to sell the horses sooner or later. Chances were she'd assign him the chore of wrangling the best bargain. Their acquaintance might be little more than an hour old, but she was already issuing him orders as quickly as a jumped-up Army general with a West Point diploma and next to no field experience or sense. And considering he'd served under such an officer, J. W. knew exactly what he was up against. He intended to do exactly what he'd done in the late war, too. Let the general rattle on, then do what was needed, whether his actions coincided with orders or not.

In the case of Mrs. Burgess's barely tamed team, when the time came to dispose of them he'd pay someone to take them off his hands and just give her twice their worth from his own stash of ready money. In the meantime, he kept an eye peeled for anything of value she might have missed in her hurried packing. She was going to need every saleable item the miserable little ranch offered. So far the only item of any true value he'd found had been tucked out of sight in the loft in the barn: a nicely tooled and ornamented Spanish saddle. The quality of the piece made him curious about the late Frank Burgess, but only briefly. He'd met enough men to know there were those who had skewed ideas when it came to which was most valuable, a wife or a saddle. In fact, considering the quality of the saddle, he was surprised that Burgess hadn't possessed better firearms. The two often went together. And considering that the carved-out niche beneath the cabin had a lived-in feel to it, J. W. was fairly sure a good set of irons had been important to Burgess. More important than caring for his lovely wife, at any rate.

Just because Burgess hadn't done his duty by her in his lifetime didn't mean Louisa couldn't benefit from her husband's leavings now. And so J. W. had tossed the saddle in the wagon. He doubted she had even noticed the addition yet, although when his own saddle was added, the two took up a hunk of space.

"There's the small valise yet to manage, if you could, Mr. Walford," Mrs. Burgess said as she dumped the bedding just behind the buckboard's well-sprung seat. He hoped she had an oiled cloth to cover the items in the event of rain. For that matter, some rain gear to cover herself and the baby. The frilly little parasol she'd pulled from somewhere was good only for shading a lady from the sun at a tea party. The furled fabric would leak like a sieve if she tried to use it during a spring downpour.

"Oh, and Angelina's cradle. It will go just here." A wave of her hand indicated the nest she had made with the quilt. "That way she can be comforted by the sight of us."

Us, he thought. How easily the term sprang to her lips. How adept she was at maneuvering things so that he was at her beck and call. If indeed her suggestion that they travel together did allow him to slip free of the posse, he would be even more in her debt than he already was. How did a man ever repay an obligation like that?

With lots of legal tender, he hoped. He'd have little need of it where he was no doubt bound.

He couldn't help wondering where he'd be right now if she hadn't been lying unconscious by the well, if he had simply helped himself to a horse and ridden on.

Probably dangling from the business end of a rope, that's where he'd be. The posse had turned up close on his heels, after all, and they hadn't exactly been in a mood to see that he got a proper trial from the beginning. Particularly since he was innocent.

Well, maybe not entirely innocent. He had been gunning for Uriah Roane. But it had been a fair fight with Roane drawing his pistol first. He couldn't help it that the former Reb preferred a fast, wildly aimed shot. A successful gunman took his time and aimed carefully. As he had.

Mrs. Burgess paused before returning to the cabin, her eyes turning for perhaps the sixth time toward the already darkening eastern sky. She was sensibly dressed for clandestine travel, her clothing as naturally colored as the landscape and showing definite signs of daily use. They were a well-matched pair, her turn-out as age-worn as his own.

"Exactly what direction did the posse ride when they left?" J. W. asked belatedly. He rubbed his hand in a last soothing stroke along the now calmed bay's neck, watching his hostess only from the corner of his eye.

Mrs. Burgess started. "What? Oh, to the north. They probably think you were making for Alto since it is on the main road. There would be a better chance of replacing your horse there."

If he'd known where Alto was in the first place, he probably would have headed there instead of winding up on her doorstep.

"Then what's that way?" J. W. asked, jerking his head to indicate the direction that kept reclaiming her attention.

"Peaceful," she said. Rather than look at him, she fussed with her skirt, endeavoring to shake some of the newly accumulated dust from the hem. "The town where Frank was killed."

J. W. kicked himself mentally. What a louse he was, too busy dealing with the events of the day to spare a moment for how she was feeling.

Her husband was so recently dead. At the most, a week, she had said. He remembered only too well how he'd felt upon hearing of Claire's death. Devastated. Lost. So much so that in the years since the war had ended, he had not had the courage to return to Kansas to visit her grave. Or the grave of his son.

Even if he personally thought Frank Burgess could have done better by her, it didn't mean she felt the same. In standing off the posse earlier she had certainly demonstrated that it hadn't been her first such showdown. She was probably one of those women who loved her man blindly, purposely overlooking his faults and trumping up any spare virtues he might possess. Whether Burgess deserved it or not, his wife was likely missing him fiercely.

So why was she so ready to run?

She gave her skirts a final shake and, as if unable to stop herself from doing so, gazed off in the direction of the town once more, to the place where her husband had died.

"You miss him, don't you?" J. W. asked. "I know how you feel."

She turned to look at him over her shoulder. "No, Mr. Walford, I doubt you do. We shouldn't waste any more time. The light will soon be gone and delaying much longer would be incredibly dangerous for both of us," she said, her voice surprisingly quiet and calm, he thought, considering her choice of words. "If you could get the valise and cradle, I will get Angelina and we can be on our way," she added.

Apparently there wasn't time to explain further. However, since the shadows were growing longer and the light dimming toward the haze of twilight, he agreed with her. It was getting more dangerous by the minute for him to stay. Why it was also dangerous for her, well, he could only hope that she would trust him enough to explain once they were on the trail.

J. W. released the once skittish mare's bridle and, feeling rather like an obedient hound dog, followed Mrs. Burgess back into the dim recesses of the cabin.

The town of Peaceful lived up to its name, Claude Morgan mused as his horse ambled down the main street behind a handful of other posse members. At the far end of the street there was a church spire spreading its influence over a dozen single-story wooden structures, of which only one appeared to be a saloon. He counted two dry goods stores, a livery stable, a bank, and a sheriff's office. On other buildings were shingles hung proudly announcing that a doctor, barber, lawyer, and undertaker called Peaceful home. A token sort of building laid claim to being a schoolhouse. The sound of a blacksmith's hammer still rang from within the livery stable but there wasn't a peep being heard from the open door of the saloon, nor was there a bell to be rung in the church steeple that he could see. A couple of lounging citizens made the effort to turn their heads, following the course of the horsemen as they trouped to a stop before the sheriff's office, but other than that and a handful of lights beginning to glow in various windows as the sun called it a day, there was very little to cause excitement in Peaceful.

That wouldn't last long, Morgan thought. Particularly if Walford had stumbled into town.

"Evenin', gents," the man taking his ease before the sheriff's office said without bothering to take his boots off the hitching rail or drop his tilted chair back on all four legs. "See yer wearin' tin. Where from?"

The man Detmer had put in charge of their party brushed back his coat to better display the tin badge fastened to his weskit. "Lone Tree," he said.

"Bit out of yer jurisdiction, ain't ya?" the local law observed.

"A bit," Detmer's deputy answered. "Chasin' an escaped murderer. Wondered if he'd been through here. Tall feller, dark hair 'n' eyes, beard."

Peaceful's sheriff pushed the brim of his hat back a spare inch. "Sounds like most strangers passin' this way," he said. "Killer, you say?"

"Shot a man in cold blood," Detmer's man said, needlessly clarifying the matter.

Damn idiot, Morgan thought.

"Don't say. Might check with 'em down at the saloon. Most strangers make a stop there if only to fortify themselves."

Detmer's deputy put a hand to the brim of his hat in a casual salute. "My thanks. There someplace my men can bunk tonight? Be nice to have a bed fer a change."

"No hotel, but I'll ask around," the sheriff promised, although he made no effort to get to his feet.

Morgan backed his horse and turned its head in the direction of the saloon. It was time to give the posse his notice to quit. Walford would have them riding in circles soon, if they weren't already. And if not Walford, then Detmer would. They'd been barely out of sight of the broken down ranch house before Detmer had decided to divide up the men. Some rode with him toward Alto in case Walford had made it to the main road. Some hied back across the Angelina River to Nacogdoches in the event that Walford had doubled back, tricking them with the sign they'd read at the riverbank. The remainder had turned south to Peaceful. Morgan had chosen to join the last group with an eye to making a return visit to the rifle-wielding hellcat who'd faced them off. After grueling hours in the saddle, he couldn't say that he had an abiding interest in catching Walford at the moment. It would be much easier to give Detmer's deputy his temporary star than give it back to the sheriff himself. Uriah Roane had greeted him as a friend before eating a last meal of Walford's lead. Some of the Lone Tree men would find it damn strange that he was leaving the chase after his compadre's killer.

However, riding with a man during the war and being his friend were two entirely different situations, Morgan knew, and it had only been the reward that had turned him into a tin-wearing posse member to begin with. That and curiosity over why Walford had a grudge to cure when it came to Roane. Walford had growled something under his breath that had pushed Roane to hastily slap leather. "Lawrence, Kansas" was all Morgan had caught of the exchange, but it was enough to gnaw away at his peace of mind.

Before sidling into the saloon, Morgan slipped the thin hammered piece of tin from the rolled lapel of his dark wool vest. If he was going to distance himself from the Lone Tree horde, doing so immediately struck him as a mighty fine idea. He made it to the long rough bar before the other deputies had finished hitching their horses outside.

"Beer," he told the bartender. The beverage slid his way was weak compared to the brews he remembered with longing from St. Louis and Cincinnati. His name had been something different in each of the river cities in those other lifetimes. But then, so had the names of a lot of folks. But that had been before the war, before people had started to spill west in ever-increasing numbers. Too many knew him as Claude Morgan now to make a switch of identity a smart move. Particularly with the profitable prospect of a change of profession in his immediate future. But first his most recent past needed to be erased, particularly his connection to Wes Dalhert and the atrocities they'd committed in the name of the Confederacy.

Two years he'd ridden with Dalhert. Morgan couldn't say it had been because he was all fired up over the views held by Johnny Rebs, but then raiding groups like Dalhert's and Quantrill's hadn't been officially recognized by Jeff Davis's administration like Mosby's men in the Shenandoah Valley were. Mosby was a gentleman guerrilla fighter who had followed the rules of engagement even if he had become a thorn in the Yankees' side. Even the nom de plume Mosby had acquired, The Grey Ghost, had a gentlemanly sound to it. The epithet "bloody" was more likely to be attached to the name of men like Bill Quantrill and Wes Dalhert, rangers who'd been nothing more than westerners with deep-seated grudges. Particularly when it came to the Free-Soilers of Kansas.

Dalhert hadn't been choosy over whom he rode with. If he took a liking to a man in a saloon, Wes was willing to christen his newfound friend as a raider. Christenings were in Yankee blood. At first Morgan had ridden with the raiders out of boredom. After that, it had been from madness.

The madness had passed, just as the war had. Now all that remained was cool-eyed determination. There was wealth to be gained in a system set to legally rape the former Confederate states, but not for a man who'd ridden with a western guerrilla group. Out of all the men who had fought for the South, the Missouri rangers were the only ones to whom the plug hat gents in Washington refused to grant amnesty. In riding with Dalhert he had lost rights that even dirt-poor ignorant sharecroppers could exercise if they had the gumption. Things like voting and running for and holding a political office.

Morgan nearly laughed at the irony of the situation. He hadn't cared a jot about politics during a war fraught with political dissension. He still didn't care for anything but the easiest way to line his pockets with gold. Too bad the slickest way to do that was to be elected as a representative of the people.

After a life of drifting, he had a fancy to settle down and enjoy the pleasures that graft had to offer. But to do so he had to cover his disreputable past, distance himself from the Claude Morgan who'd been Dalhert's right-hand demon. The best way to do that was to make sure the handful of men who had known him as a ranger were six feet under.

When the Lone Tree men pushed through the saloon's door, Morgan picked up his beer and looked around for an empty table. Seeing none, he was about to down his beer and leave when a prosperous-looking gent signaled him, indicating one of the empty chairs at his table in the corner.

"Appreciate the offer," Morgan said, putting his glass down and taking a seat, his back to the wall.

"Glad for the company," the other man insisted. His well-made dark suit and weskit fit comfortably over a girth that was still in the building stage. A broad-linked gold watch chain looped across the girth, broadcasting the man's personal prosperity, and the starched collar and lily-white shirt front he wore looked fresh, as if he'd changed before visiting the saloon. His face was florid, his nose prominent, and the carefully maintained beard and mustache below it were speckled with gray. "You with those other fellers that rode in?" the man asked.

Morgan considered a moment before answering. "Was," he allowed. "Decided I didn't like riding with them."

"Notice they're wearing badges. That mean you're a man of the law, too?" his host persisted.

"Occasionally," Morgan said and grinned. If he'd been a religious man, no doubt lightning would have struck him down on the spot. But then a religious man would never have done the things he'd done. Besides, he doubted signing on to hunt Walford counted as being a real man of the law. Roane's chums were nothing more than glorified rangers of the worst sort. After all, no one knew the type better than he did, Morgan mused.

Considering his host's turnout, Morgan doubted the man all that law-abiding himself. Unless knowing how to take personal advantage of the Reconstruction laws governing things in Texas could be accounted as law abiding. The fellow looked like another of the plug hat gents, never having had to dirty his hands with manual labor. And since Morgan had heard that this neck of Texas, the whole of Angelina County, had rejected secession back in 1861, the man had no doubt managed to keep his hands clean during the war, too.

"Name's Titus Gillette," his well-suited, newfound friend said. "I own the local bank, which means I also own most of the land in these parts. Let me buy you a drink, Mr. . . . ?"

Morgan took a long slow swallow of warm beer before accepting and giving his name. "You sound like a man who's looking for something in return, Gillette."

The banker signaled the bartender for a fresh round. "I am, Mr. Morgan. I am that. And from the way you wear that gun on your belt, I think you just may be that something."

Lou felt the seconds ticking away, robbing her of sanity as she hastened to load the wagon. Surely she was forgetting something in her rush to escape the cage Titus Gillette had built around her. It was overwhelming to think how easily he had accomplished it, how quickly one terrible event had followed another. And sad that among those terrible events she did not number Frank's sudden demise as one of them. No, things had only begun to go awry when Gillette had arrived at her door and shown her Frank's hastily scribbled signature deeding the ranch and everything on it to the banker. Including, apparently, her.

She guessed that it had been barely a week ago that events began to conspire against her. Gillette hadn't been long in arriving at the ranch after word reached her of Frank's death. His well-sprung buggy and carefully groomed team had driven smartly up to the door. She had watched as he heaved himself from the equipage and tipped his hat. The courtesy had not prepared her for what was to come.

"A terrible thing about your husband, my dear. Tragic. Particularly in view of Frank's wager in that fateful game," Gillette had said, settling himself at her table.

At first, Lou had thought he was going to give her the opportunity to reclaim the property, gather a modest herd, repay Frank's debt, and build a new life. She could have done it, she knew. As a forgotten child on her grandfather's ranchero, she had been eager to learn everything about the daily operation of the place in the hope that Don Felipe de la Vaca would find her interest worthy of note. She knew how to raise cattle. Had always been eager to ride out with the vaqueros, to learn along with the boys all she could of roping and riding. As the *patrone*'s granddaughter she was forbidden to work with the women in the hacienda or kitchens, and had taken advantage of her grandfather's oversight in regards to chores usually taught to the boys.

But her eagerness and knowledge had not been valued by her grandfather. As the daughter of a hated American who had eloped with Don Felipe's only child, Xaverina, Lou belatedly realized her grandfather considered her an embarrassment. One he was well rid of in bartering a generous dowry to Frank Burgess for wedding her. And, just as she'd been wrong about what would interest her grandfather, Lou realized she erred in regard to Gillette's intention, too.

"It was wrong of Frank to gamble away your home, my dear," the banker said, "but it was a fair wager under the law, although I doubt the property will prove to be worth much."

The words seemed a slur considering she had worked hard to keep the ranch buildings neat, clean, and in repair. There hadn't been much else she could do since, other than the wild mustangs her husband had occasionally rounded up, there had been no livestock in either the small corral or the disreputably built barn. The dreams she had fostered of having a profitable cattle ranch had not been shared by Frank, who claimed to value cunning over hard work. Only she seemed to recognize that when it came to actually being cunning, Frank didn't measure up.

Whether Titus Gillette was cunning or not, he most certainly had the upper hand.

"Your personal items, such as clothing and the child's things, are yours to keep, of course," Gillette allowed. "However, the rest is forfeit."

When his gaze swept over her rather than the meager furnishings in the cabin, a chill ran up Lou's spine.

"Forfeit," she repeated dully.

"At your husband's wish," Gillette said. "You are no doubt wondering what your prospects are. Wondering when you need to move into town. Wondering if Frank arranged for his daughter's care or for your care, my dear Louisa."

She had known then that Frank had bartered her as well as the ranch in the fateful card game. And why shouldn't he? Hadn't her own grandfather done nearly the same thing, conspiring to punish her for being the offspring of a hated American by purchasing another American as her bridegroom? When she'd learned the truth, she had vowed never to despise anyone as wholly as Don Felipe had despised her. Now the vow was broken, shattered as Lou savored the first pungent taste of true hate.

Gillette left without spelling out the abominable future that awaited her, promising only to return once she had buried Frank and realized the true hopelessness of her situation. "I'm sure that you will soon see the sense in accepting a strong arm and aid from one who cares for your well being, Louisa," Gillette said, then added, "and that of tiny, helpless Angelina."

The slight emphasis he put on the word *helpless* left Lou feeling the words were nothing less than a threat. The fact that a couple of Frank's cronies had arrived with more blatant suggestions on how she was to survive merely made her situation appear more hopeless. Gillette hadn't voiced the idea aloud yet, but he would in the coming days, Lou knew. The choice they all gave her was one of beds: either she share an outlaw's or the banker's.

Neither was acceptable.

Thus she had stood at Frank's graveside silently cursing him as shovel after shovel full of mud was dropped on his rain-soaked coffin. She had married him for better or for worse, not realizing her release from that vow would leave her in still more deplorable circumstances than she had known as his wife. Yet without the means to leave, Lou had felt as helpless as her infant daughter was.

Worn with worry and drenched by a cold spring rain, she had been struck down by fever that had robbed her of what little strength remained. When Gillette had installed his handmaiden, Widow Rosa, in her home, Lou had felt all hope desert her. But it had returned when a stranger arrived to find her in a swoon at the foot of the well.

A stranger who was probably no better than her late husband had been, but who in a short span of hours had taken on the mantle of her childhood hero, Santo Jorge, slayer of dragons. Mr. Walford was a killer of men, of that Lou had no doubt. He was a man on the run from the law, a man with a posse on his trail. Yet, if the papers Titus Gillette had waved in her face represented the letter of that same law, then she, too, was a breaker of the code, stealing not only the buckboard and horses, but herself away as well.

She was doing Walford no favor in helping him elude the posse. Her own escape and the safety of her child were all that mattered to her. If they were caught, he would hang as a horse thief as well as a murderer. But her own situation would be worse. She would live, controlled once more by a man she despised.

Unable to stop herself, Lou stared in the direction of Peaceful one last time, then accepted Walford's hand to climb aboard the wagon. "We head due west, Mr. Walford," she directed as he settled beside her and picked up the reins.

"Into the forest," he said, his tone indicating reluctance.

Lou nodded. "Into the forest. Tomorrow we will join El Camino Real at Crockett and blend in with other travelers."

"Yes, ma'am," he murmured. "Whatever you say."

That's right, Lou thought. *Whatever I say*. She hoped he would be as agreeable when he found out exactly what else she planned to say. Particularly when it came to putting distance—and Mr. Walford—between herself and Titus Gillette.

Chapter Five

Their way wended briefly through a flower-studded meadow before entering the ancient growth of woodlands. The path was not wide, stretching little more than the width of the buckboard in places, which made speed one element of their getaway impossible to achieve. But Lou had chosen the trail because it was rarely used, willing to sacrifice speed for the relative safety of the forest trace.

She wasn't sure Walford appreciated the distinction though. He sat hunched at her side, the reins held loosely in his hands as he allowed the horses to pick their own way over the barely visible track. Although he'd settled the borrowed hat low over his eyes, Lou could tell from his expression that he was frowning. Whether it was because she was taking unkind advantage of him or because their way was growing more difficult to discern, she couldn't tell. She wouldn't apologize. She did admit, if only to herself, that the light was fading far too fast. Would they be able to put enough distance between the rundown ranch and themselves before it was too dark to continue farther on their way?

The sun had already dipped below the western horizon, though some of its reflected glow lingered like an afterthought. Their way was further shadowed by the tall stands of trees. Cypress, hickory, oak, gum, and magnolia were common to the area, mingling with various species of pine, mulberry, white ash, and maple. Although Lou had never visited the neighboring state of Louisiana, Frank had told her the terrain was much the same there as in Angelina County. It too harbored marshy areas like the bog they skirted near the Neches River.

Walford eased the team to a halt as they approached the water's edge. "You didn't happen to mention there was another river to cross, Mrs. Burgess," he murmured, a slight edge to his voice.

In his place, Lou was sure she would have felt much the same. The comment also told her he was a stranger to Texas; he didn't realize that there were still a dozen other rivers or creeks they would be crossing before reaching the Rio Grande. If, that was, she convinced him to escort her even that far.

"It's a shallow ford," she promised of the Neches crossing. "Nearly as shallow as the one the main road crosses below Alto."

"Nearly," he repeated, his voice flat and, she supposed, tired. How long had he been on the run that day already? She knew so little about him, yet trusted him so completely.

She hoped doing so wouldn't prove to be another horrible error on her part.

The Neches was streaming higher on its banks than usual, and without the glint of sun sparkling on its normally shade-dappled surface, the ford looked anything but welcoming. Over the noise of the rushing water, Lou caught a trill of sound. Tilting her head to the side, she listened once more for the ominous call of the bird to be repeated. When it was, she touched Walford's arm lightly.

"We really shouldn't delay, Mr. Walford," Lou said softly. "The ford truly is quite safe and if we don't find a sheltered place to stop further along our trail, I'm afraid we'll lose our way in the rain."

"Rain!" He glanced quickly at the scrap of softly graying sky just visible above the treetops. "There's barely a cloud to be seen."

This had nothing to do with clouds though. At least, not yet, Lou thought as she noted another of nature's signs. The breeze had turned. Its gentle touch was no longer caressing her cheek as it had only moments earlier, but pressed instead at her back. Lou turned so that the slight wind tugged at the wide brim of her hat and sent the dangling tails of the tied ribbon dancing forward around her face. "Didn't you hear the quail?" she asked. "It has called twice already."

"I've heard a number of birds chattering, Mrs. Burgess. Forgive me for neglecting to identify each magpie as it spoke," Walford growled, slapping the reins to coax the team down the bank and into the river. When the temperamental mares balked, he passed the reins into Lou's care and stepped down from the buckboard.

He was being facetious, she thought. There were no magpies in the area. Any number of other species of birds, of course, from woodpeckers to bald eagles, but not that she had heard, a single magpie. "It was a quail's whistle," Lou said. "If you hear one after sundown, you can expect rain."

Walford resettled her husband's old hat more firmly over his eyes, took hold of the far side horse's bridle and tugged the resistant mares forward into the river. The jangle of the harness mingled with the bright sound of hooves splashing through the shallows, then hushed as the team reached deeper water. Although she was sure the water was still quite chilly this early in the year, Walford didn't flinch or falter as it rose from ankle depth to mid calf within two of his long strides.

"Forgive me for being skeptical, ma'am," Walford said, dragging the team along, "but I'd be more inclined to guess your quail is chiding her family into settling in for the night."

"Well, yes, that might be one translation," Lou agreed as the river rose around the wagon wheels. Having crossed this particular ford only on horseback before her pregnancy when she'd barely dampened the hem of her riding skirt, she hadn't considered that the path might be more treacherous for a team and buckboard. Or recalled that storms to the north might have swelled its size. When the Neches reached no higher than Walford's knees, she breathed a quiet sigh of relief before feeling guilty over his now sodden boots and trouser legs.

Walford clucked his tongue, urging the horses up the opposite bank and along the narrow path. Rather than pause to wring water from his cavalry trousers or empty it from his boots, he strode into the woods, his hand still gripping the bay's bridle. "Perhaps your quail was merely commenting on the weather to her neighbors," he suggested, "wondering if rain would keep other damn fools from crossing the river in less than ideal conditions."

Lou decided that he was referring to the failing light, and couldn't really blame him for that. What choice had they had though? The posse was sure to return when they found no trace of him elsewhere, and though she had no idea how long it had been since Titus Gillette had last visited the ranch, the fact that there had been little in the way of fresh supplies in the cabin for Widow Rosa's use argued that someone would be coming to restock the vittles, if not to check on her own recovery. She, Walford, and the baby had had to leave immediately or risk losing their chance at freedom.

"It isn't merely the quail's call that suggests rain," Lou explained as Walford forged along the little used trail. "The wind is from the east, too, which is another indication of a coming storm. When the two instances are consecutive, there can be only one result."

"Rain," Walford said.

"Rain," Lou agreed.

The forest seemed alive with the news as well. There was a whisper in the trees overhead as branches swayed gently in the newly risen breeze. Birds continued their twilight gossip. The creak of the buckboard, the sound the wheels made as they rolled over lightly packed soil, and the jarring ring of the harness when one of the horses unexpectedly tossed its head, all seemed unnaturally loud in the wilderness. Present but unseen, Lou fancied their progress was noted by curious ringtail opossums, cottontails, gray foxes, and bobcats. Somewhere back along the river a bull frog commented to his companions on their passing. Ahead on the right, a quick movement in the brush allowed her to spot the white tail of a deer rushing away at their approach.

Would the landscape be anything like this where she was bound, Lou wondered? Even if there were hardwood forests and flower bedecked meadows in Mexico, her mother lived in a city, a totally foreign environment compared to Lou's own experience. She had grown up on a large ranch, one of the remaining Spanish grants, then had moved to a small rundown homestead. She had done little more than visit San Antonio briefly, and even though she had lived in Angelina County a number of years now, her visits to Peaceful itself had been rare. What would it be like to live so close to neighbors that she would be aware of their comings and goings on a daily basis?

Of course, there was little point in wondering about such

things at the moment. There was always the chance that her mother's husband would refuse to welcome her and Angelina. They would be arriving on his doorstep unheralded by letter or wire. If they made it all the way to Mexico City, that was.

What would she do if Walford refused to escort her so far? Or if he were recognized, arrested, and thus forced to abandon them?

She had not thought things out clearly, Lou realized. But how could she have when time had been so scarce? The need to run had been so great and the window of opportunity so small. Was it any wonder that she had barely thought ahead to what awaited her in the future, and only rushed through the quickly vanishing present? The enormity of the ordeal yet to come was enough to leave her feeling uncommonly weak again, and that was a luxury that she could ill afford. As if the action itself would strengthen her and clear her mind of the drug's aftereffects, Lou glanced back at her sleeping baby. Her daughter was so at peace with the world, so sure that all would be well, that her mother would protect her and see to all her needs. Such innocence. Such wonder to have created that perfect little being.

Lou squared her shoulders, straightened her drooping posture on the wagon seat. For Angelina's sake, there was no obstacle she could not—would not—surmount. Some way, some how, she would find the strength to see them through the journey. And the first step along that journey was to see them safely through the night.

Rather than return to her side on the wagon's narrow bench, Walford continued to walk at the bay's side, calming the skittish horse when unseen creatures scurried in the brush at the edge of the path. "Did that quail mention anything about how long before the rain is set to commence?" he asked.

"No," Lou admitted. "It isn't as exact a science as counting the rings around the moon."

"Rings around the moon," he muttered, just loudly enough for her to hear. "I suppose they tell the exact hour to expect the downpour."

"Days until the downpour," she corrected. "You didn't grow up in the countryside, did you, Mr. Walford?"

"Meaning, I'd know this particular set of superstitions if I did?"

"Indications, not superstitions," Lou insisted. "Perhaps they differ in the North though."

He glanced back at her. "What makes you think I'm from the North?"

What a silly question. "Shall we say you don't sound like any Texian I've ever encountered," she said. "You are wearing cavalry trousers, too, Union ones. Unless you appropriated them from a man no longer in need of them—"

"You mean a dead man, I take it," Walford said.

Lou ignored the interruption. "—then they were yours to begin with. But that is neither here nor there, is it? We were discussing your obvious city origins."

"No, ma'am, we were discussing the likelihood of rain and when it was planning on arriving," Walford corrected. "And I don't hail from the city, merely from an area where the quail keep their thoughts to themselves when it comes to the topic of the weather."

The damp fabric of his trousers no doubt chafed as he walked, she thought. River water might yet slosh within his boots since he hadn't stopped to empty them. Both these discomforts gave him good reason to be short with her. Still, it hadn't been at her behest that he'd waded into the river. Men could be so difficult to deal with at times. Even relatively gentle men, as Mr. Walford appeared to be when dealing with a female.

"I merely thought you'd prefer to be forewarned," Lou said stiffly.

"Appreciate the thought, ma'am," Walford murmured, resolutely leading the team deeper into the woods.

She doubted it. Miffed, she remained silent. He was no doubt equally irritated with her since he remained on foot, rather than return to the wagon. The reins dangled in her hands uselessly. She had little to do but stare at the broad expanse of his back, although in the building gloom even that was becoming difficult to discern.

There was very little light to guide them now. Even though she knew the trail, at night it would be difficult to find her way unless on foot, and even then it would be so easy to miss the path. Yet Walford, a stranger to the area, seemed to find the way effortlessly.

He was in truth a guardian sent in answer to her prayers. If not Santo Jorge, then an archangel, one of Heaven's fighting brethren.

"Did you really kill him?" she asked quietly.

The sounds of the forest seemed stilled, as if waiting for his answer as well.

"The man back in Lone Tree? Yes," Walford said.

The forest continued to hold its breath, only the sound of the horses' hooves and the creak of the wagon breaking the silence. "It's not too late for you to turn back, you know," he said after a bit.

But it was. "It isn't much farther to the clearing, Mr. Walford. I don't think we should chance a fire, but I believe we can enjoy a cold supper. Are you partial to beans?" Lou asked.

*   *   *

Was he partial to beans? J. W. shook his head, wondering at her calm, complacent tone. She'd just asked him if he'd killed a man then brushed off his answer as though it barely mattered.

He had killed so many men, adding one more to his tally shouldn't matter to him. But it did matter. During the war the enemy had been relatively faceless. A man killed or was killed. Survival had depended as much on luck as on skill. It had become commonplace to fire his pistols, draw and use his sword. To shout orders and encouragement to his men until he was hoarse and only realized it after the smoke cleared from their killing field. Killing was the adrenaline that kept fear at a distance. Or it did in the thick of the battle. Before and after an engagement, fear was a soldier's constant companion.

So why was it that now, when face-to-face with his enemy, when he had more reason to kill his foe than a command given, fear never entered the picture? Was that what the fever of revenge did to a man?

Or was it that having lost Claire and their son, he no longer cared whether he lived or died?

If that was the case, why did he still see Roane's startled expression in his mind's eye? The raider had been confident that the outcome of their confrontation would be in his favor. The realization that the pistol ball had been more than a bumblebee whizzing by had truly stunned the Secesh. A hand to his chest and confusion in his eyes, Roane had buckled and his handgun had dropped to the saloon floor, its clatter like a loud report in the stillness of the room. He himself had immediately been jumped by the fallen rogue's friends, but it was Uriah Roane's disbelieving face that remained clear as life in J. W.'s memory, not what had followed.

The trouble was, while Roane haunted him, the visage he longed to remember had faded. He hadn't even the small portrait of Claire that had accompanied him to war. It had been lost during one of the so frequent hours he'd spent in brevet hell, those frozen-in-time moments of the battle itself.

He tried again to raise her ghost, to rebuild the contours of her face, to remember the exact shade of her golden hair. Instead the weary exhaustion that Louisa Burgess tried to hide came to mind, bringing with it the memory of her scent, the way she had felt tucked against his chest as he carried her into the cabin. What perfume had Claire preferred? How had *she* fit against him when they danced, when they made love? He should be able to recall. Claire had been his world. But, try as he might to bring her mentally back to life, it seemed Claire's image was doomed to be overshadowed by his awareness of Mrs. Burgess's resolve and current proximity.

J. W. trudged on. He was becoming more of a philosopher than he'd ever been in his former life. The one where the law had truly mattered to him. Only Diamond ever mentioned that he'd once been a lawyer. A good one, she said. Now he took the law into his own hands. That fact, as well as the ghosts of the men he'd gunned down, haunted him.

What choice had there been though? Though Wes Dalhert's ranger unit had been denied amnesty after the war, there had been no legally sanctioned action taken to punish him and his men for the atrocities they had committed. No, that chore had been left to his discretion. His and Diamond's. Without his sister's aid, the revenge he sought would probably have lain festering in his soul.

Or what was left of his soul, if he possessed one yet. Uriah Roane had been the third of Dalhert's former raiders he'd sent to meet their Maker. There were still at least four others yet to find: Egan O'Brien, Quentin Winters, Dalhert himself, and the mysterious man known only as Morg.

As if to remind him it dwelt more in the present than his mind, his stomach growled. Cold or not, dinner was going to be welcome. Extremely welcome, considering he had traveled on an empty stomach all day.

"I've dealt with worse than just beans for a meal," Walford said, answering his lovely traveling companion's query. If one of the men he hunted was a bit of a mystery, the fellow had nothing on the lovely woman who'd thrust him into the position of being her escort.

"You haven't tasted these beans yet," Mrs. Burgess said. At times she seemed so set on keeping the conversation going, he wondered if she was one of those women who couldn't stand the sound of silence. Though he was fairly sure they were in no danger of being overheard on such a forgotten scrap of trail, he hoped if the posse put in another appearance that she could restrain her need for a running commentary.

"We also have some tortillas, but they aren't freshly made, nor of my own creation," she continued. "I appropriated them, considering Rosa's need of them less urgent than my own."

Nearly anything was an improvement over the field rations he'd lived on during the war. There had been a reason the men referred to the dehydrated lumps of vegetables they were issued as *desecrated vegetables*. "Sounds like an improvement over hellfire stew," J. W. said.

"Hellfire stew?" He could hear the humor in Mrs. Burgess's voice. Unfortunately, the sound if it reminded him of Claire, of how she had always claimed the only thing she needed to be serious about was how much she loved him.

"Yes, ma'am. It's an adaptable recipe. You take some pulverized hardtack, soak it in water, then fry it in pork fat or anything else that comes to hand," J. W. explained. "Standard Army fare."

"It sounds . . . er, intriguingly imaginative," she said.

It had been better than nothing, but not much better.

"This the clearing you had in mind?" J. W. asked as the path widened. He judged there was a spare ten feet on either side of the path. Barely enough room to get the buckboard off the track but enough space to bivouac for the night. Particularly if she was right and rain was coming.

He'd barely drawn the team up when Mrs. Burgess set the hand brake, wrapped the reins around it, and lowered herself down from the wagon. "It looks much smaller at night," she murmured when she joined him. "Will it suffice, Mr. Walford? We could go on, but I'd rather not."

She looked ready to drop in her tracks. Determination alone was probably keeping her on her feet.

"It will suffice, Mrs. Burgess," J. W. said. Before long, he doubted it would be possible to see his hand in front of his face, much less the way through the woods. On his own, he would have chanced it, the desire to put as much distance between himself and the noose back in Lone Tree driving him to take a gamble. He would not do so with a woman and infant in tow.

The assurance seemed to relieve her mind. "The way will improve greatly tomorrow, Mr. Walford," she promised. "In fact, unless the shower tonight affects the path, we should be able to join the main road before noon and be in Crockett before sundown."

Without a map to enlighten him on the matter, J. W. figured he'd just have to take her word on it. "And we'd be headed in what direction when we do?" he asked.

"West," she said.

West, he thought, exasperated anew. That told him a whole hell of a lot. He was bone tired and wouldn't have the comfort of a fire, coffee, or a hot meal that night. Nor would he have the leisure to dry out from his second baptism of the day before he was drenched in an apparently quail-induced rainstorm. But at least he knew he was headed west.

Women!

Unaware of his frustration, Mrs. Burgess picked her way across the token clearing, sizing up the choicest spot to make camp. "The bushes should act as a bit of a windbreak here, don't you agree, Mr. Walford?" She gestured grandly, the fringe on her shawl swaying with the movement. "If we can find some suitable branches, they can support the tarpaulin, leaving room for all three of us to stay safe and dry beneath it."

Safe? Maybe. Dry? Debatable. The piece of oiled canvas would serve as little more than a crude shelter, what they'd called a shebang in the Army. "I'll make my bed under the wagon, ma'am," J. W. said. "I'll be fine there."

She turned to him, hands on her hips and a slight smile of amusement curving her lips. Even drawn with exhaustion and recent illness, she was an incredibly fine-looking woman. "Make your bed with what, Mr. Walford?" she asked. "You haven't a blanket and I've none to spare."

"I'll be fine," he repeated.

"You'll be cold," Mrs. Burgess corrected.

He wondered if she'd been a schoolmarm before getting married. Her voice had the same admonishing tone in it that he associated with the office.

"It won't be the first time," J. W. said.

"You need to change out of that damp clothing," she announced and, not waiting for a response, headed back to the wagon. She was getting stronger, he noted. She only steadied herself briefly before clambering into the wagon bed. "I'm afraid Frank never had much of a wardrobe, but I brought along what was left. I'll just check on Angelina, unearth the change of clothes for you, and see to the horses while you change."

She sounded like his sister did when there was no arguing with her. She reminded him of Claire, determined to take charge when he was perfectly capable of unharnessing the team, setting up the makeshift tent, and making do under the wagon.

But she was sadly mistaken if she thought he was the kind of man who stood by while a woman did a man's work. Particularly a woman who was already pushing herself beyond her natural limits. What sort of husband had Burgess been that she felt obliged to do things entirely by herself?

"One thing at a time, Mrs. Burgess," J. W. counseled. "But *I'll* move the wagon off the road, unhitch the horses, and do something about a shelter. You see to your little girl. While I'd appreciate dry duds, if that quail of yours is right, I might as well stay in the ones that are already damp."

She paused, sat down abruptly on the buckboard seat, and opened her lovely mouth as if to repudiate his decision, then appeared to think better of it. The effort cost her though. Her lips were pressed together so tightly they looked thin and pale. "As you wish, Mr. Walford. I hope you don't mind if I set out our rough meal."

"Not at all, ma'am," he conceded. "Fact is, I'd appreciate the service."

She wasn't ready to leave him to the chores quite yet. "I'm not helpless, you know," she said.

"Of course not," J. W. agreed.

"I'm ill, but more from the potion Rosa forced on me than from physical weakness," she continued.

Considering he'd found her in a swoon outside her cabin, J. W. wondered what she did consider physical weakness. "All right," he said.

"You've already been more than kind in helping me," she said. "And no doubt you could put far more distance between yourself and that posse without Angelina and me, which means I was silly even to suggest your wearing Frank's suit and passing as a family man to elude them."

Okay, so he had thought the idea a bit insane, but it had grown on him. Although the idea of wearing what was without a doubt the ugliest getup he'd ever seen didn't appeal to him, he was prepared to do it. At least till there was enough distance between him and the determined hanging party. After that, she was welcome to keep the plaid monstrosity for the pleasant memories it no doubt held for her.

"No, ma'am. Though it means thrusting myself on you a bit longer, I've grown partial to the plan," J. W. said, hoping the assurance would ease her mind.

What little light remained was fading fast. As it was, he could see little but the oval curve of her face in the gloom. With the deep colors of the patterned shawl wrapped around her shoulders for warmth and her dark riding skirt blending with the forest tones, his lovely companion would be well concealed against discovery that night. Unless, that was, she continued to be quite so loquacious.

"You're being kind to say so," she said. "I know I forced the idea on you."

"No—"

She threw him a look he hadn't the heart to repudiate.

"All right, maybe you did," he conceded. "But it makes sense. I think it will work."

"You're sure?"

Hell, no, he wasn't sure. "Absolutely," J. W. said.

Her gaze held his for a rare, quiet moment. "Thank you, Mr. Walford," she said and burst into tears.

Chapter Six

Lou hastily wiped her eyes with the edge of her shawl. "I'm sorry, Mr. Walford," she said, sobbing, for some reason unable to stop the flow and, at the same time, mortified to show such weakness before him. He was probably wishing her to the devil only, being a different sort of man than Frank had ever been, was polite enough not to mutter the words out loud.

She did hear him give a muffled sort of curse before the buckboard shifted and she found herself pulled into the comforting circle of his arms. "Go ahead and cry, Mrs. Burgess," he murmured softly, taking no exception when she hid her damp face against his shirtfront. "You've had quite a day. If any woman deserves to let it loose, I think you're the one."

When she shook her head in denial, brushing her cheek

against the solid breadth of his chest, the faint scent of wildflowers rose anew from the soft, worn flannel of his shirt. The edge of his loosely tied neckerchief soaked up the worst of her tears. She had already, inadvertently, soaked his lower regions with river water, now she was drenching his upper regions as well. If she'd put her mind to it, Lou doubted she could have given him better reasons than those to abandon her and Angelina.

The night around them was growing cooler, the temperature dropping quickly now that the sun had departed. The forest was moist and cloying, the trees pressing uncomfortably close rather than protectively near. Or was it merely in her imagination that they felt so? Protection and comfort lay in the warm embrace of a man she had no claim on, but who held her without the slightest hint of distaste in his tone or in his touch. And who showed no inclination to let her loose quite yet either.

Oh, he was nothing like Frank. Nothing at all like Frank, thank goodness.

"No, no." Lou hiccuped, trying to regain control. "I think perhaps your day has been worse than mine."

Walford surprised her by chuckling at the comment. Snuggled as she was against him, she felt the gentle rumble of laughter as well as heard it. "You may be right, ma'am. But it won't be the first bad day I've had. Nor the last," he said.

Lou took a deep, calming breath and, though loath to do so, forced herself to push free from his arms. "Still, I should have been able to control myself better. It is simply that you've been so kind."

"Merely paying my debt, Mrs. Burgess," he claimed.

She was glad when he lingered rather than immediately deserting her as she expected him to do. "You owe me nothing, Mr. Walford. But if you really don't mind posing as Frank tomorrow—"

"I don't," he assured, his mouth turning up in a rather quirky half smile that she found devastatingly attractive. Perhaps even intimate.

And considering how briefly she'd been a widow, the fact that she found it so flustered Lou far more than the fact that she'd accepted the comfort of his arms in that moment of ungoverned distress.

"Then I think you'd best call me Lou rather than Mrs. Burgess," she said.

Walford's grin grew wider with amusement. "Lou?"

"Short for Louisa," she confessed, "although I've never really felt much like a Louisa."

"Never?"

The query sent a rush of warm color into her cheeks. She had always preferred the shortened, more masculine version of her name because the only person who ever called her *Louisa* had been her grandfather. And his tone had always been one of distaste when he said her name.

"Never," Lou said flatly. "The sheriff told me your name was Walford, but he didn't give your first name. I suppose it probably wouldn't be wise to use it anyway. Will you mind greatly if I call you Frank or Mr. Burgess if we are stopped for any reason?"

Walford sent the wagon swaying slightly as he stepped down from it once more. "I'm more concerned over how you feel about that, Mrs. Burgess," he said.

He wasn't reluctant to offer her consolation in his arms but he was reluctant to use her first name, Lou mused. Now why did that make him even more intriguing to her? And more determined to hear her name on his lips?

She was giving his actions reasons that had no relation

to what was really in his mind. He had put physical distance between them by getting out of the buckboard, but he still stood only a few feet away, observing her closely.

"You're so recently bereaved. It must hurt to lend your husband's name to a stranger, even if for a brief time," he said.

"Is it wise to use your own?" she asked.

When his mouth curved this time, it appeared more in self-derision than amusement. "No, ma'am. If you'll forgive my speech, I consider it damn unwise. Now, if you'll excuse me, I've got a wagon to move. If you'll ease the brake off, I'll take care of the rest," Walford said, and left Lou alone with her thoughts.

Tess Ramsdale looked up from her cards when she heard the saloon door swing open behind her. It was becoming a bad habit to do so. Before long the men around her table would begin considering the action a tell, an unconscious signal that she was holding a winning hand or trying to bluff them into either raising the stakes or dropping out of the game.

"The way yer actin', Diamond, I'd swear there was somebody gunnin' fer ya," said the man directly across the table.

"That's a terrible thing to say to a lady," the player to his right claimed. "But if'n it were true, and if'n you were a gentleman, Orson, you'd offer to change seats with Miz Diamond to protect her back."

Orson shook his head, concentrating on the cards fanned out in his hand. "Not when it's proved to be a winnin' seat tonight. Diamond understands that, don't ya, ma'am?"

Oh, she understood it all right, Tess thought. Winning

at cards was how she supposedly made her living. Not the most desirable state of employment for a woman, but one that she had found she excelled at while following the drum with her husband during the war. Bart's friends had thought it a great joke when she laid down the winning hand time after time during their friendly games in the sagging canvas tent. They hadn't realized that her "luck" was anything but. It was merely one of the pranks Bart enjoyed playing on his former West Point classmates. *Larks*, he called them. He had even considered going off to war nothing more than a great adventure that had the promise of promotion as an added carrot. Having her follow him, traveling in the caravan of the Army of the Tennessee, had been a lark at the beginning. One that had given her a nodding acquaintance with generals Grant and Sherman by the time the Army moved deeper into the South.

The great adventure Bart had envisioned had lost its shine long before the Shiloh engagement. That massacre had taken the last of the light from Bart's eyes, turning him into the sort of officer he should always have been: capable, stoic, and deadly serious. He had wanted her to return home then, but the war had changed her as well.

Perhaps she wouldn't be as nervous about J. W.'s whereabouts if she hadn't relived the hellish trail to Vicksburg again in her sleep the night before.

When the Army headed down the Mississippi River toward Vicksburg, she had volunteered her services with the ambulances. And the night before she had been there again, feeling the weight of her own haversack with four days of rations, tucking up her skirts to more easily climb the steep ridges or make it through the dense woods, suffering the heat, clouds of dust, and two days of nearly constant rain along with the men. She had been aboard one of the floating hospitals when Grant took Champion Hill, surrounded by the sound of men's cries and moans, taking in the scent of blood, death, and fear with every breath she drew, wondering if she would ever survive the living hell she'd wandered into in search of a wondrous adventure.

And then Bart had come aboard, a broken, battered, bloodied shell of the brash young officer she'd wed. Helpless to do anything for him, she had watched him die. Again.

Was it any wonder she was skittish over her brother's unexplained absence? But she couldn't let the emotion show. Too much depended on the goodwill of the men at her table, even if presently she did nothing to deserve it.

"Stay right where you are, sugar," Tess told Orson, adding the honey-dipped lilt of the South to her voice. In the five years since Bart's death, she had become quite the accomplished actress. The only time she ever dropped the assumed accent was when she was with her chaperone-companion, Neddy, or around her brother, and even then she didn't do so, if there was a chance that they would be overheard. The success of their venture depended on her ability to be accepted as one of the now homeless Southerners who wandered the West, and thus overhear information that would never be dropped if the speaker realized Northern ears were listening.

But no matter how she tried, it was impossible to be attuned to the conversations around her that night. Until J. W. walked through the swinging doors of the saloon, she would continue waiting for, and worrying over, her brother.

"You just keep warming that seat, Orson," she told the grizzled-looking man across from her, "because it won't be long before Lady Luck realizes she has made a grievous error in honoring you thus far tonight."

"Yeah," another of the players agreed. "It's 'cause ya ain't took that darn hat off even though yer in the presence of a lady like our Diamond."

"Ain't neither," Orson said.

"Cain't take his hat off, Lem," the man on Orson's right declared. "He's bald as a bean under there and knows wimmen like a feller with a full head o' hair ta run their fingers through." He shook back his own untamed and overgrown mane as if to prove his point. "Didn't I call your hand least five minutes ago?"

"Not more'n two minutes, if that," Orson said as he meticulously rearranged the cards in his hand. "There're some ladies that prefer a shiny pate, as this clearly shows." With great care, he spread the winning hand out before his companions' astonished eyes.

Tess laughed lightly, although she had known what cards Orson held, having dealt them to him herself. It wasn't only her accent and her name that were counterfeit. So was her legendary luck at the poker table. She was not above using the sleight-of-hand tricks Bart had taught her to control play at her table. At first she had tried to convince herself that she did so in tribute to his memory. Now she knew it was merely an expeditious way to gain a particular player's trust.

Orson offered to buy a round of drinks, wisely sharing the benefits of his winnings with his friends. He'd unwittingly shared a lot more her first day in Austin, which was why Tess had gone out of her way to keep him coming back to her table. It was Orson who had dropped the name she'd been waiting for months to hear: Wes Dalhert.

Unfortunately, if her brother didn't turn up soon, the

lead they had on the former Confederate raider would become useless. He would have moved on. Not that Dalhert was in Austin himself. According to Orson, outlaws were rallying to the guerilla captain somewhere outside of San Antonio. Austin was merely a rendezvous point for the men who had ridden under Dalhert's leadership during the war, men who figured the experience gave them the cachet to become lieutenants in his new army of outlaws.

Men whose names appeared on J. W.'s vengeance list.

Considering how fast her brother was used to traveling, Tess had expected him to walk through the saloon's swinging door more than twenty-four hours ago. Had the telegram she'd sent missed him in Louisiana? She didn't want to consider any other reason for his delay. Too many of those she loved had already been lost to her. She couldn't lose J. W., too.

"Would you gentlemen be kind enough to hold my place at the table for a bit?" Tess cooed, getting to her feet.

Even if he had kept his battered felt hat on in her presence, Orson was gentleman enough to surge up out of his chair as she rose. He batted Lem up the back of his head when the other man was slower to show his manners. "Wouldn't think o' givin' it away, ma'am. Appreciate yer company too much ta do such a thing," he claimed.

Tess dipped her head slightly in acknowledgment. "I won't be long. It's become a trifle chilly tonight, don't you think? I'll be back once I've fetched a warmer wrap."

"We'll be waitin'," Orson promised.

Although she made her way slowly to the adjoining hotel, knowing the men in the saloon watched the erotic sway of her ruby-red silk skirts as she moved, Tess's mind was whirling at a frantic pace. Should she lead the conversation at the table to the atrocities inflicted during the war in the hope of learning more about Dalhert and his men, or should she do as she had done so far and merely let the men ramble on, boasting of their deeds or of those they admired? And where in the world was J. W.? She needed more than just a heavier scarf to drape around her shoulders. She needed Neddy's advice.

When Tess entered the second-floor room they shared it was to find Nedra Edwards bent near a lamp as she repaired a tear in the hemline of one of Tess's modified evening gowns. The circle of light found gleaming highlights in the tightly woven braids that encircled the young black woman's head. Although it was long past the hour when most people were in bed, Neddy was still dressed in one of the neat, conservatively dark calico dresses she favored. The high, modest neckline and frill of cream-colored lace along its edge accented the queenly curve of her long neck and the warm chocolate tone of her skin. Her hands were narrow, their motions elegant as Neddy plied the needle expertly, regularly refurbishing and updating gowns that had once graced the elite ballrooms near West Point.

It wasn't Neddy's skill at dressmaking or her constant, unswerving friendship that bound Tess to her though. It was shared loss.

Tess had barely shut the door behind her when Neddy dropped the work in her lap and glanced up eagerly. "Mr. Jeff has arrived then?" she asked.

Tossing aside the fine lace shawl draped loosely over her arm, Tess sat gingerly on the edge of the bed, her ruby skirts spilling around her. She had worn the gown the night she met Bart at an evening recital in her aunt's home, but with new black satin cording accenting the now lower-cut bodice and the flat-fronted skirt, the dress had found new life in Neddy's hands. "No, he hasn't," she answered. "What could be keeping him? He said he would be staying in Shreveport until we sent word. Could the telegram have gone astray?"

"Not with him checking at the office daily. You know that's what he does. That and fret. You're both good at fretting," Neddy said. "But I know that's not what you're really afraid of, Miss Tess."

Tess sighed deeply. She and Neddy had been through so much together. At times she could almost swear Nedra Edwards could read her thoughts. She certainly could judge her moods well. Tess felt as close to Neddy as she would to a sister, closer in fact than she'd ever felt to her sister-in-law Claire. She thought Neddy felt the same about her. The woman was well educated, had taught in one of the abolitionist schools that Claire's father had sponsored. But, in spite of all that, the young black woman refused to address either J. W. or herself as equals, her excuse for clinging to a servant's sort of formality being that "other people wouldn't understand, particularly white folks." While Tess chafed at such unjustness, she knew there were as many Northerners as there were Southerners who had difficulty seeing the former slaves as fellow human beings. The fact that Neddy and her husband had both been born free carried no weight when it came to changing that frame of mind.

Coming to terms with the name Neddy preferred to call her wasn't Neddy's problem but her own, Tess knew. If she had once been young enough to believe it was possible to change the world, traveling with the Army had soon shown her the error of her ways.

"You know what Miss Claire would say about your brother?" Neddy asked.

Tess shook her head. Neddy and her husband, Ezra Edwards, had lived on Claire's father's farm, on the outskirts of Lawrence, Kansas. Tess had met them when she joined Claire there after Bart's death. A few weeks after her arrival, Wes Dalhert and his men had ridden in the yard, and left Tess's life in further ruins.

"She'd say her man had a stubborn streak more than a mile wide, but he kept his word no matter what. Particularly to you," Neddy said.

"Me!"

Neddy grinned. "Don't look so surprised. You know very well he was always protective of you. Men usually are of their little sisters."

Tess gave a ladylike snort. "Protective? Overbearing, I'd say. He didn't think Bart was good enough for me, you know. He even abandoned his law clients and rushed to our aunt's house in West Point, determined to drag me back to Iowa. Called Bart a 'trumped-up jackass with more brass on his uniform than brains in his head.' "

"That sounds like Mr. Jeff," Neddy agreed. "And was he right?"

"At the time? Yes, he was right," Tess admitted. She doubted even Bart would think the admission traitorous. He *had* been exactly that, but she'd loved him all the same.

"And he'll be here. It's a long way from Shreveport to Austin, and saint though you think him, the man hasn't got wings."

She did not think her brother was a saint, Tess corrected silently. A saint would forget the sins of the war; a saint would forgive the sinners. J. W. neither forgot nor forgave. There were preachers galore ready to remind that the Lord claimed vengeance was His alone. J. W. was likely to tell them he was merely giving the Lord a helping hand. When it came to the deeds of Wes Dalhert and his men, the Lord needed all the vengeful helping hands he could get.

Or so Tess had once thought. Neddy, she knew, had never believed it, yet she had refused to let Tess travel alone.

"You always know the right thing to say," Tess told her friend.

"You just think I do," Neddy said. "Now, what excuse did you give those men downstairs to let them think you would be leaving their pockets full at the end of the night?"

Her spirits renewed, Tess got to her feet. "Not a good enough excuse," she said, retrieving from the dresser the soft black cashmere wrap Bart had given her on their last anniversary. As a barrier against the evening chill, it was little better than the lace shawl. It did enhance the pale cream of her skin as it draped over her slender bare arms. If the jet-black cord trim on the gown didn't draw every male eye to the deep decolletage of her bodice, the cling of the cashmere would. Distracting a man from his cards was essential, and her gowns had all been modified with that goal in mind.

Tess perused her appearance in the washstand mirror, smoothing down the richly colored silk over her impossibly narrow waist, checking the catch on her dangling, red crystal earbobs. Three perfect soft, pale brown sausage curls swayed from the twist of hair at her crown when she turned her head. They brushed against the faint diamond-shaped scar on her unadorned shoulder, a souvenir of her headlong tumble from the hayrack as a child, and the inspiration behind the only name she ever used now: Diamond.

Pleased with the overall effect, Diamond smiled faintly at her reflection. "You're right," she told Neddy. "J. W. has merely been delayed. I'll stop worrying this minute and do what I'm here to do. Just how many of those twenty-dollar gold pieces should I relieve the gentlemen's pockets of tonight, do you think?"

The quail had been right, J. W. admitted when he woke. It had rained during the night. More than a mist but less than a downpour. A helpful sort of rain, the kind that would have obliterated their tracks from the ranch into the woods, but had not been disturbing enough to spook the skittish mustangs. That in itself was a blessing, considering he would have been the one crawling from their rough shelter to calm the beasts.

He had compromised with Mrs. Burgess, fixing the length of oilcloth so that it draped from the bed of the buckboard, forming a poorly shaped triangle beneath which they had all sheltered. He lay partly beneath the wagon with the baby's cradle between them, creating a far more effective bundling board than any of his ancestors had ever used. Mrs. Burgess had tried to find a way to share her lone quilt with him, insisting the evening drop in temperature would ruin his health should he go without sufficient cover. Which just went to show that she'd made a quick recovery from her unexpected fit of vapors earlier. He wasn't sure if she was trying to boss him around or mother him. More likely the latter since she had produced a pair of knitted socks, insisting he pull them on to keep his feet warm while his boots dried. In the end he had given in to her insistence that he at least change out of his damp clothes and had donned the despised wool suit—trousers, shirt, weskit, and jacket—to placate her. Doing so had given him a chance to remove his waterlogged boots and extract the hidden cache of now sodden greenbacks and gold coins without her knowledge.

Thank goodness he hadn't tucked the horde in his now-lost, never-to-be-returned saddlebags. The total would have given the deputy who discovered the loot one hell of a night on the town. Fortunately, his better judgment had prevailed. The money had remained hidden in his boots, divided and wrapped in flat neat packets that rested beneath the soles of his feet. While sheltered from his traveling companion's sight, he'd transferred enough of the money into the inner pocket of the borrowed wool weskit, prepared to supplement their limited supplies at the first dry goods store he spotted when they reached any sort of town.

He had tried to keep himself alert that night by mentally cataloguing the items Mrs. Burgess had packed in the buckboard's bed and creating a quartermaster's list of things they needed. The dreaded getup he'd resisted wearing had actually kept him fairly warm and comfortable all night long, and the tally had been cut short. Morpheus had had his way, even though that way had been broken and fretful at times.

Both infant and mother had slept the night through, waking only when the birds stirred in the trees around them.

Snuggled beneath her quilt, Mrs. Burgess lingered, obviously loath to relinquish her cocoon of warmth. She looked quite young and innocent, not the least like the mother of a healthy infant. Even less like someone who answered to the name *Lou*.

"Good morning, Mr. Walford," she murmured, blinking sleep from her eyes. "I hope you had a restful night."

As restful a night as any man could have lying within two feet of a lovely woman, he thought.

"Were you warm enough?" she asked.

J. W. grunted noncommittally. There had been those passing warm thoughts involving her proximity, after all. He didn't think she'd cotton to hearing about them, even if they had raised his temperature a mite.

"Well, things will improve this evening when we can have a fire once more. Personally, I'm looking forward to a cup of tea," Mrs. Burgess promised and confessed all in one breath.

"Coffee'll be sorely missed this morning," J. W. said, "but we'll also get on our way quicker without lingering over breakfast."

"Yes, we will," she agreed, rolling to her side. Rather than toss the bedding aside though, she snaked one arm from within its warmth and propped her head against her hand. Although she'd woven her long black hair into a single braid before retiring, a very mesmerizing and domestic task he'd enjoyed watching, strands had pulled loose in her sleep to fly attractively around her face. "Do you think anyone returned to the cabin last night?" she asked.

He'd been wondering the same thing himself. "Might have," J. W. admitted cautiously.

Mrs. Burgess's expression was lost to him in the shadowed lee of the makeshift tent. "If Rosa woke from her stupor and returned to the cabin, she still wouldn't be able to tell them anything about you. Perhaps they'll give up their hunt."

J. W. doubted it. "But you think she'll have someone looking for you," he said.

"Possibly," she said, and sat up, tossing the quilt aside. "Gillette will want the horses and buckboard back. Even if they are sorry excuses for transportation, the terms of Frank's bet include them in the ranch's property. We shouldn't delay here in any case. Unfortunately, it will take a few moments for me to see to Angelina's needs, but I've never been one to dawdle over changing my clothing, Mr. Walford."

If that was the truth, she had to be the only woman in creation not to do so. "Just shake your skirts out and rebraid your hair as we drive, ma'am," J. W. suggested. "You'll look fine."

"With you looking stalwart and conventional in that suit, sir? I think not!" she countered as she backed from beneath the oilcloth and stood. In the growing light of dawn he noticed she was smiling. "If we are to pass casual inspection, then I need to be as proper and formally dressed as you are." Her grin widened, turning her expression impish. "We shall go unnoticed as Mr. and Mrs. Frank Burgess."

J. W. maneuvered from beneath the wagon himself and stood up, flexing a sore muscle in his shoulder as he did so. That was what he got from spending too much time lying on his side admiring the pale glow of her face during the night.

"I've been thinking about that," he said. "About how your cabin had a convenient outlaw hole, about your husband being recently dead."

The smile she'd sported fell as quick as a front line infantryman charging a freshly loaded row of sharpshooters' rifles. "You're leaving us?" she asked faintly, fearfully.

Even if it was a faster way of saving his own skin, he wasn't cad enough to abandon a woman alone with a child in this wilderness. "I'm saying it isn't a good idea to use your husband's name," J. W. explained hastily.

"But I thought we had agreed that it isn't safe to—"

"Use my own name either," he finished, cutting her off. "No, it isn't. That's why I'm proposing that, if asked, we claim to be Bartley Ramsdale and his wife, Theresa."

"The Ramsdales," Mrs. Burgess repeated, as if tasting the flavor of the new name on her tongue. "Are they a real couple?"

J. W. knew he looked uncomfortable over the answer. "In a manner of speaking," he said. "Believe me, neither of them is currently using the name. Considering our need, it would be a shame to let it go to waste, don't you think?"

Chapter Seven

Lou was relieved when Angelina hurried through her morning meal. The baby had nursed quickly, acting as hungry as Lou felt. A shared jar of the beans she had raised and canned, a couple of tasteless confiscated tortillas, and some of the remaining venison jerky from Frank's last hunting effort hadn't sufficed as a dinner, particularly when served cold and washed down by tepid water from a battered canteen. Perhaps she should have followed Mr. Walford's example and taken a swallow or so of the whiskey. For medicinal purposes, of course. It would have warmed her and deadened her tastebuds. But she had never become accustomed to the fiery taste of the liquor under her husband's tutelage and had no intention of attempting to do so now. The last thing Angelina needed was a mother who escaped her problems in drink.

The unprepossessing dinner would be followed that

morning by an even slimmer breakfast menu. With the tortillas gone, and the taste of dried venison lingering on her tongue, Lou opted for a breakfast they could eat easily as they drove. That evening, at least, it would be possible to have a campfire and hot food. Not that the items featured on the menu would differ; her foodstuffs were painfully limited. If Miss Nottingham had not sent back East for a wedding gift—the dozen Mason jars with their clever porcelain-lined lids—canning her own produce would never have been possible. Other than the tidy row of preserved vegetables in the sealed jars, her supplies consisted of dried meat, dried fruit, and more vegetables—dried this time. She had a handful of tea leaves, a little flour, no sugar, some potatoes, a bit of salt and pepper, and three cherished apples. A very meager larder considering she had a long way to travel, no money to replenish her supplies, and a grown man to sustain.

Still, her mind was clearer and her stamina was on the mend. A full night of undrugged sleep had worked miracles. Today she wouldn't be quite as useless as she had felt the evening before.

But then, if her knight in shining armor didn't think she needed him for even the simplest tasks anymore, would he stay with them?

Even as the question formed in her mind, Lou tried to brush it away. She wasn't going to like the answer, she knew, so why even bother to think the question? He would say the dreaded words out loud before long anyway.

Lou folded the quilt and placed it over a carpet of thick, though slightly damp, pine needles. Then, laying the baby on her stomach on the bedding's padded bright patchwork surface, she rummaged among her meager store of supplies in the wagon for two of her carefully hoarded apples. They had been wrapped in paper to protect them but even the covering hadn't safeguarded them sufficiently as they wintered in the root cellar. The once rosy red skins had darkened and were beginning to wrinkle, but taking a bite of one, she decided they were still an excellent choice for breakfast. She hoped Mr. Walford would agree with her. He really had very little choice considering he was as anxious as she to put distance between the tiny ranch and themselves. He could travel so much faster without her. Would he slip away, leaving her on her own when they reached Crockett? And if he did, what should she do then?

Drat it! Even when she tried to keep the inevitable answer away, her thoughts continued returning to it constantly. Was that because she had no options? He would at some time leave her to her own resources. She had no way to hold him long, not even if she bartered herself as payment. Life with Frank had proven that. A wife at home did not mean a man eschewed a jolly old time in one of the high flyers' bedrooms above the saloon. Frank had thought her a burden at home; Walford no doubt already thought her a burden for a man on the run. Her grandfather had certainly made her feel like an unwanted burden in his hacienda.

Lou sighed deeply, girding herself for the inevitable. She would soon be on her own. And, given no other option, she would continue on. Alone.

That didn't mean she couldn't delay the inevitable by any means at hand.

In the event Walford was considering cutting loose from her that very day, Lou unearthed her last apple and placed the offering on the buckboard's seat. The two apples with their dark, aging skin looked quite pathetic as a lure to keep him by her side, but they were all she could offer at the moment.

Unless he was willing to consider herself as payment. Prolonging their parting even a few days would put her farther along the road to Mexico City and much farther from Peaceful and Titus Gillette's control.

She should be blushing at the impropriety of the idea. What had happened to that vow she'd made to avoid men in the future?

And what had become of the lessons drummed into her by the local padre in San Marcos and, in his absence, by Miss Nottingham, her governess? Ladies, *real ladies*, did not contemplate selling themselves to a man, much less relish the idea.

But then, real ladies would not have had to live with Frank Burgess either. Real ladies would not be faced with the alternatives of becoming Gillette's plaything or a convenience for one of Frank's outlaw friends, both of which were repugnant to her. However, the thought of being intimate with Mr. Walford was anything but repugnant.

Louisa Keating Burgess, what is the matter with you? Lou murmured silently in reproof. She was spending far too much time thinking about Mr. Walford, wondering when he would take to his heels, wondering how she would manage without him, wondering what his first name might possibly be. Remembering far too warmly how good it felt to be held in his strong arms.

Well, it was his own fault! She hadn't asked for him to scoop her up the day before, nor had she thrown herself against his chest the evening before. If her thoughts tended to dwell on how wonderful such tender mercies had felt, it was only because she was human, female, and starved for any demonstration of kindness. Her nerves were showing the strain of the past week. Possibly even the past few years. That was why she was even entertaining thoughts of such outrageous behavior.

However, if she didn't hurry and get ready to leave, Mr. Walford wouldn't be interested in any offer she might be tempted to make, immoral or not.

Lou gathered her change of clothing from the wagon, throwing the little-worn visiting dress over her arm. The fabric was hopelessly creased, not only from the years it had languished in her trunk but also from her hasty packing when she had shoved it haphazardly into the much smaller valise. Considering it was no doubt long out of fashion as well, she would look like a country bumpkin. Would she look like a Theresa Ramsdale? She would have to ask Mr. Walford about the real Mrs. Ramsdale. Who she was. Why she was not—how had he put it?—"currently using the name."

Taking shelter behind a nearby bush, Lou quickly shed her sturdy riding skirt, drab blouse, and the well-worn boots she had pulled on in what seemed another lifetime. Had it really only been yesterday afternoon that she'd awoken to find Rosa in a drunken stupor and shoved her feet in Frank's old boots before heading for the well?

The elegant copper-colored light wool of her gown felt as refreshing as a waterfall as it fell over her head and settled around her hips. It had been made with a crinoline in mind, but the full, stiff underskirt had died a valiant death the year before, annexed by rodents as both bed and meal larder. Lou hoped her pleated and gathered skirt would retain its shape without aid. Even lacking the support of the underskirt, the gown made her feel better. Twin rows of braiding in green and black trimmed the bodice both front and back, following the contour of her

103

shoulders and angling to form a V at her waist. The braid
was repeated along the tail ends of her sash as they spilled
over the trailing skirt back and her hips. She struggled
slightly with the tape ties and hook eyes, but at last managed to secure both the bodice and skirt in place. Fortunately the tiny hand-painted black straw hat, with its froth
of noire net veiling in front and spilling green and bronze
ribbons at the crown, had been overlooked in the wildlife
invasion, as had the square-toe cloth boots with leather
heels and silk lined tongue inset. She would need to lace
the sides once seated in the wagon, but felt Mr. Walford
would be notably impressed with the speed with which she
had accomplished her conversion from bedraggled waif to
composed matron. It was amazing what being dressed
properly again could do for a woman's spirits.

Angelina's warm squeal of delight echoed in the clearing, challenging the calls of the birds in the surrounding
trees. Lou glanced to where her daughter still lay, belly
down on the quilt. The baby was testing herself, lifting her
head to look around and arching her back so that hands,
arms, legs, and feet were all suspended, if briefly, off the
ground.

It was her newest trick, one that showed she was growing quickly. More surprising, however, was the fact that
Walford was lying nearly nose to nose with Angelina, talking softly to her.

"That'a girl," he murmured. "You're flying like a bird,
if a bit more grounded. Mama's going to be proud of you."

"Mama's very proud of you," Lou agreed, moving from
behind the bush. She paused only to drop her discarded
clothing near the valise in the buckboard, before strolling
casually over to where Walford and Angelina lay. The baby
turned her head at the sound of a familiar voice and im-

mediately lost her temporary buoyancy. Toes, knees, and hands touched down on the bedding once more.

Lou bent to swoop her child up into her arms. Angelina gurgled a host of welcoming sounds. Breathing in the intoxicating scent of the baby's skin, Lou nuzzled her daughter's cheek. "At this rate you'll be dancing in no time, my dove," she said and turned to the man still reclining at her feet.

He had rolled to his side and was supporting his head on his hand, staring up at them, looking like a man who had all the time in the world. And not the least like a wanted felon. In fact, in the borrowed suit, he looked quite the reverse and rather handsome. He was hatless at the moment, leaving his dark hair subject to the breeze. It was overlong for a respectable gentleman, but he was dashing all the same. Even with damp pine needles from the forest floor now clinging to his clothing.

She was also undergoing inspection, Lou noted. She could almost feel his eyes moving over her from head to foot, lingering on her various curves before sweeping back up to rest on the frivolous confection on her head. Did he approve of her overall improved appearance?

"Do I look anything like Theresa Ramsdale?" Lou asked, putting the baby to her shoulder. Angelina reached for the veil of her hat as it fluttered slightly in the morning breeze.

"Not a bit," Walford said, sitting up and getting to his feet. Rather than meet her eyes, he bent to dust the clinging debris from his trousers. "But then, considering that she's my sister, I've never considered her truly beautiful," he added.

Unable to prevent it, Lou felt color rising to her face. Did that mean he considered *her* beautiful? She hadn't taken the time to fix her hair, making do with her fingers for a comb and twisting it up into a knot at the crown of her head. Hopefully, the veil and ribbons of her hat would hide the haphazardness of her coiffure. By the time they reached Crockett, travel along the road would account for her dishevelment. Or she hoped it would.

But beautiful? No, she sincerely doubted she could lay claim to the term. He was being kind.

She didn't want him to be kind. She wanted him to honestly think she was beautiful.

It wasn't a thing a woman could ask a man she'd known less than twenty-four hours.

"Your sister!" Lou exclaimed to cover her own confusion.

"A lot of men have them," Walford drawled, tossing her a fond smile. Or perhaps the look had been for the baby. Lou couldn't be sure which of them he'd been looking at. He had been conversing with her daughter rather intently. Thank goodness Angelina wasn't old enough to inadvertently give away any of her mother's secrets!

Walford circled her, eyeing her crumpled finery from all sides. Angelina squealed in delight when she caught sight of him and then discovered the ribbons that trailed from the back of the hat.

"Yes, I suppose that's true," Lou said, grabbing for her headgear as the fine black cord ties that held it in place gave way. "I am just surprised that you've lent me her name so readily. I mean, you barely know me, Mr. Walford."

He came to a rest before her. "Bart Ramsdale, remember?" he coached.

Her hands full, one supporting the now squirming baby,

and the other holding her hat in place, Lou didn't answer him at first.

"Our safety depends on your remembering the name, Mrs. *Ramsdale*," he said.

"Yes, yes," Lou mumbled, distracted. "Angelina! Let go!"

"Here," Walford offered. "I'll take her."

"She's not used to being held by—" Lou began.

Angelina, rather than scream in fright as she had the few times Frank had tried to hold his daughter, actually gurgled with pleasure and reached for Walford.

"Oh," Lou said. "I guess she's willing to make exceptions."

"All the easier to pass as a family, wouldn't you say, Mrs. Ramsdale?" Walford asked.

With both hands free again, Lou reached to set her hat in place once more, then watched Angelina flirt outrageously with their benefactor. As if recognizing her father was indifferent to her, the child had never warmed to him. With Walford, Angelina appeared intent on making her first male conquest. Lou watched in amazement as her daughter began the quite feminine process of twisting their Santo Jorge around her little finger.

"Yes, Mr. *Ramsdale*, I suppose it does," she said. "It would help if you looked more like a man who answers to the name *Bart* though."

Engaged in rescuing his nose from Angelina's grip, Walford's reply was a bit muffled. "Why, thank you, my dear. That's the nicest compliment anyone ever gave me," he said with honest pleasure. "But if that is a sly way of trying to find out what my real first name is, you are out of luck."

Stunned at the casual endearment as well as his response, Lou watched as Walford ambled over to the waiting, already hitched team, and guided Angelina's chubby little hand in a caress down the less skittish sorrel's glistening neck. Left on her own, Lou retrieved her quilt and shook it out. By the time she had scrambled aboard the buckboard and stowed her meager possessions, Walford was once again at her side, Angelina still cooing with delight in his arms.

The incredibly fetching outfit Mrs. Burgess had donned caught him by surprise. Oh, he'd seen the fabric, recognizing it as a proper gown, long before she'd tossed it over the sheltering bush and changed. He'd even opted to further his acquaintance with her baby in an effort to keep his mind from mentally picturing her slipping free of the sensible blouse and skirt. From wondering if her skin was as satiny to the touch as he imagined it to be.

Rather than torture himself with erotic thoughts, J. W. had gotten down on the child's level, stretching out before her, uncaring whether his borrowed duds suffered from further contact with the forest floor. He'd already slept in the suit, so there was little more damage he could deal it. Unless it was to earn it a bullet hole and a generous dousing in blood.

There was another benefit to lying full length on the ground. He would be able to feel the approach of riders if they were galloping recklessly down the woodland trail. Not that it would be much of a warning. It wasn't as if he could defend himself or Mrs. Burgess and her baby against any marauders, whether they be tin-toting legal types or outlaws set to separate unwary travelers from their possessions. The only decent firepower his lovely companion possessed was a time-worn Beecher's Bible, a nearly decade-old Sharp's rifle like those Henry Ward Beecher had shipped at no cost to the Free-Soilers in Kansas in the 1850s. His father-in-law had been the proud owner of one, even though he hadn't moved his family to Kansas until late in the unofficial war between the slavocrats of Missouri and the abolitionists of Kansas. As the precursor of the War Between the States, the squabbles between the frontier neighbors had set the stage for violence and hatred long before Fort Sumter was fired on or the first Southern state voted to secede from the Union.

It was better to keep his mind far from thoughts of Kansas though. Better to live in the present, enjoy the small pleasures that came his way. Like the frequently frustrating yet enticing company of Louisa Burgess and her tiny, equally enticing, daughter.

There was little of the mother in the child yet. Louisa was so finely crafted and the baby yet so roundly tufted. Angelina's dimple was all her own, as was the fine, much paler tuft of hair that graced her crown. Would the baby's currently blue eyes melt in time to the soft green of her mother's? Or would Angelina take after her father, a man she would not remember but whose image she might glimpse when she looked in the mirror?

"So who are you going to resemble the most?" J. W. whispered to the baby.

She had been contentedly lying on the quilt, but at the sound of his voice, the infant raised her head. It bobbed slightly, showing she was still practicing this new craft. As she had the day before, she grinned, flashing her dimple at him, and cooed an unintelligible greeting.

J. W. offered her two fingers to grip in a baby-sized handshake. "What do you make of it all, Angel?" he asked. "Your mother is frantic about something, but I haven't the right to ask what. I'm not exactly the right sort for either

109

of you to consort with, even though it looks like your father might not have been either. But let's you and I face it, Mama's a lady and you're going to be one yourself. You both need a steadier fella than me around to help you."

Angelina gave her opinion on that and, though he couldn't understand the burbled answer, J. W. had a feeling it was the same one Louisa Burgess would have given him.

"You can tell me not to be ridiculous all you want, Angel. It doesn't change the circumstances. Wherever you're bound, I can't be with you the whole way," he said.

He was serious, but Angelina took the whole thing as a big joke and laughed at him. This time when her head bobbed up, it took her other limbs with it, so that she rested only on her well-rounded tummy, arms and legs in the air. She had a long way to go on the road to independence, but she was already learning it was a necessary ingredient when it came to survival on the frontier.

J. W. complimented the baby on her achievement then felt his gut twist in primeval knots as the infant's mother moved from the shelter, newly gowned and curious about her child's excitement.

When she bent to sweep Angelina into her arms, J. W. hastened to get control of himself. He'd known the gown would be inappropriate for travel, but he hadn't been prepared for how lovely she would look in it. There was a ridiculous wisp of a hat perched on her head with veiling and ribbons that both fluttered in the breeze. It was a town hat, perfectly matched to the rich, elegant copper-colored fabric and green and black trim of her dress. And the whole getup was as out of place in rural Texas as his ludicrous borrowed plaid suit was.

He had the impression that the baby was looking at him

knowingly. *No wonder you laughed when I said I couldn't stay,* J. W. thought, sure that the silent communication had been received by the tiny charmer. The bob of her head against her mother's shoulder certainly seemed an acknowledgment of his belated concession.

"Do I look anything like Theresa Ramsdale?" Mrs. Burgess asked.

"Not a bit," he said and got to his feet. In fact, no one could look less like his sister, Tess. Was that because he had become used to seeing her as the woman she pretended to be, even gotten used to calling her *Diamond?* Or was it because Mrs. Burgess, whether dressed in sensible clothes, a nightgown and robe, or this extravagant bit of conservative nonsense, was exotic as all hell. She was a true beauty, lovely no matter what the circumstance. His sister, on the other hand . . .

When Mrs. Burgess exclaimed, J. W. realized his mouth had kept moving while his mind was elsewhere. Best to distract her before she compiled too many questions for the tally of answers he was willing to trade.

Angelina seemed of a mind with him, chipping in her two bits by tugging on any available part of her mother's hat that came to hand.

"Bart Ramsdale, remember?" he said, using the same tone of voice he'd used as an officer. Best to get the marching order understood by all concerned, he'd always felt.

She took no notice of the sound of authority, busily engaged in saving her hat from the baby's curious fingers.

Perhaps if he used a bit more force, pulled full rank, as it were. "Our safety depends on your remembering the name, Mrs. *Ramsdale,*" he said sternly.

"Yes, yes," she responded.

Hadn't heard a word he'd said, J. W. thought. It was a

good thing there had been no babies challenging him for command during the war because, from the way things were going, he would have been the fellow left out. Angelina was in firm control. There was only one way to regain command of the situation.

"Here," he offered. "I'll take her."

Mrs. Burgess looked at him in true surprise. Why, he couldn't tell. She had seen him groveling at the baby's level only moments before.

"She's not—"

Angelina's drowned out the rest of her words.

But it was the way the tiny creature felt against his chest, more than the baby's babbling sounds, that distracted him. It wasn't the first time he'd held her. He had put the infant in her mother's bed the day before. Had held her sleeping form as Mrs. Burgess scrambled up onto the buckboard the evening before. But those times the miniature charmer hadn't been interacting with him. She was now, and not being a bit subtle in her conquest.

Was it the baby's demand to be recognized as a person in her own right that had him wondering if his son had been the same way at that age? Timothy, the boy he'd never met.

As if divining that his thoughts had strayed from her, Angelina smacked J. W. in the nose with one waving miniature hand. It was apparent that women, no matter what their age, didn't like it when a man's attention strayed from them.

If they were going to pretend to be a family, he was going to have to be more attentive to Angelina's mother, too. Such hardship a man could only pray for.

Particularly since Mrs. Burgess's stance as she fixed her

hat in place once more seemed to accent the lush rise of her breasts and the slimness of her waist.

"It would help if you looked more like a man who answers to the name *Bart* though," she said.

His mind had been wandering again while his mouth continued to hold its own. However, for a man who had taken an instant dislike to Bart Ramsdale when he'd met him, her words fell like manna from Heaven.

"Why, thank you, my dear," he said as Angelina latched on to his nose, the strength in her tiny fingers taking him by surprise.

Mrs. Burgess gave him a startled, if pleased, look. What had he said? Something about her simple statement being a compliment.

". . . if that is a sly way of trying to find out what my real first name is, you are out of luck," J. W. announced breezily, hoping she wouldn't feel any sting in the words. Just in case she misunderstood, he thought a temporary retreat was wise, and headed for the newly hitched horses.

By the time he'd introduced the baby to the team, Mrs. Burgess had stowed the last of her possessions and was seated on the buckboard devouring an apple.

The scent of it reached out to him. Enticed him. Nearly as much as she did. Was she playing Eve to his Adam? No. Her husband was barely in his grave. The only intent she had was to supply breakfast. The fact that there were two apples resting on the buckboard seat in his place proved that. It was his own acute awareness of her that had conjured up the faint hope that she would offer him—Eve-like—forbidden fruit.

J. W. tucked her baby in the crib directly behind the wagon seat, then claimed his place next to the lovely young widow. "All set to break rank and march?" he asked.

"More than ready," she answered with a bright smile.

With the reins in one hand, J. W. palmed an apple and bit into it. The tart, tangy taste of it was sheer pleasure. But it was the memory of her smile that was going to sustain him. And it would do so long after they parted company.

The pounding on the bedroom door came at an inopportune time, Claude Morgan thought. While dawn wasn't breaking on the horizon any longer, he was still in the act of having a final soiree with his paid partner of the evening and not in the mood for any other sort of business.

But Titus Gillette was insistent. The saloon girl squealed when the banker walked into the room, picked up her discarded wrapper, and tossed it to her. "Find us some coffee and vittles, Dulcie," he ordered, strong-arming her from the room before she could dress.

Morgan sat up and tucked the lone bed pillow behind him, in no hurry to jump to Gillette's tune himself. "I'm paying for that," he said, jerking his bristled chin to indicate the woman in the hall.

"We'll find you better," Gillette said and closed the door.

"I'll find my own," Morgan countered. "In fact, I've got one in mind."

Gillette moved over to the window, pushed the curtain back an inch and looked down into the street. "The men you rode in with know about her, too," he said. "A hellcat with an uncommon dislike of strangers."

As no response seemed necessary, Morgan reached for his trousers and pulled them on.

"Funny thing about that hellcat," Gillette murmured. "She doesn't exist."

"The hell she doesn't."

"Cabin standing just clear of a stand of hardwood trees? Token sort of barn and corral out back? Black-haired bit of a girl with a baby?"

"And a steady rifle at her shoulder," Morgan added. "Know her, do you?"

Gillette dropped the curtain. "Own her. Own the ranch. More importantly, I now own that stand of hardwood."

"You've got a strange way of ranking things," Morgan said.

"If you knew the kind of profit made in the lumber business, you'd rearrange your priorities, too," Gillette commented. "However, the matter of this hellcat's existence still stands. The woman living in that cabin is recent widow Louisa Burgess and, on every occasion I have met the lady, she has been well spoken, although not cooperative."

It didn't have to be spelled out for him. If the usually well-spoken lady had a wanted man hidden in her house, she would have good reason to put on the show she had for Detmer's band of men.

"You know that job I mentioned in passing last night?" Gillette asked. "It's changed. I rode out to the Burgess place earlier. Other than the drunken sot I left watching the Burgess woman, the place was empty. She's run off, taking a buckboard and team of horses with her."

Morgan donned his shirt and pulled up his suspenders. "Don't tell me. They belong to you, too."

"Damn right they do. I want you to retrieve them. And her."

For this the bastard had interrupted his morning calisthenics with Dulcie? Morgan dropped back down on the bed, not bothering to shove his boots on. "The hell with you," he said. "Go fetch the wretch back yourself. She can't have gotten far."

Gillette shook his head, an odd smile twisting his features in the morning light. "She's not alone. Someone dragged the sot out to the barn, and you can bet Louisa wasn't the one doing it. Your gunslinger was with her."

Morgan chose a cigar from the selection he'd left on the washstand next to the bed, bit off the end, and lit it. "Then you don't need me," he said, sucking smoke back into his lungs, enjoying the taste and sensation of his first draw. "Detmer's posse will find them."

The banker's lips distorted unpleasantly. "Not when they rode off in the wrong direction," he said as he reached for the door. "It might interest you to know there has been a new development overnight in regards to your gunman. Seems the bounty has been raised."

"Yeah?" Morgan grunted around his cigar.

"Doubled," Gillette answered. "And now it will be paid out whether he's brought back dead or alive."

Chapter Eight

The journey out of the forest and cross country over flower-filled meadows to the dry, beaten path of the Old San Antonio Road was accomplished without interruption. At least, without interruption by a posse. Angelina's frequent cries demanded that they halt so that her mother could change her, feed her, or merely coddle her. By the time Crockett came in sight later that afternoon, J. W. realized it was going to take the better part of a week to travel the distance he usually covered on his own in a single long day in the saddle. He kept the frustration to himself though, well able to hear the embarrassment in Mrs. Burgess's voice each time she asked him to halt. No matter how often he brushed off her apologies, each time he pulled the team up, his tired companion apologized anew for the delay.

When Angelina's clarion sounded this time, J. W. tried to forestall the child's harassed young mother. "Not a word," he said, guiding the team to the side of the well-traveled trail before the request to stop came. "Angel's not holding us up. She's helping us pass as a respectable couple."

"Are you sure? If I didn't know better, I'd think she had a burr under her saddle," Louisa said, exasperated.

Unprepared for the aptness of her words, J. W. hastily turned the chuckle that rose in his throat into a strangled sounding cough, and readjusted the angle of his borrowed hat to better hide his expression. She didn't look like a woman prepared to see the lighter side of the situation. And he had enough experience of women to know when to keep his amusement to himself.

"Perhaps she's just tired of traveling," Louisa murmured, casting a glance back at the baby.

He could tell from the weariness in her voice that his traveling companion most definitely was ready to quit running for the day. He also knew her well enough to know she wouldn't utter a word of complaint.

As civilization came into sight, traffic picked up. A stagecoach whisked by them, the driver already beginning to slow his horses from their headlong flight prior to entering the main street. A freight wagon trolled along behind a long string of mules on the opposite side of the road, headed out of Crockett. The man holding the reins nodded companionably to them as he passed, then expertly spit a stream of tobacco juice in an arch that landed in the dirt. He barely missed two lone riders who bounced in their saddles as they swerved around the buckboard, their mounts' hooves a steady *clop clop* of sound as they trotted toward town.

Idly, J. W. wondered where the mule skinner was headed, how long he'd been practicing spitting, and then whether the horsemen knew the best saloon in town, or planned on settling for the first one they hit. For himself, there would be no whiskey that night. All day long he'd been dreaming of an entirely different elixir, one he had no intention of going without any longer.

"We are so close to town," Louisa said wistfully. "Perhaps Angelina will quiet when she hears other commotion around us."

The baby continued to whimper, quite obviously having a decidedly different plan in mind. She was used to demanding and receiving immediate attention. Considering his acquaintance with her during the last twenty-four hours, J. W. figured he just might have a better understanding of what exactly that entailed than a lot of other men. Fathers weren't, after all, around their offspring for such a continuous span of hours usually, having chores to keep up that kept them away.

As a father himself, he hadn't even been around to make his son's acquaintance, much less acquire practical experience of baby rearing. Not that he hadn't wanted to. The war had kept him away.

J. W. pushed the maudlin thought away. He had lived in a different world then, been a different sort of man. Now he had a posse on his tail. Somewhere.

As if his pursuers might yet be riding into sight, he looked back along the road the way they had come. No horde of galloping horsemen sent feathery plumes of dust into the air. Even if they materialized in the next few minutes, he would have to remain calm. He was, for all intents and purposes, merely a family man headed into town for supplies. And, as he reminded Louisa, Angelina's plaintive wail was all part of the charade.

The logic behind that charade was losing something in the translation, seeming less and less sensible with each hour that passed. It wasn't proof against the impotent longing he felt whenever other travelers sped by, kicking up a storm of particles so dry, he frequently wondered if rain ever fell on this side of the county. The respectability Louisa had sought in donning gown and hat was now coated in Texas powder. His concern was more with the masquerade than the attire, though.

And the snaillike progress they made. Hell, even a normally slow-moving emigrant train had passed them, most of the members walking alongside their trail-worn oxen and lumbering wagons. At least no one they met gave them more than a cursory glance and a wave. Judging by the citizens he'd met in Lone Tree, he wouldn't have thought Texians all that friendly. Working his way down the century-old road was giving him an entirely new perspective on the Texian temperament.

Unless he judged it by that displayed by young Angelina Burgess.

"What now?" Louisa exclaimed, twisting in her seat as her daughter's wail increased in volume. "You cannot be hungry. You just ate! And I changed you not five minutes ago."

J. W. wished he had his pocket watch to consult. Another possession lost to the deputies in Lone Tree. But the sun overhead had dropped the width of a finger, so he guessed it was closer to forty-five minutes since Angelina had requested her last rest stop. In any case, he guided the team even farther off the road and pulled them up short.

"Maybe she just wants to be held," he suggested. "Or she's bored. Other than when we stop, her view is of nothing more exciting than the back of our heads."

Louisa sighed deeply. "You could be right," she said and, getting to her feet, she turned and put one knee on the seat as she bent over its low back to gather the baby into her arms.

Despite his better intentions, J. W. found it impossible to keep his eyes on the distant buildings of Crockett. And he'd been doing his damnedest to avoid the enticing view she presented every time they stopped. He was human though. Given the circumstances, he doubted any man could restrain for long the natural urge to admire a woman as lovely as Louisa Burgess.

Louisa. When had he stopped thinking of her as simply Mrs. Burgess? Hours ago. Try as he might, he couldn't think of her as *Lou* though. Particularly not as she was currently dressed. Someone named Lou did not have fluttery ribbons, voluminous skirts, or delicate green bobbles dangling from her ears. He hadn't noticed the earrings until seated next to her where he could watch them swing back and forth with the motion of the wagon.

It could use better springs. Or he could use a stronger dose of self-control. Either would be an improvement.

She twisted back around and placed a sobbing Angelina on her lap so that the baby faced the tail ends of the horses and could see the sturdy buildings that comprised the town of Crockett on the prairie before them. "I'm sorry to put you through this, Mr. Walford," Louisa said.

He noticed she had glanced around to see if other travelers were near before using his own name. The time was coming when they both had to be alert. Although it had taken them a long day's drive to get near it, Crockett was much closer to her ranch than he would have liked. Sheriff Detmer could have sent a man on to alert the local lawmen to keep an eye peeled for him, or Louisa herself could be recognized. Who wouldn't remember a beauty so recently widowed if she was seen gallivanting around the countryside in her city best with a strange man at her beck and call?

It wouldn't do to let their guard down. Not when they'd made it this far undetected.

"Comes with the territory," J. W. muttered, urging the team back on the rut-filled road. "Think we'll make town in time to do some shopping?"

Louisa smoothed the rooster comb of fine fuzz on the child's head, each stroke soothing Angelina's distress away. "You're planning on going into town?"

Although she was obviously surprised at the suggestion, J. W. noticed Louisa kept her voice level rather than excite the baby once more.

"Is that wise?" Louisa asked. "I thought we'd make camp outside of Crockett or find a wagon yard and then continue on to Madisonville as early as possible tomorrow."

"We could," J. W. allowed. "Do you have a coffeepot back there?" He nodded toward the bed of the wagon where she had tucked all manner of odd possessions in the nooks and crannies around the two saddles.

"No," she admitted. "I have some tea and a couple tin cups though."

A meager offering, yet she made it sound like a treat. "I

work better with strong, hot coffee," he said.

"There's the whiskey," she reminded him hopefully.

"Coffee," J. W. intoned. "What about flour?"

"We've some," she said.

"Bacon?"

"Just jerky. We could try to trap or shoot a rabbit or prairie hen if you'd like fresh meat. I've got one of Frank's rifles, a pistol, and some ammunition."

Some ammunition. He doubted it was more like a couple of cartridges, or the fixings for them. It wasn't hunting he had on his mind though.

"Molasses or sorghum?" J. W. asked.

The baby had at last quieted, which made it all the easier to hear Louisa sigh. "No."

It was a very small sound.

"Crackers?" he asked.

"You didn't like the menu last night, did you?" Louisa said.

She sounded closer to despair than she had any time during their admittedly brief acquaintanceship. There were countless things he didn't know about her, but that she had the courage usually associated with a mountain lion, he knew very well.

She was already girding herself for whatever came now, unconsciously squaring her shoulders and taking a deep breath.

"Dinner at least can be warm tonight," she said. "Having a fire will improve it a great deal."

J. W. flicked the reins over the horses' backs, urging them to pick up the pace. "I don't know. It seems a bit windy. We've enough matches to spare if starting a fire proves tricky?" he asked.

"Matches? No, I've a flint box," Louisa explained. "It's

much more dependable. Works even after it's gotten wet."

She was getting testy now. J. W. thought that a good sign. He couldn't afford for her to weaken. His life just might depend on how well she played her part.

"What's the real reason you don't want to stop for supplies, Mrs. Ramsdale?" J. W. asked. "Are you acquainted with someone in town, afraid we might meet them?"

"I wouldn't have suggested we come here if such were the case," she said. "There will be no such gauntlet to run, Mr. Wa—Bart," she said, hastily correcting herself.

He should have chosen a different name, J. W. thought. Having to answer to his brother-in-law's moniker already irritated him, and it was the first time Louisa had called him by it.

"You relieve my mind," he murmured. "We could definitely use a few more supplies. Such as an extra blanket, perhaps? Or better weapons?"

"Weapons!" As if realizing her voice had risen, Louisa bent her head over the baby in her lap. Angelina paid her no never-mind, content to watch the activity around them. "The rifle is in perfect condition," Louisa insisted. "It was Fra—the previous owner's second best, I'll grant you, but I've maintained it scrupulously myself for the past two years."

"That Sharps was a fine rifle in its day, my dear, but we need to do better."

The team entered the town proper, the mares' movements spritely, as if they realized the trials of the day were nearly over. He would have expected them to be skittish from the commotion around them on all sides, but the mares, just like Louisa, continued to surprise him.

"You do need a blanket," she said. "The problem is, I haven't anything with which to purchase one for you.

There. I've said it. There are no available funds to spend. Are you happy?"

"Ecstatic," J. W. assured her. "If you will recall, I was on the lookout to buy a horse yesterday, and I haven't bought one yet. That would indicate, I believe, that I do have funds, both available and ready to spend."

"Oh." The sound was so small, he wasn't sure whether Louisa had answered him or Angelina was trying out her repertoire of sounds under her breath.

His lovely Mrs. Burgess was too tired to argue, J. W. decided. At least he hoped she was, because he planned to spend like a proverbial drunken sailor when they came upon a good-sized dry goods store.

"So you'll be purchasing your own blanket?" Louisa asked.

"Bedroll," J. W. corrected. "And coffee, a coffeepot, crackers, bacon, molasses—"

"Pickles?" She sounded wistful.

"As many as you like," J. W. said.

Pickles, Lou mused in wonder. It would take only one to make her feel she'd stumbled into the Garden of Eden. Such a small thing, yet capable of giving such great pleasure. It had been so long since she had enjoyed the tart taste of a treat from the pickle barrel. Frank hadn't been the sort of man to indulge his wife. Not even for a minor thing like a pickle.

But what if the reality didn't measure up to the memory? She would have wasted good money in the wanton pursuit of unfounded pleasure.

"Angelina and I couldn't impose on your kind nature, Mr. Wa—" Lou caught herself again in time. They were tooling down Crockett's main street. People bustled by on boardwalks, and crisscrossed the street with what seemed little heed for traffic. Some even rode alongside the buckboard, making her feel hemmed in. Any number of people could overhear her.

"Don't be ridiculous, Bart," she said, tempering the rebuttal with a smile. All the same she noticed he cringed slightly at her words. "If you tease me with such possibilities, I'll have no appetite whatsoever for dinner."

Walford's lips stretched in a wry grin. "I doubt that, honey," he murmured.

Unsure of whether he'd used the casual endearment for the benefit of any possible audience, or merely meant to tease her—his voice had been pitched to an intimate tone, after all—Lou felt warmed all the same.

"Well, look at that!" J. W. drawled. "A general store with the door wide open and enough room out front to leave the wagon. Looks like fortune is smiling our way at last, sweetheart."

Two endearments within the space of a minute! If he kept this up, she'd swoon dead away, Lou thought. Even the enticements of fresh pickles faded under such an onslaught!

She knew her cheeks burned brightly. How would he read the blushing color? As embarrassment over the familiarity? Or as the pleasure she felt? Even when he was courting her, Frank had never bombarded her with such honeyed words. And growing up at the hacienda the closest she'd come to feeling special had been when her grandfather's cook, Constanza, and head vaquero, Ramone, called her *Loucita*—Little Lou.

Walford maneuvered the buckboard next to the boardwalk, stepped down into the street and hitched the team to a ready post, all in what seemed like a single fluid motion. "If you'll hand our little angel over to me, we can commence the shopping, dear one. After that, I promise to find you the best meal Crockett has to offer."

When he wasn't engaged in running from the law, Lou wondered whether Mr. Walford tread the boards. He took to acting the part of loving husband so easily.

Perhaps he was well practiced, having perfected his patter on a Mrs. Whatever-His-First-Name-Was Walford. Was there such a lucky woman somewhere? Lou envied her if there was.

Of course, he was merely playacting in promising to buy her dinner, but even more than the thought of savoring a pickle once more, the idea of having a meal served to her in a restaurant was enough to make her lose her head.

Be sensible, Louisa, she lectured silently. It was all a performance. When it came time for dinner, it would be she, not a hotel employee, who would be slaving over the fire. A campfire, at that. Though an improvement over cold jerky, mushy beans, and dry tortillas, the same menu served hot—minus the tortillas—was what awaited them.

Lou handed an eager Angelina over to their protector. Since a smile now dimpled her daughter's cheeks, she decided the little flirt had only been crying to get his attention, not her mother's. Lou wasn't sure whether to be relieved or jealous. Angelina had had only one center in her universe for three months. Now, it appeared, she had two.

Or was it she herself who had two universes? A strange, warm sensation crawled through her when Lou noticed Walford was standing with his free hand extended, waiting to help her down from the buckboard.

"Perhaps I should stay with the horses," Lou suggested.

"The bay does tend to be skittish in unfamiliar surroundings." She felt rather skittish herself.

"Mama's trying to be noble," Walford murmured to the baby on his shoulder. "Tell her to come have fun with us."

As if she understood what he'd suggested, Angelina extended her arm toward Lou, the action seeming to mimic his own stance. "Aah," the child said, and then rested her fuzzy tufted head against his cheek.

Her daughter was worse than a flirt. She was a dyed-in-the-wool hussy, Lou thought, amused at the baby's blatant antics.

"Well, if you're going to both gang up on me," she said, accepting Walford's aid in stepping down from the wagon, "I suppose I'll have to go with you after all. I give you fair warning not to leave me alone near that pickle barrel, though. You know I have an unnatural fondness for the things, dearest."

It felt adventurous to use an endearment of her own. Doing so made her wild and daring. But it was Walford's slow smile that sent unknown butterflies into flight in the area directly beneath her heart.

Oh dear. What had she gotten herself into now?

"And here I thought your tongue was just naturally tart," Walford drawled, waiting for her to precede him into the dark interior of the store.

Lou had barely set foot inside when another scent wiped all thought of pickles from her mind. It teased her, embraced her as she moved slowly toward the rough counter where a man in a pristine butcher's apron placed items in a customer's basket.

At her shoulder she heard Walford's breath catch. "Gingersnaps," he said, sounding like a man preparing to worship at a sacred altar. He sniffed the air again, as if believing his nose had mistaken the heavenly aroma. "Lord, I hope the fellow's wife sells baked goods as well as the fixings."

Lou grinned up at him. "You aren't planning on running off with her as well are you, Bart Ramsdale?"

"Never!" he vowed, smiling down at her.

Outside the shop windows, twilight was edging down the streets, heralding the return of evening. A tall, gangly limbed boy was quietly moving through the store lighting lamps in already dim corners. But, unaware that they should be settling in for the night, the butterflies kicked into action again, their fluttering beneath her rib cage worse this time. As if to still them, Lou pressed her hand flat against her stomach. Unsuspecting that he was the cause of her pleasant distress, Walford made the situation worse.

"Don't worry, my love," he murmured in a tender, teasingly deep voice. "I'd come home to you once the cookies were gone."

Good Lord! How much of this fond teasing could she take and not find herself falling hopelessly in love with him? Already her heart was behaving like a circus acrobat, doing flips every time he smiled her way. *You barely know the man*, Lou reminded herself sternly. It was all playacting, not real. She was probably the only one who wished it could be real.

Mentally, Lou took a deep breath to steady herself. "At least until a fresh batch was baked," she countered, determined to play her part of happy helpmeet.

Was the verbal wordplay a reflection of the way people in love acted? Was the casual, lightly possessive touch of Walford's hand on her arm, her waist, merely another pleasure she had never enjoyed as Frank's bride? How wonderful it must be to feel so loved that you knew nothing could break that bond. Did wedded lovers touch each other when they thought no one was watching?

Walford's hand rested lightly in the center of her back, sending more pleasant, bittersweet tremors of warmth through Lou's body. "I believe it is our turn, Tess," he said, giving her a slight push.

Tess. He meant her. She must stop musing on what she had missed and remember who she was now, temporarily. Later she would allow herself the luxury of daydreaming. Much later.

Lou stepped up to the counter.

"How you doing, folks?" the shopkeeper greeted. "Don't believe I've seen you here before, but what can I help you with?"

Walford offered his hand to the man. "Bart Ramsdale," he said by way of introduction. "My wife, little girl, and I are bound for Austin and need a few more supplies."

"Glad to help," the shopkeeper said and introduced himself. "What can we start with?" he asked.

If Mr. Walford said weapons they were doomed, Lou thought. And he would do it. She had seen that look on a man's face often enough before. He was already looking past the man behind the counter to the display of pistols behind him.

"Cookies," she said brightly. "And after that, a pound of flour, some yeast powder, salted pork, crackers, cheese, nuts, a tin of condensed milk, oatmeal, brown sugar, and coffee."

When they left the shop Lou felt rather guilty. Not only had Mr. Walford paid for what she felt were her extravagant purchases, he had added orange marmalade, raisins, navy beans, molasses, and peanut brittle to the tally. And a coffeepot.

While the staples were gathered, he had roamed around the shop, apparently aimlessly, happening on items that he discussed the purchase of with Angelina, who was quite content with her station at his shoulder. When their circuit of the store was complete, he tossed two pairs of saddle-bags on the counter and something he termed a "dog tent" that would be "an improvement over their current hous-ing." She received a wide-brimmed felt hat with rawhide ties as another improvement, an item Walford assured her would make her look more like a frontier woman than her bonnet did. "Didn't have things like this back in St. Louis," he told the shopkeeper.

Before long she would need to take notes if she was to remember the places they had supposedly been and the places they had lived.

Angelina hadn't been overlooked either, Lou noted. Still content against her presumed father's shoulder, she chewed happily on the arm of a rag doll they had found.

The purchasing wasn't over yet though. Walford had nearly forgotten the bedroll he needed but had not over-looked a Winchester .44 caliber carbine with a twenty-inch-long barrel that held thirteen rounds, and boasted of lever action and calibrated sights. A discussion had ensued with the shopkeeper about the danger of Indian attacks, but even though he had been assured that the Indian ques-tion had been answered in all but the westernmost stretches of the state, Walford had added a Starr Double Action Army .44 self-cocking revolver, enough ball, black powder, and percussion caps to roll his own ammunition, and a holster in which to keep it.

The ecstatic shopkeeper was totaling the purchases

when Walford tossed a pair of trousers made of sturdy cotton jeaning on the counter and a new hat, over which he took considerable time adjusting the pinch in the crown and the curve of the brim before leaving the store.

"Wife doesn't care for the jim-dandy headgear I bought off a down-and-out fellow in Nacogdoches," Walford explained in a man-to-man confidence with the understanding merchant.

Lou stared at the trousers. Obviously, the suit was not being booked for a return engagement the following day, but she could hardly blame him. She had only intended it for use within hailing distance of Peaceful. If all went well, by dusk the next day they would be close to fifty miles away from Titus Gillette, and nearing Madisonville. Should she mention that there was another river to cross? Best not to. Walford had been wet enough the evening before. He might not sleep well if he knew the Trinity awaited. Knowing he was resting so near, separated from her only by Angelina's cradle, would keep her awake at their campsite that night. How could a woman choose to sleep when her mind had the option of reliving each familiar yet light touch of his hand, or better yet, every single endearment he'd dropped so casually as they pretended to be husband and wife? She hadn't had those distractions the night before, only vague restless dreams about Frank and Titus Gillette.

With thoughts of the evening ahead already filling her head, Lou was startled enough to drop the intricately carved hair comb the shopkeeper's wife was showing her when she heard Walford ask one last question.

"Is there a decent hotel nearby with a nice restaurant?"

Lou bit back the protest that rose to her lips. Surely he was not serious! He couldn't be. With all the fresh supplies, why would he choose to stay in town rather than camp near other travelers? Surely, it was far too dangerous. In a room, they could be surprised without warning. In the open, it would be possible to see Banker Gillette's buggy or the sheriff from Peaceful's stallion long before they were discovered.

Or the arrival of the posse. Walford did not know she was fleeing for her life, after all. She had specifically neglected to tell him thus far. However, he did have his own reasons to be alert. Just because they had left Angelina County behind in crossing the Neches, that did not mean the lawmen had given up the chase.

But perhaps the supplies and request for a hotel were for him alone. Perhaps this was where he would abandon her to her own devices.

It would be so lovely to eat in a hotel again. She had only done so a handful of times, all during her wedding trip from San Marcos to the tatty little ranch in Angelina County.

It did little good to dream about it. When Walford sat down to a dinner served by an attentive serving girl or waiter, she would not be with him. She would be gnawing on jerky and sipping water gathered at the fresh oasis of the Crockett Spring.

"Well, I believe we made little impression on anyone at this stop," Lou declared as they left the shop. She accepted Walford's hand to climb aboard the buckboard once more, acting as she presumed a perfect, doting wife would. "They'll barely remember us if anyone asks."

"Sarcasm does not suit you, my dear," Walford chided as he passed the now dozing Angelina back into her care.

"What happens if anyone asks after us at the hotel? Won't it be suspicious that we didn't stay there?" She would not give in to the need to demand whether he was setting off on his own. At least not while they were within hearing of the helpful shopkeeper and his wife.

"No," Walford said, joining her on the wagon seat. "Because we are going to stay there."

Both flabbergasted and delighted, Lou stared at him. "Mr. Wa—"

He gave her a warning glance, reminding her of the danger of giving away their masquerade.

"Mr. What-is-money-for-if-not-to-spend-it!" she continued, undaunted. Surely she sounded very wifely. "We need to marshall our funds against the future, not spend them willy-nilly on things like hotels when we have a perfectly good—and new—shelter. Isn't that why you bought the tent?"

He raised one brow in question, looking delightfully wicked in the process. The corners of his mouth turned up slightly, as if he were fighting to disguise his amusement. "Perfectly good?" he echoed. "It's a tent!"

"All right, adequate," Lou admitted. "We didn't need everything you bought, you know."

Walford slapped the reins lightly against the mares' backs. "I'll admit the peanut brittle was an extravagance."

How easily he discounted the doll and her new hat! They were precious to her because he had been so generous. Charade or not, they were still unnecessary items.

"The peanut brittle?" Lou sputtered.

"Think of it as a present," he said. "You had to forego the pickles. Who would have thought a shopkeeper would run out of such a popular staple?"

"Now who's being sarcastic?" Lou asked. "We aren't really going to the hotel, are we?"

He guided the buckboard around a corner and down a

street that had the feel of permanence to it. A large home with Greek Revival aspirations rose to their left, its interior appearing to glow with warm golden light. It looked settled on the land, boasting the type of permanence only buildings that predated the late war managed to achieve.

"Darn right we are staying at the hotel, madam. Nothing is too good for my bride. Think about how nice a feather bed will feel."

Considering she wasn't really his bride and had never had anything better than a straw-filled mattress before, Lou couldn't imagine the comfort. She could imagine what might happen in regards to such a bed if it were being shared. He had been using a superfluous number of endearments the past hour. Though she had treasured every one, there was an outside chance that he'd been using them to charm his way under her blanket that night.

It was the sort of thing Frank would have done, though probably with another woman. Never with her. He had thought her too conventional. Or so he had once told her before heading off for the saloon.

"And will this bed be big enough for three?" Lou asked.

"It will be big enough for two," Walford said. "You and the impish Angel. I, my dear, will make do with the floor."

Chapter Nine

J. W. spent another fairly sleepless night, this time listening to Louisa's restlessness in the bed. He would have liked to think she couldn't sleep for the same reasons he was wide awake, but doubted women ever had what Claire had always jokingly termed his "lascivious" thoughts.

At least he'd hoped she was joking. There had been times when he wasn't sure whether Claire had been teasing or was quite serious. Particularly when it came to the physical side of their marriage.

In any event, he had pretended to be asleep, forcing each breath to be evenly drawn when just the thought of Louisa in bed had the power to make his breathing downright ragged. Their acquaintance was not of long duration but the circumstances made it feel as if they'd done a considerable amount of living together.

But even if there was a certain rhythm to the way they interacted, even teased each other naturally as a husband and wife might do, he had no call even to think about husbandly rights. He was no longer a man who could settle down. His gun, and a certain proficiency with it, had turned him into one of the soulless drifters who watched their backs and never stayed anywhere for long. Louisa was a woman who needed something more than he could ever offer. She needed the man he'd been. No woman needed the kind of man he'd become.

Exhaustion at last claimed her, making it a bit easier for him to doze. He'd learned to get by on practically no sleep while in the Army. Still, when the sun crested and the floorboards began to complain as other hotel guests rolled from the sheets, J. W. quietly dressed in the sturdy jeaning trousers and one of Frank Burgess's well-laundered calico shirts, settled his new hat on his head, and crept from the room.

Downstairs, the intoxicating aromas of freshly brewed coffee and frying bacon drew him into the dining room. They had eaten there the night before. Louisa had been jumpy when he registered them as Mr. and Mrs. Bartley

Ramsdale and daughter. Her nervousness had continued as they were served a rich beef stew and fresh-baked bread, but her appetite had been unaffected by anxiety. When had she last been able to satisfy her hunger? She had eaten little of the supper shared in the woods that first night. Knowing now how meager her supply of foodstuffs had been, he realized she had been fearful of running out on the trail. And, if she indeed intended to make it to some undisclosed location in Mexico, running short had definitely been an eventuality. In fact, even if he hadn't been along to share the grub, he doubted she would have made it as far as San Antonio before being destitute.

He didn't like to think of her in such a situation. Perhaps he could find her lodgings, arrange for a bank draft on which she could draw until he finished his mission. In the event he survived it, he could return to her, taking the necessary time to escort her wherever the hell she was bound.

J. W. dug into his breakfast, enjoying the quantity of fried eggs, bacon, bread, and coffee the waitress brought to the table. But though there was a lot of it, when it came to quality he didn't think it matched up to the two apples Louisa had given him the morning before. In retrospect, they seemed more like an offering than a meal. As strong as she pretended to be, at heart she obviously knew she needed a man's protection on the trail. Weighed against the dearth of supplies she'd had, those apples had been more precious than gold.

Fortunately, he had gold enough to offer.

"More coffee?" the waitress asked.

His mouth full of food, J. W. nodded and hastily swallowed. "Is there a telegraph office in town?" he asked. "It's taking my wife and me longer to get where we're going than I expected. We've got family waiting on us, and they're probably concerned over our whereabouts."

"That's real thoughtful of you, sir. Yes, we've got a telegraph line. What you need to do is turn right out the front door, then . . ."

J. W. made a mental note of the directions and thanked her. Now the only problem was deciding how to word his wire to Diamond.

By the time he'd finished the coffee the content was set in his mind. *Delayed week or two. Jeff.* No one but Claire's family had ever called him Jeff, but he couldn't exactly sign his name when there might soon be wanted posters circulating with it. And working in the fact that he'd killed Roane and was traveling with a beautiful widow and her child in an effort to avoid a posse was an equally bad idea. Not only would they be throwing a hemp necktie over the nearest tree limb before he got a block away from the telegraph office, he'd be worrying Diamond needlessly to even mention such details. Knowing his sister's temperament, J. W. figured she'd read the message and call him one of the unladylike words she'd learned while trailing Ramsdale's coattails with the Army. Considering he was using her jackanapes late husband's name, he no doubt was deserving of it. Bartley Ramsdale had certainly lived up to every epithet J. W. had ever called him.

With the telegram sent, he was ready to leave the office when a roughly dressed man pushed through the door. "Ya got anything come fer a Egan O'Brien today?" he asked. "Be from a feller name Roane. Uriah Roane."

J. W. nearly halted in mid-stride. He hadn't expected to hear Roane's name again, much less have it uttered by a man who didn't know the bastard was dead. A man who happened to answer to one of the other names on his list.

So J. W. lingered, pretending to read a notice tacked to the wall.

O'Brien was a couple inches taller than Roane had been and had a shock of unkempt red hair on his head and another equally unruly on his chin. Other than that there was little difference between this former raider and Roane. O'Brien was as well armed as his compadre had been, and as destitute looking otherwise. J. W. had no doubt that this man, too, deserved to die.

The telegraph operator shook his head. "Same answer as yesterday, Mr. O'Brien. There's been no message. Would you care to send one?"

"Seein' as I don't know where the hell he is, I don't rightly think so," O'Brien said, and left, letting the door slam shut loudly behind him.

J. W. looked after him. "Friendly type, ain't he?" he murmured to the telegraph operator.

"You said it, mister," the man said in heartfelt agreement and turned back to his work.

J. W. surreptitiously watched through the storefront's window as O'Brien sauntered down the street, then left the building to shadow the former raider's progress down the street. It was a good thing the wire to Diamond had already been sent, he thought, because he was about to get into another serious bit of trouble.

Lou bolted upright in the bed, not sure what had awakened her. The sheet was tangled around her, as if she had been thrashing in her sleep. She had been dreaming, she remembered, picturing Frank shoving his pistol under his belt, and walking through the open doorway of a saloon. A normal enough event, all things considered, if one she had never actually witnessed. Frank hadn't allowed her to go into town very often, and she had never been near a saloon in her life. But she had pictured it enough times to give the dream a stage on which to play out. Particularly this dream.

It wasn't the first time she had had it. It had surfaced the night after she learned of Frank's murder, and had especially haunted her during the hours of drug-induced slumber at Widow Rosa's hands. It always played out the same, like a carefully scripted theater performance. When someone in the saloon called his name, Frank always spun, fumbling to get his gun free.

But this time when the hand came up waving the revolver, it was Walford's face she saw rather than Frank's.

Was the act of pretending to be Walford's wife confusing her dreams? Or was there some portent intended in the substitution?

Down the way, the door to one of the hotel rooms slammed shut, the sound as startling and loud as the report of a fired gun. Another such noise had no doubt been what jolted her from the dream. It didn't explain why she still had the uneasy feeling that something was wrong.

The blanket Walford had used was neatly folded and tossed over the foot rail of the bed. The suit he'd worn and Frank's old hat were tossed aside on a chair. The new Winchester was propped against the wall but the double-action revolver and its holster were missing from the top of the dresser. At least he would be coming back, she thought. He would never leave the rifle behind. He had cleaned and loaded each of the weapons the night before with a reverence some reserved for their Sunday morning church meeting. Frank had shown a like reverence, only the objects of his affection had been a deck of cards and a whiskey bottle.

Next to the bed, Angelina was awake in her crib, engaged in chewing on the edge of her miniature quilt. "It's nothing to worry about, is it, darling?" Lou asked the infant. "It was just a dream. He's just gone out to give us privacy. Even with the door closed, I can smell the coffee they're serving in the dining room. He's merely having a cup while waiting for us to join him there, isn't he?"

Rather than reassure her, Angelina whimpered. That made two of them worried. Lou grabbed her clothes.

Within moments she was dressed once more in the sensible dark riding skirt, cotton blouse, and boots she'd fled the cabin in. Rather than take time with her hair, she pulled it back, tying it at her nape with Walford's neglected neckerchief. She would apologize for appropriating one of his possessions later.

It took a bit longer to change and reassure Angelina, but within ten minutes of waking, Lou had the baby in her arms and was on her way downstairs.

"Good morning, Mrs. Ramsdale," the hotel clerk greeted from behind his desk in the narrow, dark wallpapered lobby. "Looking for your husband?"

Lou took a deep calming breath. "Yes. Have you seen him? I'm afraid I overslept."

"Traveling takes the wind out of a person but good, don't it?" the man asked. "Mr. Ramsdale probably went down to the livery stable to settle up."

"Yes, of course," Lou murmured. It was logical that he do so. Particularly since he had paid extra to insure that no one raided the items in the wagon bed.

That didn't mean that he wasn't in trouble. That he hadn't been spotted by someone from the posse. She had last seen his pursuers headed in the direction of Alto, but they could easily have followed the road as it ambled southwest toward Crockett. And if such was the case, Walford needed her help.

Lou switched the baby to her other arm, angling the infant so that Angelina faced the man behind the desk. "Is there someone who could watch my daughter while I run down there to see if he is about ready to go?" she asked. "I'll be able to get there and back much faster if I'm not carrying her."

As Lou had hoped, Angelina gurgled some of her incoherent sounds and smiled, flashing the adorable dimple in her cheek, ready to make up to yet another susceptible man. There was something to be said for the timeliness of the baby's newly honed talents as a charmer. Lou wished she could take the time to nuzzle her daughter's plump little neck in approval. But there wasn't time. Not if Walford really was in trouble.

"She's going to be a beauty one of these days," the hotel clerk declared, grinning back at the baby. "I'll nip back to the kitchen and see if my Greta has a few minutes to spare."

Greta, a comfortably rounded woman of middle age, bustled into the narrow lobby barely a minute later, eager to care for Angelina.

Lou wasted no time in handing her daughter over. "I won't be long," she promised, but doubted Greta heard her. The woman was already engaged in a one-sided conversation with the now subdued baby. Afraid that Angelina would notice her leaving and begin to cry, Lou nearly sprinted for the door.

The livery stable held center stage on the next street, the size of the building proving that the owner was in the progress of making his fortune in caring for and renting out horses and equipages. Although slightly out of the way of the normal run of traffic in town, business had not been lacking when they had driven to the door the evening before. Each stall had been filled, but the owner had willingly turned a couple of his own horses free in the corral to make room in the stalls for the two mustangs. He had even helped maneuver the buckboard into the building, watching as Walford secured the oilcloth over their possessions in the wagon bed and tied it down tight.

There was little sign that anyone was on duty as Lou approached the gray clapboard building. Where could Walford be if not there? Not, she hoped, at one of the saloons. She had the courage to do a lot of things, but entering a saloon alone was not one of them.

The large double barn doors were closed and apparently bolted from the inside. They didn't give when she pulled on one. That was strange considering the morning was advancing quickly toward noon. She could not imagine why Walford had let her sleep so long. They needed to put far more miles between them and any pursuit, be it from Peaceful at Banker Gillette's behest, or from the gentlemen of Sheriff Detmer's bloodthirsty posse. But if Walford was not at the livery stable, and not at the hotel, there was very little she could do short of asking another hotel employee to scour the saloons for him.

She was just about to turn away when the sound of hooves striking wood and the panicked whinny of a horse at the rear of the stable made Lou change her mind. Whatever was going on in the corral, there would be someone who could tell her whether her "husband" had been there that morning.

A narrow alleyway led between the stable and the whitewashed wooden building next door. Lou followed it, feeling as if the clapboard walls on either side of her were pressing closer. Quite obviously she would never be comfortable as a city dweller. She had lived too long in the open spaces. But until she reached her mother's home, there was little reason to dwell on the problem. One issue at a time was all she could handle. Finding her absent benefactor was currently top on the list.

The narrow passageway did more than merely close in on her though. It amplified sounds, so that they echoed ringingly back from the corral. Two men were talking, she realized, antagonizing each other. There was the sound of a scuffle, of boots against hard-packed ground, the ring of spurs as quick steps were taken. A horse whinnied again, and must have reared slightly for she heard hooves strike the dirt, then something else hit the earth as well.

An unknown man grunted, then swore. "You bloody blue belly," he said, growling. "I ain't goin' down as easy as Roane."

"You're still going straight to hell," Walford's familiar tones announced quietly. He sounded quite calm, Lou thought.

"I'll show you hell," the other man said, snarling. There was a crash, the thud of something heavy striking the outer stable wall, then a gurgling that boded ill for one of the men. Lou's hesitation evaporated. She raced around the corner of the building, sliding to a frightened stop when she saw the combatants on the ground.

A saddled horse sidestepped them, its eyes wide and rolling. In the corral, another mount circled the confined area nervously, looking for escape from the sprawled, unmoving body by the watering trough.

But it was the two men battling for supremacy of a pistol that held Lou breathlessly still at the alley's edge. An unknown redheaded assailant was trying to turn Walford's own gun on him.

Walford's back was in the dust, putting him in a seemingly helpless position. Yet, as she watched in horror, he twisted, throwing the other man off balance and sending the Starr .44 flying from the fellow's hand so that it skittered across the yard out of reach.

Out of her reach as well, Lou realized, since the men were between her and where the pistol lay just yards from the nervously dancing saddled horse.

Though their struggle for possession of the gun was over, the redheaded man wasn't finished. With both his hands free, he pressed down on Walford's neck, trying to strangle him.

"Ain't it 'vengeance is mine' that the preachers claim the Almighty says?" he demanded, his gruff tone indicating he cared very little for Scripture or preachers.

His own fingers ineffectual in loosening the man's grip around his throat, Walford rammed his knee up between his assailant's legs. When the man rolled away, his hands sheltering his groin, Walford leaped to his feet, gasping to get his breath back. "Who says I'm not working for the Lord, O'Brien?" he rasped. "He needs all the help he can get to deal out retribution for what your kind did in Lawrence."

"Kansas? Hell, that was war and you know it, Yankee," O'Brien muttered. Moving carefully, he, too, got to his feet, his arms held in apelike readiness away from his body.

Lou pressed back out of sight, her spine flat against the livery building. Vaguely she recalled hearing of Lawrence, Kansas. What had happened there? There had been so many horrific stories of what man did to man throughout the four long years of the war. Somehow such atrocities had brought these two men within inches of killing each other. One of them she needed alive.

Peering around the side of the barn once more, Lou watched as they circled each other. Neither of the men appeared anxious to rush into combat yet. Both eyed each other cautiously. The standoff wouldn't last for long though. Townspeople would be stopping by the livery just as she had. They would find their way around back, see the livery man injured—surely not dead!—on the ground. With one of their own attacked, it wouldn't matter which of the men yet standing was responsible. They would call in the law. Both Walford and O'Brien would be arrested.

And then her Santo Jorge would be hanged. At times it was difficult for her to remember that he was a murderer on the run. Now was not one of those times.

As he waited for the moment to strike, she could see he was quite a different person from the kind, considerate Walford who'd come to her rescue. This man was a killer. There was no doubt in her mind at all. And if it was his profession, he was quite obviously very good at it.

She couldn't say the same for his opponent. However, there was animal cunning revealed in O'Brien's face when he smiled evilly at Walford. Killer though he was, she judged Walford to be a man who lived by a code. His opponent was more akin to Frank's more dangerous friends, men who killed for the thrill of it.

Lou shivered. She could not lose Walford to such a man.

"Lawrence wasn't war," Walford said, his voice modulated, even calm. But there was a ruthlessness in the tone that she had never heard him use before. A dead certainty that he was in the right and that when it visited, death would be dealt from his hand. "It was killing innocent civilians, Reb."

O'Brien snorted in disgust. "No such thing as an innocent civilian in Kansas," he claimed. "Only Bible-thumping abolitionists. Yeah, we went in firing. Took out every living man or boy we saw. Left the buildings burning and the women weeping."

"Not all the women," Walford corrected. "You killed one. Shot her down."

O'Brien's lips twisted in an unpleasant smile. "Your woman, huh? Damn, guess I do deserve to die. Ain't like there aren't enough widows to pick a new one from, is there?"

Lou saw it coming. The moment when Walford snapped. He lunged at O'Brien, catching the man around the knees, knocking him back against the watering trough. Water sloshed over both men, but neither apparently felt it. As one they rolled in the dust, fists hammering into soft flesh, unaware that they were dangerously close to the nervous, saddled bronc, which reared slightly in fear.

The animal's hooves came down inches from Walford's body. Lou watched as he fought on, recklessly, seeming not to care whether he survived as long as he took O'Brien with him when he went to meet his Maker. But O'Brien was canny, baiting Walford to throw repeated punches. And Lou saw why.

With every blow Walford landed, O'Brien fell back a foot closer to the Starr .44 lying forgotten on the ground. The pistol she had watched Walford so carefully load the evening before, inserting each freshly rolled bit of ammunition, carefully insuring that each fit neatly in the waiting chamber.

The men were still between her and the handgun, but that didn't mean she had to stand by helplessly and watch her guardian angel be felled before her eyes. She needed some way to stop the fight without calling the attention of the townspeople. And she needed to do it quickly.

No longer caring whether either of the men saw her, Lou dashed into the barn. In the center aisle her buckboard waited patiently. The bay and the sorrel were the only horses still residing in the stalls. She could see their tails flicking idly at irritating flies. And outside the nearest stall was the answer to her unconscious prayer.

A shovel.

Quickly grabbing it, Lou ran back into the yard. O'Brien's back was to her, but he was barely two feet away from the Starr. Without considering what she was about to do, Lou swung the shovel with all her might. The broad metal scoop smashed with a sickening sound against the back of O'Brien's head, sending him stumbling forward into Walford.

"The hell!" Walford cursed, stumbling back as he caught the unconscious man. A rather mild exclamation, Lou thought, considering some she'd heard her late husband and his friends use.

There was blood on the broad surface of the shovel. She looked in fear from it to O'Brien, as Walford let him drop full length on to the dry, hard beaten earth. "Is he dead?" she asked faintly.

"Not yet," Walford said. In a single movement he reclaimed his pistol, seized her hand and pulled her from the stable yard.

Barely aware that they were not retracing her steps to the street, but hurrying past the corral and behind the adjacent houses, Lou tried to hang back. She felt the need to explain herself. She wasn't a violent person yet she had just attacked a man, and done so behind his back, at that.

"He was going for it," Lou said. "He was going to shoot you down with your own gun."

Walford shoved the Starr back in the holster on his belt as he moved. "Hard thing to do with an empty pistol."

"*A what!*" Lou demanded, pulling free of his hand. "It was emp—"

He moved swiftly, taking her by surprise when he pinned her back to the nearest building. "Empty," Walford said quietly, his voice an intimate, teasing murmur. "But thank you all the same," he added; then he kissed her.

It was hard, fast, and the most wonderful thing she had ever experienced. And it was over far, far too quickly.

"Come on, beautiful," Walford said. "Let's get back to the hotel. I think it might be wise to leave town attired as we arrived, don't you? Too bad I hate that damn suit."

In Austin, Diamond watched activity in the street below her hotel window, hanging back from the window just enough not to be noticed by passersby. She knew what the women would think of her, a woman living in a succession of hotel rooms, nearly always on the move, her livelihood seemingly dependent on the turn of a card. Good women didn't trespass in the male dominion of saloons. They didn't gamble, drink, or cheat. Once she had been like them. Now their world was alien to her.

The late nights at the card table were beginning to tell on her. Or was that merely the number of restless hours she spent wondering how much longer the trail to revenge would be. For more than two long years she had been wandering in search of information, rarely hearing more than a whisper of the name of one of the men for whom she searched. But here in Austin, things were coming together swiftly. Or they would once her brother arrived. If he ever arrived.

Despite Neddy's assurances, she still feared something had happened to J. W. He had never been out of touch with her this long before. When one moved on with their quest, the other was always given a new location where he or she could be reached. The last she had heard from him he had followed a lead from St. Louis to Shreveport, assuring her that he would await word from her there. And word she had sent, news guaranteed to have him traveling nearly night and day to reach Austin before circumstances changed.

That had been ten days ago. Surely he could cover a couple hundred miles easily within that time. The stagecoach did; a lone horseman usually managed to travel faster.

As no horseman with J. W.'s recognizable seat in the saddle was trotting along the street below, Diamond moved away from the window. Soon it would be time to dress, go down to dinner and on to her evening in the saloon. For now, it was the ravages of a string of sleepless nights she needed to repair.

Diamond studied her face in the dresser mirror, checking the precision with which she applied powder and rouge to hide the circles under her eyes. It didn't do to look haggard when a woman was engaged in finessing information from men without their knowing it. Not that she had learned much lately. The only tales that had been told in the past few nights at her table were the same ones she had heard before. If Dalhert's men were gathering in Austin, either they were lying low or were yet on the trail. In the event some of them began to put in an appearance, she needed to be ready. But ready to do what, she didn't know.

Usually she merely gathered information. J. W. acted upon it.

Behind her the door opened quietly. Diamond heard the gentle whisper of Neddy's skirts before the black woman's face appeared at her shoulder in the mirror.

"I think you'll feel better when you read this, Miss Tess," Neddy said, passing her a folded slip of paper.

"From J. W.?" Diamond reached eagerly for it, then dropped her hand before her fingers touched the telegram. Instead she pulled her wrapper closer around her torso and shoulders. "What's it say?"

"Only that he's delayed. Possibly as long as two weeks," Neddy said and paused a moment before adding more. "He signed it 'Jeff.' "

Diamond sat down abruptly on the lone chair in the room. "Not a good sign, is it? Do you think we've been found out?"

Neddy opened her reticule and took out a box of matches. "I think we needn't jump to conclusions that are unfounded," she cautioned and struck the match against the striking plate. When it flamed to life she waited a moment before holding it to an edge of the folded paper. "Do you want to read it yourself first?"

Diamond waved the offer away. "No. We're being overly cautious, aren't we? It's a telegram, not incriminating evidence," she said.

"I didn't think it was a judge or jury that you were worried about, Miss Tess," Neddy reminded quietly. "It was the chance someone in that man's camp learned who you were and what you are doing."

That man. Neddy never called Dalhert anything else, as if using his name evoked an unspeakable evil. In a way, Diamond thought, her friend was right.

"Go on, send it on its way," she said. "I suppose we'll just have to be patient and wait until J. W. arrives to learn any more. Sometimes I think he wallows in being mysterious. Do you think he ever uses another name to escape notice? Do the men he has murdered know who he is and why he in particular is their executioner?"

Neddy held the burning match to the message, waiting until the furthermost edges were black and curling before dropping it in the waiting saucer on the dresser. "We'll probably never know. Your brother has never been one to confide in anyone. It was one of the things that irritated Miss Claire the most about him."

Diamond watched as the telegram turned to dark ash. "Do you ever think about it?" she asked. "About what happened the day Ezra and Claire died?"

"Is that why you didn't sleep again last night? I heard you tossing and turning," Neddy said.

"If you'd be sensible and sleep in the bed instead of on that pallet on the floor, you could have felt me tossing and turning as well," Diamond answered. "Do you think about it?"

Neddy busied herself shaking out the skirts of a midnight blue evening gown. Ruching had lowered the neckline to what Tess Walford would once have considered a scandalous level. In her pose as a southern belle fallen on unkind times, Diamond termed the neckline's dip necessary.

"You mean do I relive it?" Neddy corrected. "That's what you do, isn't it?"

It was exactly what she did. How could she not? It was at the moment of her violation that she had stopped being Theresa Walford Ramsdale and become a nonentity called

151

Diamond. Dalhert and his men had stolen her life. Or what remained of it after Bart's death.

Neddy carefully placed the dress over the iron footboard of the bed where it would remain unmussed until Diamond put it on that evening. Perching on the edge of the bed herself, Neddy patted a spot on the utilitarian blanket next to her. "Come sit with me," she urged.

When Diamond joined her friend, Neddy took both her hands and squeezed them lightly, although whether Neddy was drawing courage to speak herself or giving comfort, Diamond didn't know. The mahogany-skinned woman's back was as straight as the ramrod of a rifle, her feet in their laced cloth boots were properly situated on the floor. Neddy might pretend to be her maid servant, but the woman was far more proper in bearing than she herself had ever been, whether as Tess or Diamond.

"I miss my husband," Neddy said. "It wasn't right the way he died. But do I think about how it happened often?" She shook her head and let go of Diamond's hands. "No, Miss Tess, I don't."

"You're lucky then," Diamond claimed. She pulled her bare feet up beneath the trailing skirts of her nightgown and wrapper, hugging her upraised knees. "I can't stop watching the whole thing happen again and again in my head. Those men riding into the yard, their rifles and pistols out and blazing. The only things they didn't take aim at were you and me. And if Claire—"

Neddy gently put her hand over Diamond's once more. "Miss Claire always did go her own way. You know she enjoyed the freedom of dressing in your brother's old clothes when she helped Ezra in the barn. That's why they thought she was a boy, why they shot her down."

"But if I'd been the one out there, Claire would be alive

now and so would J. W.'s son," Diamond said.

"And it would have been Miss Claire those men—"

Diamond turned her face away. "Don't. It's bad enough that I relive it. Worse that I was as eager as J. W. when he swore to hunt down every one of them. Hell, we wouldn't even have known who the riders were if one of them hadn't called out Dalhert's name."

Neddy frowned. *Like she always does when I swear*, Diamond mused.

"Stop giving me the benefit of your schoolmarm stare," Diamond said. "You know it doesn't work. And you also know that, even if I'm tired of tracking down Dalhert and his men, as long as J. W. is on the blood trail, I will be there for him. He lost everything he cared about, or ever wanted to care about, in the war."

"You lost your husband," Neddy said softly. "He died in your arms of his wounds. Do you relive that day as well?"

Her friend wasn't playing fair. "You know I don't. Bart wouldn't want me to."

"Neither would Ezra or Miss Claire."

It was impossible to sit still with all the old emotions clamoring for release again. Diamond got to her feet and returned to the dresser. She picked up a delicate hare's-foot brush and added a dusting of powder to her cheeks. This was what Dalhert had brought her to. She had not only lost herself; she had become one of the fallen, a painted lady.

Only there was very little of the lady left in her.

"It isn't for them that it stays so fresh in my mind, Neddy," Diamond said.

"It's Mr. Jeff then?"

Diamond shook her head. "No. It's for me."

Even that was partially a lie, she knew, but it was what kept her going.

A little while later when the dark blue gown slipped over her head and settled just off her pale shoulders, Diamond took a deep breath. "Wish me luck?" she asked before leaving the room.

Neddy let the book she had been reading rest in her lap. "I wish you were able to quit this life," she said softly. "Wish you could become Tess Ramsdale again."

Her hand on the doorknob, Diamond paused. "Both wishes that can't come true, my dear friend. You, better than most, should know that Tess Ramsdale is gone. I don't think I ever could be that woman again," she said; then quietly closing the door behind her, Diamond went down to play.

Chapter Ten

"Whip 'em up, Mrs. Ramsdale!" a man yelled through the pouring rain. "Easy does it though. Don't want to leave us fellers facedown in the mud."

Lou did as she was bid, urging the mustang mares into action in an effort to pull the buckboard out of the quagmire the Brazos River crossing had become. The horses strained as the mud sucked at the wheels, drawing them down nearly to the axle. Men swore as they put their shoulders to the wagon bed and pushed. And over it all fell the blanketing sound of rain. Not a pleasant, ground renewing gentle rain, but blinding, ground-ripping torrents falling in what looked—and felt—like solid sheets of water.

They had hitched up with a group of emigrants from Pennsylvania, joining their train of wagons outside of Madisonville. Mr. Walford had called it hiding in clear view. She had silently termed it safety in numbers. Whichever it was, traveling with others had changed the way they interacted with each other, at once forcing them to behave more like husband and wife, yet making it possible to keep somewhat distant from each other. While he joined the men to care for the animals and do repairs on the wagons, she helped the women tend to the children and prepare meals that were shared by all.

But the performances they played in this public arena were intimate ones. Walford frequently rested his hand at her waist, used terms of endearment when he addressed her, and impressed the other women with his readiness to care for the baby. And occurring as these things invariably did at twilight, every evening she found herself slipping a little more in love with him.

She shouldn't let each touch, each tender word affect her that way. He was only playing a part, pretending to be her spouse, her lover. For most of the time, her heart knew it was an act. Yet there were times, like when she watched him with Angelina, that Lou found herself dreaming impossible dreams. Her daughter might have been fathered by another man, but it was Walford who was quite obviously filling that role in her baby's early life. He took joy in being around Angelina, carrying on one-sided conversations with her, helping her play pattycake with the other children, and always materializing when she was fussy, ready to help calm her. He would make someone a wonderful father, Lou thought. If only that someone could be Angelina.

Which was a ridiculous thing even to consider in passing. He was, after all, an outlaw on the run from the law. Did that make him much different from her though? She hadn't killed anyone, not even the man she'd bashed with the shovel, but Titus Gillette would term her a thief for stealing away from the pathetic little ranch with what few vendable items had been left. She even had the richly tooled saddle her grandfather had presented Frank on their wedding day, which was probably worth more than everything else she owned combined. And she only had it because Walford had thrown it in the wagon, no doubt believing it had sentimental value for her. How far from the truth that was!

It rested behind her in the wagon even now, hidden from sight beneath the canvas tarpaulin. Though with the fierceness of the driving rain, the saddle was probably as drenched as the rest of her possessions at the moment, and of absolutely no use to anyone engaged in prying her buckboard from the grasping mud.

"Halt! Pull 'em up, Tess!" Walford yelled, his voice carrying clearly through the storm. He'd probably honed his vocal cords as an officer, shouting encouragement to his troops during a battle, trying to be heard over the barrage of cannon fire, she mused. He hadn't told her much about his past, beyond confessing that he'd killed the man that the posse from Lone Tree was riled over, but he had admitted to having been a Northern officer. He hadn't mentioned from what state, or whether he'd been among those engaged in the fights at places like Gettysburg in the East or Chattanooga in the West, or whether he had marched with Sherman through Georgia. He hadn't explained why he'd tried tricking the redheaded man, O'Brien, into drawing an empty gun on him, or why they had squared off against each other. The references to

Lawrence, Kansas, meant little to her, the name sounding familiar only because it numbered among the many locations visited by atrocities during the war.

But it wasn't those things that she wondered about as she lay sleepless within the narrow dog tent every night. No, she wondered about the woman who had been killed, the one Walford was quite obviously set on avenging. Who was she? How had she been murdered?

Had she been the real Tess Ramsdale?

"Let's give it a rest, Tess," Walford urged, materializing from the storm at her side. Rather than risk his new hat, he'd rammed Frank's old one back on when the rain commenced. Now it drooped, rain running from various dips in the soaked rim. Mud covered his trousers thickly to the knee and, despite the downpour, clung in splatters to his shirt. In fact, everything he wore clung to him, plastered to his leanly muscled body.

She was in little better case. The oilcloth poncho and two layers of petticoats she'd added to combat the cold and damp had proven unequal to the task. In fact, all the layers of sodden skirt made her every movement as lumbering as she'd felt in the final weeks of her pregnancy. The clinging fabric was confining when wet, and since her skirts were more than just a little wet, she probably weighed as much as the elephant she had seen when Frank took her to see the traveling circus. The outing had taken place early in his courtship and, probably because it had been one of the very few treats she had ever enjoyed, the memory had remained clear in her mind. However, even that elephant had been more agile than she currently was. In fact, with splashes of mud on her drenched clothing and her long hair clinging like the dark tentacles of a sea creature Miss Nottingham had shown her in a book, she probably looked worse than Walford did.

That made them a very sorry-looking pair. At the moment it also made them blend in incredibly well with the other couples in the emigrant train.

"Henry says his missus has hot coffee available," Walford continued. Through the torrent, she could barely see his lips curve in the now-familiar grin of amusement. "Claims it was her ability to always keep a pot of it handy and blistering hot that led him to the altar. That and her father's old shotgun."

Lou tied the wet reins around the hand brake and scooted through the puddle forming in an indentation in the wagon seat. "Even though I prefer tea, coffee sounds wonderful at the moment," she confessed, leaning forward to place her hands on his shoulders. When his hands encircled her waist and he lifted her to the ground, Lou found herself holding her breath. She had done so every time he touched her, wondering if this time he would kiss her again. She had been waiting for a repeat of that brief yet thorough embrace for four days.

Four days in which she had pretended to be Tess Ramsdale.

Four days of continued curiosity over whether she measured up to the real Tess Ramsdale. She knew no more now about Walford's sister than she had the day he had presented her with Tess Ramsdale's name.

But then, considering how long they had been posing as husband and wife, she knew even less about Walford himself.

After that surprising kiss, he had put a distance between them again. No, she thought, it was more like an unscalable stone wall. She should do the same, follow such an excellent example. She had lost her heart to Frank, if only briefly. Hadn't she sworn never to let a man get close to her again? A woman should watch what she vowed, particularly over a freshly filled grave. Such ultimatums tempted fate too much to put her in the path of temptation.

That's what Walford was. Temptation. No matter how well, or how often, she instructed her heart to stay clear of him, it seemed determined to pay her no heed. Even now, the touch of his hands at her waist, effortlessly lifting her cumbersome form free of the wagon, appeared to give her simple heart enough reason to indulge in ardent daydreams. A woman with a young daughter to rear should be sensible enough to squash such fantasies.

At the moment there didn't seem to be a single sensible bone in her entire body.

She needed to listen more closely to the strictures her better self listed each night. He was a killer and he was hunting men to avenge a woman he had loved. Men like that were best forgotten because they would soon either abandon one or be gunned down themselves. Better that he leave her than force her to stand alongside another grave.

As soon as Lou's feet hit the muddy ground, Walford released her and stepped back. "You all right?"

"Just tired and wet, which the rest of you are, too," she said.

"I'd go beyond wet, in this case," he drawled lazily. "We all look a hair shy of drowned."

When he grinned down at her, despite the cold rain, Lou felt warmth flood through her veins. *Do not fall in love with him, Louisa Keating Burgess*, she silently reminded herself once more, as if the admonishment would cure or correct the error already made. Not fall in love with him? Ha! She had already been halfway there within twenty-four hours of meeting him.

"Angelina's probably wondering what happened to me," she said, settling the dripping poncho back in place over her shoulders.

"Or enjoying the company of her latest conquest, the Lindstroms' little boy," Walford countered cheerfully. Being drenched by the spring storm hadn't dampened his spirits. If anything, it seemed to have invigorated him. "Soon as we get the wagon out, we'll all be looking for some of that coffee though," he said. "You head in, have a cup, and find some dry clothes."

Dry clothes was a relative notion, Lou decided. Although the emigrants had grouped their old Conestoga wagons in as close a circle as possible, tying down oiled tarpaulins to block the encroaching rain, even things packed in trunks would probably be damp by now. Everyone had spent time in the storm, either setting up the hastily drawn camp or working to free the vehicles from the greedy mud. People set on pioneering carried supplies, not extensive wardrobes. And on a night like this, Lou suspected even the Queen of England would be hard-pressed to find a dry item in her traveling cases.

Rather than linger in the rain, she nodded in acceptance of Walford's suggestion and headed for the circle of wagons. She hoped Henry was right about his wife's coffee. She was so badly chilled, her teeth were inclined to chatter.

"Oh, you poor dear!" one of the women exclaimed, sweeping the sheltering canvas aside when Lou knocked on the side of the wagon bed rather than enter unannounced. "Get in here this very minute, Mrs. Ramsdale. Look at her, Helen! I've never seen a more drowned soul in my life."

"Wait until the men get here," Lou warned as she climbed carefully inside. "I think they're in worse shape than I am. After all, I was only trying to drive the team. They were stuck on the river's edge being sucked down in the mud."

"Well, it's what we brought them along for, isn't it?" the woman said lightly. "I mean, what else are they good for?"

Helen chuckled appreciatively. "At times, not much," she agreed. "Here, I've got a nice toasty blanket ready for you, Mrs. Ramsdale. But strip down as near the skin as possible before wrapping up in it. If you stay in those clothes, you'll have an ague by morning. Then where will your husband and little girl be?"

"Other than stranded in the middle of Texas," her friend said.

"I don't think we've reached the middle of Texas yet, have we?" Helen asked, helping Lou struggle out of her things.

"With this rain, I think we could sail right over it and never notice. Too bad none of the men answer to the name of Noah," the other woman muttered as she gathered up Lou's discarded clothing.

"Why, Irene Adams!" Helen exclaimed. "I never thought I'd see the day when you turned on the Good Book."

Mrs. Adams held one of Lou's drenched petticoats over a bucket and began squeezing water from it. "I'm merely pointing out that it is wet enough to need an ark," she insisted. "You know quite well we're all God-fearing folk in this train."

At least *they* were, Lou corrected silently as she huddled in the blanket. It felt clammy against her skin, but then so did her camisole, drawers, and corset.

Was she a God-fearing woman though? Compared to the kind Samaritans of the wagon train, she doubted it. She'd always been too fearful of her grandfather's ire, and then of Frank's temper, to worry much about the deity. What would these women think of her if they knew she was traveling with a man who was not her husband? That she wasn't the woman she claimed to be?

And even worse, in their eyes, that she had been wishing Walford would forget she wasn't his wife in truth and would entertain—and act on—conjugal thoughts when lying so close to her each night.

Oh yes. To their traveling companions she would most definitely be seen as a woman who had fallen from the path of righteousness. Yet, if such were the truth, why did what she was doing feel so right?

"Here," Helen said, handing her a china teacup from which steam rose enticingly. "Mind the chip in the rim. My grandmother brought this set with her when she left Darmstadt to come to America. They've survived two generations of daily use intact, but they have not taken well to travel, I'm afraid."

Lou took the cup gratefully, curving her chilled hands around the warm surface. "You're lucky to have family things to bring with you," she said wistfully. "I'm afraid all I have from my family is Angelina's cradle."

Irene Adams folded the wrung-out petticoat neatly and put it aside before reaching for the second one and repeating the process all over again. "It's a lovely piece. A bit more sturdy than Helen's china and less bulky than my great-grandmother's spinet."

"She had to sell it," Helen murmured in a soft undertone near Lou's ear. "There was no room in the wagon."

"I can hear you, Helen," Irene said, a bit testy. "Besides, bringing the spinet along would have been foolish. It would have been so badly out of tune from all the jostling on the trail anyway."

Lou didn't think Irene sounded convinced. She sounded sad. Resigned.

"There was no way of knowing if San Marcos would have a decent piano tuner, so I let it go. I think my husband managed to buy one of the oxen with the sorry sum it fetched. The way things are now, folks just don't have the ready money to buy nice things."

But Lou wasn't interested in the price of either spinets or oxen. "San Marcos?" she croaked, her voice seeming to fail her.

Irene worked the last drops of water from the second petticoat. "Yes. Is that where you and Mr. Ramsdale are headed as well? Helen and her family are going there, too. Henry and my man want to try their hands at ranching. We heard San Marcos was a good area in which to raise cattle."

San Marcos was a ranching community, but it was also the last place Lou wanted to be. And yet, since the wagon road followed the older Spanish trace, if they continued along it, she would find herself back in San Marcos. And much too close to her grandfather's ranchero for comfort.

"No, Mr. Ramsdale has relatives in Austin," she said. At least that was the story she'd heard Walford give when asked. As to where they really were bound, she hadn't thought much beyond the necessity of putting a sufficient number of miles between herself and the greedy banker in Peaceful. It was time to begin looking ahead, not behind her. She had left the rundown cabin determined to seek sanctuary with her mother, but the plan had always been rather nebulous. Exactly how far was it to Mexico City? She didn't know. Did the Camino Real continue on to Mexico City? Probably, but was it as safe and well traveled as the San Antonio Road in Texas? Doubtful. It would be wise to find out, and in the event the news proved unwelcome, to come up with a secondary plan which she could act on if necessary.

Lou had a feeling it was going to be very necessary, very soon. Particularly if Walford was indeed only going as far as Austin. She would have to ask him if they ever had a moment's privacy. A difficult feat to accomplish when sharing accommodations with the kind families who had welcomed them, shared with them, and unwittingly provided further shading to the charade she and Walford played.

The sudden keening of an infant's voice broke into Lou's thoughts.

"Sounds like someone knows her mother is once more at hand," Helen said. "Angelina is probably hungry. We can't offer much privacy, but there's a niche between two barrels where we can fashion a screen if you'd like to feed her."

Rather than grapple with thoughts about her looming future, Lou took Helen up on the offer.

J. W. put his shoulder once more to the wagon's tail board, straining as he and three other men pushed hard, their feet slipping in the mud or driving deeper into it as they sought for purchase. Although the other wagons were heavier and should have sunk farther in the muck, as the last vehicle in line it had been the buckboard that became bogged down in the muddy ruts at the ford. They were lucky that, although the rain seemed to arrive in overflowing buckets, the river had yet to rise from the deluge. It wouldn't be long until it did, but the other wagons had found higher ground on which to set up camp. The buckboard would join them soon. At least he hoped it would be soon.

"Ya, ya!" yelled the man who had taken Louisa's place at the reins, snapping the leads over the mustangs' backs. The mottled bay reared in her traces, sending the wagon rocking back into the grasping, muddy rut rather than out of it.

"Ah, hell," the fellow next to J. W. muttered as he jumped back out of the way. "Thought we'd have it that time. Maybe we should bring up the oxen to yank 'er free."

"Let's give it one last try," J. W. suggested, then raised his voice. "Once more on the count of three, Hershel!"

"Come on, girls. Give it yer all!" Hershel urged the mares.

This time when the reins snapped, the team jerked forward with sufficient power to wrench the buckboard free at last. Spinning mud back onto the men, the wheels slipped and slid on the slick ground. Then with a sudden lurch over an unseen obstacle, the wagon crashed down hard on the left rear wheel. A moment before it had hung slightly suspended, spinning freely, but when the wagon tilted, the wheel splintered, rim and spokes crumbling into bits of tinder. Even with the noise of the rain ringing in his ears, J. W. heard the unwelcome crack of even sounder wood snapping.

"Whoa! Whoa!" the man handling the reins yelled, trying to find purchase on the wet, tipping seat and still stop the horses.

"Double hell," someone swore. "There's no fixing that,

Ramsdale. Not only do we not have a wheel that will fit, I think the axle itself is gone."

The euphoria of working to correct a problem rather than keep an eye on his back faded abruptly. Well, what could he expect? They had probably been lucky to make it this far in that sad excuse for transportation. The poor opinion he'd been working on in regards to Frank Burgess dropped to a new level. What had the man done? He certainly hadn't taken decent care of his wife, his ranch, his weapons, or this damn buckboard.

"What'll you do, Bart?" another of the men asked.

If he was smart he'd leave Louisa and the baby in the care of these good-hearted people, throw his saddle over one of her horses and hightail it to Austin to face down the dwindling number of Dalhert's Raiders his sister had reported were gathering there. Trouble was, when it came to Louisa Burgess, his actions were anything but smart. They might each have started the disastrous adventure to escape a personal devil, but she had grown on him to the extent that he thought more of her safety than he did of his own. Leave her to fend for herself, even if it was among kind folk like those of the wagon train? He couldn't see himself doing it. Certainly not now that he had lost his head and kissed her.

That had been four long days ago but he could still remember the taste of her and the feel of her soft curves against his body as he pressed her back against the side of the building. Even the cold, drenching rain couldn't cure the rise of enthusiasm the memory elicited. He'd been a damned fool.

And he wanted to be exactly the same kind of damned fool again.

"Think we can pull the buckboard's sorry carcass far

enough off the road to let it rot in peace?" J. W. asked. "I know you haven't got much room to spare in your wagons, but if you can transport our stuff into Caldwell, maybe I can find another wagon there. Even if the baby could handle traveling on horseback, we still couldn't carry the rest of our gear that way."

"Your kin are in Austin, ain't they? Maybe they've got a wagon you can use."

Since Diamond was the only kin waiting for him in Austin, it seemed highly unlikely, J. W. mused. "Austin's still a couple long days' ride away. Even if I plant my wife and baby in lodgings in Caldwell, she'd fret for my safety if I was gone that long."

"Yours, too?" Henry asked. "The war did that to my Helen. She had to do without hearing from me for long spells, and made me swear not to leave her imagining the worst ever again."

J. W. nodded. "That's the way of it," he agreed. Had Claire felt the same way? He didn't have to wonder about Louisa Burgess's reaction. He knew she would worry, not only over his safety but over whether he was coming back for her. No, he couldn't leave her. At least not yet.

"We'll find spots for your stuff, Bart. And if there isn't a wagon to spare in Caldwell, you and your family are welcome to stay with us as long as necessary," Henry assured him. "Hell, this isn't the kind of country where you abandon a fella and his two pretty ladies. Just ain't fittin' to do so."

" 'Sides," another of the men said, "Helen would ride him somethin' terrible if he ever considered it."

"All our wives would," a third man added.

"Get those nags moving again, Hershel! We've got coffee awaitin' on us," Henry yelled. "Come on, Bart. Let's head for drier ground."

"You're planning to do what?" Louisa demanded the next morning. She knew her voice had risen, but hoped the others would find that a wifely sort of reaction.

"I'll saddle up one of our horses to ride alongside the train. Henry assures me Helen will welcome you in their wagon. There's got to be a wagon for sale in Caldwell," Walford explained calmly. "Besides, we haven't got much choice, Tess. The wheel is next to sawdust and the axle is snapped clean through. Nothing for it but to abandon the buckboard."

How easily her assumed name fell from his tongue, Lou thought. She was constantly reminding herself to call him Bart or Mr. Ramsdale. Partly because he looked uncomfortable every time someone called him by either name. Partly because he did not look like someone named Bart, much less Bartley. If she ever learned his real name, would it fit the man she knew? Or would he never be more than Mr. Walford to her? Hero, saint, and guardian angel all rolled into one.

Lou took a deep breath. "It can't be done," she announced.

Walford frowned down his nose at her. Such a handsomely shaped nose, Lou thought, then wondered absently whether Angelina's face would assume Frank's features in a few years or grow into a reflection of her own. Walford's nose would look well on any child. Too bad Angelina hadn't been given the chance to choose a better father. At least when it came to noses. Frank's had been . . . well, not nearly as fine as Walford's.

"What do you mean it can't be done?" Walford de-

NAME: _____

ADDRESS: _____

_____

_____

TELEPHONE: _____

E-MAIL: _____

____ I want to pay by credit card.

__ Visa   __ MasterCard   __ Discover

Account Number: _____

Expiration date: _____

SIGNATURE: _____

Send this form, along with $2.00 shipping and handling for your FREE books, to:

Historical Romance Book Club
20 Academy Street
Norwalk, CT 06850-4032

Or fax (must include credit card information!) to: 610.995.9274.
You can also sign up on the Web at www.dorchesterpub.com.

Offer open to residents of the U.S. and Canada only. Canadian residents, please call 1.800.481.9191 for pricing information.

If under 18, a parent or guardian must sign. Terms, prices and conditions subject to change. Subscription subject to acceptance. Dorchester Publishing reserves the right to reject any order or cancel any subscription

manded. "We've been lugging along two saddles. Mine and your—"

Lou threw a frown of her own his way. Hadn't she just been admiring how well he carried off their charade? But he had nearly slipped, had nearly said the highly tooled saddle had belonged to her husband.

Walford had the foresight to bury his much admired nose in a tin cup of steaming coffee. Would anyone who had overheard think he'd said "mine and yours"? They wouldn't if they had gotten a good look at both the saddles. She had practically grown up on horseback, but the richly tooled Spanish saddle was too heavy for her to swing up on the back of any horse. Particularly either of the barely broken mustangs.

"Don't you remember?" Lou asked sweetly. "The man you got the horses from told you that one of them hadn't been broken to the saddle and that the other was only getting acquainted with the idea of having a rider on her back."

Walford nearly choked on the coffee. "He said what?"

Lou leaned closer and dropped her voice to the barest whisper. "Frank hadn't broken either of the mares to anything but the harness yet. You're welcome to try to mount the bay. She's had a saddle on her back briefly. But if you try the sorrel, we'll no doubt start planning a funeral."

"For the mare, I hope."

Lou merely looked at him.

Walford put his cup down. "He can't have started with that damn skittish bay. She's afraid of her own shadow. Damn it, Lo—" He caught himself up short. "I mean, my—"

"I *know* what you mean, Mr. *Ramsdale*," Lou said haughtily. As usual, he barely managed to restrain a sneer of repugnance at the name. Whatever had possessed him to adopt it? Couldn't they have as easily been Mr. and Mrs. Smith?

"There is no need to use that sort of language around me, Bartley Ramsdale!" Lou declared, enjoying his discomfort over the name this time. " 'Unruly tongues lead to unruly ways,' or so Miss Nottingham, my governess, often said," she said stiffly.

From the amused glances the other couples threw each other, she was fairly sure they bought her false indignation.

Whether Walford thought it real or an act, she wasn't as sure. "Tess, I'm sorry," he said. "Miss Nottingham obviously was bent on correcting mankind's errors."

"She was," Lou agreed primly before dropping her voice to a whisper. "And as a man you should know exactly why Frank chose to start with the bay. She was a challenge."

"He was an idiot," Walford grumbled.

Lou grinned. "Well, we're in agreement on one thing at least."

Pushing his hat back off his forehead, Walford stared up at the sky. The storm had blown itself out overnight, leaving the sky a marginally lighter shade of gray this morning, but dry nonetheless. That didn't mean the road would be any easier to travel, Lou knew. The ruts would be deeper and the mud a long way from drying. Dust trails were one thing that wouldn't taint the horizon that day. But then, she doubted Walford watched for signs of trailing horsemen anymore. They were a long way from Angelina County. Even Titus Gillette was unlikely to hunt her this far from Peaceful.

"The bay's had a saddle on her back before then?" Walford asked. "She's used to the feel of it?"

"Used to the feel of a saddle? Moderately used to it at best," Lou answered.

"And the sorrel? The *calm* one?"

"Not even a nodding acquaintance with a rider. She probably thinks a mounted man is just another breed, like a centaur, I suppose."

"Ah, hell," Walford said, groaning mildly as he pushed to his feet. "The bay it is," he said. "I'll go get my saddle. You tell Henry and the others that the entertainment is about to commence."

Chapter Eleven

"It's a wonder there are any men left considering the various and sundry ways they find to kill themselves, isn't it?" Irene Adams murmured from her perch on the high wagon seat. "Does your husband know what he's about, Mrs. Ramsdale? Has he ever broken a horse to the saddle before?"

From her seat on the lowered wagon tongue, Lou looked across the muddy meadow to where Walford and the other men were gathered, one at the mare's head with a firm grip on the bridle, another tossing a blanket then the saddle on her back. Walford was pulling on a pair of leather gloves and looking none too thrilled about the prospect ahead of him.

"Lord only knows," Lou said. "You think you know a man inside and out and then he goes and does something like this." Not that she knew Walford all that well, but she still hadn't thought him the sort of man who worked regularly around horses. Not to make a living at it as Frank had now and then.

"I wonder why he never thought to ask the liveryman who sold him the horses whether they were trained to the saddle," Helen mused from her seat on an upended wooden box next to Lou.

"Does your Henry think to ask questions like that?" Irene asked.

For answer, Helen chuckled. "Don't be ridiculous. He might if left on his own, but if anyone was around to hear, you know perfectly well he'd act as if he knew everything there was to know in the world."

"Pitiful, that's what I call it," Irene murmured.

"But at times endearing," Helen added.

On that Lou had to agree, but only when it came to Walford. Unlike her late and unlamented husband, deep down Walford was a good man. He wouldn't be traveling with her if he wasn't. Most men would have abandoned her that first night. Frank most certainly would have.

No, though there might be a posse on Walford's trail and a certain lack of common sense in his current venture, he was the kind of man a woman dreamed of marrying. The kind who would take care of his family. The kind of man who risked his own life to right a perceived wrong. A man who stood by his word.

"Your husband is a bit of a mystery, isn't he, Mrs. Ramsdale?" Irene said. "I mean, he's got a tough side but I took him for a city feller."

"It's the war," Helen said. "It made men do things they weren't accustomed to and now they aren't content to find more sensible ways around things. I mean, he could have borrowed one of the other men's horses or driven one of the wagons into Caldwell. He just didn't consider the logic of it. At times it seems to me that only women are born with common sense."

Lou shook her head. "No, that's not it. Men can't resist a challenge. Any sort of challenge."

Irene nodded her agreement. "Not a brain in their handsome heads at times."

"How true," Helen agreed with a sigh. "I've got bandages and splints ready just in case."

Lou smiled her thanks but quickly turned back to the proceedings at hand. The saddle was cinched tight and the mare, newly aware of the unwelcome weight on her back, was dancing sideways. The horse shook, trying to dislodge the saddle, then tried to nip at it with her teeth.

Sensing it was safer to put distance between the mustang and themselves, the men backed out of the way.

Walford alone stood his ground. He gave a last tug on his hat to fix it firmly in place, but didn't take up the reins or mount immediately. Instead he stroked the mare's face, his leather gloved fingers drifting lightly over her muzzle. Lou heard him murmuring softly as he had done on many other occasions to calm the skittish animal. The horse's ears flicked back and forth as she listened to his voice. Once she tossed her head, sending the bridle jingling crisply in the clear, cool morning air, nearly ripping it free from Walford's grip. On a more intelligent or biddable animal, the action could be construed as answering a question Walford had asked, but Lou doubted the ornery beast was in the mood to be agreeable.

Whether she was or wasn't, when at last Walford let go of the bridle and grabbed hold of the saddle horn, things began to happen fast. One moment he was standing alongside the mustang, the next he appeared to flow up into the saddle. The athletic grace apparent in the single fluid movement took her breath away.

Nearby, both Helen and Irene sighed faintly in appreciation. Even though he was not her husband in truth, their patent admiration made Lou glow with warm pride over Walford's expertise.

But even the beauty of his effortless mount didn't distract her from noticing that he wasn't wearing his spurs. How strange. She could remember hearing them ring with each step he took as he carried her back inside the cabin that first day. He had stowed them in the wagon when he changed into Frank's wedding suit, and had not had a reason to wear them while driving the buckboard. Frank had never gone near the corral without a vicious-looking pair of rowels at his heels. The flanks of a horse were usually bloodied before he considered it sufficiently broken. Was the oversight an indication that Walford really was attempting to further tame the mare from bravado alone?

He wore a determined scowl beneath the curved brim of his new pinched crown hat. And his mounting had been sheer poetry. Frank had never moved like that. Perhaps Walford did know what he was doing. She should stop expecting him to act as Frank had. No two men could be less alike. Wasn't that why her heart was in such danger of being lost?

The men backed even farther away as Walford settled tentatively in the saddle. He did well to remain alert, Lou thought. The last time the bay had worn a saddle, the creature had nearly fallen over backward in her eagerness to be rid of the man on her back. Frank had jumped free, but he'd sworn to put a bullet in the mare's head if she tried that again. Fortunately for the bay, before he had a chance to make another attempt to break her spirit, someone had rid them both of Frank via that well-placed bullet in his heart.

The bay's ears flicked back. While astride her back, Walford was still talking to the animal, Lou realized. Reasoning with her or soothing her? The mare quivered uneasily. Walford leaned slightly forward, running his hand down the mustang's glistening neck. "Easy, girl," Lou heard him say to the frightened animal.

Don't break his neck, girl, Lou pleaded silently. *We need him.*

I need him.

Rather than pay heed to the mental request, the mare took a leap forward and bucked her back legs high in the air. Walford rocked violently backward then forward in the saddle, one hand on the reins, the other gripping the saddle horn in an effort to keep his seat.

"Whoa!" a couple of the men called out, their arms spread to ward the irate steed back to the center of the campground. When the bay twisted in midair again, they scrambled anxiously between the waiting wagons' tongues to avoid the flying hooves and the flying clumps of mud they kicked up.

Amazingly, Walford was still in the saddle, although his hat had sailed free. Lou wasn't sure how he managed to stay mounted. Even if he'd once been in the cavalry, there had been officer's braiding on his uniform, and officers didn't break their own horses that she'd ever heard. Like Irene Adams, she had thought him city bred. Yet Walford stuck like glue to the mare, staying in the saddle no matter how creative the creature was in trying to dislodge him from her back. The bay twisted, bucked, reared, even tried to unseat him by arching back too far. Walford merely moved with the mustang, his rowel-free heels managing to stay close to her flanks.

The bay was persistent though. With a tremendous leap forward, her rear legs kicked high and finally sent Walford sailing free of the saddle.

Careless of whether the horse's hooves were still flying, Lou darted forward to where he lay flat on his back, his arms outstretched. She fell to her knees in the mud at his side.

"Dear Lord!" she cried. "Are you all right?"

Walford's eyes were closed. "Let's just say I've felt better," he muttered, then groaned when he tried to sit up. "Damn but I hate that horse."

Lou moved so that his head could rest in her lap. Of their own accord, her fingers found their way into his tousled hair, combing it back from his brow tenderly.

But she wasn't the only female interested in his health. The mare ambled up, calm now that her back was free of his weight. With the reins trailing along the ground, the horse pushed her muzzle into the center of his chest in a fond nudge.

The watching crowd laughed at the mustang's antics. "I think she's in love, Bart," one of the men called out.

"Go away," Walford said.

Lou thought he meant her. Frank had hated having her near the corral. He hadn't liked the idea that she might witness one of his failures. Walford obviously felt the same.

"Not you, sweet," he murmured, catching her hand when she made to get up. "This almost makes the whole thing worth my while."

Lou sank back into place readily. "Does it now?" she asked, stealing pleasure from the moment herself.

"Absolutely," Walford said quietly. "If every bone in my

body didn't ache, I'd think I'd gone to heaven."

Unsure of how to answer, Lou continued to trail her fingers through his hair.

The mare wasn't content to leave him be though. When the horse nudged him again, Walford groaned and grabbed the bridle to push her away. "Go on now. You've done your worst. Enjoy the moment, you abominable nag," he snapped.

"That's no way to talk to her," Lou admonished lightly. "You've won her heart."

Walford sighed. "Ah, but I've none left to give in return. And so I'd tell her if I knew her name."

Lou stole one last fond caress, then shifted position, preparing to get to her feet. "We never named her, so I suppose the honor is yours alone now. What name suits her best?"

"Trouble," Walford said, grunting as he rolled to his feet. "I think she can live up to a name like that. Most women, in my experience, do."

Lou froze, her spine stiffening at his words. He meant her. He had to mean her. After all, it was a woman he was set to avenge. She had heard the redheaded man taunt him about it. Surely that meant that not all the women he had known were difficult. In needing his company on the trail, only she deserved to be considered a troublesome female.

"I don't mean you, love," Walford said, dropping his arm around her shoulders.

She knew the endearment was murmured for the benefit of those around them, as was the fond seeming embrace, but both melted the ice that had formed so swiftly in her veins. Was it because he was such a convincing actor? Or was it because she needed so dearly to hear sweet words? There had been so few of them directed in her life.

"You'd better not mean me," Lou countered, holding up her end of the charade. "Do you think Trouble will let you ride her now? If not, you could ride in the wagons as Angelina and I are doing."

"Oh, I'll ride her," he said, although Lou thought the words were uttered through gritted teeth. Then he left her, striding off to reclaim his hat from where it had landed in the center of the field.

"And we all know why he'll ride her," Helen said as she and Irene rejoined Lou. "It's the challenge, just like you said, Mrs. Ramsdale."

"Yes," Irene agreed. "Oh, but didn't he look magnificent?"

Lou followed Walford with her eyes. The mare was nuzzling him again, happy to have his full attention. "Yes, he did," she murmured softly. And because he had been so magnificent, she was currently extremely jealous of one very mottled bay mustang.

Back in Crockett, Claude Morgan enjoyed a glass of fine Irish whiskey with his beefsteak at his favorite saloon, in no hurry to find either a card game or a willing woman that evening. Gillette had paid him well to hunt down Louisa Burgess and drag her back to Angelina County. He hadn't decided if the irate banker intended to marry her or abuse her. Whatever the case, he couldn't see the hellcat who had faced down the posse acceding to either without a fight. Let her enjoy a brief freedom, he thought, then when given the choice of being unceremoniously dragged back to Gillette's far from tender care or trading her favors for a chance at freedom, the dark haired beauty would no doubt be a very willing bed partner.

Of course, he'd still see that she was returned to Gillette.

A man interested in profiting from the system had to be a man of his word. At least when it was given to a man who was in a position to grant other favors. Women were, and always had been, merely chattel.

The enjoyment of his meal was nearly ruined when Egan O'Brien stumbled up to the bar and banged on it for service. Morgan barely paused as he chewed. Having run into Uriah Roane in Lone Tree prior to the man's untimely demise, he wasn't surprised to find another of his old comrade-in-arms fetching up in East Texas. Roane had told him Dalhert had put out a call to his men, figuring they would find the prospect of preying on travelers and townsfolk a pleasing one. It was what they had done most often during the war, their allegiance to the Confederacy merely words rather than conviction. The move to outright outlawry was a natural one. But Morgan still wasn't prepared for the way O'Brien looked.

The whole side of the man's face was one massive dark bruise. Both eyes had been blackened and his knuckles sported fresh abrasions. However, it was the matted hair at the back of his skull that looked the most painful. Blood had turned the redheaded man's hair to dark rust over the spot.

The barkeep filled a glass with the poisonous-looking substance served to men of few funds and pushed it toward O'Brien, then scraped the coin the battered man had tossed down from the counter. O'Brien leaned heavily on the bar, his eyes on the mirror behind it as he monitored the men reflected in its long length.

Morgan knew the moment when the man spotted him alone at a table against the wall. "Well, hell," O'Brien mumbled. "See Wes found you, too, Morg."

Their former captain hadn't, but that hardly mattered.

179

"Looks like someone besides Dalhert found you," Morgan said, tearing off a chunk of bread from the loaf on the table.

It didn't seem to bother O'Brien that he hadn't been invited to take a seat. The man merely grabbed his glass from the bar and ambled over, his motion stiff as if the act of moving caused pain.

"Damn mean-minded blue belly, he was," O'Brien growled, falling in the chair next to Morgan. "Woulda cooked his hash good if'n he hadn't had a friend bidin' time behind ma back."

Morgan didn't doubt O'Brien. He'd seen the man kill for the enjoyment of it. Rather than comment, he forked another succulent piece of beef into his mouth.

O'Brien watched with the open hunger of a predator. He wiped the back of his hand across his battered mouth. "That taste as good as it looks?" he asked.

"Tastes as good as it cost," Morgan countered.

"Yeah, I'll bet," O'Brien said. "Ain't had a decent meal since I got to this damn town. Been livin' on whiskey since bein' blindsided by that cuss."

Ignoring the redheaded man's fascination with his meal, Morgan used the bread to sop juice from his plate. "So he robbed you, too?"

"Picked nearly clean."

If the scenario had played out as O'Brien claimed, the thief probably hadn't gotten far on the ill-gotten gain. During the war O'Brien hadn't been a man to hang on to a coin long if there was a faro table nearby. Morgan doubted the fellow had changed in the ensuing years.

"I suppose you were trying to loosen his pocket first," Morgan said.

"Woulda," O'Brien admitted, "if'n he hadn't jumped me

first. I'd already knocked the livery fella out and helped maself to his funds. Woulda had the other feller, too—"

"But for his friend," Morgan supplied. "You see a doctor about that head?"

"Docs won't look sideways at ya without a bit of ready in yer hand or a pistol trained on their gut. You know that, Morg."

Hippocratic oath aside, Morgan doubted there was a doctor alive who thought repairing an animal like O'Brien worth a groat. However, a revolver had tipped the scales in the past. If O'Brien had had one to wield.

"I wouldn't let Dalhert hear you're in need of a weapon." he mused. "He'd as soon shoot you as supply one."

"Worse if he learned it was a damned female that give me this," O'Brien said, pointing to the back of his head.

In the act of raising his glass, Morgan froze. "A woman? You sure?"

"Caught sight of a skirt 'fore I blacked out," O'Brien said. "Hell of a place, this town. If I wasn't waitin' fer Roane to show, I'd hightail it to where Wes is waitin' fer us in Austin."

Morgan set his whiskey back on the table carefully. "What did this blue belly look like?"

O'Brien downed his own poisonous dust cutter before answering. "Dark hair, clean-lookin' gent. Tall feller. Had a nice new Starr .44 on his belt. It was what attracted me ta him, if ya get my meanin'."

The description was vague enough to fit a couple dozen men in the town. Himself included, Morgan thought. "What made you think he was a Union man? Was he wearing Army issue cavalry trousers?"

"Naw. What he was doin' was jawin' on about what happened in Kansas back in '63. You remember that?" O'Brien asked.

There was another man who couldn't forget what had happened in Lawrence, Kansas. A dark-haired bastard with a Yankee accent and a shootist's deadly skill.

"I wouldn't wait around for Roane if I were you," Morgan said. "Your man killed him back in Lone Tree more'n a week ago. He was worked up about Kansas then, too."

O'Brien took the news of their old compadre's death in stride. "So Roane's roasting with Old Scratch hisself now, is he? Couldn't shoot worth a damn, but had a way with the ladies."

Morgan thought of the angry, vengeful vixen back in Lone Tree who had put a price on Walford's head and wondered anew what the tart had seen in Roane. "Not all ladies," he said, his mind moving back to the very personal battle Walford was fighting. "There were those two in Kansas. Roane shot one down, didn't he?"

"Tried," O'Brien said. " 'Course we didn't know she was a female till after she was dead. Damn waste of a good time. But the orders was ta kill every damn thing in pants, man or boy, and when yer lookin' down the business end of a rifle, you ain't gonna check ta see how well them pants is bein' filled out now, are ya?"

"So Roane's in hell for something you did?"

"Me or Quent Winters. We let the bumblebees fly near the same time. Uproar of it echoed something awful in that damn barn." O'Brien stared forlornly at his empty tumbler on the table. "We should drink a toast to old Roane. Ain't fittin' to let a feller in arms go to his just reward without whiskey to wash the taste of the proceedings away."

Morgan gestured to the bartender, indicating O'Brien's

glass. "You're a damned sentimental cuss, aren't you?"

"Am when there's a drink in it," O'Brien said. "So you gunning for the Yank?"

"For the woman," Morgan corrected. "Looking for her for a feller. Respectable type with a ready pocket."

His glass refilled, O'Brien got maudlin. "Ain't right ta kill a woman. Leastwise not unless she's asking for it."

Morgan pushed his chair back, angling it to tilt against the wall. "This one probably gave you that split head. If she's the same female I'm hunting, that is. Too bad you don't know what she looked like. I could pay for the information."

O'Brien fingered his refreshed rotgut, twisting the glass back and forth against the scarred surface of the table. "How much?"

Flipping a twenty-dollar gold piece onto the table, Morgan put temptation in clear sight. But when O'Brien eagerly reached for it, the chair dropped back in place and Morgan's hand smashed down, pinning the other man's fingers in place. "You said you only saw a bit of skirt," he reminded quietly. "Could have been the tail end of a cowhand's duster or a stackwad's chaps, and no skirt at all." With the ready money almost within his grasp, Morgan knew O'Brien wouldn't take long to deliver more.

When Morgan released him, O'Brien wiped his hand across his mouth once more. "Was a woman. I tracked 'em down."

Morgan smiled complacently. "You still didn't see her."

"Black-haired beauty, the hotel feller said she was. Seemed taken with her. Even told me her eyes were green and she was shapely as ever a man could please. A Mrs. Bartley Ramsdale, traveling with her baby and husband," O'Brien said. "That's who she was."

"Not my girl then," Morgan said, reaching to reclaim the gold piece. "Mine's a hellcat and a widow."

He knew O'Brien wasn't about to lose the chance to put the twenty-dollar coin in his pocket though, so Morgan waited.

"You think anybody but a hellcat would manage to bash in my head?" O'Brien demanded. "Oh, she's the same gal. Had her so-called husband described ta me, too. Same black-hearted cuss I faced down in that stable yard."

"If that's so, why haven't you killed him yet?" Morgan asked calmly.

"Don't think I wouldn't have if they was still here," O'Brien said, snarling. "But they'd lit out. Got gussied up and climbed into a damn buckboard and drove out of town lookin' as innocent as a Sunday school preacher."

"How long ago?"

"Couple days. If I'da known Roane had bought it, I woulda trailed after 'em afore this," O'Brien insisted. "Don't ya think I wouldn't. I owe that cuss."

"And not the woman?" Morgan asked.

O'Brien's face twisted in hate. "Oh, I'll make her pay when I catch 'em."

Not, Morgan thought, *if I get to them first*. "Which way were they headed?"

At long last, O'Brien gave in to the need to down his latest dose of rotgut. "Same way we are," he said, slapping the now empty glass back on the table. "Southwest to Austin."

Chapter Twelve

The landscape began to change subtly as they left the Brazos River behind. While there were still some belts of trees, they weren't as thick as the woodlands in Angelina County. Here the countryside spread out into increasingly large spans of prairie grasslands, making it ideal country in which to raise cattle. White-tailed deer were still abundant, as were quail and warblers, but Lou also began to see pocket gophers disappearing into the meadows that rolled away on either side of the road.

The road itself was far from enchanting though. She had traveled it only once, and in a different season—a dry season—and was unprepared for the quagmire of muddy ruts that tended to bog down both man and animal, much less the weighty wagons.

If only the sun would shine, Lou thought wistfully. Surely the way would clear then, the surface grow hard and fast so that they reached their destination quickly. She thought no farther ahead than Caldwell where another buckboard might be found. She was too tired at the end of the day to see beyond that goal.

They had been told at a stagecoach station that Caldwell was a short day's distance on, but at the rate the wagons traveled, it had taken a full day longer. Now with the cloud-shrouded sun barely a hand's width above the western horizon, they were trailing through the town toward a wagon yard where camp would be made for the night ahead.

There was a hotel in Caldwell with a reputation that travelers up and down the Old San Antonio Road admired. It had been in place for well over a decade. Lou had seen the outside of it when on her wedding trip with Frank nearly three years earlier, but that was all he had allowed her to see of the place. As the wagons rolled through town, Lou looked longingly at the finely maintained building. How nice it would be to afford such luxury, she thought, then pushed the thought aside.

"Nice place," Walford said, reining Trouble up next to the plodding oxen. He tipped his head in the direction of the hotel. "Care to give it a try?"

"Don't be ridiculous, Mr. Ramsdale," she said primly. "You know quite well we need to husband our resources if we are to start life anew here on the frontier."

Walford gave her a wolfish grin. "That's what I like the most about you, Tess. Always mindful of your husband's pocket."

"I'm mindful of a vehicle we must purchase, sir. One that I hope will be able to withstand the rigors of the remaining trip," Lou insisted.

"You could still stay at the hotel. Think about it, my dear. A soft, rock-free bed, a roof that you don't have to get on your knees to get beneath, and a restaurant where someone brings you the food already prepared."

It was tempting, but then it was also unfair to flaunt such luxury before their traveling companions. The emigrants traveled with meager possessions and even fewer monetary resources.

"If your wife doesn't take you up on that offer, Mr. Ramsdale, I may well," Helen said from her position on the wagon bench next to Lou.

"Welcome to it, ma'am," he insisted. "Can't see a reason

why any of you ladies should do without a bit of comfort now and again."

Helen's husband rode up next to Walford. "Then you can't have taken in the awesome scope of the folks you've been trailing with the best part of a week, Bart," he said and laughed. "Hell, you think we men could survive without a woman to cook for us? We'd all be rangier than some of those coyotes we chased off last night, if they took to such a life of luxury."

"Henry!" his wife snapped, although Lou noticed there was a teasing glint of laughter in Helen's eyes. "Mind your tongue. If you don't behave yourself, you can do without my slaving over a smokey campfire, and I will take advantage not only of Mr. Ramsdale's offer but also of the fine offer Texas has made to us women."

"Think you could handle 640 acres of land without me, woman?" he asked.

"I'm handling you, aren't I?" she returned quickly.

Henry chuckled in appreciation and after touching the brim of his hat to them both, pulled up his horse so that the wagon rolled on by.

Walford was still alongside though. "What's he talking about?"

Helen clucked her tongue, encouraging her team of oxen to pick up their pace. "For a fellow set on settling in Texas, you've been mighty lax, Mr. Ramsdale."

"The decision to relocate was made rather swiftly," Lou said. It was the truth, she thought. Between the posse and Titus Gillette, conditions had favored a very quick retreat from Angelina County.

"Very swiftly," Walford agreed, exchanging a look with Lou.

Helen chuckled. "If I was much of a reader when it came

to novels, I'd find something monstrously romantic in that idea."

Walford sighed dramatically. "She's found us out, my love," he told Lou. "It's getting so a fellow can't run off with another man's wife in peace anymore."

"And why should she when she can file for her own homestead in Texas?" Helen countered, quite obviously believing he had been kidding rather than telling the truth.

Lou looked at her friend in surprise. "She can?"

"Absolutely. All she'd need to say was that she was a widow, and if a child is involved, like your sweet little Angelina, she can be counted as head of her own family. My cousin's wife was considering coming with us to do just that. She lost him in the war and some of the states back East aren't as forward thinking as Texas is," Helen explained. "Here a woman qualifies to own 640 acres as long as she stays on the property and works it for three years."

A spread of her own, Lou thought. She could file for such a homestead. She was a widow with a child. If she could put a herd together, in time she would not only be self-sufficient, she would be able to send Angelina away to school to become a proper lady.

"But your cousin's widow didn't come with you," Lou said. "Why not?"

Helen flicked the reins over the yoked oxen again. "Fear," she said. "Even though Henry explained that as long as we stayed far south or east of Fort Worth there was nothing to fear from Comanche or Apache raids, she wouldn't believe him. Last we heard she was working in a garment factory, making men's shirts sixteen hours a day, and her boys were shining gentlemen's shoes to help her make ends meet in the city." Helen shook her head sadly. "I keep hoping she'll change her mind and join us."

Lou's mind wasn't on her friend's story though. It had turned to her own prospects, ones that had seemed far too slim and less than encouraging. She intended to give her grandfather's ranchero as wide a berth as she could, but the question of whether she would even be welcomed at her mother's home troubled her. If she could qualify for land under the homestead laws of Texas, there was a chance that she could be her own woman at last. There would be no need to worry about whether she would be welcome at her mother's in Mexico City, or whether she could adapt to town life, Lou thought. Establishing her own ranch would be hard work, but everything she worked for would be hers alone. Her life would be hers alone.

"If your cousin does decide to come to Texas, how would she go about filing for a homestead?" she asked.

The question had been directed at Helen, but it was Walford who answered. "She'd be best advised to find a lawyer to handle things for her. A trustworthy one."

Helen tilted her head and grinned. "Is there such a thing as a trustworthy lawyer, Mr. Ramsdale?"

"Absolutely, ma'am. I'm sure because you're looking at one," he said.

"A lawyer!" Helen exclaimed.

Taken by surprise, Lou had nearly bleated the same words.

"Or rather, I was one once," Walford corrected. "Before the war. Living in brevet hell changed my mind about continuing in the profession."

Helen jogged Lou with her elbow. "Make him reconsider, Mrs. Ramsdale. A country as wide as this needs all the honest fellows it can get. Particularly with these reconstruction laws to deal with. My Henry claims he had no idea how confusing or how unfair a set of laws could be until he started to look into things here in the South."

While Lou knew that Texas hadn't been officially accepted back into the Union yet, she had never considered her native land as being part of the South. Daily concerns at her grandfather's ranchero had nothing to do with being Confederate or Union since he had despised all Americans equally. His fealty was still with Mexico and always would be.

He was an autocratic tyrant living in the past, praying for a return to earlier years. Despite his refusal to treat her as the granddaughter of the patrone, Lou suddenly felt very sorry for Don Felipe de la Vaca.

It didn't mean she would run to him for help though. Maturity might allow her to understand him better, but it did not mean she had to forgive him. Growing up unwanted and unloved was something she would never forget.

"Ah," Walford said, glancing ahead. "The wagon yard at last. Best head them in, ladies. If you change your mind about the hotel, just let me know."

Touching his heels to the bay's flanks, Walford urged his horse into a lazy canter that quickly outdistanced the more plodding oxen pulling the wagon.

"Typical man," Helen muttered. "Why does he want to give up a fine profession and tend cattle instead?"

Since she hadn't heard that version of the tall tale Mr. Walford had spun for the emigrants, Lou answered honestly. "I have no idea."

Helen gave a quite unladylike snort of disgust. "Well, even if our menfolk don't think we've the intelligence to understand their reasoning, at least the State of Texas does. If my Henry doesn't mind his p's and q's, I just may file for some homestead land for myself."

Lou knew her friend was joking, but for herself, she was deadly serious. "I can't think of a better opportunity for a widow with a child. If I were your late cousin's wife, I'd file right away."

"Good for you, Mrs. Ramsdale," Helen declared. "If you were a widow determined to make her own way, I'd welcome you as a neighbor."

No, you wouldn't, Lou thought. *Because I'm not the woman you think me. My name isn't really Theresa Ramsdale.*

"Are you really a lawyer?" Lou asked as she helped Walford set up the dog tent a little while later.

He grinned at her. "I was. Ironic considering the circumstances in which we met, isn't it?"

She knew he wanted her to let the subject rest, but that was impossible. "Helen says Texas needs all the honest men it can get, particularly men who know the law."

"Laws change," Walford said.

"Which is why we need more people who understand them and can deal with them," Lou insisted.

Walford made a slight adjustment to the canvas and then set the front tent pole firmly in place with a sharp blow or two from his hammer. "Is it for Henry's family that you're advocating for my return to the straight and narrow path?"

Lou kept her face averted, fussing with the canvas herself. "Of course," she said.

"Louisa," he murmured, his voice quiet, a mere undertone to the activity around them, "I saw the way you reacted to the homestead offer. You're interested in a place of your own but are leery of any paperwork it involves because I opened my fat mouth and set that worry in place. That's the real truth of it, isn't it?"

"Maybe," she admitted, finding new busywork in tossing a small stone away from the tent's entrance.

"I thought you were headed for Mexico."

"I was," she said, then took a chance, looking up to meet the concern in his gray eyes. "I'm just not sure of my welcome there."

"And not sure how you'd get there either, unless I miss my guess," Walford added.

Lou shrugged, trying to make light of it. "We've been taking things an hour at a time on this trip, doing what was necessary, whether it was leaving Angelina County at dusk or—"

"Chucking a shovel at a man's skull?"

She frowned at him, unhappy to be reminded of her action. Not only had she discovered herself capable of true violence that day, but the memory always brought her back to the quick, ardent kiss they'd shared. An incident that he seemed to have forgotten, much to her chagrin.

"Or posing as husband and wife," Lou snapped, irritated with him.

"That was at your suggestion," Walford reminded her.

"Originally, yes," she agreed. "But we've outdistanced that sheriff's posse and put well over a hundred miles between Peaceful and here. Can you fault me for beginning to wonder what happens next? Or what will happen to me if you taunt another man as you did the man in Crockett? You planned to kill him, didn't you?"

When Walford remained silent, Lou sighed deeply. "Isn't one man's blood on your hands enough?" she asked softly.

"In this case?" he answered. "No. I don't expect you to understand."

"And you won't try to explain," she countered.

He gave the tent post another whack, the sound of the

strike seeming to echo across the wagon yard. "What about you, ma'am? Care to tell me who or what you're running away from?"

He had reversed their roles, Lou realized. Putting her on the defensive rather than giving her answers. "You really are a lawyer, aren't you?" she asked, raising her chin in defiance. "As I am not on trial, I can refuse to answer that question. It is impertinent, sir."

Walford chuckled, but it wasn't a cheerful sound now. "If you were on trial, ma'am, we lawyer types would call what you're trying 'hiding behind the Constitution.' "

"The fifth amendment, I assume?" It was more than the set of her chin that challenged him now, she realized. Her shoulders were squared and her back was rigid. Had she learned nothing through her years with Frank? Such an attitude had earned her a bruised cheek or a swollen eye far too many times. How would Walford react? Her eyes dropped briefly to his hands, to the hammer swinging laxly from his fingers.

Walford chuckled again, this time with a return to his normal good humor. "Don't know why you think you need a fella like me, honey. That look would scare off a battalion of Seceshs faster than a fusillade of black powder bumblebees."

She was in no mood to be cajoled into a better frame of mind. "And what pray tell is a Secesh?"

"Someone from a state that seceded from the Union. In other words, a Southerner," he said.

Lou narrowed her eyes. "In other words, someone like me," she declared. "Or has it escaped your attention that I am a native-born Texian, a person from a state that seceded from your precious Union?"

"Lo—" he began.

"Tess," she hissed. "Thanks to you, I believe everyone here thinks my name is Tess."

"I—"

But she had no intention of letting him twist her words back on her again. With her chin in the air and her back still ramrod straight, Lou swept off across the wagon yard, leaving Walford to finish setting up camp on his own.

"Insufferable man," Lou mumbled, glancing back at where Walford worked, apparently unconcerned that she had left in a huff.

"Lover's spat?" Helen asked kindly. She had Angelina to her shoulder and was gently patting the baby's back in a soothing manner.

"I tried to get him to consider returning to the law profession," Lou said. Her explanation was half true, anyway. "Is Angelina all right?"

Helen nodded but continued to rock back and forth on her feet. "The boys were a bit too boisterous at their play and gave her a little scare. She's fine. I'm not so sure about you."

"I'll be all right. I just have to calm down," Lou answered, reaching for her child.

Helen handed the baby over, realizing as only another woman would that cuddling Angelina would make everything right in her world, Lou thought. Was it only women who had any sense?

"Yes, it is," Helen said.

Lou felt embarrassed. "I said that out loud, didn't I? I didn't mean to. It's just that he makes me so mad sometimes."

"How long have you known him?" her friend asked. "Unless I miss my guess, not much more than the year it took to create this little wonder." Helen brushed her hand lightly over Angelina's flyaway hair.

Lou felt color flood her cheeks. She had certainly been dreaming of someone like Walford, wishing for him to ride up to the door of the depressing little cabin and rescue her a year ago. Her Santo Jorge had been a bit late in showing up though, and when he had it had been without a horse to carry her off. So much for dreams coming true, she thought sadly.

"We met after the war," Lou confessed, thankful that she could be totally truthful in at least one answer. "I don't know why it never crossed my mind to ask him what he had done before it. All our plans revolved around Texas."

Happy to be with her mother once more, Angelina patted her cheek excitedly, then yanked on a lock of her hair. Helen reached over to help untangle the strands from the baby's chubby little fingers. "And waiting for Angelina's arrival probably made him antsy to be moving, I'll bet. It would my Henry, and most times he is the most patient of men. I'm inclined to think your husband is a little less disposed that way. What did he do in the war?"

At least it was an answer she knew. "He was an officer in the cavalry," she said.

"A man of action rather than one of waiting, which Henry was in the infantry. His letters home always spoke of the waiting," Helen said. "I would guess that the cavalry was usually on the move for one reason or another."

Lou nodded. Although she knew little of war or armies, it made sense. When she was small and there were occasional Indian raiding parties still roaming the settlements near San Marcos, they were frequently visited by ranger units that had been called up to police the area. They rarely stayed anywhere long, but roamed on horseback, carrying only the minimum in supplies, but the maximum in weapons and ammunition. Her grandfather hadn't been very welcoming since most were transplanted Americans rather than Mexican or Spanish like himself. She had even wondered whether her father, Neil Keating, the man she had never known, had been like the rough volunteers who made up the ranger forces. All she knew of him was that he had wooed and won her mother's heart, arranged an elopement, and then shortly after had managed to get himself killed. Perhaps being attracted to men of action was in her blood.

"You just make up your mind to what you want, and he'll come around," Helen advised. "He's a good man, which means he'll do the right thing in the end. They can't help being stubborn as old mules, but if a man wants the comforts of a warm bed, he'll soon change his tune."

The idea of Walford's tall, manly form enjoying the comforts of her bed made Lou's face color even more brightly.

Helen laughed and ran her hand gently over Angelina's fuzz-covered head once more. "Despite this little joy, you're still in the newlywed stage. You'll learn what it takes to keep him close to your skirts. We all do."

"You make husbands sound like lap dogs," Lou said to cover her new embarrassment.

"That's right," Helen agreed and looked fondly across the compound to where her husband and sons jostled one another in a mock sparring match. "And even as shaggy and grizzled as Henry looks out here on the trail, you know, I wouldn't change him for the world. You take my advice. If your husband doesn't fancy practicing law anymore, pressing him to do it will make him buck worse than that partly tamed bay mare he rides now. Bide your time and things will turn out for the best. They always do with Henry and me. They will with you two, too."

Bide my time, Lou thought. The trouble was, time would not wait around to be bided or anything else. And as her claim on Walford was at best tentative, there was very little chance that things would turn out for the best.

"I do hope you're right," Lou murmured, her eyes drifting back to Walford's tall form.

"I hope I'm right, too," Helen said.

Chapter Thirteen

J. W. kicked at the rock Louisa had moved to the side earlier, not caring whether it rolled back under the tent to bother one of them—probably him—later or not. Damn her! Things had been going along fine and now he was riled up. There was no reasoning with women. Hadn't he reconciled himself to that idea yet? Hell, Claire had kept him jumping to her tune before they wed as well as afterward. And even his sister had not allowed him to leave her behind when he went after Dalhert and his men, no matter what he said. And now Louisa—hell, Lou! She was strong-minded enough to be a man, might as well use the shortened, male-sounding version that she had told him she preferred.

Contrary, stubborn, single-minded woman! Return to the law? Hell, he'd broken so many laws, civil, federal, and moral, that if he bothered to run a tally it was sure to show he had put in more time making himself a bona fide black-hearted devil than he had ever put into reading the law.

There was no going back. The deeds were done, his soul was already thoroughly singed by hellfire, and before the crusade to punish Dalhert's Raiders was over his heart would no doubt be even blacker than his soul. If she would just take a good, long look at him, she'd see there was no redeeming the man he'd become.

"I've seen that expression on a man's face often enough before," Henry drawled, strolling up. "Trouble with the little woman."

J. W. grinned wryly at the other man. "Don't you know it," he muttered. "They ever settle down enough so as a man can understand them?"

"Nope," Henry answered shortly. "Care to talk it out? Wasn't a soul in camp that couldn't see a battle was raging even if we couldn't catch a word of it. 'Course, yours wasn't the first marital showdown we've witnessed; it was merely the latest. If you'd rather steam on your lonesome though, I'll leave you be."

J. W. struck the last tent peg in place with a violent blow, putting his so-called steam to work, driving it deep into the dirt. At least they were no longer setting up camp in the mud, which was a pleasant change, if only a minor one. "Much obliged, but in the universal scheme of things, a fight with my wife is pretty petty stuff."

Henry buffeted him on the shoulder. "Universal scheme or not, Bart, let's just say we'll all be expecting the two of you to retire a mite early tonight to patch things up. Hell, that's why we keep battling with 'em, isn't it?"

J. W. agreed for the sake of agreeing, having no choice but to keep his own counsel. Particularly as a vision of Lou with her lustrous, long black hair spilling over her shoulders came to mind. He'd seen her in a nightgown so often, he had no trouble starting his dream at that point and moving on to the more interesting parts of the game.

She was an incredibly beautiful woman, though she appeared unaware of that fact. Even in a country where lovelies with Spanish ancestry abounded, she stood out. Was it because he was from northern climes that he found her so exotic? Or was it simply that her warm skin tone and dark hair didn't conflict with his memory of Claire's pale complexion and blond tresses?

Who was he kidding? Claire's likeness had been hard to grasp long before he'd trailed up to Lou's door. How many days had it been since he'd last tried to evoke his late wife's memory? More than he would have thought possible once upon a time. Her image had nearly faded from recall, limited to items that were just words now. He could tell someone how tall she'd stood when next to him, that her hair had been pale, her eyes blue—or had they been brown or green? Damn, even the litany of her traits that he had once chanted proudly to his fellow officers was becoming impossible to repeat now. Lou—flesh-and-blood and incredibly alive and captivating Lou—had made him forget.

Which was probably why he'd ended up fighting with her. *You're a damn fool*, he told himself. Might as well just shoot himself in the foot as het up a woman, particularly one he was partial to. All right, obsessed with. What else could a man call having his thoughts turn to her every few seconds rather than keep centered on the job he'd set out to do after the war?

Of course, as it had been their first bona fide argument and it had been waged before an interested audience, the fight had probably put the stamp of authenticity on their charade as husband and wife. Only an honestly wedded couple would be thought capable of getting on each other's nerves the way they had done.

Was that a big part of the problem between them? At least for his part, it was. The more he played at being her husband—touching her, sleeping next to her, being cosseted by her attentions—the more he thought about the one right a husband had that he couldn't indulge in. There were times when that was all he could think about, and if anything had the power to drive a man insane it was being celibate around a woman like Louisa Burgess. In fact, now that Henry put him in mind of the way marital squabbles were usually patched up, his body was making plans his mind knew couldn't be acted upon.

Damn her for being so beautiful, not only physically but in spirit, too. Though he might have lost Claire's face to time, Lou's was vivid, intoxicating, and before him nearly every hour of the day. In his mind's eye he could still see the way she'd looked lobbing the business end of a shovel at O'Brien's head. An Amazon warrior incarnate, that's what she'd been. It hadn't been the first time she'd taken his safety into her hands. He might not have seen her in action that first day when she'd held off the posse, but he'd certainly heard the challenge in her voice. And she had been dropping with near exhaustion when she'd done it.

Hell, how could a man not be taken with her?

But how could a man let a woman blind him to the course he rode? A path he had set out on to right a wrong, to avenge the death of the woman he'd loved.

The same way Lou made him forget they were just playing a part, that's how.

Had she noticed his slip of tongue earlier? J. W. wondered. Not only had he not referred to her as Tess, as he should have, but for the first time in their acquaintance, he had dared to use her own Christian name out loud rather than the more formal *Mrs. Burgess* that he'd stuck to so religiously to this point. Not only had he called her *Louisa* once, he'd nearly done so twice, tempting fate that no one in the camp would overhear him, or read the name on his lips.

Perhaps she had noticed and taken offense at the familiarity. She'd certainly cut him off with that snapped reminder that her name was supposed to be *Tess*, her tone implying an accusation that it was all his fault that she now answered to it.

Women!

"Mr. Ramsdale?" One of Henry's boys interrupted his useless thoughts. J. W. nearly thanked him for the interruption. "Pa says that if you're interested, he and a couple o' the other men are going into town to ask about conditions farther down the road." The boy dropped his voice and leaned closer, giving away to anyone who happened to be watching that he was about to relay a confidence his father had entrusted him to deliver. "They're gonna be at a saloon, only don't let Ma or the other ladies know."

J. W. nodded shortly. "Appreciate it, boy. They won't hear of it from me." But the women would learn of it one way or another. At least the furious glances and cold shoulders the other men received when they all returned would keep curious eyes from turning toward his tent that night.

With that comforting thought in mind, J. W. headed into town to ask a few questions of his own.

He waited until long after nightfall to return to the camp, knowing that Lou would have turned in long ago. With little more than the light of their campfire to see by, there was little she or anyone else could do once twilight passed.

As expected, the rock he'd been stupid enough to kick back into the tent was lodged under his bedroll. It bit into his knee through the thin layer of wool when he crawled beneath the low pitch of the tent roof.

Angelina's cradle held center stage between his bedroll and Lou's, the baby still acting as both barricade and deterrent to any move he might be foolish enough to make. As had become his habit, J. W. checked on the infant, insuring she hadn't managed to tangle her miniature bedding around her limbs. Even within the dark confines of the tent he could see the lighter glow of her fair skin. Her cheek rested against the soft body of the doll he'd bought her in Crockett. The fact that Lou had put it in the cradle beside her daughter, even though she was furious with him, touched his heart. She was a fair-minded woman when all was said and done. A better woman than he would ever deserve, at any rate.

Careful not to disturb either of his sleeping charges, J. W. set his hat aside and carefully pulled off his boots.

"Titus Gillette," Lou's voice said softly in the dark.

He assumed she was dreaming, mumbling in her sleep, so he said nothing.

"He's the banker in Peaceful," she said. "He's the man I'm running from."

J. W. set his boots aside carefully, leaning them upright against the side of the tent. "You didn't need to tell me. I had no right to hurl that question at you earlier."

The campfire outside was already burning low, but the light it threw into the narrow tent was sufficient for him to see her shift within her quilted cocoon to face him. "You had every right. I needed your help to get away, so I spun a web of reasons why having the baby and me with you would deceive the posse. The reality was, I felt your presence made us invisible on the trail."

"Yet all three of us seem to have escaped detection," he

reminded her. "Besides, I'm the one who had the most to lose. I left the necktie party during the planning stages back in Lone Tree, you know. I'll always be grateful to you for saving my life. I hope you know that."

Lou sat up. Her face was draped in shadows, but he already knew every lovely plane of it. Knew that her beautiful eyes turned from the color of tender new leaves in spring to the more mysterious, dark swirling shade of murky water when she was troubled. They would be that hue now, touched with a hint of brown and solemn, the spark that he caught a flash of occasionally would be gone, pinched out by sorrow and worry.

She shook her head, sending the midnight strands of her nearly blue-black hair tumbling free from the loose braid he knew she would have fashioned before retiring. He'd thought about the ritual while propping up a bar in town, experiencing a bittersweet regret that he wasn't witnessing the nightly routine, yet making no move to toss off the whiskey he was nursing so he could return to her.

"Your own escape was merely a pleasant bonus, Mr. Walford," she whispered into the night. "I was willing to do anything to escape Gillette." She paused a moment before adding, "I still am."

Those plans his body had made earlier rushed to mind, but J. W. doubted she had meant what the offer had sounded like to him. She was a good woman and good women didn't offer themselves to men like him.

There was something in her tone that reined his libido up short though. "What exactly were you afraid this Gillette might do?" he asked.

She answered with a question. "Other than take my ranch? Well, considering he claimed to have won it from my husband in a card game, I suppose he had a right to it."

"But you don't think he did," J. W. said quietly. "You suspect he arranged to win that game."

Her lips twisted into a grim smile that boded ill for Titus Gillette should he come within rifle range. "I'm quite sure he did arrange the game, just as he no doubt arranged Frank's untimely demise." Lou's eyes dropped, her lashes not only shading the emotions reflected in them but creating crescent moons against her sun-darkened skin. "He threatened to take Angelina away from me. He wanted to—"

"I can guess what else he wanted," J. W. muttered. If he'd had Gillette in his own sights, the next property the banker would be closely associating with would be a neat six-foot deep plot in the local churchyard.

"Yes," Lou said. "He was going to do whatever it took to get his hands on the forest land. That meant he was going to have to get rid of me, too."

The announcement was totally unexpected. "He wanted the lumber?" J. W. demanded. "I thought that he wanted—"

"Me?" she asked, her voice incredibly calm. "Yes, he did. But I'm frequently not a very cooperative woman. I thought you might have noticed that sorry trait."

If he had, he wasn't going to be ungentlemanly enough to mention it.

"The land and the trees were going to be of interest far longer than I ever would be," Lou said. "I've noticed that men tend to lose interest in a woman once they've, er . . ." She stumbled for words. "Availed themselves of her," she finished, her voice barely audible.

Not only was she no longer meeting his eyes, her fingers

plucked nervously at a loose stitch on the quilt.

J. W. physically reached across the abyss created by their earlier argument. The gentle touch of his hand over hers stilled her fretting movements. "You're safe, Mrs. Burgess. He can't touch you or Angelina now."

"That's what I keep telling myself," she murmured.

Although she didn't voice the thought, he heard the omission. "But you're afraid of what will happen when I leave."

She must have been holding her breath, for when a quiet sigh escaped her, J. W. knew he'd chosen the wrong phrase.

"When you leave," Lou repeated, her voice sadly accepting in tone.

If—why hadn't he said *if? Because you can't offer her anything else*, he told himself, furious that fate had played them both so wrongly. Between them there could be no hope, no promises for the future. There could only be today and possibly tomorrow, but little beyond the bounds of the present.

"Gillette has the ranch," J. W. said. "He has the woodlands. What reason could he have for pursuing you?"

She looked up at that. "For a reason I thought you would understand very well," Lou whispered. "Revenge."

Diamond could feel the touch of unknown eyes on her. The sensation made the tendons of her slender neck rigid, put her nerves on edge.

Whoever watched her appeared content to let the tension grow. The saloon was crowded with men. Only a handful of women were ever on hand, the waiter girls who did duty both in the saloon serving customers drinks at the tables downstairs and brief doses of paradise on the mattresses upstairs. They dressed in garish gowns that displayed their wares well. The men, on the other hand, had wardrobes that varied from the perfection of starched white shirtfronts and tailor-made dark suits, the trousers of which fell over well-buffed, custom-made leather shoes, to frayed and faded calico shirts and woolen weight pantaloons shoved into knee-high, scuffed, mass-made boots. That night there was even a scattering of Army uniforms in the crowd, although the men who wore them were being given a wide berth by those nearest them. With the reinstatement of statehood still hanging in the balance, Texas was patrolled by the unwelcome Army rather than by their own.

Her own refashioned evening gown was of unrelieved jet silk that night, even the lace edging the dipping bodice and minuscule sleeves. A small, cream-backed cameo pin was fastened to a length of black satin ribbon so that it lay in the hollow of her throat. A trio of ringlets spilled from her upswept soft brown hair and smaller cream cameo earrings dangled just above her bare shoulders.

March had turned to April now and the weather offered fewer cool evenings. As a result, the saloon was nearly stifling with a mixture of closely packed bodies and a haze of cigar and cigarillo smoke befouling the air.

Diamond fanned herself lightly with a fan of hand-painted rice paper, stirring the thick atmosphere somewhat. "I fold," she told the dealer, her voice nearly dripping with honeyed Southern tones. "It is perilously close in here tonight, isn't it? Would you gentlemen forgive me if I stepped outside briefly? The press this evening is making me a bit faint."

Two of the men, regulars at her table, pushed back their chairs immediately.

"Ya needful of a drink, Miz Diamond?" one asked.

"I'll escort ya, ma'am," the other offered.

As neither had tossed his hand of cards on the table to indicate abdication from the game, but rather held the pasteboards yet fanned in their hands but close to their bodies, she shook her head and urged them to remain where they were.

"I won't be but a moment or so, I promise," she said. "But in the event that I don't make it back in time for the next hand, would you deal me out and merely save my seat at the table?"

"A pleasure, ma'am."

"Your chair is reserved for no other, fair lady."

"Make it quick, honey," the grizzled fellow across from her growled. "I came ta play, and an empty chair don't make for a well-rounded game."

Her two gallants frowned at him for the ungentlemanly display. "As you say, sir," Diamond drawled. "I shall inhale sufficiently of the evening breeze to sustain me for the duration of your stay at our table." *Which will be damn short if I have anything to do with it*, she added silently.

Rather than appear annoyed, she kept her movements leisurely, her steps as measured as the tread in a reserved country dance. If the sway of her skirts appeared enticing, all the better. Perhaps whomever watched her would be lured to the doorway in her wake. And if he was not? Well, she could always use the smoky atmosphere and heat as a reason to return to her quarters at the hotel earlier than usual. If there was one thing that J. W. had drummed into her head before agreeing to let her "ride point" on their quest, it was never to take chances.

As Diamond made her way through the crowd toward the saloon doors, she slipped her hand in the hidden pocket of her skirt, curling her fingers around the smooth ivory handle of the short-barreled, single-shot derringer secreted there.

She stopped short of actually pushing through the swinging doors and leaving the saloon, though. It was too dangerous to do so. Too easy for the unknown who watched her to drag her from the board walkway and into the nearby alleyway. But she also dared not step out on the porch and expose herself to the stares of decent people. Although she had begun her career as a gambler three years past, the disapproving glares and hastily quickened steps to avoid her still had the power to wound. Rather than tempt fate in any manner, Diamond contented herself with whatever breeze penetrated the dank atmosphere of the barroom behind her.

No one sought her company in the lee of the door yet the sensation of being under observation remained. Who was it that watched her? J. W.? Surely her brother would have ambled over to the table ostensibly to watch the play just to let her know he had arrived at long last. But even a quick scan of the saloon proper offered her no glimpse of his tall form. Was it an enemy then? Though she made it a habit never to skin any man's pocket too deeply, there were those who didn't take a loss to a female gambler with good will. Gamblers were considered among the lowest human beings on the social ladder in the West, a fact she had always thought odd considering the number of men who willingly threw their hard-earned wages away at faro and poker tables in every town she had visited. If knights of the felt table were held as no-accounts, a female of the order ranked below the shabbiest prostitute. Prostitutes, at least, were honest in selling their soiled wares.

Diamond couldn't fault them for that. She did manipulate the cards, though not to insure her own wins usually. Usually. She was tempted to make an exception with the grizzled boor across from her at the table that night. If not for his ill-manners, then for the noxious odor of the long nine clamped between his yellowed teeth. Although his features were nothing like the other man who favored the cheap nine-inch-long cigars, the fellow put her too much in mind of Wes Dalhert, and that was not a happy circumstance. Particularly for him.

She and Neddy were in need of a few more twenty-dollar gold pieces. Lingering on in Austin as they waited for J. W. had pinched their purse tight. Bart had not left her with much to live on, and a widow's pension was more likely to be paid to women with greater need and a permanent address, neither of which she had. In part, it had been her lack of finances that had led her to accept Claire's offer of a home after Bart's death.

Until her arrival in Kansas, she had known very little about her sister-in-law other than that J. W. worshiped her and Claire's father had held a rather high position in the government in Washington. As what, Diamond had never thought to ask. Claire's parents had died in an influenza epidemic in much the same way her own parents had died of cholera, within weeks of each other. But Claire Naughton Walford's parents had left her a recently purchased farm in Kansas and a bank account capable of keeping her very comfortable for the rest of her life.

It had been nice to live in comfort, even if Claire had rather quickly assigned her nursemaid duties with Timothy, Claire and J. W.'s far from robust infant son. At times, Diamond had wondered if her sister-in-law even loved the baby, she spent so little time with him.

But whether she was an unnatural mother or not, Claire

had soon been dead, shot down by the trigger-happy members of Wes Dalhert's guerrilla company, who mistook her for a boy in the trousers she delighted in wearing while working in the barn yard. The horsemen had torched the barn and the house with little care as to whether there were other occupants inside. Neddy had run into the narrow stand of trees near the creek, young Timmy bundled in her arms. It had been a brave act, Diamond thought, and a selfless one. Only moments before Neddy had watched the riders open fire on her husband, a gentle man who had religiously refused to learn to handle either rifle or pistol.

A quick death from a bullet had not been her own fate. No, the raiders had reserved a living hell for her. Dalhert had reigned his horse up near the already blazing house, pulling the tall gray stallion into a flashy rear, its hooves pawing the air. "Do as ya will with the women, boys," he'd shouted. "Word in town is they're Yankee officers' wives and not from these parts. That means they ain't got kin we might know ta be bothered with what happens ta 'em."

When the raiders had ridden out, they had left her bleeding and abused in the yard, her gown little more than shredded rags.

The women in Lawrence fared better, but their homes were reduced to ashes just as the buildings on the Naughton farm were. With nowhere to shelter from the elements, she and Neddy had done what they could for the baby but Timmy's far from robust little form had followed his mother into a shallow grave barely three days later.

Yet, though Claire and Timothy were both gone, the Naughton money continued to provide for Neddy and herself through J. W.'s generosity. He had thought it only right that Claire's inheritance pave the way to retribution for his wife's death. If they were penniless by the time Wes

Dalhert and his men were brought to justice, a swift one delivered via her brother's deadly pistol, then so be it. For her part, Diamond felt that whatever awaited her in the future would be well deserved, be it poverty or a hangman's noose for her part in J. W.'s vigilante-style justice. She had set out on this course of her own accord, but it had never been to avenge Claire Naughton Walford's untimely demise. It had been to cleanse her soul.

Instead she had further tarnished it.

Perhaps that all too likely future was closer than she would like now. Diamond wasn't sure. But when no one took the clearly offered opportunity to join her near the door, she wondered if the feeling of being under observation was more an act of her recently overactive conscience or an enemy in truth. The thought that the onlooker might have been an admirer never entered her mind. She was no longer the fresh young girl Bartley Ramsdale had wed. That pretty child had died a little at each battlefield visited until, when brutally ravished by Dalhert's men, she had ceased to exist. What looks she possessed were of the painted version, subtly drawn with a deft brush and a well-trained hand. Besides, despite the flowery compliments men were still wont to give her, Diamond knew quite well that not a one of them would have taken her to wife. She was no longer pure enough to share a man's name.

Waving her fan idly before her face, stirring a breath of cooler air, Diamond turned and made her way through the crowd to the table she had abandoned only minutes before.

There was a new player seated among the familiar faces. The grizzled man had absented himself without the aid of a series of ill-favored hands. His retreat relieved her. Every time she manipulated the cards there was a chance that a sharp-eyed player would catch her sleight of hand and denounce her to the saloon at large. She knew what happened to men so exposed. They received either a quick bullet from a disgruntled player's pistol or a swift escort out of town by the sheriff. But what retribution would be meted out to a female gambler?

Nothing that hadn't happened to her before, of that Diamond was sure. Still, the fact that she could continue to play a clean hand cheered her.

"I trust you gentlemen were not overly discomfitted by my absence," she drawled softly, smiling over her shoulder at the gallant who had leaped to his feet to hold her chair for her.

"Not at all, ma'am. But we lost a man while you were gone," he said. "Although he was no loss, to my mind."

" 'Fact, a replacement was readily found and he assures us he's willin' ta empty his pockets ta us. In sore need of entertainment, ain't ya, captain?" another of the men asked, turning to face the newcomer.

"Sore need," a familiar voice said quietly.

Diamond glanced at him, her mind and emotions at odds. It had been nearly six years since she had heard that voice or met the cool blue of those eyes. He was in uniform, Army blue with gold trimmings, although the glory of his kit was dimmed by a coating of fresh Texas dust. The lieutenant's insignia she recalled on his collar had been replaced by the newer, higher ranking mark of a captaincy, but the slightly tarnished tone of his fair hair was the same.

He straightened slightly, leaning on the scarred wooden arms of his chair. "Ma'am," he murmured, with a slight bow before dropping back into his place. She remembered only too well the way he oftentimes had loomed over her, his height always seeming to put her at a disadvantage. But she also recalled the feel of his hand at her waist as he led her in a waltz, the admiration that had warmed his otherwise cold seeming eyes.

There was neither warmth nor admiration in his glance now. "You put me in mind of a woman I used to know, a Mrs. Bartley Ramsdale," he said.

"Do tell," Diamond said, her heart fluttering at a rate she was sure could be heard by her nearest neighbors at the table. "I'm afraid I've not the lady's acquaintance."

"No loss, ma'am," he said, slumping a bit in his chair. "She had abominable taste in husbands."

"Really?" Diamond asked, fighting to keep from spitting the word from between gritted teeth. It was an effort, but she smiled knowingly at him and dredged up a piece of what felt like ancient history. The time she had spent being courted in West Point felt as if it had happened in a different era, a different world. "Am I to understand that the lady turned down your own proposal, sir?" she inquired pertly.

The captain grinned widely, although without a hint of amusement. "Gentlemen, you were quite right in estimating that your fair lady player would be an entertainment in herself. My apologies, ma'am, if I set your teeth on edge. Name's Jack Landrey." He offered his hand across the table. "And you would be—?"

"Less than interested in entertaining you, captain," Diamond said, pushing back her chair. "Good evening, gentlemen. Please do your damnedest to empty Captain Landrey's pockets in my absence."

And without a backward glance, Diamond strode firmly to the saloon door and back to her room at the hotel.

Chapter Fourteen

J. W. lay on his back on his bedroll just outside the dog tent, his head resting on Lou's neatly rolled quilt, Angelina sprawled happily on his chest. He could tell the baby was happy from the contented sounds she made, warbling her vowellike words, though whether to herself or to him, J. W. wasn't sure. For the most part Angelina preferred to rest her rosy cheek against his shirt and watch her mother put together the simple fare of their breakfast.

He watched Lou as well, but more surreptitiously, as she wrapped an edge of her skirt around the handle of the coffeepot before pouring the early-morning elixir into a cup for him. It was all a part of their morning ritual, and had become his favorite time of the day. While the camp around them sometimes was chaos incarnate with men cursing oxen and mothers shouting at children, Lou made their corner both tranquil and domestic.

"The coffee is quite hot this morning, Bart," she said without turning from her self-imposed duties. He had told her he was perfectly able to make his own coffee each morning, but Lou had paid him no never-mind and continued to brew it anyway. "I suggest you wait a bit before attempting a sip."

At the sound of her mother's voice, Angelina's head bobbed up but, instead of looking at Lou, she looked straight at him and grinned widely. "Charmer," he teased, smoothing down a particularly wild tuft of the baby's hair. "You named her after the river, didn't you?"

"I take it that was directed at me, not Angelina?" Lou asked. "Yes. I'm surprised you haven't asked before, considering how taken you both are with each other."

"It's her blue eyes," J. W. said. "They remind me of a river on a bright, sunny day. Not that that's the way I remember the Angelina, though. It did its damnedest to drown me when I crossed it."

"Spring floods have a way of doing that," Lou agreed as she packed away their surplus supplies. Beyond his coffee and her tea, they made do with a biscuit each and a bit of jerky for breakfast each day. In a way, he missed the apples she had given him that first day, missed the implied offering, the Evelike quality of the gesture.

But weren't all her movements like those of the biblical Eve? It seemed so to his eyes. Lou was never less than graceful, womanly, and wholly desirable. Despite her belief that the banker back in Peaceful was more interested in the woodland than her, J. W. doubted she was right. No man in his right mind would turn aside from a creature as enticing as Louisa.

He thought briefly of what she'd said the evening before, about a man losing interest in a woman once he had enjoyed her favors. Obviously Frank Burgess had been even more of an idiot than he'd originally thought. She was too innocent, too young, to have experience beyond her late husband when it came to men. If only he had the right to teach her that all men were not like Burgess. That some of them would consider her a treasure of the highest order, one to be honored, cared for. Cherished.

"Which route would you prefer to take to Austin?" J. W. asked.

He'd taken her by surprise with the question. He could

tell by the way her head jerked in his direction. "What did you say?" she murmured.

"I wasn't merely catering to my wounded ego with whiskey last night. I asked about the best way to reach Austin," he said. "Caldwell is sort of a jumping-off spot. We can either head to Lexington, then directly west or continue down the road with the others until we reach Bastrop and follow the Colorado River northwest up to the city."

Lou sat back on her heels, her dark, serviceable skirt swirling in a puddle on the ground around her. "You're asking me to go to Austin with you?"

"Hush, my dear. Why wouldn't I take my wife to Austin if that's where I'm bound?" He sat up, sweeping the baby up with him. "Mama just isn't thinking, is she?" he asked Angelina.

She gurgled an answer, much more in accord with him than Lou was at the moment.

"Yes, but I thought—" Lou babbled a bit incoherently. She stopped herself, biting her lower lip as if to still the words before they tumbled out. "You're really asking my opinion about our route?"

The idea seemed to astound her. Burgess had without a doubt been a total jackass of a man. "More than just your opinion. I'm letting you choose the route."

Whether it was to hide her expression from him or to give herself time to think, Lou went back to her packing. "What sort of conditions can we expect if we leave the road?" she asked, all business. "Is the way well traveled? Are there watering holes or stage stations on the way?"

"There are and there aren't," he admitted. "That's why I'm torn over which way to take. A man alone on a horse could make the trip faster by leaving the old road. He wouldn't be as likely to be spotted by outlaws as a slower moving wagon would."

"There are outlaws preying on travelers on this road, too," she reminded him, her face still turned away from him. "That was part of the reason we joined this train, to avoid becoming their target. But you are anxious to reach Austin, aren't you? We've already held you up, Angelina and I."

He hated it when she got all noble. "I haven't minded," J. W. said, not totally truthful.

"Liar," Lou murmured under her breath.

All right, there had been times when he had itched to take off. But he hadn't. He'd stayed, and not merely because she needed him. The reasoning behind the decision wasn't something he cared to look into closely yet. Perhaps never. That wasn't the matter at hand though.

Ignoring the accusation, he let Angelina latch onto his finger before engaging in a mock tug-of-war with her. "Past Lexington the western route cuts close to a place with thickly wooded hills and valleys, so it sounds peaceful."

"I doubt you'd be bringing it up if it actually was," Lou said.

J. W. grinned widely. "One of the things I like best about you is your quick intelligence, my dear. Yes, it only sounds peaceful. It appears that outlaws have taken a fancy to it since the end of the war. The area is a known hideaway for villains." In fact, if he was really as interested in tracking down Dalhert's men as he should be, he would have ridden out at dawn alone. If Diamond was right and they were answering their former captain's call, a known outlaw hideout would sound like paradise found to most of them. Or at least a good place to meet others of their kind.

Lou paused in her busywork to consider the matter. "Will that man back in Crockett be likely to head there?" she asked.

"Perhaps," he allowed. "If he moved on."

She continued to sit where she was, resting on her heels, her hands flat against her skirt-covered thighs, both her packing and her breakfast forgotten for the moment. Her jet-black hair still hung in its long braid down her back, although she had tucked the flyaway strands he had admired the night before back into the thick weave. "What is in Austin that makes it so important to reach the place?" she asked at last.

Another chance for revenge, he thought. Another chance to get himself killed. She didn't need to hear either of those possibilities, so he gave her the only answer that he could.

"The real Tess Ramsdale," J. W. said quietly. "She's been waiting for me to turn up for the last couple of weeks."

Lou felt weak with relief. The real Tess Ramsdale was waiting for him. It meant that his sister wasn't the woman who had been killed. But if she wasn't, who had been?

Walford was on his feet, Angelina contentedly trying to gnaw on his knuckles as he held her. The baby had no idea of the sort of trouble she had gotten them into by manipulating him into escorting them. But then, neither had she. She had thought an irate posse was all they had to deal with. Instead there had been the redheaded man in Crockett, and a mysterious quest for revenge of which she knew little.

Lou watched as her baby gurgled happily, obviously feeling safe and sheltered within his keeping. In staying with him, was she putting her child's life at stake? Should she use the common sense Miss Nottingham had applauded in her nature and part company with him? Or should she have faith in Angelina's and her own instincts and trust him?

"Then, if you don't mind, we'll take the San Antonio Road," Lou decided swiftly and accepted the hand he held out to pull her to her feet. "The way may be a bit longer, but it sounds the safer route. I think your sister would prefer that you arrive whole and healthy."

He grinned lazily, a wicked gleam of mischief in his eyes. Though gray, they never seemed to stay the same shade to her. At times they were the color of gunmetal, not only hard but flat, determined and inflexible, but at the moment they were lighter, the color of a dove's wing, although she was sure he would hate the comparison. A dove was peaceful and there was nothing of a peacemaker about Walford.

Would he ever tell her what drove him? Who it was that he was set on avenging? Though relieved that it wasn't the woman she had been pretending to be for the past week, she still couldn't help being curious. And even though she had confessed part of her sorry past, he hadn't reciprocated. What a curious man he was. He offered her a say in their route, but didn't trust her enough to share the burden that haunted him.

Why should he, though? They were travelers on different paths, together only because those paths had intersected back in Angelina County. In the ever nearing future, their paths would take them in different directions. Would they diverge in Austin? And if they did, where would that leave her?

219

"Then we're off to Bastrop," Walford said.

Lou reached for Angelina, needing the baby's closeness to calm her thoughts. "Not unless you happened upon a wagon while you were holding down that bar in town last night," she reminded him. "We can't continue to impose on the folks of this train. Their goods and families are already crowding the wagons."

Walford sighed deeply as if chagrined, but as a glint of laughter flitted in his eyes, Lou knew he was merely amused. "Nothing a fella likes least than to start the day being chided by his wife," he murmured. "Isn't that so, Henry?"

Lou glanced behind her to see Helen's husband strolling toward them.

"We're all in their black books this morning, Bart," Henry said. "Mornin', ma'am. Gonna be a lovely one to-day."

Lou nodded to him. "I hope so, sir, but if my husband hasn't found us a new vehicle, we can't in all fairness continue with the train. We've imposed enough already."

"Nonsense." Henry brushed aside the idea. "Besides, Bart and me have got you a dandy buggy lined up. Found it 'fore dinner yesterday. I sent my boys over to the livery stable to get it for you. Had 'em take your sorrel mare along to hitch her up. Now that Bart's broke the bay to the saddle, I know he intends to keep her out of yoke."

"He does?" she asked suspiciously.

Walford hastily turned away to bury his nose in the still steaming cup of coffee. After one quick gulp he frowned at Helen's husband. "Hell, Henry, I was just buttering her up, too. You've damn near ruined my day now," he grumbled.

As Henry chuckled, Lou shifted Angelina to her hip.

"And what, pray, will I do with only a single draft horse, Mr. Ramsdale?"

"Oh, you don't need but a lone nag, ma'am," Henry hastened to assure her. "You didn't need a freight wagon and we couldn't find another buckboard, so we got you the next best thing. A real dandy of a wagon."

The jangle of harness traces preceded the appearance of the sorrel. It was hitched to what appeared to be a tinker's van, and one that had seen better days at that.

"You're not serious," Lou said. There had once been a slogan painted along the boxed sides of the wagon, though time and weather had worn most of it away. However, she could still read what it advertised.

Helen's oldest boy was holding the reins. He pulled the sorrel up near where she stood. "Ain't it dandy, ma'am?" his younger brother called out from his perch on the driver's box next to him.

"*Isn't* it dandy," Lou corrected automatically, just as she had often heard Helen do.

"Glad you like it, honey," Walford said, dropping a hand on her shoulder. "Fella who was selling it said it was a sweet moving little buggy."

Lou looked at him. "It's a medicine man's wagon," she said. "You can still read his name and product on the side. 'Dr. Theobald G. Hilliard's Prime Elixir.' "

"It's faint," Walford claimed. "Real faint, Tess."

"I am not driving that vehicle," she insisted. "People would be constantly stopping me and asking to buy tonic."

"Not if they'd ever had a swig of Hilliard's Prime, they wouldn't," Henry said. "Evil-tasting stuff. Only thing it's good for is giving a man a dandy pain in the . . . well, I won't say particularly where, ma'am, if you get my gist."

"I appreciate your reticence," Lou murmured. "Was there nothing else available?"

Walford's fingers tightened on her shoulder slightly in what she took to be a comforting motion. "Caldwell isn't exactly the wagon making capitol of south central Texas, Tess," he said. "Think of it as more than just a wagon. It's shelter from storms, a comfy place to sleep, a place out of the sun to feed the baby."

"It's a tinker's van," she said.

"It's sound. We can slap some whitewash on the sides to cover the doc's legend some. The sides may rattle a bit, but the wheels and axles are sturdy and well oiled. This wagon will make it to wherever you want to take it," Walford insisted, then dropped his voice so that only she could hear. "Wherever you need to take it," he said.

It was to be a gift, she realized. Payment for her aid in helping him escape the posse. Their paths really were about to go in separate directions. And soon, oh, far too soon.

"It's a tinker's van," Lou said again, then sighed in resignation. "I'll drive it if I must, but the least you could do is find me a dozen bottles to fill. Perhaps I can finance part of this trip through selling an elixir of my own."

Walford gave her a one-armed hug. "That's my girl," he said and dropped a kiss on her brow. "We'll finish off breakfast, break camp, and be loaded and ready to roll within fifteen minutes, Henry. How about the rest of the train?"

Lou absently jiggled Angelina in her arms as Walford went to retrieve the rest of her belongings from the other wagons. "His girl," she murmured to the baby. "Too bad neither of us really can be that."

As if in total agreement, Angelina whimpered.

*   *   *

Claude Morgan trailed into Lexington with Egan O'Brien at his side. He hadn't wanted company on the ride, but had been unable to shake O'Brien. His former comrade in arms took it for granted that they were both bound for Dalhert's reunion and saw no reason why the ride couldn't be companionable. Which was probably because O'Brien didn't have to listen to his own drivel constantly, Morgan thought. The small-minded idiot had but a single theme that he harped on about, and that was getting the draw on Walford.

"You think he's here?" O'Brien asked, snarling, eyeing the lineup of saloons on the western side of the town square. They marched cheek-by-jowl in a row, making it easy for a man to stagger from one to the other. Morgan had no doubt that was exactly what O'Brien would do until thrown out of the last one later that night.

"We missed him in Caldwell," Morgan said shortly. "And he was asking about the quickest way to Austin."

"Probably thinkin' he can gun down Wes there like he did Roane in—" O'Brien frowned. "Where was that?"

"Lone Tree," Morgan reminded. If Wes Dalhert had respected intelligence rather than viciousness in a man, he would never have managed to scrape together a unit of guerrilla fighters. But then, Dalhert himself never thought beyond the moment, Morgan mused. Witness the insanity the former raider chief was proposing in gathering his men together once more. The object was nothing more than immediate gratification bought with gold acquired from another man's pocket. It didn't take sitting down at a table with Wes to know his band would content themselves with robbing an occasional bank, rustling a few longhorns, and holding up travelers along the most barren stretches of road. Thieving had always been Dalhert's life. It had always been O'Brien's life. Not that that made either of them any different from the other rangers who'd ridden with Dalhert during the war. They all had nefarious pasts, himself included, Morgan admitted.

But rather than be content with a fresh bottle of rotgut whiskey and a well-paid woman, he wanted status in a community and the power to shape it as he wished. That took not only money, it took connections within the government agencies that currently ran things in Texas.

It wouldn't be long before the state was reinstated in the Union. He needed to have made powerful friends by then, needed to have erased evidence of his own sin-laden past.

And so he rode with O'Brien at his side, waiting for the chance to rid himself of one part of that past. If they caught up with Walford, he could simply let the man take O'Brien on, and take care of whoever was left standing himself. The tin badge he carried in his pocket would be enough to condone his own killing as upholding the law. There was probably even bounty money in it, though the amount for a no account like O'Brien wasn't likely to be much. Walford was another matter.

But first they had to catch up with Walford.

"I hope that bastard is in town," O'Brien said, growling.

"My sentiments exactly," Morgan agreed. Having witnessed Walford's careful draw, he had no doubt that O'Brien would be the first to fall. The only thing that bothered him was why the former Yankee officer hadn't killed the idiot back in Crockett. If O'Brien was right, and Louisa Burgess had leveled him with a shovel, there would have been ample time to slit O'Brien's throat. So why hadn't Walford done it?

Louisa Burgess was why.

Morgan smiled to himself. The two were traveling together. The beauty and the outlaw. Walford no doubt felt indebted to her for holding off the posse with her hellcat act that day at the cabin. And she? Hell, Walford had whisked her away from beneath old Gillette's greedy thumb. If not sweet on each other, they were both damn grateful to each other.

Though he didn't know what sort of man Walford was, he was fairly sure he had Louisa Burgess's number. She was a beautiful woman neglected and mistreated by a weak husband. Gillette might talk about the lumber rights he'd gobbled up in arranging for her husband's gambling loss and untimely demise, but he wouldn't have been interested in her if she hadn't been a proper lady, even if circumstances had brought her to abject poverty. She was a good woman. But she was a brave one, too, brave in a way that only a female bred on the frontier ever managed to be.

Gillette would never have been able to break her. Walford would probably never even try. If he had let O'Brien live, it had been because Louisa Burgess was on hand watching what he did. And a man who couldn't kill in front of a woman was a man with a weakness.

Morgan guided his horse toward a handy watering trough and reined in, letting it quench its thirst before seeing to his own. "Why don't you start asking after him in the bars starting at that end of the square and I'll start at this end," he suggested to O'Brien. "If you find him, let the lead fly. If he isn't here, we'll meet up midway and ride out."

O'Brien wiped the back of his hand across his mouth. "Sure could use a drink," he said. "Bartenders are always more willin' ta talk if'n yer drinkin'."

Morgan took a twenty-dollar gold piece from the pocket

of his vest and flipped it to O'Brien before dismounting. "Put something more than just rotgut in your stomach while you're asking around," he recommended. "We'll need to travel fast and light out of this town, whether we find Walford here or not."

O'Brien bit down on the coin, testing it. Mistrustful bastard, Morgan growled silently to himself.

"Obliged," O'Brien mumbled. "Bit a grub'd go down fine 'bout now."

Morgan stayed where he was momentarily, watching as O'Brien slumped off down the boardwalk, thankful to get free of his noxious shadow, if only for a short time. The water droplets that splashed him when his horse jerked its muzzle from the water did little to dislodge the dust of the trail from Morgan's own throat. So, looping the reins around the nearest hitching post, he left the animal to doze in the street while he entered the nearest saloon.

With the sun high overhead, the heat of the day was already rising, which made the dim interior of the bar a pleasant change. Morgan took a step to the right just inside the doorway so his body wouldn't be outlined against the bright background of the street. He'd taken the precaution so many times now, the move was automatic. It took a while for his eyes to adjust to the change in light, but when they did, no familiar face stared back at him from among the handful of men loitering inside. They all cast him a quick look, sizing him up quickly before returning to games of cards or checkers.

"Afternoon, mister," the bartender greeted.

The long bar ran from front to rear along the southernmost wall, its polished finish showing that he'd found one of the better saloons in town. "Afternoon," Morgan returned. "Nice place you have here."

"We like it," the bartender said. "What can I get you?"

"Whiskey. The better stuff, if you've got it," Morgan said. He leaned casually on the bar. "And hopefully a little information."

"Real whiskey it is."

Morgan fished another coin from his pocket. Gillette had been generous and trusting in supplying him with a ready hoard of gold. Particularly since the majority of it had been in twenty-dollar pieces. O'Brien would have been content with a handful of smaller silver change, but chicken feed of ten dollars or less didn't buy a man information, even though it would have supplied a meal, a bottle of locally brewed tarantula juice, and a woman for the evening.

"I'm looking for a man," Morgan said. "Tall feller with dark hair and dark eyes. Might or might not be sporting chin whiskers. Has a military bearing about him, ex-cavalry man. Bit of a hand with a gun. Carrying a Starr .44, the last I heard."

The bartender slid a tumbler of whiskey over and scooped up the gold coin. He didn't test it as O'Brien had, but simply dropped it in the cash box on the counter behind him. There was also no change forthcoming. Information came at a high price in Lexington, Morgan mused.

"Lots of men come through here, mister," the bartender said. Picking up a towel, he polished the inside of a recently used glass. "I try not to look any of 'em in the eye or remember they been here, and that'll include you."

Morgan took a sip of whiskey—palatable stuff, he noticed—before extracting the tin badge from his pocket and placing it squarely on the bar. "This man managed to slip away from a necktie party we were holding in his honor in Lone Tree. I've been tracking him, but haven't managed to catch up to him yet. He might have been asking about the way to Austin."

"More likely he bypassed us and made straight for The Knobbs," a man at one of the tables said.

Morgan turned his back to the bar and leaned back on his elbows. "The Knobbs? What are they and where are they?"

"Place due west of here," yet another man said. "They're whatcha call a geologic anomaly."

The first man shook his head. "Hell, I knew it was a sad day in town when you up and married that schoolmarm," he said, then turned back to Morgan. "You got a compass?"

"Won't do you no good," the man who'd wed the schoolteacher claimed. "That's what that anomaly is all about. Something in the rock around The Knobbs makes the damn needle swing around faster than a pretty girl at a hoedown."

"You know, a drink would taste right good about now," the first man said.

Morgan placed another coin on the bar and indicated the helpful card players with a nod. "And what makes you think the man I'm after might have headed there?" he asked.

" 'Cause it's where most outlaws in these parts fetch up. What with the woods, hills, valleys, and that damn anomaly in the rock, it's one jim-dandy of a hideout, mister. If your man's anywhere, he's holed up with the rest of 'em at The Knobbs."

And if there were any more of Dalhert's men in the area, that's where he would find them, too.

But Walford wouldn't be there. If he hadn't put in an appearance in Lexington, he was still traveling with Louisa

Burgess and her baby. He wouldn't tempt fate in outlaw territory with them in tow. Which meant he'd leaped to the wrong conclusion back in Caldwell. Had made the mistake of not thinking like Walford.

Learning that a man answering Walford's description had asked after the most direct trail to Austin, he had taken that trail himself. But even if Walford was still on the Old San Antonio Road, the fact that he'd been asking about routes to Austin meant they were both headed in the same direction. Rather than catch up with the man, he'd get to town before him and be in a better position to bring him down. Maybe even flash the badge and spin the tracking tale to get the local law on his side.

But just in case Walford had merely missed this saloon when passing through, he'd spread Gillette's largess around in a few more watering holes, maybe even the local hotel. It was time to make a few friends in Lexington.

"Much obliged, gents," Morgan said. "You got a sheriff I could check in with and then someplace a man can get a decent meal before heading out?"

Chapter Fifteen

Lou could feel a change in the air the moment her tinker's wagon rolled into Austin. It wasn't merely that streets intersected regularly or that the buildings appeared taller, sturdier, or even that they marched in incredibly close-packed tandem within the narrow confines of a city block. It wasn't that traffic on the street made traveling at more than a crawl next to impossible, or that all manner of goods and services were being touted on signs displayed not only at street level, but from shingles hung at the second-story level as well. No, what really told her she had arrived in a city was the quickness of pedestrians' steps, the purpose they portrayed as they dashed across the street between wagons, and the length of their strides as they covered distances briskly on the boardwalks.

Unaware that she did so, Lou held Angelina closer. It wasn't until the baby squirmed unhappily in her lap that she forced herself to relax her grip. If she had been uneasy about adapting to city life before, now the idea of existing among the hustle and bustle of a metropolis made her downright nervous. The concept of finding a new life in Mexico City with her mother was quickly falling by the wayside.

"My goodness!" she murmured faintly when a man darted forward to slip across the road nearly beneath the sorrel's nose. The mare flinched, rearing slightly in the traces.

Walford's calming voice soothed the animal while a quick flick of the reins in his hands urged the mare onward. Lou hadn't had the nerve to mention it yet, but she was very glad that he had hitched Trouble to the rear of the wagon and climbed aboard to drive the vehicle into town for her. With so much activity going on around her, Lou doubted she would have been able to give the attention needed to guiding the sorrel through the maze the city streets represented to her leery eyes.

"Not a big-city girl, are you?" Walford said.

"None of your harem are," Lou answered. "To a woman, whether two legged or four legged, we are all country bred, and some in wilder sections than others."

"Having heard you in action with the posse, I take it

you're referring to yourself rather than to the mustangs or Angel," Walford said. "Trouble and Bother are used to running in a herd, which is basically what the folks in a city are. You, on the other hand, my dear Mrs. Burgess, strike me as a woman in a class by herself."

"Yes," Lou agreed with a sigh. "I must be. I've never met anyone else in quite the same sort of circumstances I seem to find myself in. At times I'm lucky to know my own name."

But she probably wasn't alone in that. The bay had received a name upon acceptance of a saddle, the sorrel had been dubbed Bother, for various reasons, since they had parted company with the wagon train, he had always shortened the baby's name to Angel, and she herself had spent well over a week answering to another woman's name at his behest. She was back to being Mrs. Burgess now though. Either he had forgotten the slip of tongue that had allowed him to call her Louisa once, or he was determined to keep their relationship formal. All the easier to slip out of her life when the time came, no doubt.

Of course, she had little choice about what to call him. He remained Mr. Walford simply because she still had no idea what his Christian name was.

"Are you relieved to be back to your own moniker?" Walford asked.

"Yes and no," Lou said. "There was a certain camaraderie in being Tess and Bart, even though I could tell you hated answering to your brother-in-law's name."

Walford clucked his tongue, urging Bother into a quicker step. "That transparent, was I?"

"You don't approve of him."

"Tess deserved better," he said flatly. "As he's dead now, it doesn't matter one way or the other."

What could she say to that? Offering sympathy over the demise of a man he had disliked seemed foolish. "He was from Texas then, from Austin?" Lou asked. It seemed a logical assumption since he had come to the city to visit his sister.

"Nope. Vermont."

So much for that theory. "Vermont," Lou repeated. "Then your family is also from—"

"Iowa."

Obviously Walford reveled in being a mystery. "Iowa. I see," Lou said. The conversation was beginning to resemble a geography lesson. At any moment Miss Nottingham would appear on a street corner and demand to know what the state capital was and when the area had been admitted to the Union as a bona fide state.

"It is always so nice when one receives a detailed answer," Lou murmured. "One is never left with a thousand unanswered questions. In fact, people who possess such delivery are to be applauded in my opinion. Yes, highly applauded, for they display the genuine warmth of human kindness by being so forthcoming. Don't you agree, Mr. Walford?"

He didn't answer her immediately, although a slight grin curved the corners of his mouth. She couldn't help remembering how delightful that mouth had felt when possessing her own lips, if far too briefly, that day in Crockett. How cruel he was to have kissed her so and then left her to fret over whether the embrace was ever to be repeated. With every passing day, the likelihood seemed to be less and less. It was a very lowering feeling to be teased so. To have enjoyed it so. Particularly seeing that she had been a widow whose husband was freshly in his grave at the time.

Strange to realize Frank had been dead barely a fortnight. She felt she had lived a lifetime since then. If not her own, at least a sizeable chunk of Theresa Walford Ramsdale's life. But then, being Tess, even if it had been a lie, had been much more enjoyable than anything in her own life had ever been. In fact, if she cared to carefully scrutinize her past, she was a sad failure at nearly everything anyone had ever expected her to be. Surely her grandfather would have preferred that she be a grandson. The thrill of being Frank's bride had lasted but a few hours. In fact, she was far happier as his widow, which many would find quite an irregular reaction on her part. But perhaps that happiness didn't stem entirely from Frank's convenient demise.

Lou let her eyes linger briefly on Walford's lightly curving lips before forcing herself to look away. Unseemly it might well be, but there was little doubt in her mind what—who—lay at the center of her current contentment. And who would in the end leave her far more saddened than Frank's death ever could. When Walford left, would he do so with a final bone-meltingly wonderful kiss or merely a polite salute, two fingers lightly brushing the brim of his hat, and a fondly murmured *adios?*

Walford's grin widened wryly as he glanced over at her. "So you think I'm being overly close mouthed," he said.

As her thoughts were still lingering on the chances of his kissing her again, his choice of words startled her. "Y-yes," Lou stammered slightly. "But I suppose you know little of my past, so I am guilty of extreme reticence as well. We should cry 'pax' and be done with it. Remain little more than strangers who have passed in the night."

"I had no idea you were a poet, my dear," Walford claimed. "Or do I mean, so dramatic? Has answering to Tess's name given you a taste for the stage? Shall we see your name on posters before the theaters and feel honored to watch you tread the boards?"

"You had better feel honored should I attempt to support Angelina and myself in such a fashion," Lou said. "But I would be content if you would call me anything but that hideously proper *Mrs. Burgess*. But you won't. I have found, Mr. Walford, that you are polite beyond measure."

"I am, am I?" He sounded amused.

"It's extremely tedious," Lou declared, trying to sound as world weary as she assumed women in a city—or the theater—would appear. "I suppose that is the lawyer in you, though."

"No doubt," Walford agreed. "Men of the law are a tedious bunch. Tess always thought me so, at any rate. You should take to each other instantly."

"I hope so," Lou said, seriously this time. "I've spent so much time answering to her name, I feel I should know her already, though I couldn't possibly. What is she really like?"

He surprised her by dropping a comforting hand on her knee, briefly patting it in a familiar, reassuring way. "Not an ogre like me," he said. "But she isn't the girl she once was. Events during the war changed her. Hell, they changed all of us, but Tess in particular."

Lou thought she could guess why. "Bartley Ramsdale was a soldier, wasn't he? He was killed in battle."

Walford nodded shortly. "A lot of men were lost that way."

But not her own husband, Lou thought. No, Frank had died in the most ignoble way possible. "At least Bart Ramsdale wasn't shot down because he was caught cheating at cards," she said.

"True," Walford agreed, then glanced aside at her once

more. "That doesn't mean Tess won't be, though."

And with that enigmatic comment, she had to be content, if puzzled, for he was guiding the sorrel to the side of the road and pulling the wagon to a stop before a modestly built brick building. "This is where we're staying the night, my dear," Walford announced. "Now, who shall we register as? Mr. and Mrs. Frank Burgess? Or do you have a more creative handle that we could use?"

The suggestion startled Lou. "You wouldn't prefer to use your own name?" she asked.

"There is always the chance that the telegraph has spread the news of a jailbreak in Lone Tree, adding my own damning sobriquet to the details," he said quietly. "But that wasn't your worry really, was it? I know you were quite uncomfortable sharing the room in Crockett with me. We can easily take separate rooms."

"Don't be ridiculous," Lou snapped, irritated that he could so misread her thoughts in the matter. "We've been sharing a tent and passing as a happily wed couple for nigh on two weeks now. It's just that . . ."

When she didn't finish the sentence, Walford peered closer at her. "Just what?" he prompted.

It was silly to feel this way, but felt even sillier to have to say it out loud. "I don't want to have to call you Frank," Lou said. "I know I suggested doing so originally, but I've changed my mind."

"Ah." Walford nodded, the picture of sincerity. "Yes. I can see how it would hurt you to use his name and have me answer."

"That might be the case if I'd cared a fig for the man," Lou declared, "but, as I would have thought you'd realized by now, I did not. The idea of calling you by his name is simply distasteful." She paused a moment, then added,

"Extremely distasteful. Please don't make me do it."

Walford wrapped the reins around the wagon's brake and stepped down into the street. "I will never understand you women," he muttered under his breath. "As if answering to *Frank* could be any worse than answering to *Bart*. But if it makes you feel better, we'll be whomsoever you want us to be."

Lou scooted across the wagon seat and handed Angelina into his keeping. "The Keatings," she said. "We could use my maiden name. I believe I'd like to answer to Louisa Keating once more."

He settled the baby against his shoulder. "What about you, sweetheart?" he asked the little one. "Feel like being Angel Keating now?"

As Angelina gave a gurgle of laughter at the idea, Lou felt her daughter was in perfect agreement over the choice.

"All right, we're the Keatings. Louisa, Angel, and— what's my moniker to be?"

Lou accepted his hand as she climbed down from the wagon. "Why I'm surprised you need to ask, sir. It is your own Christian name. Whatever else should it be?"

She was a minx, this pseudo wife of his, J. W. thought in amusement. He wasn't buying the innocent look though.

"What am I to call you now?" she asked, trying to appear nonchalant. Since she used the excuse of shaking the dust of the road from her skirts to avoid looking at him, J. W. waited for her patience to expire rather than answer immediately.

He hadn't long to wait. Her head came up, a frown furrowing her brow. "I am not choosing a new first name for you, sir. I think we have traveled together long enough for me to be privy to your own name."

"You wouldn't prefer to use *darling* or *dearest* or perhaps *my love*?" he teased. "I'm quite open to any of those terms of endearment."

Her lips thinned in disapproval. "I have not traveled with you *that* long, sir," she said primly.

J. W. shook his head in mock disbelief. "And here I thought that we had." At least for his part, they had. Those exact terms slipped from his lips easily around her. The fact that they pretended to wedded bliss only made the temptation to call her his love the harder to resist. Particularly when she went out of her way to do something for him, or blindly put her trust in him as she had already done so often. When she smiled at him, or merely stood close enough for him to catch the delightful scent of her in the wind, he thought of her as his woman, his darling. His life.

And as much as he had loved Claire, as often as he had missed her, longed for her, mourned for her, he had never considered her his life. No, that distinction belonged to Louisa Keating Burgess. In a little more than a handful of days, she had come to mean more to him than the woman he had once been so hellfire bent on avenging.

But Claire had never actually been the center of his life. Lou, however, was. Without making one attempt to win his total attention, she had managed to capture his heart. His soul.

Now she wanted to know his name.

"There is a slight problem," J. W. said.

"If you dare tell me it is impolite to ask what a man's name was back East, I warn you, sir, I shall scream," Lou declared fiercely.

It was an empty threat, but it didn't make her acceptance of his answer any easier. "My family doesn't use my name," he confessed. "They've always used my initials. J. W."

She relaxed her militant stance immediately. "Was that so hard?" she asked.

"Only if you persist and demand to know what the initials stand for," he said, offering her his arm.

Lou placed her hand in the crook of his elbow with dainty precision. "I will bide my time," she said and looked up at the facade of the hotel. "Is this where Mrs. Ramsdale is staying, too?"

"Yes," J. W. answered. "But unlike ourselves, she isn't using any form of her own name at present."

"Of course she isn't," Lou said. "I would never have expected it of a member of your immediate family, growing as I have to know you so well, sir. Besides, you did tell me when you presented me with it, that she wasn't using her name currently. Why isn't she?"

He stood aside so that she could enter the open front door of the hotel before him. "That, my dear, is something you will have to ask Diamond herself," he said.

The light tap on the door of her room made Diamond go unnaturally still. Around her the room was in chaos, clothing draped or folded on every available surface waiting to be tucked in the open carpet bags and small traveling trunks.

Had she been found out? Had she made a fatal slip at the worst possible moment? Everything had been going so well, then J. W. had failed to appear when expected. Then Jack Landrey had surfaced, his very presence a threat to her charade. Fortunately, the cavalry had ridden out of town on patrol the next day, taking him with it, but just knowing Jack was in Texas caused her sleepless nights. It hadn't been the first time thoughts of him had done so, but in the past he had figured as her Prince Charming.

And then she had met Bart Ramsdale and everything changed.

Well, it had done so again, disastrously, for the night before a bona fide Southern hero had been pointed out to her by a proud saloon patron. A number of men had been buying this particular hero a number of congratulatory drinks at the bar. She had only seen him from the back at first, an ordinary-looking fellow who blended in with other Westerners of his ilk. His overall appearance nondescript: faded, dust-covered butternut trousers, sturdy cotton calico shirt, colorful kerchief, scuffed boots, and a droopy felt hat from under which rather greasy, overlong hair hung in unbound strands. A thousand like him had come and gone in the various saloons she had visited in the past three years. But then he had turned slightly and she had remarked the evil-smelling long nine cigar gripped between his teeth, seen the sharp nose, lean cheeks, and cold eyes, and known J. W.'s delayed arrival was going to cost them their prey.

Wes Dalhert had run a leery eye over the assembly, but she hadn't noticed that it had lingered over long on herself. Why should it? She doubted he'd even looked at her that day in Kansas. He'd merely urged his men to make good use of "the damn Yankee's wife."

But she knew him. The faces of every one of the men who had ridden into the yard at Naughton Farm were as clear in her mind as they had been that day in August of 1863.

Rather than concentrate on her cards the rest of the evening, she had eavesdropped on every conversation of which Dalhert had been the center. From those conversations she had learned that he and the couple of men with him were doing little more than resting their horses before heading for San Antonio. The others had merely been awaiting his arrival before continuing their journey.

It all bore out what she had heard weeks ago. What she had wired J. W. about, expecting him to be on hand when Dalhert's men began gathering.

Damn her brother for his mysterious absence, and damn her own lack of courage when it came to facing Dalhert or any of his men herself. What they had done to her should make it easy to look them each in the eye and pull the trigger. But it didn't. She was damned to living in hell yet she couldn't bring herself to kill a man. Not even one who deserved to die.

Rather than move to answer the knock on her door, Diamond glanced over to where Neddy stood, as still and tense as she herself was.

"It's probably the hotel clerk with our tickets for the stage," Neddy said softly.

"Yes, of course," Diamond agreed. She slipped her hand in the hidden pocket of her skirt, taking comfort from the feel of the cool, fancy handled derringer lying within it, hoping that if Neddy was wrong and the situation merited action, she would be able to pull the trigger.

Neddy stayed to the left of the door rather than open it immediately. "Yes?" she called out. "Who is there?"

"One very dusty set of relatives," a familiar voice answered. "I'll bet you gave up on ever seeing the Keating family again."

Neddy managed to get the door open in time for Diamond to throw herself in J. W.'s arms. "You're quite right. I had nearly despaired of ever seeing you again," she cried, hugging him tightly.

He lifted her off her feet and swung her around in the

hall, careless that they would be seen. "You know I'm indestructible," he said. "Which is more than I can say for little girls who tend to take spills out of haylofts."

"I survived that tumble very well, thank you very much," Diamond insisted. She had waited for him to arrive for so long, she couldn't help feeling a bit dizzy to have him within reach once more. Loath to let her brother go, Diamond leaned weakly against him. "Don't ever make me wait quite so long for you again, Jefferson Weyland Walford."

Her use of his full name made him go quite still. "Don't confuse me with some other fellow now, Diamond. You know we *Keatings* don't fancy being reminded of the more disreputable side of the family."

Keating. Damn. And he'd even warned her, calling out the name through the door. Dalhert's appearance had rattled her more than she had thought.

But if he wasn't using his own name, which he had always done in the past, it meant that something dire had occurred.

"I have no idea why my tongue should make such a sad error in judgment," she declared, assuming her heavily accented Southern drawl once more.

"That's what comes of naming a female after some piece of jewelry rather than give her a sound name like Tess," he countered, and stepped away from her.

It was only then that Diamond noticed her brother wasn't alone. To the side stood a beautiful woman with blue-black hair. She was dressed in a serviceable dark skirt, plain collarless homespun shirt, and what looked like a man's well-worn boots. A weathered felt hat trailed from rawhide ties down her back and in her arms rested a shy but observant infant.

J. W. put his arm around the woman, the gesture both tender, possessive, and familiar. "To refresh your sad memory, I want to point out that all three of the Keatings are here now," he said. "You remember my wife Louisa, Diamond. And this"— he tousled the infant's fuzzy crest affectionately—"is Angel."

"Angelina," the dark beauty corrected as she looked at him briefly in frustration. "I can't break him of the habit of calling her Angel. But then you already know what an irritating man J. W. Keating can be, Diamond. I hope we haven't arrived at a bad time."

J. W. glanced into the room. "Looks more like we nearly missed you," he said.

He very nearly had. Unfortunately, he was still too late. She had watched surreptitiously from behind the blind of the hotel window curtain as Wes Dalhert and his handful of men had ridden out of town that morning.

"It's really good to see you again, Mr. Keating," Neddy murmured from the doorway. "But you folks shouldn't be standing about in the hall doing your visiting. Come inside. I've made room for you to sit. I could even fetch some tea from the kitchen if you like."

Neddy was being far more sensible than she herself was, Diamond realized. "Did you just get in?" she asked, linking arms with J. W.'s surprisingly lovely companion as she would have done with a woman of long and close acquaintance.

"Bare minutes ago," said the woman her brother had surprisingly termed his wife.

"I registered us, but still have to find a livery to board the horses and park the wagon," J. W. said, pulling the door to her room shut behind them.

As if it were a signal, the faint sound of the lock clicking into place immediately changed the atmosphere in the room. The masks each had worn dropped away leaving J. W. looking tense and the woman named Louisa looking worried. For her own part, Diamond knew she looked relieved. At last, the burden of making the next move was no longer hers alone to determine.

Chapter Sixteen

"What's happened?" Walford demanded at the same time his sister snapped, "Where have you been?"

Sensing the tension, Angelina fretted in Lou's arms, her once contented mumbling threatening to turn into an unhappy wail.

"Hush," Lou ordered. While the baby ignored the request, both Walford and Diamond turned to her in astonishment. "Yes, I mean you two," Lou said quietly. "As thin as these walls no doubt are, wouldn't it be best to continue to play our various parts? Or at least keep our voices lowered?"

The real Tess Ramsdale stared at her in stunned surprise, but Mr. Walford—Jefferson Weyland Walford!—glared at her. Considering it was not the first time he had done so, Lou knew his temper would calm and he'd recognize the truth of her statement in good time. From the disheveled state of the room, with partially folded clothing waiting to be packed in the open trunks, it appeared that time was not exactly something of which they had an abundance.

But then when had it ever been so? What with the posse

and Titus Gillette, the redheaded thug in Crockett, and various other unknown elements haunting their steps, time had always been short where Mr. Walford and she were concerned.

Lou sank to the side of the bed as she patted Angelina's back comfortingly. "Perhaps the most pressing concern is why you are obviously frightened, Mrs. Ramsdale, and whether it would be wisest if we all, er . . ."

"Skedaddled?" Walford offered, his scowl vanished.

Lou smiled at him, grateful that he could still be flippant when those around him appeared to be at wit's end. "Yes," she said, then faced Diamond once more. "Would it be appropriate?"

Walford's sister wilted wearily onto the opposite side of the carefully made bed. She was gowned quite elegantly, Lou thought, feeling sadly out of fashion by comparison. But then she doubted even Diamond would have worn an afternoon dress if she'd been the one driving a tinker's van and bedding down in a tent at night. Still, the long trained deep violet skirt with its decorative bands of noire and slate-toned braiding rustled so nicely as Diamond moved, and the weskit-styled bodice of richly striped pearl gray silk shot though with silver threads drew attention to her extremely narrow waist. Even the creamy lace trimmed blouse with its round collar and tight-fitting cuffs had Lou holding back a sigh of jealousy.

Heads would turn when Diamond went by, both masculine and feminine ones, drawn either by the refined style of her ensemble or by the delicate yet intoxicating scent she wore. The room itself smelled wonderful, retaining as it no doubt did the mist of perfume Diamond would spray into the air from the atomizer on the dresser and then walk into. Miss Nottingham had taught her that trick when she had first graduated to long skirts. It allowed a woman to be subtle rather than obvious in her choice of scent. It had been a long time since she had even thought of, much less longed to be able to perform the very feminine ritual. But then, Diamond was the sort of woman who appeared to have a proclivity for elegance. Growing up on the de la Vaca ranch, her own predilection had always been for sensible, sturdy work clothes. While the scent of hothouse flowers created an alluring aura around Diamond, Lou speculated that the scent wafting near her was one of horses, dust, and open campfires.

Though she had never seen him turned out in as richly appointed garments—Frank's wedding suit hardly measured up to that description—Walford himself had the same air of style as did his sister. Even when she had first seen him in his faded cavalry trousers and flannel shirt, his kerchief tied loosely at his collar, he had been an impressive-looking man. If he were dressed in the dark tailored suit she associated with men who read the law, he would be quite commanding. In fact, in his dress uniform during the war, he had probably won the hearts of ladies wherever he went.

As he had inadvertently won hers while wearing the trappings of a common man.

But J. W. Walford was not common any more than his sister was. No, they were a pair with presence, the brother and sister, a matched set of individuals who had no connection with the world she had grown up in, the world she knew.

The world in which she belonged.

Though they were very alike in coloring and appearance, easily identifiable as blood relations, there were subtle differences between the two. Diamond's hair was paler than her brother's, a soft brown that was pulled back simply into a thick chignon. There was a similarity of feature about their faces, although hers was more delicately fashioned while his was strong, lean, and most definitely masculine. Their eyes were the same changeable gray, both currently the shade the sheriff leading the posse had described: dark as the sky during a blue norther.

When his sister hesitated, Walford spoke up. "Would it help if you knew that Louisa and I have been posing as husband and wife for a fortnight now? Without her help, I probably would be buzzard bait, swinging from a hempen necktie in a convenient tree. We've been on the move constantly, if not rapidly, so if it is wisest not to linger, say so. Our wagon is still loaded and ready to head out."

"No, you needn't leave yet, not immediately," Diamond admitted, the honeyed sound of the South slipping away from her voice once more. "Wes Dalhert himself was in town yesterday. He and some of his men rode toward San Antonio this morning. I was afraid that if I didn't follow, we'd lose them again."

Again? Lou echoed the word silently. Though she had not heard the name of the man Walford was after before, she had heard of Dalhert.

"How many men are with him? Do you know who they were?" Walford asked.

Diamond shook her head. "He is the only one I knew by appearance as well as name. The rest are only well-remembered faces."

He took his sister's hands in his and hunkered down before her. "It's been nearly five years, Tess. You can't remember them that well anymore."

Lou watched the two siblings, wondering about the mystery that drove them. Diamond didn't pull free from his touch, but she glared fiercely at her brother.

"It will never matter how much time goes by," she said, her teeth gritted in her intensity. "I'll always remember their faces. Each and every one of them. It isn't just their appearance that is burned into my soul, it's their touch, their scent, their—"

The black woman laid her hand gently on Diamond's shoulder. "He knows, Miss Tess. Leave it be," she advised.

Walford released Diamond's hands and got to his feet. "You stay here. I'll go after them."

"Alone?" Lou asked.

They seemed to have forgotten her presence, because all three faces turned toward her in surprise.

"Dalhert is a dangerous man," Lou said. "Even other men outside the law give him a wide berth. If he's the man you are after, then you'll never be fully avenged without help."

Mr. Walford—no, J. W., she thought—leaned back against the dresser, his hands resting on the edge where a frieze of carved fruit and leaves curved downward, dipping toward the topmost drawer. "You know of Wes Dalhert? How?"

Angelina whimpered in her arms. Without conscious thought, Lou cradled her baby, rocking the infant. "Through Frank, of course. I overheard him and his friends talking about Dalhert. He was a Confederate guerrilla leader during the war, wasn't he?"

"He was and still is a butcher who merely claimed his crimes were done for the honor of the Confederate States," the black woman corrected quietly. Her voice was calm, but even though her tone held the modulation of an educated woman bred in the Northern states, Lou heard hatred echoing in her voice. Although the charade they'd played out in the hall had not allowed for proper introductions, this neatly gowned, well groomed woman was obviously as much a part of the Walfords' crusade as they themselves were.

Lou nodded in agreement. "That was the consensus of my husband and the men he rode with, too," she said. "But Dalhert never rode alone." She met J. W.'s eyes. "The man you killed in Lone Tree. He was one of Dalhert's men?"

Although Diamond had remained slumped, her spirit temporarily spent by her outburst, she straightened at the news. "You managed to dispatch another of them? Who was it?"

"Uriah Roane," he said. Idly, his fingers drummed against the front of the dresser, the cadence sounding faintly like the regular thuds of a cantering horse's hooves. Or perhaps the rhythm merely reflected his restless thoughts, Lou mused. She was resigned to losing his companionship, his strength, humor, and casual affection, but did not want it to be at the hands of a devil like Wes Dalhert.

J. W. pushed himself away from the dresser, too restive now to stand still, Lou figured. Within two paces he was at the window, but when he looked down on the activity in the street outside, Lou doubted he saw a thing. His thoughts were elsewhere, dwelling on what was to come and what had already passed.

"Roane's the reason I was delayed," he said. "There was a slight disagreement between his friends and me over whether he deserved to die." He paused a moment to glance at her and smiled faintly. "Mrs. Burgess here helped me elude a very determined posse," he said, at last explaining how she'd come to be part of their adventure.

Lou sighed. "Will you ever stop calling me that?" she

asked wearily. "I quite detest the sound of that despicable *Mrs. Burgess*."

If nothing else, the complaint brought a genuine, though still faint, smile to his lips, but he didn't correct himself. "My beautiful companion here nearly wiped another name from our list, Diamond," he said. "Although she didn't kill him, she left a dandy impression on the back of Egan O'Brien's head when she swung a shovel his way."

"You did?" From the expression on Diamond's face, Lou felt she had just gone up in the woman's estimation. Would she then forgive her for slowing J. W. down on the road to Austin? Perhaps, but not if Wes Dalhert escaped unscathed. Even knowing Dalhert's reputation, Diamond was clearly hell-bent on destroying him, and probably herself and her brother as well. If only there were a way to prevent such an inevitable conclusion. But how? She was only one woman, a widow with a child, a formerly tolerated wife and unwanted grandchild. She had no special talents to work miracles. And going on what she'd learned of the man from Frank and his cohorts, surviving a showdown with Wes Dalhert and his men would take a lifetime of miracles.

"I wish you wouldn't bring up my part in Mr. O'Brien's disablement," Lou said in exasperation. "I thought he was about to shoot you with your own gun! And I still don't understand why it was unloaded. I was under the impression that you loved that pistol. You had just spent the evening before caressing it—"

"Cleaning and loading it," J. W. corrected.

"Which is why I was under the mistaken impression that it was loaded," Lou insisted.

Diamond looked from her brother to Lou and shook her head. "I can understand why you've been able to pass yourselves off as husband and wife," she said. "You bicker like a long-wed couple."

"We do not," Lou and J. W. said in unison.

Either the discussion had upset Angelina or the baby had sensed the same feeling of dread Lou felt was building in her heart. Whatever the reason, Angelina burst into tears, her wail of unhappiness penetrating enough to echo through a half dozen of the thin hotel room walls.

J. W. was at her side immediately. "Come here, Angel," he crooned softly, taking the baby from Lou. She handed her child over easily, getting to her feet to move out of his way. Their time together had taught her that Angelina quieted much more quickly for him than she did for her own mother. Did that mean her daughter would miss him even more than she would when he left? Would his attachment to the baby temper his decisions when it came to forcing a face-to-face confrontation with Dalhert? Perhaps Angelina would produce that much-needed miracle. At the moment, Lou knew she could only hope and pray that something would.

It wasn't until Angelina's cries had turned to unhappy whimpers that Lou noticed J. W.'s sister and the black woman were exchanging what Miss Nottingham would most definitely have termed "speaking glances." Was it because the baby responded to him so well? Or was it simply that men rarely interacted with infants? At least they never had in her experience. Frank had gone out of his way to avoid being in his daughter's vicinity, and her own grandfather had never spared either her or any of the other ranchero children a second glance.

"He's very good with her," Lou said, feeling she needed to explain what might seem an unmotherly desertion on her part.

"So it seems," Diamond murmured, her expression closed and closely guarded.

"It's good to see him happy again," the black woman said and smiled warmly. "I'm Nedra Edwards. What you might call a friend of the family. I've been with Diamond ever since we left Kansas at the end of the war," she added.

Pleased at the obviously heartfelt introduction, Lou extended her hand in greeting. Nedra hesitated a moment, then slid her own forward. "Louisa Keating," Lou said. "Widow of an unlamented Frank Burgess. I'm afraid Angelina and I are the reason it took so long to get here, but it seemed a good idea at the time to travel as a family newly arrived in Texas and in search of a homestead."

"And you have a wagon and team to board yet," Nedra Edwards said.

J. W. had stretched out on the bed, letting the now-quieted Angelina sprawl in her favorite position on his chest, but at mention of their horses and the tinker's van, he sat upright quickly, one arm securely holding the baby in her place.

"Damn," he muttered under his breath. "You're right, Neddy. I'm wasting time. Do we stay, Diamond, or do we load up?"

Still apparently dazzled by the sight of her brother caring for the baby, Diamond shook her head. "How long is it since you slept in a bed?"

J. W. glanced at Lou. "Crockett, wasn't it?"

"Longer than that for you. You slept on the floor there," she reminded him.

"Then it was in Lone Tree," he said with a grimace of distaste. "And the bed was nothing more than straw padding on an unyielding board in a jail cell."

"Then stay in Austin," Diamond suggested. "I'll go

ahead with my plans to take the next stage to San Antonio. You can get a good night's rest and follow Neddy and me in the morning."

Lou could tell he wasn't happy with the suggested plan. "Will Dalhert really disappear if you wait another day or two?" she asked.

"No," Diamond admitted. "He's planning to meet up with more of his former men in San Antonio. He'll probably wait for them there, but I'd rather be where I can collect more information."

Nedra Edwards folded her arms across her chest and stared at Diamond as if willing her to say more. When she didn't, Nedra shook her head slowly, clearly disappointed in the other woman. "That's not the real reason," she said.

"Then what is?" J. W. demanded. "Has someone accused you of manipulating the cards? Is it safer for you to leave than to stay in Austin?"

Diamond grimaced in irritation and turned away, picking up a pile of folded clothes and placing them carefully inside an open valise. "Don't be ridiculous. I'm careful, and I rarely favor myself when dealing."

"Then why the hurry to leave when Mrs. Burg—when Louisa and I have just arrived?" he persisted.

The fact that he had caught himself and corrected her name, even if it was to the more formal Louisa, warmed Lou's heart.

"It's not a why," Nedra said. "It's a who. Captain Jack Landrey of the Sixth Cavalry's occupational force."

J. W. frowned. "And who is this Landrey? He isn't one of Dalhert's men."

"True," Diamond agreed as she folded a gown with little regard for the creases she created in the rich fabric. "But he's dangerous all the same."

252

"He knows who she really is," Nedra supplied.

"And that makes him dangerous?" Lou asked. She hadn't stopped to wonder why Diamond was not using her own name. The realization merely reminded her that she knew very little about the people in the room. Yet she doubted whether a single one of them would be willingly forthcoming about their past, or what drove them now if she asked.

"Who the hell is Jack Landrey?" J. W. demanded, his eyes narrowed apprehensively.

Diamond went on with her packing, purposely not meeting his eyes, Lou felt. "No one in particular other than the man who nearly became your brother-in-law," she said.

J. W. handed his sister's luggage over to the handler to load into the back of the waiting stagecoach. "You're sure about this?" he asked. It had to be the hundredth time he'd said the words in the past few hours, but it never hurt to try to get through her Iowa stubbornness one more time. It was probably his own damn Iowa stubbornness that allowed him to be so damn persistent himself, which merely meant neither of them ever won a contest of wills. Although, now that he considered it, he hadn't won many of those contests with Lou either, and she hadn't a drop of Iowa blood in her veins of which he knew.

Diamond fussed with her fine kidskin gloves, adjusting the fit around her fingers. "We've been over this, J. W.," she claimed, her adopted accent back in place once more, turning her voice to a ladylike drawl. "I've learned all there is to learn in Austin. Even if others still pass through the city on the way to San Antonio, I don't need to be here. I need to be in place when word leaks out about the nature and location of the rendezvous. It's what I've been doing for the last three years, and you haven't tried to stop me before, so why now?"

She was wrong. He had tried to stop her before, three years ago when she'd met him in St. Louis and they had designed Dalhert's downfall to their satisfaction. He'd told her then it was too dangerous for a woman to be involved. But she and Neddy had been on the next stage out, headed to the most likely place Dalhert's name and location would surface first: his hometown.

Since then Diamond had proved herself an invaluable conspirator, even though gathering information and hunting down men who had scattered into hiding after Lee's surrender had been a slow and painstaking process. While she had begun the hunt, he had returned to Iowa, sold what was left of their family's holdings, then contacted a man of business to do the same with Claire's family's estate. Neither he nor Diamond had needed a home to return to, but they had needed ready cash to support their personal crusade. Even he had been surprised at the total deposited in the bank in St. Louis when all the papers had been signed and the legacies of their ancestors were reduced to a monetary total. An amount that even after three years of nearly unregulated spending was still quite generous. An amount he doubted either he or Diamond would be around to enjoy much longer. No matter how often she had promised him that she would let him pull the trigger on each of the men they stalked, he had an inkling that she intended to break that promise in the end.

"You're sure you aren't using Dalhert as an excuse to avoid this Jack Landrey character?" J. W. demanded.

"Jack isn't the problem," Diamond said patly. "He's merely someone from the past, and I was careful not to give away that I knew him. He no doubt left believing he'd merely met a woman who looked like someone he'd once known."

"Someone he'd once wanted to wed, you mean. A man doesn't forget a woman like that. Not even if the properly behaved Northern lady he knew is now sounding like a dipped in honey Georgia belle and dealing from the bottom of the deck," he insisted.

She tried to look unconcerned. "Sir, if you are set to try this lady's patience with such talk, I give you notice that it will not work." He noticed she had accentuated every Southern sounding nuance in her voice, probably to irritate him. "Actually," she said softly so that he had to bend his head closer to hear her. "Jack knows I was never all that proper and that Bart taught me to cheat at cards. They were classmates at West Point, you see. But he is not the problem. In fact, he isn't even in the vicinity. Until Texas is readmitted to the Union, the Army is kept quite busy enforcing the law, chasing Indians, and performing various other tasks, although searching out disenchanted women is not, that I've heard, among those duties.

"By the way, I like your Louisa," she added.

"Don't try to change the subject," J. W. said, growling. He turned to where Neddy stood patiently at the edge of the boardwalk. "Talk to her, Neddy. You know she doesn't need to be this close to the game anymore."

The black woman shook her head slightly, allowing the modest ribbons at the back of her bonnet to flutter slightly to and fro. "I know nothing of the sort, sir," she claimed in her best servant's voice, ever conscious that they were in public rather than the moderately private sanctuary of the hotel room. "But I do agree that Louisa and her little girl are good for you. If anyone should consider giving up right now, it's you."

The idea so stunned him, J. W. nearly gaped at her.

"Ready to load up, folks," the stagecoach driver announced, striding back from a final check of the harnesses of his double team of horses. "It's nigh on eighty miles to San Antone, but we travel at a spankin' rate. Not like the old days when we bogged down every five miles or so. If all goes well, we'll be there in three days or considerably less."

"And it will go well," Diamond declared. She raised herself on her toes to plant a kiss on J. W.'s cheek. "Neddy and I will see you in San Antonio very soon."

"Not as soon as all that," he warned as he helped her mount the step into the stage. There were already four other passengers inside, but it was built to accommodate nine. She and Neddy would be comfortable rather than crushed. "You didn't get a look at our wagon. Don't look for us for another four or maybe even five days."

Diamond swept her voluminous skirts inside, arranging them so that Neddy could join her, their backs to the horses. She grinned out at him as he handed Neddy up as well. "Now you take good care of that little darlin' on the trip down," she urged.

"If you knew Lou better, you'd know she doesn't need me to get along perfectly fine," J. W. said, swinging the door of the vehicle shut.

"Well, of course, she can. I was speaking of Angelina," Diamond insisted.

Claude Morgan hung back in the doorway of a cigar shop, careful to stay out sight as the stagecoach driver snapped the reins and set his four horses in motion. As the equipage clattered down the dusty street, the sound of its departure echoing back from the solid brick and stone buildings of

Austin, he watched J. W. Walford readjust the angle of his hat to better shade his eyes from the sun before crossing to the opposite boardwalk.

It was tempting to follow him, for Walford would lead him to Louisa Burgess. But though Titus Gillette was itching to get his hands on the lovely lady, Morgan decided he wasn't in as much of a hurry. Besides, if he was late meeting O'Brien and Quentin Winters, the two idiots would most likely start combing the streets for him and run into Walford themselves, which would ruin everything.

He had hoped to conveniently dispose of O'Brien along the way, but as they had neared the area known as The Knobbs, Winters had ridden out from behind a stand of trees, his kerchief pulled up to partially disguise his face, and ordered them to "dish out or be shot." O'Brien had nearly fallen out of his saddle laughing over the idea that a man they'd once ridden with had tried to hold them up. Unfortunately, Winters had decided to tag along with them rather than return to his outlaw's roost, which meant he'd been saddled with not one, but two men he would prefer to see dead.

Morgan waited until Walford turned another corner and was out of sight before leaving his blind to head for Scholz's beer garden. Something else was nagging at him, and it wasn't that he'd nearly run smack into Walford in Austin. He'd been trailing the man, and though he'd lost the scent after Caldwell, he'd always known Walford would surface in Austin. This far from Lone Tree, Walford was feeling confident, acting like he hadn't a hangman's noose waiting for him. Which it would be, if not back in Lone Tree, then some other place farther along the road. But using Walford to silence Dalhert and the rest of them was just too convenient a plan to overlook. Not only would it leave him in the clear, if he brought Walford in for trial—a hasty one with the jury paid off to bring in the right verdict—it would give him the caché to step into the sort of government paid position that let a man line his pockets with other men's gold. And all more or less legally.

He might have given lip service to the Confederacy while riding with Dalhert, but damned if he didn't love the Union now. You couldn't beat Uncle Sam when it came to handing out undeserved rewards, particularly to men eager to stomp 'em in the unrepentant South.

His mind still pondering what it was that seemed naggingly familiar, Morgan entered Scholz's.

He would have preferred a less public meeting place considering he planned to disassociate himself from O'Brien and Winters while maneuvering them into Walford's killing field, but they had both been het up to visit the beer garden, having heard of it somewhere along their separate trails. It was a fairly new place, having opened in 1866, but business was brisk and that encouraged Morgan to believe the clientele wouldn't pay close attention to whom he was drinking with.

"There ya are," O'Brien boomed. "Hell, thought ya'd run out on us, Morg."

"Or found a filly with a finer face than Irish's here," Winters said. "What kept ya?"

"Business," Morgan said, signaling the barkeep for a beer. "Our business."

They exchanged puzzled looks, but it was what he would have expected of the buffoons.

"Remember how fast we all traveled during the war?

And how damn slow we've been trailing?" he asked. "That remind you of anything in particular?"

Winters took his nose out of his beer long enough to grunt. "Ya mean when Quantrill was drivin' us," he said. "You 'member that, Irish?"

"Hell, yeah," O'Brien answered. "Back the summer of '63, weren't it? There were so damn many of us in on that raid in Kansas it took near all day just to bring every dang man up a bare ten miles. Wes was beside himself, weren't he? Would a thought he was riding with God almighty instead of Bill Quantrill. Still, that was a day, weren't it, Morg? We got the honor of hieing out to the Yankee's place."

The Yankee's place, Morgan thought. Damn, but he was as much an idiot as these two! He knew exactly to whom that Yankee's place had belonged now. J. W. Walford. He'd heard the cold-eyed gunman mention Lawrence, Kansas, the day he turned the lead loose on Uriah Roane, and O'Brien had said Walford had mentioned it in Crockett, too.

Did he still remember that day? Like it was yesterday. While one of the others had shot down one of the women, mistaking her for a boy, he'd had the honor of taming a pretty little brown-haired wildcat.

A wildcat he had a suspicion he'd just seen get on the stage for San Antonio. It would be interesting to catch up with her, to see if she had a small scar on her shoulder, one shaped like the profile of a cut-and-polished diamond.

Things were getting more interesting by the minute. Of course, if it was indeed the same woman, she'd have to be removed as well. There could be no witnesses to the things he'd done in the past if he was to succeed.

"Do you remember what happened to Gaines at the

Yankee's farm?" Morgan asked his two companions quietly.

"Hell, yes. Ya shot the bastard dead rather than let him have first go with that Yankee's wife," Winters said.

"Surprised the hell out of him, too," O'Brien added.

"Well, if the two of you aren't ready to ride at dawn tomorrow, I'll do the same to you," Morgan warned. "You see, while you've been drinking, I've been asking around. Seems Wes and some of the others just left Austin this morning. We're a day behind them, and I aim to catch up."

Chapter Seventeen

The hotel restaurant was only half filled, many diners having departed for more convivial entertainments at the theatres, saloons, and billiard parlors. J. W. was glad that only a few of the tables were occupied around them, partly because Lou had fretted about bringing Angelina into the neatly appointed room, afraid that the baby would disturb other guests, and partly because he could tell she was building up to one hell of a conversation, one he probably would have preferred foregoing.

But the inevitable had a way of coming around whether a man wanted it to or not. He'd felt that way about Tess's marriage to Bart Ramsdale; about the opening salvos of the war. Even about finding himself behind bars back in Lone Tree.

She hadn't started the barrage of questions yet, thank goodness, which allowed them both—well, him at least—

to enjoy a pleasant dinner. While others around them relished meals of oysters, whether steamed, fried, boiled, or baked, he and Lou had chosen simple beefsteaks with potatoes. After the monotonous meals on the trail, the tender, juicy meat was a feast in itself. When a bowl of the cook's specially made ketchup arrived on the table, he'd thought he'd gone to culinary heaven. Funny how a fella could miss a simple thing like ketchup. Lou had passed on spooning it over the beefsteak, but when he'd taken the baby from her so she could make equal headway on her meal, he'd dabbed some on Angelina's fingertips. She took to the stuff immediately, contentedly sucking the new taste off rather than causing a commotion.

"I'm not sure that's good for her," Lou said as he added a dollop more to the baby's fingers.

"She seems to like it," J. W. pointed out. Mothers quite obviously took all the fun out of a baby's life, regulating it beyond measure. Had Claire been that way? Somehow he couldn't picture his late wife even being a mother, much less a cautious one, which she no doubt had been, considering her letters to him had fretted over their infant son's frailty.

"Just remember you said that if she gets sick during the night," Lou threatened.

Lou took another bite of her meal in silence. Whether she was enjoying it or not was difficult to tell since her gaze strayed, lighting first on one set of diners, then another. He thought she sighed, but the sound was so soft he couldn't be sure. "Are you feeling all right?" J. W. asked.

"Yes, of course. Why wouldn't I be?" she answered, but the easy words didn't convince him. Then she sighed again, a bit more audibly, and put down her fork. "This is very dear. The meal, the hotel. We should have found a wagon yard in which to stay rather than put the horses and van up at a livery stable again. Angelina and I have already been such a drain on your resources—"

"Hush, my dear. You are both delightful drains," he said flippantly.

Rather than grin in appreciation of his wit—or what passed for it—as she had done innumerable times before, Lou's lips thinned. She put her fork down. "Delightful or not, we shouldn't be dependent on your pocket. You've already spent a great deal on us."

Obviously they had reached the point when the dreaded conversation was to begin. To avoid meeting her eyes, he bent his head to Angelina, shifting her slightly in his lap so that she couldn't reach the edge of the table. Lou's daughter appreciated what her mother saw as extravagance. At least she was trying to reach for the ketchup bowl.

"There is still a great deal left of those resources, so you needn't worry. You did save my life. A bit of change spent here and there hardly cancels a debt like that," he reminded her.

"Still—"

This time he did meet her fretful glance. "That's not really what's bothering you, is it?"

She looked ready to argue the point, then thought better of it. "No, you're right, it isn't really, although I've just had to be a miser for so long, I do feel guilty over every penny you spend. It's foolish."

"Indeed it is," J. W. agreed.

"But—"

He grinned at her wryly. "Now why am I not surprised you have an exception to raise?"

She didn't exactly smile, but the edges of her mouth

curved up slightly, which reassured him. "So what's the problem?" he demanded.

Lou pushed her plate back a bit, leaving a good deal of her meal untouched. "I don't belong here," she said. "Not in this hotel with its elegant furnishings, fashionable diners, and extravagant food."

"The ketchup was superb," he agreed, even if it hadn't been as good as his mother's recipe. "Why do you think you don't belong?"

The question earned him the kind of look Claire used to give him for being obtuse. "I'm a product of the frontier, J. W. I haven't the manners, the style, the—"

"Wardrobe? We can fix that," he offered.

"I don't want to fix it. Not at your expense, I don't. But I also don't know what happens next," Lou said. Even though he knew she had no intention of eating, she picked up her fork again and poked listlessly at what remained on her plate. "You're headed to San Antonio, but I don't know where I'm going. What's going to happen now? Particularly if . . ."

When she didn't finish the statement, he did. "If I go and get myself killed."

His bluntness startled her, he could see. Her eyes flew up to meet his, serious and tragic. Such lovely eyes they were. In a world where all went right, he would have the opportunity to simply lose himself in those soft green eyes.

Or would he? In a world made right, wouldn't Claire still be alive, and young Timothy? Wouldn't it be his son, not Lou's daughter, whom he dandled on his knee?

"Where would you be now if I hadn't shown up at the cabin that day?" he asked quietly.

"In Titus Gillette's control," she said.

"And if you'd circumvented his designs and made it to the San Antonio Road?"

"That would have taken a miracle, J. W. You know I was in no shape to—"

"Miracles do happen," he murmured. And they did, he thought. Hadn't he found a reason to live after chasing the Grim Reaper's tail for so many years? He'd lost the will to live when he'd heard Claire had been killed, that Timothy had died. And yet here he was, a survivor of war, both national and personal, sitting across the table from the loveliest woman he had ever met. Which Lou was. Even Claire, as much as he'd cared for her, had not been as brave or self-sacrificing as Louisa Keating Burgess was. She was a reason for a man to want to live, to love again.

She put the fork down once more. "If a miracle had happened, one that didn't involve your appearance, then I might have made it as far as the Brazos, where the buckboard would have fallen apart at the crossing. Or I could simply have been murdered by outlaws. Or starved to death. Or been bitten by a rattlesnake, a scorpion, or any number of dire creatures."

She was being downright theatrical now, he thought, her imagination run amok with fancied disasters. "Or might have met up with the very same wagon train we joined," he suggested. "In which case you would have continued on with Henry's family, filed that homestead claim on land next to theirs and found yourself a good man to give Angel here a handful of brothers and sisters." Strange how quickly he could come to hate a man who existed only in the scenario he had spun, but he did. Despised the fellow. Envied the hell out of him.

Lou shook her head sadly. The fabric of her dress rustled as she moved restlessly in her chair. It was her best gown, the copper-colored one that made him want to peel each proper layer away, if only he had the right to. With great delicacy she took the pristine linen napkin from her lap and folded it nicely before tucking it under the corner of her plate. "All of that would indeed have been a true miracle, sir. But, even if events had played out as you suggest, I couldn't have lived where Helen's family intended to settle."

He couldn't imagine why not. Henry's wife had taken Lou under her wing, openly offering friendship and affection. Helen would have done the same, perhaps faster, had Lou been a stranded widow, alone with her child and in need of aid.

"You see," Lou continued, "they planned to settle in San Marcos." She fussed a bit more with an edge of the napkin, smoothing the hem with her index finger. "My grandfather lives outside of San Marcos," she said.

"Then—"

She cut him off with an angry glance. He had never seen her look so fierce. Not even when she'd swung the shovel at Egan O'Brien's head.

"I'll never live anywhere near that man," Lou swore. He could tell it was a vow, not merely a statement. And a vow she had made more than once.

If anyone knew about the consequences of emotionally sworn vows, it was he. At some time she would wish to take it back. "He's much closer than Mexico City," J. W. said. "He's family."

Her eyes narrowed at the suggestion. "He may be a blood relation, but he is *not* family!"

At the fierceness in her mother's voice, Angelina's eyes widened. Around the fingers in her mouth, she whimpered, frightened by the change in the atmosphere.

"Oh, dear," Lou murmured. "I'm sorry, darling. You'd better give her to me."

He rather hoped that she'd called him darling, but knew the term of affection had been for the baby. "Don't be ridiculous. She's fine with me," J. W. insisted, putting Angelina to his shoulder. It only took a few comforting pats of his hand on her back to settle her down. Idly, he wished it was possible to calm Lou the same way. The trouble was he wanted to do more than merely comfort her.

Lou was strong though. She proved it by reining in her emotions quickly. "Angelina is going to miss you," she said.

"Don't try to change the subject, sweetheart. Just explain things to me," he urged.

"All right." It still took her a moment to compose her thoughts though. He could almost see her considering what to tell and what to leave out. He could accept that. There were a number of things he hadn't told her yet, and doubted that he ever would. Things like the fact that he was in love with her.

Lou took a deep breath, fortifying herself for the story to come. "Don Felipe de la Vaca, my mother's father, rules the area just south of San Marcos. His ranchero is one of the old Spanish land grants," she explained. "He was less than pleased when his only child eloped with an American. When my father was killed in a stampede, my grandfather quickly arranged for Mother to marry a man in Mexico City, but would not allow her to take me with her."

"Didn't want to lose his heir," J. W. mused.

"Hardly," Lou said flatly. "He couldn't abide my presence as a child on the ranchero, much less as a grown woman. It's why he paid Frank to marry me and drag me to the opposite end of Texas. In fact, that damn saddle you found in the barn and dumped in the wagon is part of the bounty paid." She wilted slightly, her shoulders slumping now that the weight of the secret was off them. "I hate that thing," she whispered under her breath.

There was only one thing he could say, J. W. thought. "I'll get rid of it tonight."

She forced a tentative smile to her lips. "Don't be ridiculous. Even I know it's a wonderful piece of workmanship."

"But seeing it causes you pain—damn it, Lou! I had no idea. It was the one thing of any value you seemed to own. That's the only reason I—I'm sorry I brought it with us."

"Take it," she said. "In payment for keeping Angelina and me."

"Like hell I will," J. W. declared.

Lou's heart did a complicated flip, rather akin to a leap she'd been amazed to see an acrobat do during her lone trip to the circus. He was swearing at her and he'd finally called her Lou! Perverse female that she was, both of those things cheered her.

J. W., on the other hand, looked anything but cheered. "I would have thought it was quite clear by now that I'm nothing like Frank Burgess," he insisted, scowling at the very idea.

"Yes," Lou said softly. "I know."

His brow cleared, but he was clearly not a happy man. "I'm also no saint," he insisted, all the while patting Angelina's back softly. Her baby's fears were not only soothed, Lou saw, but Angelina had nestled her cheek on his shoulder and fallen asleep. He was more than a saint. He was their protector.

"You are a saint," Lou contended. "Before I knew your

267

full name, you were my Santo Jorge, even Angelina's and my guardian angel at times."

"Thank you very much. Just what a man wants to hear," J. W. declared, as though insulted. She knew him too well to believe that he was. "I'm still not taking that damn saddle," he added.

"But you are leaving us," she said, solemn once more.

"Lou—"

"Shh," she murmured. "You'll wake Angelina. Why don't we just go to bed?"

He didn't move from his chair. "Don't tempt me, madam," he said far too softly. "I know what you think you're doing. Paying me back. If I won't take the saddle, maybe I'll settle for you. That's the way you think."

"I do not," Lou said. But she had been.

J. W. stayed where he was, holding her with his gaze. Oh, those storm-colored eyes of his most definitely carried the same intensity as the thunderheads that preceded a downpour. But she didn't care.

"I can't promise you a tomorrow, Louisa," he said. "Even if they were headed for San Marcos, you should have stayed with Henry's family."

He was right. It was the sensible thing to do. Just because she lived in the vicinity did not mean she need have anything to do with Don Felipe. And Henry would help her file for a homestead of her own. She could find where Miss Nottingham had gone after leaving the ranch, see if her former governess would be interested in making a home with her, in teaching Angelina everything the woman had once taught her.

It was what she should do.

"No," Lou said quietly. "If you will let us, Angelina and

I will stay with you as long as you let us, J. W. As long as it is safe to do so."

"Lou, I—"

"Hush," she murmured. "At least as far as San Antonio, please."

"And then?" he asked.

Lou pushed her chair back and stood. "And then I'll do whatever seems best."

"You'll consider returning to San Marcos?"

"I'll consider it," she promised, knowing she would never return there. How could she? "I'll consider it on one condition," she bartered.

"And that's?"

"That you tell me how to explain to Helen and her Henry that my name is not Tess Ramsdale," Lou said.

It wasn't the unyielding floorboards that kept J. W. awake most of the night. He lay there, once more listening to Lou toss and turn in the bed only a few feet from where his bedroll had been flung. Was she restless because of the promise he'd forced her to make? If things were different, he knew exactly what he would do. Drive the ridiculous tinker's van up to the front door of Don Felipe de la Vaca's hacienda, pound on the stout boards until the man himself came to see what the commotion was about, and then toss that damn fancy saddle right in Lou's grandfather's face.

How could any man treat his own kin as if they were nothing more than chattel to be bargained away? It was the middle of the nineteenth century, not the Middle Ages! He could sympathize with de la Vaca when it came to seeing a loved one wed the wrong man. Though Bartley Ramsdale had been in his grave a number of years, his former brother-in-law's name had the power to irritate him yet. A little fact he'd conveniently overlooked in appropriating it for his own use along the trail. But considering the type of person Lou was, he couldn't see her father as a bounder like Bart. No, considering her mother had bowed to de la Vaca's wishes and abandoned Lou for an unknown bridegroom in Mexico, he preferred to think Lou had inherited her strength of character from her father.

It was men like de la Vaca who made him realize women had been sadly overlooked by the law in regards to their rights as human beings. Someone needed to correct that oversight. If things were different, he might have considered taking up the cause, running for office, forcing through changes in the law to take care of the omissions when common sense and family loyalty failed to provide for a woman. *Damn idiot! You're thinking like a lawyer again*, the voice of reason insisted in his head. The law was certainly not a profession for a vigilante such as he had become. No matter what Lou thought.

Ah, but if things were different . . .

Different in that he wouldn't be lying on the floor but would be beneath the sheets with Lou, making no effort to find sleep, but making great headway toward having a future again.

A future? Hell, he'd had only one future waiting for him ever since killing the first of Dalhert's men. And he hadn't improved those odds any by going and doing the same damn thing again. And again.

J. W. yanked on the corner of his blanket and turned over. *You're worse than an idiot, Walford, you're a fool to boot*, he growled silently to himself. Here he was being an ass of a gentleman, refusing the opportunity to do the only thing he seemed capable of thinking about anymore: making love with Lou.

She would be soft, he knew. Her skin warm velvet to the touch and two-toned, part bronze where the sun had touched her face, throat, wrists, and hands, and part ivory. Her womanly curves weren't opulent, but they were very satisfying to his eye. They would be even more so to the touch. But he wouldn't rush things, no matter how loudly his blood clamored to do so. No, first he would loose her long raven's wing hair, unraveling it from the conservative braid until it fell like a shining veil around her shoulders.

They weren't bare shoulders yet either. No, that was another thing to take his time over, the slow winning of her trust, the ribbons and buttons of her nightgown unfastened at a rate that told her he was willing to take all night.

But it wouldn't take all night. Not in the least. As leisurely as he might plan it, the exploration couldn't wait, it needed to be advanced to the point that he was not only touching her but tasting her, moving from her lushly welcoming lips down the arched glory of her slender neck to the enticing hollow of her throat. He'd seen it bared frequently when the day warmed and she freed the topmost button of her shirt. He'd also glimpsed it and the hint of her breasts when she prepared to nurse her child. The gentleman in him had always turned away, but the memory lingered.

However, when the nightgown was tossed aside, the feast would begin in truth.

Would she moan softly with pleasure when his lips began their exploration? He knew his own senses would be intoxicated by her natural scent. It had enticed him when they sat shoulder to shoulder in the wagon, when they lay within touching distance in the tent at night, separated only by the baby's cradle. The elation of at long last being enfolded in her arms, drawn close to each womanly curve and dip of her, would be better than any opiate and even more addicting.

And when his fingertips traveled at a leisurely pace from calf to knee to thigh, how would she react then? Would she arch against his hand? Cry out in her need to draw him deep within her? And when they were one, their flesh melded into a single being with but one thought, would he be able to hold that moment in his mind, his heart? Would he be able to leave her with no regrets?

J. W. rolled over once more, allowing his eyes to rest on the woman in the bed. She was still now, her fretting and the activities of the day finally taking their toll, allowing her to sleep. In the haze of moonlight drifting through the lace curtain at the window he could see the gentle rise and fall of her breasts beneath her worn and faded nightgown. Could hear the gentle sigh of her breath as she slumbered. She was at peace but there would be no peace for him that night. His mind was too alive to rest. Sleep would rob him of the pleasure of just watching her, aching for her. Silently loving her.

Somehow, somewhere along the trail, she had unknowingly branded him as hers forevermore. Her mark was on his heart. But all he could leave her with was remorse. So he would keep his distance and lose his sanity in dreams of her. For it was only in those dreams that things could ever be different.

Only in dreams that he had the right.

Chapter Eighteen

"Señorita Loucita!"

Lou nearly flinched when she heard the familiar voice of Ramone, her grandfather's head vaquero, call her name.

"Is it really you, señorita?"

She had hoped when they reached San Marcos that it would be at an early enough hour to make pushing on toward San Antonio reasonable. But instead they'd arrived in the Anglo-American town just as the sun disappeared over the distant horizon.

If J. W. hadn't lingered over his coffee, asking question after question about the area, they could have been well on their way as the sun crested that morning. But he had lingered, had asked all those questions.

In other circumstances, she might have been gratified by them, for he seemed fascinated with the countryside. He could see, he claimed, that everything the members of the wagon train had heard of San Marcos was true. The green meadows, majestic hills and endless plains of grass were wondrous to her own eyes after an absence of three years. To new eyes, they were no doubt even more impressive.

But it hadn't been just the scenery that caught his eye. It was the prospects the land offered that interested him as well. How many head of cattle had her grandfather run? he wanted to know. Which direction was the de la Vaca property from the town? How far away from it? The town looked fairly new, he said. Which it was. Although one would have thought founding a settlement at the headwaters of the San Marcos River would have appealed to the Spanish and Mexican settlers who had come before, it had been left to the Americans to carve a niche at the lovely site barely seventeen years before.

The headspring was prolific and beautiful, tumbling over rock and shaded by cypress, the cold water attracting wildlife as well as men. White-tailed deer were as plentiful here as in Angelina County, but they were joined by creatures quite foreign to Eastern Texas: ring-tailed armadillo, tarantulas, and javelina, the wild pigs who had always managed to find their way into the ranchero's kitchen garden.

She shouldn't let thoughts of life at the hacienda intrude, but just the sight of the rolling plains of indian, buffalo, and switch grass brought so many episodes from her childhood tumbling back. They hadn't all been bad, Lou admitted. If her grandfather hadn't cared much for her presence, there were others who had. Ramone's wife, Consuelo, the hacienda's cook, in particular.

And so she turned with an honest smile to greet Ramone as he galloped up, pulling his horse to a stop alongside the tinker's van.

"Ramone! I didn't expect to see you this far north," Lou exclaimed. She had in fact been praying that none of her grandfather's people would have a reason to be near the town, much less near the San Antonio Road. If there had been any other way of rejoining the old trail without passing through San Marcos, she would have urged J. W. to do so. But there hadn't been. Either her prayers had not been sincere enough, or she had not been judged worthy of having them granted. At least they had not run into Helen, Henry, or any of the other members of the wagon train, for which she was grateful.

"Ah, but I forget," Ramone declared, his deeply bronzed

face alight with pleasure over their chance meeting. "You are a señora now. Is Señor Burgess not with you, Loucita?"

"Senor Burgess is dead, Ramone," Lou said, trying to keep from her voice the relief even the thought of Frank's passing brought bubbling forth.

"My sympathies, señora. Does that mean our meeting was fated? That you are returning to the ranchero to live?"

Before she could disabuse him of the idea, Ramone's expression changed drastically.

"It would be good to have you home, Loucita. The patrone, he is not so well these days. His strength ebbs, you see. He can see that the time to join his sainted wife in Heaven grows nearer and, I think, as does my good Consuelo, that he is a bit sorry to have treated your mama and you not as he should have. At least, that is what is in Consuelo's mind."

Though Ramone and his wife might believe Don Felipe capable of remorse, Lou could not picture her grandfather ever doubting his own decisions. He would stand by them, inflexible as always. Even if he thought he was dying. And that was why she refused to see him.

But she couldn't say that to Ramone—kind, devotedly loyal Ramone. He would think she had inherited such an unfeeling attitude from her grandfather.

Had she? Lou wondered, never before having considered her own reaction as similar in any way to Don Felipe's. Now that it had occurred to her, she couldn't help dwelling on the possibility. Was she in turn being inflexible, unwilling to forgive the past, unable to believe people she thought she knew were able to change?

Dear Lord! She couldn't be just like her grandfather, could she?

"No, Ramone, I'm en route to San Antonio just now.

275

But I will come for a visit when my business there is completed," she promised. And unlike the promise she had made to J. W., this one Lou told herself she would keep.

It didn't mean she would stay, though.

J. W. had ridden ahead to check out conditions along the road, but he came cantering back to draw Trouble up beside Ramone's horse. "*Hola, señor!*" he greeted the vaquero before asking, "Is this an old friend, Lou?"

She could see Ramone measuring the sort of man J. W. Walford was as she introduced them. Had he done the same with Frank? Had he seen the flaws but kept silent about them, believing it was not his place to object to the patrone's choice of a husband for his granddaughter? Probably. But had he worried what would become of her? She was sure that Consuelo had, for the woman's eyes had been guarded when they said their farewells.

"We must be on our way, Ramone. You will give my love to your wife and the others?" she asked.

"I will, Loucita. Consuelo will be pleased to know you have a good man this time," he said, and then with a grin, he touched his heels to his mount's sides and was off.

So he had known Frank was an ill choice, Lou mused. If only there hadn't been a social barrier that kept the staff at the ranchero from giving advice to the family, even to a marginal member such as herself, perhaps she would have been warned. But would she have accepted their advice? Probably not, she admitted. She not only had thought herself in love, she was most definitely the patrone's granddaughter. She was of the de la Vaca bloodline. If it was a hereditary trait, then blind stubbornness did run through her veins.

"Ramone seemed genuinely pleased to see you, sweetheart," J. W. observed as he watched the vaquero's horse gain speed over the grassy plain. "Are you sure avoiding your family's place is what you want to do? After all, I could see that you were fond of this fellow. Outside of your grandfather, aren't there other reasons that perhaps you should visit the hacienda?"

Lou looked ahead, her eyes on the road as Bother ambled along. "There are," she admitted. "But not yet. Not today. I doubt whether your sister could take the strain of a further delay. We need to reach San Antonio."

He nodded absently. "You're probably right. And the sooner the better. The road seems to be in good repair ahead, so why don't you pull over and I'll hitch Trouble to the wagon's tail and join you on the box."

She did as he suggested, willing to turn the reins over to him. She had, after all, a lot to think about. Was she truly as inflexible as her grandfather? And, if so, could she change? The answer was long in coming, for Lou realized days later that they had reached the lights of San Antonio before the question was resolved to her satisfaction.

J. W. pulled the wagon to a halt before the grand edifice of the Menger Hotel. It stood two and a half stories high and was built of finely cut stone. Considering the appearance of the clientele that passed through the door as he watched, he wondered if the management would even consent to give him a room. As he and Lou were both covered in dust from the trail, they certainly didn't match the quality of Menger's usual guests.

He could tell the same thought was on Lou's mind from the way she looked.

"It's not too dear," he said, anticipating her excuse. "We are not staying in a wagon yard, and if you feel too much like a country mouse, there is a simple cure for that. Go shopping."

"This is where Diamond and Mrs. Edwards are staying?" she asked.

It took him a minute to realize she meant Neddy. As a dear friend of Claire's family, Nedra Edwards had never been addressed as Mrs. Edwards in his presence before, although that's who she was, Ezra's widow as much as he was a widower through Claire's loss.

"Absolutely," he said. "Diamond never stays anywhere but at the best hotels if she can help it. She claims doing so is part of her pretense as a successful gambler, but I think that's just an excuse to indulge herself."

Lou pulled a large handkerchief from a pocket hidden in the folds of her skirt and tried to wipe away some of the dust from her face. The handkerchief wasn't a dainty, decorated square of fine linen such as his late wife had always carried. It was a man's, another of Frank Burgess's leftovers with which Lou made do, unable to cure the poverty her husband had brought her to.

No, that was going to be left to him, J. W. decided. While he needed to discuss the matter with Diamond, he was sure that she would be in agreement over the disposal of his estate. Before leaving San Antonio, he intended to draw up a will, visit a local lawyer, and leave his share of the bank account back in St. Louis to Lou and Angelina. He would have no use for it in his grave, and the amount could easily be transferred to a bank either in San Antonio, Mexico City, or San Marcos. He hoped she returned to San Marcos, even if doing so meant explaining to Helen and Henry why she'd been posing as his wife and going by another woman's name.

She was right in saying that lying to the kind members

of the wagon train had not been the best of his ideas thus far. But it had been necessary. At least at the time.

It still wasn't a wise idea to use his own name in San Antonio, so he was sticking with the name Keating. Considering Egan O'Brien was still alive when he left Crockett and there was a chance that one of Uriah Roane's friends had stayed on his trail long past Lou's cabin, Dalhert's men could be on the lookout for a fella named Walford. He couldn't take the chance of being found out and shot down before arranging for Lou's future security.

"Do you think Diamond has a dress I could borrow?" Lou asked. "Our meeting was so brief last time, but I would suspect that we can spend more time together here in San Antone."

J. W. smiled. Her accent was such a delightful mixture of proper Eastern breeding and Mexican flavor. But her shortening of the city's name was pure Texian.

"That can all probably be arranged," he agreed. "Ready to run the gauntlet of the lobby stares, my dear?"

She scooped a contentedly gurgling Angelina from her crib behind the seat before squaring her shoulders. "Lead on, MacDuff," she said brightly.

It pleased him that she was in good spirits. Since leaving San Marcos behind, she had been introverted, quiet, thoughtful. He'd worried that she was dwelling too much on the coming confrontation and what would happen.

He'd already played the showdown out in his mind so often, the reality would be more like a repeat performance. Only with live ammunition, this time. He'd even seen himself falling beneath Dalhert's lead, but only when the last of them was down. He hoped he wasn't being overly optimistic on that count. If a single one of the raider captain's men was left standing after his death, it would mean his quest had failed. No, as the self-appointed avenging hand of righteousness, he needed to punish them all.

But despite that need, he had been regretting things, wishing for things.

Although he had written his own death into the scenario, figuring only a miracle would save a lone man against a half dozen or so villains, he now wished he hadn't found so many compelling reasons to go after Dalhert and his men in the first place. Belatedly he realized that Claire did not need avenging. Her death had been tragic, but in some ways, one of the mishaps of war. She had been shot by mistake. Even his sister had wavered in her determination to punish the men outside of the law at times. She hadn't mentioned it when they were in Austin, but he half expected her to bring it up once they knew where Dalhert and his men were making camp.

And she would do it for the same reason he was questioning their mission himself at the moment.

Lou.

The clerk behind the desk looked a touch taken aback when he glanced out at the street and saw their sad-looking conveyance, but J. W. was relieved when the fellow didn't try to throw them out. Just to be on the safe side, he asked the man if there was someplace in town where a better wagon could be found, explaining briefly that the tinker's van had been all they'd been able to get when their own vehicle had broken an axle. With a more welcoming smile, the clerk had said he'd be glad to recommend a couple of firms.

Not that J. W. had any intention of replacing the rattling medicine wagon. He'd bought it specifically because it could serve Lou as a structure in which to live while a solid house was being built. From the first time she'd heard that she could file for a homestead of her own, he knew her plans had changed. She no longer intended to continue on to Mexico. She wanted the security of knowing no man could ever take her land away from her again. With the money he left her, he would be helping her fulfill that wish.

As the hotel clerk handed over the key to a room on the second floor, Lou touched his arm. "Don't forget why we're here, darling," she said.

Darling. She'd finally called him darling. It didn't even matter that it was part of their usual performance as husband and wife. A man desperate for certain words couldn't let a little thing like playacting stand in his way of enjoying the sound of them.

She looked quite adorable, still retaining a faint coating of dust across her cheeks and nose. The attempt to clean her face with the handkerchief had merely smeared the dust into streaks.

"As if I'd forget a thing like that, my love," he teased, handing her the key and taking a wide-eyed Angelina from her arms before turning back to the hotel man. "I believe you have a Miss Diamond staying here as well? Could someone let her know that her brother and his family have arrived?"

From the fellow's reaction, J. W. could tell Diamond had greased a few hands before his arrival. Money was a wonderful miracle worker, they'd both found. It opened both previously locked doors and unbuttoned closed lips.

"If you'd like, Mr. Keating, I can have someone bring your luggage in and see about boarding the, er"— he looked past them to the tinker's van and its worn but readable snake oil message—"vehicle and horses at a livery not far from here."

"There's just this one valise to come in," J. W. said, indicating Lou's well-stuffed carpetbag on the floor at his feet, "but for the rest, I'd like it immensely. And Mrs. Keating would be very grateful if a bath could be arranged. I assume you have such conveniences?"

"Absolutely," the clerk agreed, accurately foreseeing a generous monetary handout for arranging things. Yes, Diamond had most definitely paved the way for their arrival.

The man at the lobby desk was no slouch himself though. Within minutes of getting to their room, both Diamond and Neddy arrived at the door. The black woman was as neatly turned out as usual, her very demeanor kind and comforting. His sister, on the other hand, wore the signs of nerves too finely stretched.

"Word at the tables must be scant," J. W. observed once Neddy had joined Lou in caring for the baby.

"Yes and no," Diamond admitted quietly. "They were in town, and I don't mean just Dalhert. I've heard every one of their names mentioned in some context or another, even our elusive Morg, but then they apparently disappeared. Word dried up practically overnight. It's nearly two days since I heard anything." Apparently unaware that she did so, Diamond knitted her hands together, twisting them nervously. "Perhaps it's just that I've been in the wrong saloons. There are, after all, some that even I dare not enter. Unfortunately, those are the exact types of places that Dalhert and his men *would* frequent."

J. W. nodded in agreement. "As soon as Lou and Angel are settled, I'll go out and visit a few of those places myself. At the moment, I think I might fit in rather well."

One edge of his sister's mouth tweaked in sardonic agreement. "You do look rather disreputable and dangerous. What happened to the razor you were using to look a bit more civilized?"

"Stropping strap bit the dust yesterday," he said.

"It isn't just your beard that's a bit thick," Diamond mused, running the pad of her finger over his bristled jaw. The tip came away covered with a faint coating of dust.

"Cover for me while I slip away," J. W. murmured. "Because if Lou knew—"

"Because if Lou knew, she'd tell you both that you'd overlooked one shockingly evident thing," Lou said, interrupting their hushed conversation.

Angelina squealed happily, but a glance showed him that the baby was being entertained by Neddy at the head of the bed. Lou was curled up against the iron footboard, one arm resting along its top rung.

"You are, you know," she reiterated. "These are outlaws, correct?"

When both Diamond and he nodded, Lou smiled complacently.

"It may have skipped your attention, but until his untimely death, I was living with a man who was more outlaw than solid citizen. He was small time, but still, he and his friends discussed things within my hearing. The one thing that any of them did consistently was stock up on supplies before making camp anywhere."

He agreed with that idea. And if there were more than just a couple of men, as there were with Dalhert's horde—

"I'm not saying they'd actually *purchase* the goods," Lou continued, "but they wouldn't ride out without having them."

"She's right," Diamond said. "But I still wouldn't rule out those other saloons. Whiskey will be high on the list of things any of them would want in camp."

"And women," Neddy added quietly.

When they all looked at her, she shrugged. "Even though you are all keeping your voices down, it is a small room, my friends, and I am far from either deaf or unconcerned." Laying Angelina on her stomach in the center of the bed, Neddy stood. "While you visit the saloons, I'll go to the dry goods shops."

Lou stopped her, reaching out to take Neddy's hand in hers. "No, I'll go," she said, getting to her feet. J. W. admired the way his feisty little dust-covered Texian faced the neatly gowned black woman. "Angelina is already comfortable with you, Mrs. Edwards. And while I hope you won't take offense at the notion, please consider which of us a shopkeeper is more likely to confide in."

When Neddy didn't at first answer, Lou let one more reality of life drop. "This is Texas, Mrs. Edwards. It was a slave state and it hasn't been readmitted to the Union yet."

He hadn't noticed how stiffly Neddy's shoulders had been held, how like a ramrod her posture was, until she melted. "You're right," she said quietly. "A shopkeeper will be much more forthcoming with you, Mrs. Burgess."

"Lou," Louisa suggested. "I'd like it if you called me Lou. It's what my friends call me."

Neddy's smile was one of true pleasure, J. W. was pleased to note. "I would be honored to be considered one of your friends, Lou," Neddy said.

J. W. figured he knew an opening when he saw one. "Then can you please stop calling me Mr. Jeff?" he asked. "Even though the Naughtons always called me Jeff, I never could get the hang of answering to it. I'd rather be simply J. W."

"And for you, my dear stalwart companion," Diamond

murmured, "could you simply call me Tess in private? I really detest having that deferential *miss* tacked on even when there is no one around to overhear."

J. W. thought he could see tears shining in Neddy's eyes, but she blinked them back quickly. "After all, what did I go off to war for if not for the pleasure of having *all* my friends call me by the same name?" he demanded.

This time a tear or two did escape Neddy's control. "You're all finer people than any of the Naughtons," she said, dabbing at her eyes with a tiny lace-hemmed handkerchief. "Though they supported the school Ezra and I ran, we could see they still enjoyed the deference implied in a servant's form of address. It may be ill to speak so of the dead, but it is the truth. I'm lucky to have friends such as you."

No, J. W. thought, *we're lucky to have a friend in you*. But it had taken wonderful, kind-hearted, determined Lou to truly make them all equal. Did that make him even a bigger fool than usual, planning as he was to get himself killed?

Damn right it did.

There hadn't been time to indulge in the promised tub bath, which seemed to be a continuing theme in her life, Lou thought. She'd vetoed the luxury back at the cabin so that they could make it into the forest before it was too dark. This time, at least, the pleasure of sinking into heated and scented water, of letting every ache and pain gathered on the trail seep away along with the steam, would merely be delayed. She would be able to savor the prospect of such a treat, which in itself was a pleasure beyond measure. But first there were things to be done, information to be gathered. A point to be made concerning the logic of her own suggestion. Quite obviously, neither of the Walfords had had to deal with the mundane aspects of life. At least not in the manner she had had to do so. How nice it must be to never worry about whether there would be sufficient funds, sufficient foodstuffs, sufficient fuel to survive. Her life with Frank had been no life at all, so closely bound as it was by need, worry, and disappointment. Would her life be much different after J. W. left her? Considering contemplation of his loss and of the trials that awaited her in the all too near future enough to crush the most buoyant spirit, Lou pushed them aside. She was on a mission, and for the nonce, that must come first on her list of priorities.

And so, with her face freshly washed, her hair upswept into a more fashionable coiffeur, and the luxurious feel of one of Diamond's afternoon gowns nipping at her tightly corseted waist, Lou preceded J. W. down the hotel staircase, at long last feeling as if she really belonged in the grand building.

He looked disreputably threatening in the jeaning trousers, Frank's shirt, and the hat he'd spent the past few weeks fitting to his head. And, of course, he hadn't yet shaved. A new stropping strap was on her shopping itinerary. As dangerously handsome as he looked unshaven, Lou decided she liked seeing his whole face even more so.

It wasn't merely that she was finely gowned, more so than at any period in her life, but that she had a stack of neatly folded greenbacks in her borrowed purse that kept her spirits high. J. W. had tried to give her a couple twenty-dollar gold pieces to take with her, but Diamond had vetoed the notion, pointing out that the coins would be more welcome where he was going. Ladies, and the shops they patronized, preferred to use lighter weight paper money in smaller, and thus more convenient, denominations.

J. W. had appeared doubtful. "I was under the impression that greenbacks were considered suspect considering that so many different banks print them."

"You would feel that way, naturally," his sister had said, giving Lou a sideways glance that spoke volumes when it came to female solidarity. "You're a man," Diamond said, "and in my experience, men rarely trust anything they can't bite."

Lou had had difficulty not laughing at the disgusted face J. W. had made, but she herself had watched Frank test the authenticity of a coin by putting his teeth to its edge too many times not to side with Diamond.

"You're in awfully good spirits considering the mission you're on," J. W. observed as he followed a step behind her down to the hotel lobby.

"Don't remind me," Lou said. "I'd rather not think about the result."

"Getting myself killed."

"Yes. I'm just glad that you're letting me help rather than cutting me off from this crusade," she said.

"Damned stupid though it is," he muttered. "At least you haven't told me I'm a fool."

"That's because you already know that and are doing it anyway," Lou declared as they crossed the lobby. "I suppose it's a code or something."

J. W. pulled the outer door open and held it for her. "Women rarely understand codes," he agreed conversationally.

When he joined her on the boardwalk, Lou rested her hand in the crook of his proffered arm. They would part within a short city block or so, but she was pleased at being treated as a lady. J. W. had never treated her as less though, no matter how many times she could tell he was irritated beyond measure with her.

"Codes don't take common sense into consideration very often," Lou said. "That's why they don't appeal to women. We're the ones left behind to deal with things, and it takes a plethora of common sense to do that."

J. W. patted her hand, giving her one of his more lopsided grins. "Yes, I can see that. There was common sense to spare when you hustled me into taking you with me back at the cabin," he agreed with a straight face.

She loved it when his eyes were so full of laughter. Loved him hopelessly even when they were quite sober.

"I believe the most eloquent example of my superb common sense was when I hit poor Mr. O'Brien with the shovel," Lou said. "Wouldn't you agree?"

J. W. slowed his step, put his hand over hers where it rested on his arm. Through the thin fabric of her visiting gloves, Lou could feel the warmth of his touch. It made her feel cared for, protected, all the things she had longed for in her reveries of dashing, rescuing conquistadors months before.

Yet when she glanced up into his eyes, it was to see that, in the space of a single heartbeat, the laughter had died out of them.

"I kissed you that day," he said, the humor she had come to expect also absent from his voice. "It was a weak moment. You were so glorious in battle, I couldn't stop myself."

It was an all too brief moment in time that she drew up in memory to savor frequently herself. "I didn't mind," Lou admitted. "In fact, I've wondered ever since why you haven't kissed me again."

"Blame it on another of my damn codes," J. W. muttered.

Lou bit her lip, considering whether she should say the words that trembled on her lips. "I wanted you to kiss me again," she said, taking a chance. "I wanted you to do more than merely kiss me, and it has nothing to do with paying you for taking such good care of Angelina and me."

"Doesn't it?" he asked.

They had reached the intersection where they would part, he to head for the more disreputable side of town in search of information, she to lose herself in the mercantile stores on the same quest. Lou stayed him with her hand, holding him back.

"Answer me one question before you go," she demanded, amazed that her daring had reached the stage where she was ready to cross the borders they had each drawn nearly three hundred miles ago in Angelina County.

He slipped free of her touch, but waited patiently, one booted foot in the street while the other rested yet on the raised boardwalk.

"Who are the Naughtons?" Lou asked quietly.

He looked down at his feet a moment, as if considering whether to honor her request with an answer.

"My late wife, Claire's family," he said; then he turned and left her standing alone.

At least now she knew the woman he was set on avenging, Lou thought. Claire Naughton. His wife. A memory she hadn't the least hope of measuring up to, much less besting.

Her once high spirits deflated by the realization, Lou picked up her borrowed skirts and continued on her way.

Chapter Nineteen

Although her intended destination had been a dry goods store, it was the milliner's window that drew Lou in. Displayed prominently in the center, as if on a stage, sat a hat of gloriously wonderful design. It had long black and white feathers cascading from a partly curved, painted straw brim; a low, flat crown; and satin ribbons. A small nest, featuring a tiny, colorfully plumed avian resident, nestled cozily among all the trimmings. Unaware that she had stopped to stare, Lou touched the modest jocket hat Diamond had thrust on her. It was round-crowned, had a small, curved brim and was decorated with but a single rooster feather and a band of forest green ribbon, which J. W.'s sister had insisted made the softer green of her eyes particularly enchanting. Even if that was true, the smaller headgear seemed insignificant compared to the flamboyant creation in the window.

"Breathtaking, isn't it?" a woman in a modest yet elegant dark gown said from the adjacent doorway.

"It leaves me nearly speechless," Lou confessed. "Do ladies truly wear such complicated bonnets nowadays? I'm afraid I've been hopelessly rural of late and thus lacking in fashion knowledge."

She could see the woman's eyes run over her borrowed ensemble, calculating the amount spent on the turnout. Lou hadn't liked to ask Diamond about the deep green gown, afraid that she would be too nervous to wear it if the cost had been beyond her wildest dreams. It hadn't been just the dress with its cleverly caught up train, gold braid trimmed overskirt, richly figured underskirt, and form-fitting bodice. No, she was also wearing a most ingenious crinoline that collapsed neatly for packing when traveling, and cloth boots with satin inset tongues of gold-toned silk. And, of course, the tiny conservative jocket hat matched the ensemble perfectly.

"I wish I had somewhere to wear such a beautiful creation," Lou said of the hat on display, "but I'm afraid that wearing it on the ranch would start a stampede faster than a clap of thunder."

The woman, quite obviously the proprietor of the shop, held the door open. "You're probably right, but that is neither here nor there when it comes to trying it on, is it?"

With a last glance at the chapeau, Lou hesitated only a moment. "You're quite right," she agreed. There was no reason not to try it on, but purchasing the extravagant confection was quite beyond her currently borrowed means as well as far from an example of her well-lauded common sense in action. However, the milliner was just the type of person who could save her considerable time. "Let's do try it on," Lou said.

"Not everyone appreciates the complexity of this piece," the shopkeeper said once they were inside the shop proper, "but it is the wave of the future, my dear lady. The wave of the future. Already in Paris, London, and New York the women are crying out for something different. Particularly the fashionable women in New York are ready to flout convention after the hardships endured during the late war. Extravagance of expression will become their by-word."

Sitting on a low bench before a tall mirror, Lou looked

at her own rather extravagantly gowned image and had trouble believing the woman in the reflection was indeed herself. The rich fabric of Diamond's dress hugged her form and appeared to ripple with light when she moved. She had never had quite so elegant a coiffeur before either, and wondered how Nedra had managed to arrange her usually uncooperative mass of hair in such a short time. She looked quite unlike herself, and yet wonderfully sophisticated. What had the milliner thought when she'd brought up the subject of cows? The woman who stared back at her from the mirror should have no working knowledge of livestock. She was more the sort to flit from one dance to the next, waltzing with various gallants, while saving her love for just one.

What had J. W. thought of her fashionable turnout? Lou wondered as she removed the jocket hat. Had he thought her beautiful? He'd termed her so in the past, but always to others, never to her personally really. At least not so that she felt she was being complimented. Had she looked as much like a stranger to him as she did to herself in her borrowed finery?

As the milliner settled the wondrous hat from the shop window on her head, the woman sighed. "Of course, you know only a few of us are ready to anticipate the advance of fashion."

"Yes," Lou agreed, trying for a world-weary tone she felt matched Diamond's gorgeous green afternoon dress. "It is Texas, and still sadly backward in many ways, and quite evidently still the wildest frontier. While en route here, I must say I heard any number of frightening stories."

The milliner adjusted her creation, running a finger tenderly along one of the long, trailing feathers. "Where are you traveling from?" she asked.

"St. Louis," Lou said, choosing at will what she felt was an appropriate setting. It had the added cachet of being a city she'd heard J. W. mention when questioned about their fictional past together.

"You no doubt thought you'd be carried off by Indians," the shopkeeper said. "I certainly thought that would be my fate when I first journeyed here. Fortunately, all the Indian trouble is further North nowadays. Those poor people west of Fort Worth are not so lucky as we are here in San Antonio."

When Lou nodded, the hat threatened to slip from her head. "Oh, dear!" she cried, putting a hand up to steady it. "I suppose I'm just too used to my modest little caps."

"Then let's try on another similar to the one you are wearing, shall we?" the milliner suggested.

"Let's," Lou agreed, lifting the more extravagant hat from her head and setting it aside on the counter. If the price wasn't too dear, and the woman supplied the sort of information she was in search of, then she would purchase a new hat, though one more fitting of the woman she knew herself to be. "No, it wasn't Indians we feared," she said. "My husband has heard such terrible tales of the outlaws along the roads that I nearly told him to go purchase the ranch he has taken it in his mind to want, and send for me only when the area was fully tamed."

"I'm afraid it would be a long wait if you'd done so," the shopkeeper said as she gathered a more modest set of bonnets for review. "Things have been particularly bad in nearly every western town since the war. Too many men wandering about with guns and too used to firing them with little forethought. I suppose it was a worthy reaction during the war itself, but the war is over. Unfortunately, there are also far too many feckless drifters about."

"If only they were willing to work like God-fearing folks should," Lou declared, "I'm sure that things would become as civilized here as they are in the East."

"We can only hope," the milliner agreed.

"Still," Lou persisted, "there are always some who never want to work for what they can take at gunpoint."

"So true," the woman said. "Shall we see how this one looks?"

Rather than consult the mirror as to the looks of the bonnet the woman had placed on her head, Lou watched the shopkeeper herself. "Do you know, I myself saw two men battling with their fists in broad daylight when we passed through Crockett," she confessed. "One was a ferocious-looking fellow with unruly red hair and a decidedly unattractive expression. I was under the impression that he had tried to rob someone and his crime had been interrupted by a concerned citizen, although that man looked little better than the ruffian he was accosting. Oh, I do like this hat! You wouldn't happen to have something similar with dove gray ribbon? Now that I consider the matter, I have a gown that is sadly in need of a fetching bonnet. Something appropriate for church on Sunday mornings perhaps?"

"I believe I do have one that would suit," the woman said. Considering Lou had spotted the hat when she came in from the street, she would have been surprised if the milliner had not presented it. "Not everyone is as fortunate as the person in Crockett," the milliner added. "Why just down the way at Mr. Firebaugh's dry goods, three men entered the store and took what they pleased a mere two days ago. I believe one of them had red hair, too. An Irishman, no doubt. That sort are always causing trouble."

Lou waited hopefully while the new chapeau was

perched carefully on her upswept locks. "Was the mercantile busy at the time? Was anyone hurt?" she asked when the woman stepped back to observe the total effect of her latest offering. The mirror showed a modest three gray ribbons trailing from the crown nearly to her shoulders.

The shopkeeper fussed with minute imperfections in the way the ribbons lay. "It was near closing time so Mr. Firebaugh was alone. However, the poor man was physically abused by one of the men, being beaten about the head with the handle of the man's pistol, even though he was careful not to rile them. Still, he feels he was fortunate not to have been shot. But truly, the incident is not one that is repeated often. Civilization is on our doorstep. Why, with every passing day, San Antonio becomes a better, safer place to live. Was your husband thinking of ranching in this area?"

Knowing the woman was asking in regards to perhaps future hat sales, Lou nodded. "He is out looking at properties as we speak." She turned her head from side to side, watching the way the ribbons fluttered with each movement. Never in her life had she owned something so elegant. Even the bonnet that matched her bronze gown paled by comparison, though the confection currently balanced on her newly arranged hair was quite modest. "Do you know, I believe this one will suit me nicely," Lou said. "Do you have a box I can carry it in?"

The milliner beamed happily at her, obviously relieved to have made a sale, even if it was not the extravagant creation that had first caught Lou's eye. But then it was a quite unlikely choice for a woman with the sufficiency of common sense she had.

"If you wish, I can have it delivered to wherever you are staying," the milliner offered.

"How delightful," Lou cried. "Just as would happen in St. Louis." At least she hoped it would. Surely, what one city's retailers practiced, all cities' retailers practiced? "We're staying at the Menger Hotel and I'm Mrs. Keating."

"I'll have it there for you later this afternoon," the woman promised before announcing the cost of the bonnet. "I hope that the rest of your afternoon is as delightful as our time here has been," she added.

Lou smiled and handed over the number of greenbacks the woman requested. It was an exorbitant sum for one small, modestly decorated cap, but reasonable when the information she'd been inadvertently given was figured into the cost.

"I'm sure it will be," she said. Well, perhaps not *delightful* but certainly successful. How could it help but be once she'd visited Firebaugh's Mercantile?

J. W. could hear the babble of feminine voices before he even tapped on the door of the room he shared with Lou and Angelina at the Menger. He hoped that meant Lou had been more successful in her news gathering venture than he had been.

Oh, he'd heard about some of the fellows they were chasing. One bartender he'd spoken with had turned downright unfriendly when O'Brien was described. Well, J. W. couldn't fault him for that. O'Brien was a nasty character. Other than that, he knew no more than what Diamond had discovered—that Dalhert was gathering men, and while the men who'd ridden with him in the war were the nucleus, they were bringing newly met friends with them. They'd even lured a couple of the flash girls from the upstairs rooms at one saloon to go with them, which irritated the owner a good bit. When asked if he knew where exactly they'd gone, the man had snarled that if he knew that, he'd ride out and drag the ungrateful women back by their badly hennaed hair. Not a soul in the saloon had believed him, of course. To a man they'd all known that going after Dalhert's group was a quick way to end up on the undertaker's slab.

Hell, he knew it himself, J. W. thought. But it wouldn't be stopping him. He'd come too far and killed too often to stop when the end was in sight. His own as well as Dalhert's and his men's. If they hadn't been gathering to take up where they'd left off at the end of the war, he might have been able to hang up his guns, decide to let the Almighty finish the job he'd begun, and settle down with Lou. Live like he'd always wanted to live: quietly, peacefully, and with a woman so beautiful and good, he knew he didn't deserve her.

But they were gathering. Were planning renewed mayhem on an entirely new batch of innocent folks. Whether he was motivated by revenge, some damn code, or a lingering respect for what was right and wrong under the law, once he found out where they were holed up, he was riding out.

Alone.

Thank God he didn't have to be alone at the moment though, J. W. thought as he tapped on the door, waiting for it to be opened.

Diamond answered his knock. Behind her on the bed, he could see Neddy counting Angelina's chubby little toes to the baby's delight. Her squeals and chuckles were enough to break his heart. He wouldn't be around to see her grow up, become as lovely a woman as her mother.

"Lou back?" he asked.

"Over here," he heard her sing out as Diamond nodded over her shoulder, indicating where Lou stood.

She was admiring herself in the mirror atop the dresser, turning her head this way and that. Shiny gray ribbons fluttered from the tiny hat on her head. She had it perched at a quite attractive and jaunty angle, he thought. "I pay for that?"

Lou spun, her eyes glowing brightly. "Yes! And it was quite, quite dear."

He smiled upon hearing what he felt had to be her favorite word. But then, given the circumstances in which he'd found her, the common necessities of everyday life had been "dear" compared to the state of her finances. She had had good reason to fear the price of things. She wouldn't have to for much longer. He'd leave her with the wherewithal to be reasonably comfortable for the rest of her life.

Mischief danced in her lovely face at the moment, making her appear far too young to be a matron with a child, much less the sort of woman who had endured a brutish husband and then the punishing life of the trail these past weeks.

"If you were in fact my husband," Lou declared coquettishly, "you would have nothing to do with me for being so extravagant!"

He doubted that. She looked too delightful, too lovely. Too desirable. If she were his wife in fact, he would gladly let her bankrupt him to have her looking so happy.

"Did you learn anything?" Diamond asked, finding a perch on the lone straight chair in the room. Neddy and Lou always gravitated to the bed, preferring the comfort offered by the thickly padded mattress. But Angelina lay on the bed. He had noticed that Diamond distanced herself from the infant whenever possible. He hadn't thought about what her reaction would be to the baby. Hadn't remembered that she blamed herself for his son's death. Timothy would have been close to Angelina's age when his frail body breathed its last. Never having seen his son, he hadn't had the same sad memories that Diamond silently harbored.

Fortunately for Lou and Angelina, Neddy had no such reticence, and delighted in playing with the good-natured little one. Would the shadow of events at Naughton Farm always taint his sister's outlook? He hoped not. Hoped that the coming showdown with Dalhert and his men would free her, enable her to find the sort of life she had once wanted. Even if that life had once been with Bart Ramsdale.

J. W. leaned back against the hotel room door, arms folded across his chest, and shook his head. "I heard the same sort of information as you did for the most part. The only bit I added was that they'd taken a couple of saloon women along for entertainment. Along where, I couldn't find out."

"Espantosa Lake," Lou said.

Diamond and he stared at her in surprise.

Lou's grin of satisfaction had a touch of superiority in it. "I told you you were overlooking the most likely places to learn information," she declared.

With the ridiculously small chip of a hat still in place, she nearly skipped to the side of the bed, her pride at having bested both himself and Diamond at their own game making her downright giddy.

"I bow to your superior knowledge, dearest," J. W. conceded. Sweeping his arm to the side theatrically, he bent at the waist, suiting action to words.

Lou beamed at him. If the others had not been present, he would have swept her up into his arms and kissed her. The hell with not being able to stop himself once he started. She was far too delightful to resist.

And she'd uncovered information that he needed. Information that would allow him to finish the chore he'd assigned himself three long years ago. Information that would not only get other men killed, but himself as well.

As if she'd just read his thoughts, Lou sobered. "Mr. Firebaugh, the grocer whose shop was ransacked, said there were just three of them, but from the things they took and the way they talked, he suspected there would be close to a dozen men in their camp. Surely even you will concede that number is far too great for a lone man to best."

"I'd by far rather hear how you pried all this information from the sadly abused Mr. Firebaugh," J. W. said, hoping to sidetrack her. It didn't matter if there were three dozen of them. There was no one but himself to take them on.

Lou wasn't about to be diverted though. "A posse could be gathered," she said. "Mr. Firebaugh is an upstanding citizen. If the men of Lone Tree were so eager to take out after you for killing a man who was anything but an upstanding citizen, surely there are right-minded men here in San Antone willing to do their civic duty."

"Not when that civic duty could get them killed," J. W. insisted. "The fellers who took after me were more interested in the reward Roane's lady friend posted for my head. Exactly where is this Espantosa Lake?"

"Mr. Firebaugh reckons it is close to a hundred miles west of here," Lou answered.

"Then you aren't going to find a local lawman ready to

gather a posse, sweetheart. The place is out of his juris-diction. It's in another county," J. W. said.

"That wouldn't matter to a deputy marshall," Lou countered. "They don't have to worry about jurisdictions, do they?"

"That doesn't count for a fig when it comes to rounding men up to ride, Lou," he insisted, beginning to get exasperated with her. Granted, she was trying to keep him from resting in some forsaken Boot Hill, but sending a group of hastily rounded up, untrained volunteers after Dalhert's group would only get a lot of innocent men killed. Better it be just himself. He sure as hell wasn't innocent anymore.

Her expression was tragic though, and he couldn't stand for her to be sad. Not yet, anyway. "Use that common sense of yours, honey," he urged. "You just said it was a hundred miles away. Men don't want to leave the comforts of the city to rough it on the trail if they aren't being forced to it."

He knew he'd said something important the moment her eyes brightened. "Of course they don't! But there are a host of trained men who *are* forced to keep the peace in Texas right now. The cavalry!" Ignoring him for the moment, Lou practically pounced on Diamond. "Do you have any idea where your friend and his men were headed?"

His sister frowned, but whether it was in irritation over having Captain Landrey termed her friend, or whether she was considering the prospect of turning their crusade over to the current official law enforcers of Texas, J. W. couldn't tell.

Lou sat on the side of the bed nearest Diamond and reached out to touch his sister's hand. "I know you were upset over seeing the captain, but isn't it worth your brother's life to find help?"

"Of course it is!" Diamond snapped. "But since I went out of my way to avoid Jack in Austin, I have no idea where his troop was headed. The old military road runs between Austin and Dallas and the Red River country. They probably make a circuit up and down it unless ordered elsewhere. If they are anywhere, it's Waco, not San Antonio."

J. W. thought that bit of news would end the discussion, but he should have known Lou wouldn't give up that easily. She was not one to lose hope. Hadn't she overcome her own physical weakness and the lingering effects of laudanum to get Angelina, herself, and him safely away from the rundown ranch back in East Texas? A woman with that sort of inner strength and determination wouldn't let a little thing like the cavalry being out of town slow her down.

No, instead she turned those incredibly lovely green eyes of hers his way. "Can the telegraph find them?" she asked.

"Probably," J. W. conceded. "But whether they can reach Espantosa Lake before Dalhert moves his base of operations is debatable. They would have to be here by morning and then ride hard to catch Dalhert's group unaware. Unless Espantosa Lake is a mass of defensible canyons, I'm guessing Dalhert will shift the location of his camp frequently. Particularly if he finds out his men can't keep secrets when liquored up."

"Surprising them at the lake is the only way to best them with a minimum of casualties, isn't it?" Lou said. "That's why you think you can take them on alone."

He shrugged. "If I have to."

"But you don't have to. Not alone," his sister said, getting to her feet. Her shoulders were squared and her stance was the equal of a well-drilled Army infantryman on parade. "I'll go with you. Bart made sure I was a fair shot with either rifle or pistol when I traveled with the Army."

He shouldn't be astonished that she was volunteering. He had always suspected Diamond wanted to be in at the end, in at the kill. Yet hearing her calmly announce that she would be riding with him had surprised him.

It was Lou who took it in stride. "Have you ever shot a man?" she asked quietly. "I mean, looked him in the eye and pulled the trigger without questioning the right of it?"

Diamond didn't answer at first. J. W. knew there were a number of things his sister hadn't told him about her life with Bart, traveling with the Army, even things she'd done since donning the mantle of a drifting gambler. Had she ever shot a man in cold blood?

Diamond sagged back into her chair. "No," she confessed, defeated.

"Then you can't go with J. W.," Lou said. "He needs someone with him who won't hesitate."

At the head of the bed, J. W. noticed Neddy smoothing down Angelina's flying rooster comb of fine hair. "Lou's right," she said. "You can't go, Tess. But I can."

J. W. ran a hand back through his hair. Once he'd been careful to keep it neatly trimmed as befitted a man of business, a man of the law. In the past year it had grown longer, ragged, and with the current coating of road grime, matted as well. "You can't go with me, Neddy. These are former Confederate raiders. They didn't touch you back in Kansas, but you can sure as hell believe they'll plug you in the wilds of Texas."

"I agree," Lou murmured. "That's why I'll be the one riding out with J. W. in the morning."

"The hell you will!" he snarled. "You've got Angel to think of."

"Diamond and Neddy can take care of her."

"Not feed her."

"I'm sure a wet nurse can be found for the time I'm gone," Lou said complacently.

J. W. wasn't buying her calm exterior though. He could see the quick beat of her pulse in the hollow of her throat.

"I'm the logical choice," Lou claimed. "I'm a native Texian and used to living on the trail. I have my own weapons, both a carbine and a pistol, and I know how to use them without wasting either powder or ball. I was born on a ranchero, which means that, although I've not had the chance to demonstrate my riding skills, I was practically born in the saddle. And, considering I love you, I think my reasons for wanting you to survive this battle are better than either Diamond's or Nedra's, although I know they care for you, too."

She loved him! She had stated it before witnesses. Calmly, coolly, matter-of-factly. But if she thought that gave her a hand up on watching him kill himself, or worse, get herself killed, she was wrong. Dead wrong.

"The hell you're going," J. W. said once more, as if repetition would make her change her mind. "I don't care if Texians are birthed with a six-shooter in each hand, a Bowie knife between their teeth, and can ride a horse while standing on their heads! You haven't cold-bloodedly shot a man either."

Lou's chin went up an inch. "But I have," she said softly. "And I killed him."

There, Lou thought, she'd confessed the one thing that made her unworthy of being considered a lady. It wasn't surprising that the only sound in the room was Angelina's contented cooing. She had shocked the others into silence. Might as well take advantage of their speechlessness and shrive her soul further.

"During the war, Indian raids were regular," Lou said. "When the tribes realized there was just a token army here after the Union turned the forts over to the Confederacy, things returned to the way they'd been when my grandfather first came to Texas. At the hacienda there wasn't an able-bodied soul who wasn't trained and drilled in the use of firearms in anticipation of a raid. We women were told the men would protect us, but that we needed to keep their rifles and pistols loaded. If in danger of being captured, we were to use the weapons on ourselves."

"Oh, Lou," Diamond whispered in sympathy.

"It never came to that." Thank God it hadn't. Lou doubted she would have been able to turn a gun on Consuelo or any of the other ranchero women, much less herself. But she had been able to sight down on painted braves.

"The men were out branding calves on the range when the hacienda came under fire," she continued, her eyes no longer focused on the well-appointed room in San Antonio but rather turned inward to the day war cries had echoed in her ears and smoke had billowed from various outbuildings. Miss Nottingham, for all her Eastern ways, had marshaled the household staff, ordering the youngest to load each rifle as it was emptied. She'd stationed the sharpshooters, Lou and herself among them, so that every side of the hacienda was defended. "They rushed us, coming from the west so that we were looking directly into the low hanging sun," Lou said. "I remember firing so quickly, my rifle was hot to the touch and soon far too warm to load. At first they were just distant figures, nightmarish forms that shouted and fell from our fire. It's much easier to kill when you can't see a man's face, can't see the expression in his eyes."

J. W. hadn't moved from his position by the door. His face was hard, closed, so that she couldn't guess what was passing through his mind. Was it distaste for her now that he knew of what she was capable? Or was he reliving his own moments in battle when the circumstances had been similar, only the faceless forms had worn gray and butternut rather than streaks of war paint.

"They were well armed themselves. The draperies jerked and danced as bullets tore through them. Plaster spit from the walls when hit. Paintings fell or tipped drunkenly on split cords. Yet still we fired, merely exchanging an overheated rifle for a pistol when necessary. And when we did so, they crept closer."

She was no longer speaking to Diamond or Nedra, only to J. W., who stared woodenly at her from five feet away.

"Somehow, one of them managed to get in the room where I was stationed. He had the twelve-year-old boy who was loading for me in his grip before I was even aware of his invasion. When the boy yelped, I spun to find a knife at his throat and a savage grinning at me. With the boy as his shield, he thought he had the upper hand. I was a woman and therefore not a threat. But I had a loaded pistol in my hand.

"He said something in his own language and motioned that I should toss the gun aside. Instead I raised it. Leveled it at him. He was laughing when I pulled the trigger and shot him in the temple.

"He deserved to die, and I killed him. I can and will do the same to any of the outlaws holed up at Espantosa Lake. Never doubt it."

It was nerve-racking to have him continue leaning back against the door, his stance so like it had been that first day when he'd tried to discourage her from leaving the cabin. That day felt as if it belonged a century in the past rather than a mere few weeks.

"In the temple," he said. "Lucky shot?"

Inside, Lou gave a sigh of relief. She hadn't won him over yet though. Raising her chin an inch, she met his eyes. "I can group shots close enough at a hundred paces to cover the hole they make with a twenty-dollar gold piece. I'm even better at close range. Before Widow Rosa was thrust on me back in Angelina County, I took the heel off the boot of one of Frank's friends when he came to *comfort* me."

"And what happens if a bullet catches you, sweetheart? What happens to Angelina if you get killed?"

He thought to deter her, but she'd already given it considerable thought. "She's too young to miss me. She doesn't really know me, isn't old enough to have memories of me. I know because my own mother had removed to Mexico City when I was Angelina's age."

Lou reached out to touch Diamond's and Nedra's hands. "If I don't come back, will you see that my baby is taken to my mother in Mexico? I've never been sure whether I would be welcome in my stepfather's home, but I can't see Mother letting him turn away her grandchild."

"I'll see to it," Nedra promised, laying her other hand over Lou's.

"We'll do as you wish," Diamond said. "She'll be well cared for even if your mother can't rear her."

Lou squeezed J. W.'s sister's hand, thankful that her darling daughter would be taken care of if something happened. "Thank you," she murmured, then turned to Nedra. "Thank you both."

But the one person whose approval she still needed was silent. Lou turned back to face J. W. "Do you really have an option?" she asked. "If nothing else, I can keep your weapons loaded. No doubt the faster they can be emptied, the safer we will be."

He was chewing a corner of his bottom lip in thought, she noticed. Weighing the chances of survival for either of them. They weren't good, Lou knew. But with surprise on their side, and two sure gun fingers on the triggers, they had an outside chance. If it were in her power, she was going to make sure he survived the coming showdown. And going with him was the only way he had even an outside chance.

"We ride at dawn then," J. W. said. "I have a few things to arrange yet today."

"And supplies to pick up at Mr. Firebaugh's mercantile," Lou said. "I took the precaution of ordering what we'd need. Since Bother isn't broken to the saddle, you'll need to rent me a horse and saddle."

Despite the nature of the business they would be riding out on the next day, J. W.'s lips twitched. "Not interested in using the Spanish saddle?"

Lou reached up to remove the elegant little hat she'd purchased at the milliner's a few hours ago. "Using it seems a dandy way to get myself killed by someone desirous of possessing it. Much better to have something previously used, don't you think? And I believe it would be far more sensible to borrow back a pair of Frank's trousers from you. I can wear them and—"

"*No!*" three voices shouted at her at once.

Lou blinked, stunned at their reaction. "I've done so before," she assured them.

Next to her, Diamond's complexion had gone three shades paler. "That's how Claire died," she whispered, her voice so faint Lou nearly didn't hear her.

"She was wearing trousers," Nedra said, her own voice none too steady. "Working in the barn, in the yard, with my husband. Those men rode in with orders to shoot men and boys. Claire was dead before they realized their error."

Claire. The ghost of his dead wife. The woman he would be avenging. The woman she could never live up to.

"Then I'll wear my usual riding skirt," Lou said.

Chapter Twenty

Diamond stood at the window staring down into the street, wondering if she would ever see her brother again. Behind her in the room, young Angelina Burgess was tucked in her crib on the floor near where Neddy sat mending. Lou's daughter was blissfully unaware that her mother had ridden off blinking back tears. The baby gurgled happily, carrying on a one-sided conversation with the doll who shared the cradle with her. Oh, to be so carefree, Diamond thought. Had she ever been that way? Perhaps when she was Angel's age. As thrilled as she had been when Bart Ramsdale proposed, even when she married him, she had not been carefree. He had been a soldier, after all, and war was brewing.

Her life seemed to have been a series of disasters since

that brief moment in time. Even before. She had gone to live with her aunt in the small town of West Point, New York, because her parents had died. Had gone to live with Claire when Bart had died. Where would she go if J. W. died?

It should be she with him, not Lou. Lou had something to live for, her child. But herself? For so long she had thought only of finding and punishing, destroying Wes Dalhert and his men. With that time at hand, she needed to know where she was bound from this point on. But she couldn't think beyond the moment, couldn't plan when her mind was riding with J. W. and Lou toward an unknown and possibly very short future.

They would be riding hard, covering the hundred or so miles to Espantosa Lake at a rate that would be punishing. She'd traveled like that with the Army, covering incredible distances in a short time to catch the enemy unaware, but never on horseback. Lou had frowned when she looked at the nag J. W. had rented for her to ride, but after walking around it and checking its hooves, she had declared it capable of maintaining a steady mile-eating canter and perhaps the occasional gallop over good terrain. That was the only way they would cover the distance quickly. They were traveling light, with only a minimum of supplies in their saddlebags, and bedrolls strapped to the backs of the saddles. Lou's worn and faded quilt had stayed behind, left for Angelina in the event she didn't return.

Would any of them ever see each other again? She could pray for her brother's and Lou's safety, but it had been a long time since she had deemed herself worthy of having prayers answered. And while Neddy believed that Ezra looked after her from the beyond, Diamond doubted either Bart or Claire bothered to check on her progress. In many ways the two had been quite similar, both more interested in themselves than in those who loved them. Claire had chosen J. W. as her groom because he was a lawyer, as her father had been. Bart had liked having an audience—her, ever grateful, ever attentive, but not always entertained.

If she was honest with herself, she knew life with Bart would soon have lost its allure. Now time had cleared the air, diffusing his charm until it was a hazy memory.

Angelina chortled at something she imagined the doll had said. A droll toy, that rag poppet, Diamond thought. J. W.'s son, Timmy, hadn't done much but cry, and a constantly fussy baby had not appealed to Claire. Had she thought his poor health a reflection on her? Diamond wondered. She herself certainly took full blame for his demise. She had done her best to keep him alive, all to no avail.

And now she had promised Lou to take care of Angelina if the unthinkable happened. A fine promise considering she was uneasy around the child.

She shouldn't have been left behind. It was her quest as much as J. W.'s. More so considering the indignities she had suffered at the hands of Dalhert's men.

"Come away from the window, Tess," Neddy urged. "When not at the table in the saloon with your cards, you spend all your time staring out the window. What are you hoping to find?"

"Enlightenment?" Diamond suggested. "There isn't much else to do but peer down on the world. I've begun to lose count of the towns I've watched from our hotel aeries."

"I doubt it's San Antonio that holds you there today," Neddy said.

Nedra Edwards, the voice of wisdom in her upside-down world, Diamond thought.

"They've been gone for nearly three hours. There's nothing more to see, Tess. Come away from there. Get acquainted with Angelina instead. She's quite unlike Timothy was, you know. Healthy, robust, and possessed of a pleasant disposition. It was clear to see your brother dotes on the child, even though she isn't his."

"That's typical of him, isn't it? J. W. always was an uncommon man," Diamond agreed, but didn't move from her station at the window. "He has to come back. They both have to. We should have listened to Lou to begin with. Even if the Army didn't manage to catch them holed up at the lake, they should have been alerted."

Neddy was right. She did spend far too much time gazing out of windows: hotel windows, stagecoach windows. She was either wondering how the evening's games would go, whether the information she sought would surface, or wondering what the next town would be like, how long it would take to get there. When this life of interminable travel would end.

There was nothing to see in the street below, no answers to be gained by staring at the normal day traffic before the Menger Hotel's door. But she couldn't turn away. Something seemed to be holding her in place.

Forcing herself to turn slightly, she looked over to where Neddy sat sewing a tear in one of the refurbished ball gowns. A gown she would probably never wear again if the long quest was at last over. "Why were we so all-fired determined to visit vengeance on them ourselves, Neddy?"

The black woman pulled a stitch through the rich fabric and took another. "Because there was no one else to do it," she said. "They were all too busy cleaning up more pressing things. Things that involved more than just the deaths of Ezra, Claire, and Timothy. We weren't the only ones who lost our souls during the war, Tess."

They hadn't lost the will to live, Diamond thought, but had that only been because the blood trail they'd been on had sustained them? What would happen now that she didn't know what came next?

"And when Dalhert and his men have been sent on their way to hell, what then? Will we have earned back our souls or sold them entirely?" she asked.

Neddy put down her mending. "I think that depends on what we do from here on in."

"Do you know what that is? Because I confess that I am at a loss." Diamond sighed quietly and turned back to the window, brushing the lace curtain aside slightly to improve the view. "How long do you think it will take them to reach the hideout?"

"At the rate your brother intended to travel? Two days. Two very long days."

"Do you think they have a chance?"

When Neddy didn't answer immediately, Diamond looked back to where her friend sat.

"No," Neddy said. "God help me, but I don't think either of them has a chance."

Diamond leaned closer to the window, craning to better see what was happening in the street below, then she dropped the curtain and grabbed up her shawl. "Then I think we'd better give them a better chance," she said, heading for the door. "Thank Ezra and whoever else is watching out for us, Neddy, because Jack Landrey and the cavalry just rode into town."

* * *

Lou wondered how J. W. could find his way, the night was so dark. Storm clouds threatened overhead, blocking the stars from sight, and restricting the moon's glow to a haze that fought to be seen behind the clouds. Somewhere in the inky blackness a coyote's mournful cry echoed, seeming like a cry from the netherworld, eerie and chilling.

She was too tired to do more than note it. Miss Nottingham had once termed the sound nature's poetry, evoking as it did so many fancies in the human mind. Lou's own fancy at the moment was to simply fall from the saddle and sleep.

They had barely stopped since leaving San Antonio at first light, not bothering to follow either the Upper or Lower Presidio roads, hoping to trim miles and make better time by heading cross country, southwest from the city, making for the Forked Lakes region west of the Nueces River. Though her riding skills hadn't deserted her, she hadn't been in the saddle in twelve long months. Longer. Frank had sold her saddle and gelded brown-and-white Indian pony a few months before Angelina had been conceived. Whatever price he got for the animal and equipage had no doubt been laid on a table at the saloon in Peaceful. It had always been where anything of value ended up.

Her body had grown unused to the gait of a horse, the feel of a saddle, but she hadn't said a word to J. W. about it. He would as soon leave her behind as have her with him when he went up against the outlaws. And so she endured in silence, pushing herself to keep up with him.

In the darkness, she nearly missed the moment when he pulled Trouble to a halt. "We'd better camp here," he said. "The horses are tired and so are we."

It took a good deal of self-control for Lou not to sigh in thanksgiving. "All right," she answered, pulling her rented nag to a stop and praying that she wouldn't tumble to the ground. Her dismount wouldn't earn any accolades, but as she kept her feet, Lou was satisfied with it.

Her mount was blowing heavily and had a crust of dried foam at the corners of its mouth where the bit rested. "Easy, boy," she murmured, running a soothing hand down the horse's chest. It was another gelding, a piebald this time. Even in the dark she could see sweat glistening on its blotched black-and-white coat, a sure sign of exhaustion even though they'd kept the horses at a walk for the last hour. "Is there water nearby?" she asked.

"A stream straight ahead," J. W. said. "I heard it, though I certainly can't see it. Watch your step. It could be at the bottom of a steep arroyo."

He sounded as tired as she felt, which was exhausted.

"I'll watch," Lou said. She could hear the bubbling sound of water tripping over rock now. A faint sound, but one that promised relief. Not bothering to loosen the saddle, she led the piebald closer. Scenting the stream, it tried to hurry her along, but Lou kept a firm grip on the bridle, using all her remaining strength to hold it back. A tumble in the dark could mean a broken leg for the animal, and a downed horse would give J. W. yet another reason to leave her behind.

The dip in the landscape was moderate though, a gentle slope with honey mesquite and a lone live oak keeping the bank from being barren or unwelcoming.

Her horse stepped lively when allowed to approach the oasis, lowering its nose eagerly to drink. But it had barely lapped a swallow's worth before jerking its head up and scrambling back a step.

Lou found J. W. at her side instantly. "What's the matter?"

She had already calmed the spooked nag though. "A tortoise. We surprised it, that's all." Could have been worse, she thought. It could have been a rattlesnake. Of course, if it had been, a single shot would have turned it from a danger into a dinner. Not her favorite meal, but better than more jerky, unless . . .

"Do you want a fire tonight? If so, I'll see if I can find something to burn and gather water while you take care of the horses," Lou suggested as Trouble pushed between them, eager to reach the water. The mare was marvelously calm compared to the skittish animal she had been under Frank's tutelage. They had all benefited from knowing J. W. Walford. The horses, Angelina, but most particularly, herself, Lou thought.

Though she couldn't see J. W. clearly, she could feel his indecision. They had become so attuned to each other, become so used to working as a team to set up camp every night, she knew his every mood, every expression. And yet she knew little of the man himself.

"Best not," J. W. murmured. "For all we know, a light could draw attention to us on the range, and this doesn't look to be the most defendable spot."

"I'll fill our canteens then and clear a spot for the bedrolls."

He didn't argue, but merely handed over his nearly empty canteen and unfastened the rolled blankets from behind their saddles.

Once the horses were staked out and the rough camp made, Lou sat on her newly purchased bedroll, too tired to chew her ration of jerky, but sleepless and apprehensive about what lay ahead. J. W. was stretched out next to her, his head resting on his saddle. They had been quiet for a considerable amount of time. She wondered what the morrow would bring, whether Angelina was missing her. Wondered what he was thinking.

"I left something for you with Diamond," he said quietly. "Yesterday afternoon I arranged for you and Angel to get my estate. You won't be able to buy many jewels with the amount, but it should be sufficient to file for your homestead and not starve while your herd is building. When the time comes, you can even send Angel to finishing school, if you wish."

Lou pulled her knees up beneath her blanket and wrapped her arms around them. "It's a shame about the jewels," she murmured. "I had a fancy for them. They probably wouldn't go with my new hat though, so I suppose I can forego them. When we get back, you can visit a jewelers and pick something out for me instead."

"Lou, I—"

She held her left hand out, her fingers spread. "I considered leaving my wedding ring behind, you know, but thought better of it. We're far enough away from Angelina County that no one will know who Frank Burgess is, but he had outlaw connections, so if you pose as Frank we might be more likely get past any lookouts they have posted. I can give you the names of men he associated with to make the masquerade have the ring of truth. But in return for all this, I expect you to buy me a new wedding band when we return to San Antonio. Perhaps something a little nicer than this one." She turned her hand back and forth, as if considering the ring she could barely see on her finger. "I'd rather not be reminded of my sad past in having a similar one, you see."

"Lou, you know that—"

She didn't want him to tell her what was more likely to happen. Would it be the next day or the one after?

"You could pretend to have been wounded by a gunshot, ride slumped in your saddle with your hat drawn down over your eyes. That way if Mr. O'Brien is on hand, he wouldn't be as liable to recognize you. We'll still have the element of surprise. It's such an important part of the plan," she said. "Do you think I'm being unladylike in pushing for marriage?"

"I think you are being foolish in picking a fellow like me for your second husband," J. W. said.

"Hmm," Lou murmured. "Of course, you could be considered my fourth husband. I have answered to Mrs. Ramsdale and Mrs. Keating recently."

"And now you'll be back to being Mrs. Burgess."

"Full circle, which is why I find it so necessary to press you toward the altar. I rather fancy being Mrs. Walford. It's quite brazen of me, isn't it? I mean, I told you I loved you, but you have not returned the compliment."

"Quite ungentlemanly of me, isn't it?"

She heard him shift position, heard the soft sound as the rowels of his spurs spun briefly when he moved. "Come here," he said.

She had laid their bedrolls out so close together that following his instruction only required her to lie down.

"You are so lovely," he murmured as his fingertips brushed lightly down her cheek. "So brave."

"But I'm not Claire," Lou said when he didn't continue. "You still want her. That's why you keep turning down my flagrant offers to join me beneath the covers."

"Is that what you think?"

She could tell he was smiling. It was in his voice. "If that's not it, then why have you stayed away?"

"Why? To begin with, because I'm not a bounder like Frank Burgess was."

"No, you're not," she agreed, and daringly lifted her hand to his tousled dark hair, letting her fingers comb through it leisurely. "And what else?"

"I have a few lingering traits one might associate with a gentleman, one of which is never to leave a lady regretting her close association with me."

"Even if she wishes to have a close association with you?"

"Particularly then," J. W. said. His fingertips slid tenderly across her lips, as if he were a sculptor wishing to memorize the shape of them, the feel of them. The warmth.

Lou closed her eyes, trying to imprint the moment, the sensation of his touch, in her memory. "You really believe they will kill you?" she asked when his hand dropped away.

"They'd be foolish not to try, wouldn't they, considering my inhospitable intentions toward them? When the firing commences, I want you out of the way, Lou. Promise me you'll do as I ask."

Her fingers drifted down the rough angle of his jaw. He caught her hand in his, turned it so that his lips could brush warmly against her palm. "Promise me, Lou."

There would be no such promise wrung from her. She knew only too well that if there was any chance of his surviving the coming fray, it would be because she was at his side, not only loading his Winchester and Starr, but her own Sharp's carbine and ancient Navy Colt, and firing them if need be.

"Are you going to marry me, Jefferson Weyland Walford?" Lou asked. "If so, swear it tonight. Here." She turned their linked hands, guiding his to rest over her own heart.

She half expected him to jerk back, he had kept such a

careful distance from her for so many miles. But he didn't.
He let his hand rest intimately between her breasts.

"I will," he said, his voice ragged. "I swear to take you,
Louisa Keating Burgess, for my wife."

"And I take you to husband, for better or worse, in sick-
ness—"

"Or in death," he finished, corrupting the words of the
service to fit his own vision of the future.

Lou wasn't of a mind to squabble over semantics. "Do
you love me?" she asked.

"I adore you," J. W. said.

"That's not the same, but it will suffice," Lou murmured
softly. "We left out one part of the service though. One
very important part," she said, arching toward him. "You
may kiss your bride."

He'd thought she would never ask.

But a kiss was all she would get. Before going into battle
some men took their women to bed in the hope of leaving
behind a son. He would not do that to Lou. Her life was
already hard enough without rearing another child on her
own. The question was, could he kiss her and still maintain
that vow?

Her lips were so close to his. Beneath his hand, her heart
beat quickly in anticipation. He should remove himself
from such temptation. The curves of her breasts rose, creating an enticing valley wherein his hand rested, eliciting
the memory of the fantasies he'd entertained of making
love to her.

The fantasies would never measure up to the real thing.
This close to her, he could feel her breath brush against
his cheek, feel the heat of her only inches away. The desert
wind stirred the brush around them, adding the scent of
mesquite to her natural perfume.

"J. W.?" she murmured, her mouth nearly brushing his.

A man could only take so much. But he would kiss her lightly, his duty done, her request fulfilled, and back away before it was too late. His personal code demanded it.

Yet when his hand rested on her waist, it was to draw her hard against him. The tender kiss turned to white heat as she melted against him, her mouth opening under his, creating a need in his soul that had nothing to do with being a gentleman, having a code, or admitting to a belated fear of the coming confrontation. He wanted her, had wanted her for so long.

He tore his lips from hers, but it wasn't to back away. It was already too late for that. Instead he tasted the cool arch of her throat, savored the quiet moan of pleasure she made. It was as he had suspected. Her skin was pure satin, her taste more intoxicating than the finest whiskey. Of their own accord, his fingers found the buttons down the front of her shirt and loosed them one by one until even more territory was open for his exploration. She drove every bit of remaining sanity from his mind when her tongue touched the hollow in his throat, following the example he had inadvertently set her moments ago. Her fingers fumbled at the buttons on his shirt so that he was forced to help her, his lips returning to hers to savor her ardor while his fingers sought to rip the stubborn fastenings free.

"I sewed them on too well," she said, her voice strangely husky. "It's one of Frank's shirts."

"Then he won't miss it," J. W. declared, rending the cloth.

Lou laughed intimately. "I trust we can retain my own buttons. Displaying my wares would be a distraction, but I'm particular about who I'm distracting."

Beth Henderson

"You have distracted me for well over three hundred miles, even with your buttons intact," he said. Her shirt slipped from her shoulders, slid down her arms. Her skin was pale ivory below the sun-bronzed brown of her throat, just as he'd dreamed it would be.

"Truly?" she asked. He was amazed that her voice could sound disbelieving and hopeful in the same instance. Amazed that she showed no hesitation in the intimate dance they played.

"Truly," J. W. vowed, shedding his shirt. "You're beautiful."

"I am?"

"You are," he said and set about proving the strength of her allure. When his hand slid beneath her skirts, it was to find her skin as soft as the finest silk but warm to the touch. Oh, so warm. She was ready for him, he realized. Eager for him. When her fingers fumbled at his belt he shed the rest of his clothing quickly, but lingered over freeing her from hers. At length the ground around them was littered with the discards and they were entwined beneath the blankets as man and woman were meant to be.

He hadn't intended to take things this far but she had unwittingly enticed him into breaking his own rules, her own lack of reticence stirring a like need in him. Once buried in her softness with her ardent cries ringing in his ears, J. W. knew that he had been given one last chance to experience Heaven before descending into hell.

Lou curled around him, holding him fast until he was drained and they both were panting. "Don't leave me, J. W.," she murmured in his ear.

And though he knew it was best not to answer, he held her close, lost in her embrace, and whispered the one vow he knew it would be impossible to keep.

"Never."

322

Chapter Twenty-one

Morgan sat in the lee of a boulder, sheltered by scrub brush, watching the man Dalhert had sent to the lookout post entertain himself by tossing a knife repeatedly at the burned-out stub of a tree. His horse was hitched out of sight but he'd unholstered his carbine and made sure it and the brace of pistols at his belt were all loaded. His former comrades thought nothing of the armaments, used to seeing him primed for whatever fight might come to hand. They joked about him itching for trouble, insisting there was no reason to be so well armed in the camp. They had no idea J. W. Walford was headed their way.

The knife quivered as it made contact with the already worried-away target. "Ya think some sorry soul set this here stump on fire to keep warm on a cold night?" the lookout asked.

"Only if he was planning to be fried over the coals by the fellas riding with him," Morgan said. "A damn fire'd be like a beacon in this country."

"Oh," the fellow said, grunting. "Whada ya figure toasted it then?"

"Lightning."

"Oh." He pried the knife out and tossed it again.

Morgan looked out over the landscape. A sorry piece of real estate if he ever saw one, made sorrier by the hastily thrown together shacks near the lake's edge. They weren't the first inhabitants, and wouldn't be the last, but he couldn't for the life of him see why any man would choose to abide in the sordid holes. Espantosa Lake had a bad air about it, to his mind, as if the ghosts of the travelers robbed then drowned beneath its surface by other miscreants in the past haunted the area still. Not that they bothered him. In fact, when O'Brien had fallen flat out drunk on his face the previous night, he'd suggested to Dalhert they drown him in the lake. Wes had laughed, as if he'd told a lurid joke, slapped him on the back, and said, "By hell I've missed that dry wit of yers, Morg."

If Walford didn't show up soon to take the blame and find his own perdition, he was going to pick them off one by one himself just to avoid being involved in any more of their brilliant conversations.

"Lightnin'," the intellectual next to him mused, tossing the knife once more.

First one to go was this idiot. He'd use the knife. Let it have some satisfaction in killing the man who blunted its tip in an endless round of tosses.

The dots on the eastern horizon were hard to distinguish at first. The rising sun hung at an angle that made him squint beneath the sheltering brim of his hat. He watched them without bothering to alert the man who was supposed to be watching for approaching riders. There was no telltale dust cloud following the twin specks, which meant they weren't the troop of horsemen Dalhert had sent out scouting the day before. He'd kept his captains close by, the men who'd ridden with him in the war, letting the new recruits handle the dogsbody jobs. Like the knife-wielding imbecile who was too bored to stay alert. Rather than draw the man's attention to the incoming riders, Morgan let them get closer. If it was Walford, the man needed all the help he could get to remove the scum that stood between himself and Reconstruction power. If it was another couple of ragtag locals looking to join the lauded war hero Wes Dalhert, then he'd merely pick them off at his leisure. There were more than enough men already living at Espantosa; he didn't need any more getting in his way.

It took them a half hour by his pocket watch to turn into recognizable forms. They were walking their horses, but making a beeline for the outlaw camp, as if they knew exactly where it lay. The front rider was a woman. He could tell by the way her skirts fell, stirring with movement when her horse tried to break into a trot. She pulled it back to a plodding walk with little trouble, glancing back over her shoulder at the nag trailing on a lead behind her. There was a body draped over the second horse.

Morgan wished he'd had the forethought to bring a telescope. He'd been patient for so long, but now he was anxious to get on with building his new life. Anxious to put both past and present association with Dalhert six feet under.

"Hello, the camp!" the woman shouted, pulling her mount to a halt.

The knife-tossing idiot jerked to attention. Reaching for his rifle, he eased up, aiming it straight at his unexpected visitor. "State yer business, missy," he yelled down.

From his sheltered position, Morgan peered down. The woman had a wide-brimmed hat on that sheltered her face. The man lying crossways over the second saddle had no hat, but his face was hidden by his dangling arms.

"He dead?" the lookout demanded.

"Dead drunk from the whiskey the fool poured down his gullet ta make him ferget the lead someone threw in his direction," she shouted, her voice radiating disgust and impatience. "Ya gonna keep me standin' in this heat all day or let us pass?"

Morgan grinned softly. He knew that voice. The last time he'd heard it, she had been taunting a posse. And more than likely, hiding Walford in her rundown cabin.

She proved him right when she pushed back her hat, letting it fall down her back, suspended by the rawhide laces common to riders in the west. The sun glistened in her raven's wing black hair. It wasn't loose and straggling over her shoulders as it had been that day at the cabin, but bound in a single thick braid that fell over her breast. A pleasantly plump bosom, it was. He would enjoy it and her other delights on the way back to Peaceful. Banker Gillette would be grateful for her return, even more pleased if she was somewhat tamed by their return.

Idly, he wondered what had become of her baby. Left at some orphanage along the way or in a shallow grave? Neither mattered as long as the brat was not his problem.

"I'm Lou Burgess," she called out. "Ma husband back there is Frank, late of Angelina County."

"How'd yer man nearly get hisself plugged?" the lookout shouted.

Morgan could tell she smiled. "Bein' a damn fool is how. Thought he could hold up the stage single handed."

"He is a damn fool," the man agreed. "So what's yer business here?"

"Heard Wes Dalhert was lookin' ta form up a new troop," she said loudly, and jerked her chin back over her shoulder. "He's hopin' ta join."

The lookout glanced aside. "What'll I do, Morg?" he asked.

Morgan grinned slowly as he watched the apparently unconscious form of the man on the nag behind her. "Hell, let the lady through," he said. And why not? J. W. Walford had at long last arrived.

Lou held her breath, waiting for the moment when she was no longer under the sights of the lookout's rifle.

"Head on in at a walk, lady," the man called, then turned. Putting his rifle down, he cupped his hands and shouted, "Incoming riders," in the direction of the camp.

Lou had already kicked her horse into action, casting a brief glance back over her shoulder to make sure J. W. was still managing to maintain his masquerade as a nearly dead body. How he'd kept from slipping off on the long walk in, she had no idea. But after working their way close to the camp the evening before, they had both decided a long, slow approach was the best way to lull the outlaws in residence. She was relieved that there were just a handful. It evened the odds, despite the fact that J. W. had given her strict orders to lie low and keep his weapons loaded. Although she'd been meticulous in maintaining Frank's old Sharp's rifle and Colt pistol, he didn't want her to use them. Just the same, she'd made sure the night before that they were fully loaded and spare ammunition was ready at hand to reload them when necessary. Soon it would all be over. She should be praying for their safe deliverance from the coming fire, but the enormity of what they were about to do left her feeling numb.

The horses' plodding steps sounded loud against the sun-baked earth. As they entered the camp, people began emerging from the handful of dilapidated shacks: two barefooted women wearing little more than partially buttoned shifts, a grizzled man in brown trousers and undervest, his braces drooping around his hips and a long ill-favored cigar clamped between his teeth, three other idlers, and the unpleasant Mr. O'Brien, his red hair looking dark from a recent dunking in the nearby lake.

Lou trooped past them all until reaching a spot where a pile of sun-bleached lumber was stacked, scrub brush growing up around it indicating the building material had waited for attention a couple of seasons already. Dismounting, she tied her reins over a prickly branch, then did the same with Trouble's lead. There were no other animals in sight, but as the camp was just stirring, the horses were no doubt in a corral behind one of the buildings. Which was the way J. W. had hoped things would be.

"Any of you gents Mr. Dalhert?" she asked of the watching men.

"Yer talkin' ta him," the man with the cigar said.

Lou nodded, as if satisfied. A last glance assured her that the rifle slung from the leather scabbard on her saddle, J. W.'s beloved Winchester, was in position for him to unsheathe and begin firing. "Ma man's of a mind ta join up if you'll have him once the licker wears off," she said, stepping clear of the horses to give J. W. an unobstructed shot.

Dalhert took the cigar from his mouth and used it to gesture toward where O'Brien sat on a plank bench, quite obviously nursing a hangover. His medicine of choice was a bottle of evil-looking rotgut whiskey. "He's proof I don't hold a taste fer the stuff agin' a man," Dalhert said. "Long as he's stone-cold sober when we're ready ta ride."

She noticed he cast no more than a cursory glance J. W.'s way, but took his time eyeing her own assets.

"Ya know how ta cook?" Dalhert asked, then indicated the two women in the doorway of the next building. "These two're good fer only one thing, and it ain't cookin'."

"I keep him fed up proper," Lou claimed, jerking her chin in J. W.'s direction.

She knew it was a mistake to draw attention to him the moment O'Brien lurched to his feet.

"Hey, I know that cuss," he declared, pointing at J. W.'s still form.

"And I know you," J. W. answered, following the words with a shot that spun O'Brien around.

Lou heard the whiskey bottle break against the side of the building, but she was already ducking behind the lumber, taking cover as J. W. had drilled into her repeatedly the evening before. His pistol had been hidden from view, holstered to his belt and sheltered by the bulk of the bedroll behind his saddle. Frank's Colt was beneath her skirts, but she had it free and ready when J. W. dived into hiding beside her, both of their rifles in hand.

"Keep your head down," he ordered as the outlaws found their own weapons and opened fire. He returned the compliment with deadly accuracy, felling another of the men.

Lou peered between a gap in the boards. The ammunition to reload his rifle was already in her hand, waiting for the moment when he passed the Winchester to her. The horses neighed in fright, trying to pull free from where she'd tied their reins, but the thorns on the branches held tight, keeping them in place. They crowded each other, with Trouble on the outside and thus more susceptible to taking a bullet. But in pushing each other aside, the animals had left a gap in their own defenses.

A man had circled around the back of the buildings and was sheltering in the lee of the furthermost one, taking a bead on their open flank. J. W. was too busy returning fire to notice. Without glancing her way, he handed his empty

Winchester to her and pulled the Starr from the holster at his belt.

Lou laid her ready Colt within his reach and put her rifle to her shoulder, quickly sighting down on the outlaw hidden from J. W.'s sight. When her shot barked, he jerked in surprise. "What the hell are—"

As if he were featherlight, the gunman slipped from hiding to crumple in the dirt by the side of the building.

"Nice shot," J. W. commented. "Is he dead?"

"Don't think so," Lou said, putting her Sharp's aside to begin reloading the Winchester.

Her shot had distracted him from the business at hand, even if it had saved one of their lives, she realized when Dalhert himself dived from cover, rushing for the horses. He was between the animals, pushing them apart, yanking down on the reins to free them.

Lou scrambled to get her pistol in hand, but with Trouble forced to be Dalhert's shield, she couldn't get a clear shot.

Across from the woodpile, another man fell to J. W.'s pistol, leaving only one man besides Dalhert standing.

But the raiders' leader was already making his bid for freedom. Throwing a leg over Trouble's back, he hung low along the bay's side, offering the horse's body as the only clear target.

Careless of the remaining man sheltering in the adjacent shack, J. W. was on his feet, angling for a shot. An impossible shot, Lou thought a moment before the pistol across the way barked twice. J. W.'s Starr spun from his hand as he crumpled at her side. With the newly loaded Winchester still in her hand, Lou stood free of their shelter and fired. Sure of an easy kill, the man had stepped into the open doorway, but now he lay shattered on its doorstep, the center of his shirt already red with blood. This time Lou knew without a doubt that she'd killed another man. There had been no option; there could be no remorse.

Next to her in the dust, J. W. lay, a blood-stained hand clutched to his right shoulder. "There's no clear shot," he said through clenched teeth. "Dalhert's going to get away."

Trouble screamed in terror once more, rearing. Dalhert had had to abandon his sheltered position or slip from the horse's back and under its plunging hooves. He yanked back on the reins viciously and dug his spurs into the bay's flanks.

Lou pitied the mare. She no doubt thought Frank had come back from the grave to torture her once more.

But if the recently calmed mustang was remembering such treatment, she also remembered how to unseat an unwelcome rider. Trouble reared once again and arched to tumble over backward on the man trapped in the saddle.

While Lou and J. W. watched in silence, Trouble hit the ground. "She's definitely a one-man horse," Lou murmured and pressed Frank's timeworn Colt into J. W.'s hand. "If you rest your arm on the rifle's stock, can you get off a shot?"

At his nod, she set the Winchester's muzzle against the ground and held it upright. Beyond the stack of lumber, the bay had scrambled back to its feet and trotted toward the lake, leaving Dalhert struggling to stand.

"The Colt pulls to the left," Lou warned. "I wouldn't want you to shoot my rented nag by mistake."

"Neither would I," J. W. said solemnly.

Dalhert was on his feet, dragging one leg slightly as he headed toward the remaining horse. Now that the firing had subsided, it had calmed and did not move away.

"Easy," Lou counseled. "Take your time."

J. W. pulled the trigger. The shot hit Dalhert in the side, but didn't down him. "Damn," J. W. muttered. "Overcompensated. He's going to get away."

Dalhert was already astride the piebald, and pulling on the reins, the rowels of his spurs cutting into the animal's sides. The horse reeled, setting off at a gallop.

"He's not getting away," Lou said as she stood and put the Winchester to her shoulder.

But J. W. had struggled to his feet as well. Pushing the rifle's muzzle toward the ground, he shook his head. "It's over, Lou."

She searched his face. It was haggard, drawn. "Are you sure?"

"I'm sure," he said.

Lou lowered the rifle from her shoulder and leaned into him. "Thank God," she murmured. "I couldn't bear to have you go after him. Couldn't bear to lose you. I love you."

J. W.'s unwounded arm settled around her, scooping her close. "And I have loved you," he said, "for nearly four hundred miles."

Four hundred miles, Lou thought happily. Four hundred miles ago they had still been in Angelina County.

She looked at the dust trail kicked up behind her fast-moving horse. How would Diamond take the news that Dalhert had escaped? she wondered. And then a shot rang out. Barely believing what had happened, Lou watched as Wes Dalhert fell from the galloping horse and lay unmoving.

"Who—?"

"Listen," J. W. said.

Then she heard it, the thunderous sound of galloping

horses. The first appeared a moment later. Men in dust-covered blue, the banner of the Sixth Cavalry flying above them, pounded into the outlaw compound and pulled to a halt.

The officer in charge trotted on to rein his horse in before them. "J. W. Walford? Mrs. Burgess?" he asked. "Jack Landrey at your service, compliments of Tess Ramsdale." He glanced around at the bodies on the ground. "I see we missed the main excitement."

"Not entirely, since you picked off Wes Dalhert, their leader," J. W. said. "My thanks for that."

"The man we passed on our way in? That shot wasn't fired by any of my men."

A man to the rear of the troop pulled his horse out of line, maneuvering it closer to his captain. "Sir? There's a horseman making off to the east. Should we follow him?"

Landrey shook his head. "There's your answer, Mr. Walford. Another lone vigilante. Not that you were one, of course."

"Wouldn't consider such a course," J. W. said, taking the Winchester from Lou's hands. "Hell, captain, I'm a law-abiding lawyer!"

The trip back to San Antonio had been downright leisurely compared to the journey out, J. W. mused five days later. His arm was in a sling, but only because Lou insisted on it. His shoulder was stiff and stung a bit yet when he forgot and put weight on it. Which he tended to do when lying next to Lou in bed. Although they hadn't gone through an official ceremony yet, she considered herself his wife and he wasn't a man to argue with a woman over something like that. Not when to do so would deprive him of

333

her company. Or at least earn him a cold shoulder for a day or two.

No, what irritated him was his sister's stubbornness. It was why they all stood on the boardwalk while the stagecoach was loaded, Diamond's cases filling up most of the available space.

"You should just hire a freight wagon to move these things and be done with it," he said.

"And where would I tell the driver to deliver things?" Diamond demanded. "Neddy and I aren't sure we'll stay in San Francisco. We just thought it might be a place we'd like to live. It has a number of things to recommend it."

"The foremost one being that it's a long way from Jack Landrey's duty station," J. W. said.

Diamond tossed her head. "Perhaps."

"You could stay," he insisted. "You could go back to being Tess Ramsdale. It's over, you know."

When Diamond glared at him, Lou rested her hand on his arm. "Leave your sister be," she counseled. "She knows there will always be a place here in Texas for her. And Nedra, too. You know you're welcome, dear friend."

Neddy had Angelina in her arms, taking advantage of the remaining moments to cuddle the little girl. "I know," she said. "But for now I'll stay with Diamond. When she decides what to do with the rest of her life, then I'll contact some of the abolitionists who ran schools and go back to teaching. Ezra would have liked for me to continue our work, and one day, I will."

The last strap was being belted in place at the coach's rear, J. W. noticed. "Find yer seat, ma'am," the driver said to Diamond. "We'll be leavin' in two minutes."

While Neddy handed Angelina back to Lou, J. W. gave his sister a one-armed hug. "You know where we'll be," he said. "San Marcos. There are a couple folks we need to straighten out about who we really are, and a saddle to return to Lou's grandfather. Then we're filing for a homestead and settling down."

"I'll be sorry to miss the wedding," Diamond said, "but I really can't stay."

"Stubborn woman," J. W. grumbled. "It is over, Tess."

"Diamond," she reminded. "I'm not sure I'll ever be Tess again."

Once Neddy had followed her into the coach, the lumbering carriage moved off at a careful rate through the city streets.

"She'll be back," Lou promised. "Sooner than you think."

He patted her hand where it rested on his good arm. "I hope you're right."

"I know I'm right," Lou said. Angelina added her own two bits, babbling and grinning happily at him.

What more did a man need when he had a beautiful wife and a darling daughter? he wondered. A good right arm again, that's what.

"What do you think you are doing, J. W. Walford?" Lou demanded when he shrugged off the sling.

"Making a full recovery," he said. "Come on, let's walk. I need to stretch my legs."

"J. W." she murmured, a veiled threat in her voice.

How like a wife she already was, he thought happily. "I'm fine, Lou. It just needs to loosen up."

"I'll let you do as you please on one condition," she bargained, shifting Angelina in her arms as they moved. "That you tell me why you let O'Brien think your pistol was loaded that day in Crockett. It has bothered me for weeks."

J. W. grinned. "Oh, that? I did it for you, dear one. We were strangers in town. If I'd shot him, the local outcry would have landed me back in the hoosegow, and where would that have left you and Angel? You'd worked so hard to convince me sticking together was necessary, I couldn't put you in the position of trying to travel on alone. So I let O'Brien think it was loaded, let him disarm me, knowing he'd grab it up if given the chance. But if someone happened upon the fight, it would look like self-defense when I killed him."

"Killed him how?" Lou asked.

"I was working on that when you laid him flat with the shovel. Satisfied?" he asked.

"Yes," she agreed.

"But I'm not," a man's voice said behind them. "No, don't stop. Keep walking. Turn into the alley ahead and head back to the rear of the building.

The building, J. W. noticed, housed one of the local undertakers and looked currently deserted.

"I'm guessing you're the last man standing," J. W. said. "Morg, isn't that what they called you?"

"You were with the posse," Lou added.

"And now I work for Titus Gillette," the man behind them said. "Temporarily, of course, but between what he pays me to drag you back, Mrs. Burgess, and the reward Roane's lady friend has posted for Walford, preferably dead, it will be a tidy enough sum to make this worth my trouble."

J. W. stepped down off the boardwalk into the alleyway, offering Lou his hand to aid her. Surreptitiously he glanced at the man behind them. Under the cover of a stockman's duster draped over his arm, he held a pistol trained on Lou's back.

"What did you have against Dalhert?" J. W. asked. "You did kill him with a shot from the lookout post, didn't you?"

"Had to, didn't I, considering you let him get away," the former raider said. "Not too fast, folks. We don't want to look like we're in a hurry here."

The alleyway was narrow, which would give him the chance to get Lou out of the gunman's sights, if only briefly, J. W. realized. He guided her ahead of him, pushing her along, a hand firmly against her spine. As if realizing all was not well, Angelina began to whimper. He couldn't blame the baby. If she knew what was about to happen, she'd be even more upset.

Though Angel couldn't read his mind, he wasn't so sure about Lou. "J. W.," she murmured.

"I love you," he said. "Love you both." Then he pushed her aside and turned to face one last enemy.

The shot echoed in the narrow confines of the alleyway. The scent of black powder was as overpowering as on the battlefield. A smell he had once thought he'd never be able to clear from his lungs. There was no pain, but the former raider's bullet could not have missed at such close range.

Then Morg's pistol tilted toward the ground and fired as his finger jerked back on the trigger, his knees buckled and he sank to a lifeless heap on the alley floor.

J. W. looked past the man's body to where his sister stood, her derringer still smoking in her hand.

"I saw him from the stage coach," she said, her voice strangely hushed.

Angelina was crying, wailing in fear at hearing the twin shots. He heard Lou trying to calm her, felt her reach for him, needing to see for herself that he was all right.

"I recognized him," Diamond said, unaware of anything

else around them. Townspeople were already arriving at the scene. "He's the one who—"

J. W. stepped over Morg's body and took the single-shot pistol from her hand.

Diamond looked up, meeting his eyes. "Lou was right," she said. "It is easier to kill a man when you can't see his face or the expression in his eyes."

"Hush," J. W. murmured, pulling her into his arms. "It's really over now, Tess."

This time she didn't quibble about his choice of names but clung to him. "Yes," she agreed. "It really is."

He didn't know how she managed it, but Lou was there beside him a moment later, Angelina still sniffling but quieted in her arms. "Don't go on to California. Come to San Marcos. I need a matron of honor and Angelina could do with a clever aunt," she said.

When Diamond gave a tentative smile, J. W. felt his heart swell even more. "I'd like being both those things," she admitted quietly.

A moment later, breathless and distraught, Neddy arrived to lead Tess away.

"Do you think Tess will give Captain Landrey another chance?" Lou asked.

"I hope so. I like the fellow. But I love you, Mrs. Soon-to-be-Walford," he murmured, helping her push through the curious crowd.

Lou grinned up at him. "I like the sound of that, Mr. Walford," she said. "In fact, considering it took you so long to say those words, I think you should repeat them to me every single day."

Careless of those around them, he pulled Lou and her baby into the shelter of his arms. "For the rest of my life," he whispered against Lou's lips. "For the rest of my life."

Author's Note

I am always curious about what things were real and which were invented in a historical novel, and have found there are other readers who feel this tug to know, too. So, here is the breakdown for At Twilight.

In the era in which this tale is set, Texans still referred to themselves as Texians.

The towns of Lone Tree and Peaceful are of my own creation, as are the de la Vaca land grant, all mercantile shops, and events at the Naughton Farm. The Menger hotel and the Scholz Beer Garden were real. Unfortunately, the raid on Lawrence, Kansas, in August 1863 by Confederate raiders was real, and the details related to Grant's march toward and the subsequent battle at Vicksburg were, too.

Any errors were my own, but I would enjoy learning where I went wrong, and where I went right. Write to Beth Henderson, P. O. Box 262, Englewood, Ohio 45322.

Crosswinds
Cindy Holby

Ty – He is honor-bound to defend the land of his fathers, even if battle takes him from the arms of the woman he pledged himself to protect.

Cole – A Texas Ranger, he thinks the conflict will pass him by until he has the chance to capture the fugitive who'd sold so many innocent girls into prostitution.

Jenny – She vows she will no longer run from the demons of the past, and if that means confronting Wade Bishop in a New York prisoner-of-war camp, so be it. No matter how far she must travel from those she holds dear, she will draw courage from the legacy of love her parents had begun so long ago.

Texas Star

Elaine Barbieri

Buck Star is a handsome cad with a love-'em-and-leave-'em attitude that broke more than one heart. But when he walks out on a beautiful New Orleans socialite, he sets into motion a chain of treachery and deceit that threatens to destroy the ranching empire he'd built and even the children he'd once hoped would inherit it. . . .

A mysterious message compels Caldwell Star to return to Lowell, Texas, after a nine-year absence. Back in Lowell, he meets a stubborn young widow who refuses his help, but needs it more than she can know. Her gentle touch and proud spirit give Cal strength to face the demons of the past, to reach out for a love that would heal his wounded soul.

Renegade Moon
Elaine Barbieri

Somewhere in the lush grasslands of the Texas hill country, three brothers and a sister fight to hold their family together, struggle to keep their ranch solvent, while they await the return of the one person who can shed light on the secrets of the past.

No sooner has he rescued spitfire Glory Townsend from deadly quicksand than Quince finds himself trapped in a quagmire of emotions far more difficult to escape. Every time he looks into her flashing green eyes he feels himself sinking deeper. Maybe it is time to stop struggling and admit that only her love can save him.